Dead End

SHIRLEY WELLS

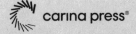

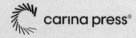

carina press®

ISBN-13: 978-0-373-00268-9

Dead End

Recycling programs for this product may not exist in your area.

www.CarinaPress.com

Printed in U.S.A.

Dear Reader,

I have the best job in the world, and I can't tell you how much I enjoyed writing *Dead End*.

A lot of my reading is done in bed and it's always during the nights that my husband is away that I hear noises. My heart races as I tell myself that our dogs would be barking if there was an intruder. Does that work? No. All I manage to do is convince myself that both dogs have gone deaf and are oblivious to the ax murderer climbing the stairs.

As a writer, however, I have great fun letting my characters hear the noises and face the killers. *Dead End* starts with Dylan receiving death threats. What would it be like to answer a phone and be told that you're going to die? I'd panic, call the police and get a couple more dogs (having tested their hearing first). Dylan doesn't panic, but as an ex-policeman who has helped send many people to prison, he soon has far too many suspects for comfort. And so it begins—the race against time.

I hope you enjoy reading *Dead End* as much as I enjoyed writing it.

I love hearing from readers, so if you'd like to chat about *Dead End*, or about anything else, you can contact me through my website: shirleywells.com.

Happy reading!

Shirley Wells

For Nick

Acknowledgments

My thanks are due to everyone at Carina Press for their dedication and professionalism. Special thanks must go to my awesome editor, Deborah Nemeth, who takes my stories and makes them shine.

ONE

HE DIDN'T KNOW where he was when he woke up. It took him a full twenty seconds to figure out which was floor and which was ceiling, and he was relieved that he hadn't slept on the ceiling. When he attempted a sitting position, sharp stabbing pains ricocheted round his head, jolted his brain back to life and slowly returned his memory. Dylan Scott, private investigator, married to Bev, who was currently undergoing treatment for cancer, father to amazing teenager Luke and cute baby Freya—

Ah yes, and a stag night that had included propping up bars in too many pubs and clubs with his mate Pikey, returning to Pikey's house and demolishing a bottle of whisky—

And someone wanted him dead. The way he felt right now, they'd be getting their wish sooner than they'd anticipated.

He vaguely remembered being offered the sofa to sleep on, which didn't explain what he was doing on the floor.

He struggled onto his knees and immediately wished he hadn't. Everything hurt. Every muscle in his body registered pain, and a wrecking ball was hard at work in his skull.

Water. He needed water. Probably a stomach pump and life support machine too.

He stood, gingerly, and leaned against the dining table. The sofa wasn't even in the same room.

Water.

He staggered to the kitchen, turned on the tap and shoved his mouth under it. A little water found its way down his throat. Most washed over his face. He found a mug, filled it, and drank it straight down. After the second mugful, he felt almost human and his mouth began to function normally again.

He filled the kettle and switched it on, and managed to hunt down a spoon and some coffee. He could walk, swallow and make a drink. All was not quite lost.

A weak April sun was trying to brighten this Sunday morning but, thanks to the neighbours' penchant for tall trees, was having little effect on the kitchen. Somewhere in the distance, church bells were ringing to summon the faithful to morning service.

"Holy crap." Pikey lurched into the kitchen wearing a The Man, The Myth, The Legend T-shirt back to front, and a pair of jeans that he hadn't bothered to fasten. "How do *you* feel?"

"About as good as you look."

"That bad, eh?" Grinning, Pikey sank down into a chair. "It was a good night, though, wasn't it?"

"God knows. I suppose it must have been."

Taking a closer look, Dylan decided he didn't feel anywhere near as good as Pikey looked. Pikey might not have managed to dress himself properly, but he still cut an impressive figure. Like Dylan, he'd passed forty, but unlike Dylan he was all muscle and energy. With his shaved head, Pikey had always looked like a thug. Detective Sergeant Pike was a damn good copper, though, a damn good man too, and Dylan missed working alongside him.

"We'll feel better with some food inside us," Pikey said. "What we need is a good fry-up."

Dylan's stomach lurched at the prospect, but by the time Pikey had rifled through the fridge for sausages, bacon and eggs, he thought he could maybe face some food after all.

Half an hour later, they sat down to plates laden with burned sausages, bacon that snapped apart and eggs that looked about to hatch. Baked beans and soggy fried bread completed the feast.

"Last night," Pikey said, "you mentioned something about wanting to pick my brain. What was that about?"

"Did I?" Dylan had planned to raise the subject but couldn't remember doing so. "Someone wants me dead." It still sounded ridiculous. Hell, it *was* ridiculous. It had to be. "I've had a couple of phone calls at the office from some jerk saying it's payback time and that I'm going to die. I know it's a long shot but I wondered if you had any ideas."

Pikey's eyebrows had risen with each word. His fork hovered level with his mouth. "You're kidding. What else have they said?"

"Nothing. The calls have been brief and to the point. No background sounds that I could make out. No clues as to an identity. Nothing. Just a quick 'it's payback time and you're going to die.'"

"Payback time? Who have you upset recently?"

"How long have you got?"

Pikey mopped up egg yolk with a piece of fried bread. "When was the first call?"

"Two weeks ago. Before then, though, Bev took

three odd calls at the house. No one said anything but she had the feeling someone was on the other end, listening."

"Hmm."

"What's that supposed to mean?"

"I can give you the name of someone recently released from prison. Someone who threatened to get you—and me, come to that."

"Come on then. Out with it."

"Leonard King. Remember him?"

"Oh, Christ. How could I forget?"

Dylan could remember every detail of the night he and Pikey had thought they were about to sort out a domestic dispute. It was one of the last things they did together as coppers.

They'd been on their way home, their stint finished for the day, when they'd heard that a huge fire at a furniture factory and two bomb scares were keeping uniformed officers busy. London was in chaos, and as he and Pikey had been less than two minutes from the property where the domestic was supposedly in full swing, they'd agreed to go and sort it.

From the moment they arrived, they'd known something was wrong.

The front door to the three-storey terraced house was open and, when they'd stepped inside, expecting to find a husband and wife in the middle of an alcohol-fuelled tiff, they quickly realised it was a setup. There was no domestic dispute.

Instead they'd stumbled into a professional drug factory where millions of pounds' worth of heroin had been processed. It was one of the biggest Class A drugs seizures the U.K. had seen.

Of course, they hadn't known that at first. They'd been too busy relieving Max Rickman, one of the U.K.'s most violent, of the samurai sword he'd been wielding.

Thankfully, the other man at the property, small-time crook Leonard King, had been unarmed but there had been no doubt in either of their minds that Rickman wouldn't hesitate to use that sword.

Rickman had started life as a football hooligan, had killed a man in a bar fight while in New York and spent several years in prison, including five in San Quentin, before being deported back to England.

Only when Rickman and King were secure and backup had finally arrived did Dylan and Pikey realise they'd stepped into a drug factory. They'd found a hundred grand in cash, a dealer list, heroin in powder and block form, a press for compressing the adulterated drug back into blocks, a cash-counting machine and another samurai sword hidden behind cushions on the sofa.

"King's out then?"

"As free as a bird," Pikey said. "The reason I know is that he was taken into custody less than twenty-four hours after his release on a drunk and disorderly charge. He was released when he'd sobered up."

"What about Rickman?"

Pikey shook his head. "Up for parole in a few months. He's late sixties now and has heart problems. Angina or something like that."

It was little consolation. Rickman was a dangerous bastard, with or without a naff ticker.

They chewed on burned sausages for a few moments, and Dylan guessed their thoughts were running along the same lines. "There was something really dodgy about that night," he said.

"Yep."

That King and Rickman had been set up, presumably by someone out for revenge or by another dealer wanting to muscle in on Rickman's territory, had been obvious. King, who'd previously spent two spells in prison for armed robbery, claimed he'd only met Rickman a few months earlier. According to him, Rickman had offered to pay him well to deliver a package. King had known Rickman was a dealer, but his story was that he'd had no idea of the scale of the operation. He'd insisted he wasn't involved and, at first, there was nothing to suggest he was.

A search of his flat had soon proved otherwise. A stash of heroin and an even bigger stash of cash had been found. King had denied all knowledge, had seemed genuinely shocked by the discovery, but it had been enough to send him down.

The phone call about the so-called domestic dispute had been made by a female and they never did find out who was responsible.

"What did King say as he was dragged from the court?" Dylan asked.

"Something like 'I'm going to get you fucking bastards,' if I recall."

"That's what I thought." Dylan wiped his plate clean with a square of bread he'd saved for the purpose. "I knew I could rely on you, Pikey. Thanks. I'll start sniffing around and see what King's up to."

"I'll see what I can find out too." Pikey flexed his impressive muscles. "If he needs sorting, we'll do it together. And if I think of anyone else who might want to end your days, I'll let you know."

"You do that. Although I'm sure it's nothing. Let's face it, if someone wants you dead—"

"—they kill you. Yeah." They did. They didn't waste time trying to frighten you.

And yet, although Dylan wasn't going to mention it, he had a bad feeling about this. There was nothing he could pinpoint, but it was making him very uneasy. Perhaps he was simply getting old. Or soft.

Pikey made coffee so strong that the spoon stood to attention in the mug. He plonked it down in front of Dylan. "Hey, do you remember that hooker we busted?"

Dylan grinned. "The pregnant one? The one you helped into the back of the car as if she were made of porcelain. The one who then gave birth to a stash of cocaine before our eyes?"

And so the reminiscing began. They'd been through a lot together, from rookie coppers who didn't have a clue what they were doing to detectives who knew how to work the system to their advantage. Time had coloured their memories, of course. It hadn't been all fun. Yet the memories that made them laugh were the ones that had to be dusted off and polished.

Dylan enjoyed his work as a private investigator, most of the time at least, but he missed working alongside Pikey. He often wondered how far he might have risen in the ranks if he hadn't been dismissed in disgrace, kicked off the force and into a prison cell.

Still, it was no use going over old ground. It had happened. It was wrong, bloody wrong, but it had happened. End of. There were far more important things to worry about—like a sick wife, two kids, a mortgage—

And the small matter of death threats.

TWO

At six o'clock on Thursday morning, the only things moving were birds. The dawn chorus was in full swing, and dozens of starlings were already squabbling like spoiled kids.

Jimmy sat in the white van he'd bought last week. It had been cheap, was suitably dented and rusting in places, and it stank of oil and something else. It was perfect.

He'd disconnected the battery and was currently blocking the driveway to a house that sat at the end of a row of similar detached executive homes. Each property came with privacy provided by tall fir trees, making it unlikely that anyone from the nearby houses would spot his van. A small lake opposite was used only by ducks so no one would see him from that angle.

All Jimmy had to do was wait, and he was good at that.

He knew the layout, knew the kitchen was at the back of the house, as was the master bedroom. It was doubtful that Brian Dowie would spot the van until he emerged from his home at 6:40 a.m. If he did, though, Jimmy would be ready for him.

Unlike the early riser she'd married, Diane Dowie liked her beauty sleep and wouldn't leave the bedroom until after nine o'clock. Their twin boys were sixteen and always managed to get themselves to school without her help. School had finished for the Easter break, though, so the boys would probably stay in bed later than usual. While her husband lorded it over employees at his car salesroom, Diane would spend his money on clothes and beauticians. Later, when her husband set off for Cardiff, Diane would open a bottle of wine, and probably follow it with another bottle.

Jimmy waited. The blood zinged through his veins and his palms began to sweat. Nothing could go wrong. He'd been patient. He'd watched the Dowie household until he knew the daily routine to the second. An inner voice reminded him that the school holidays changed that routine, but he ignored it.

Minutes ticked by. Jimmy checked his watch.

The front door opened and Dowie appeared. He aimed a remote control in the direction of the garage and the door swung up, but then he stopped to frown at the van blocking his exit. A scowl cut grooves in his face as he walked down the drive.

Jimmy jumped out the van. "Sorry. Terribly sorry. I've called the breakdown company—half an hour ago now—and they should be here any minute. If you helped push—" He gave Dowie's suit an apologetic glance. "If you'd be kind enough to sit inside while *I* push, I'm sure we'll soon have it out of your way."

"Fine." Dowie nodded reluctantly, then fished in his pocket and produced a business card. "If you're in the market for a new vehicle, here's the place to come."

Jimmy had to stifle a bubble of hysterical laughter that rose up inside him. Dowie didn't miss a trick—or the opportunity to screw someone over.

"Thanks," Jimmy said. "I'll stop by. I've been meaning to trade this in for a while now."

"Ask for me—Brian Dowie. My name's on the card."

"I will. Thanks so much. And I'm really sorry about this."

"We'll both push," Dowie said. "It'll be easier. As soon as it moves, jump inside. Okay?"

"Got it," Jimmy said.

Jimmy opened both driver's door and passenger door, then moved to the back of the van ready to push it. "Hey, check the handbrake's off, will you?"

It only took a second. Dowie leaned in through the passenger door to release the handbrake, and Jimmy picked up the crowbar that had been waiting by the rear wheel. He brought it down on the back of Dowie's head as the bloke emerged from the car.

Dowie dropped like a corpse, his car keys falling from his pocket and narrowly missing a drain. That would have buggered everything.

Christ! For one awful moment, Jimmy thought he really did have a corpse on his hands. As he bundled him into the back of the van, though, he could feel him breathing.

He quickly lifted the bonnet, reconnected the battery and climbed into the driver's seat. The engine fired at the first attempt. He reversed it a few yards, then killed then engine.

It only took a couple of minutes to tie Dowie's wrists and ankles, and gag him. Not that anyone was likely to hear him.

Confident that his prize was safe and secure, Jimmy grabbed the can of petrol, jumped out the van and locked it. He ran up the drive to Dowie's garage, went inside and fired the brand-new BMW into life. It took him a couple of attempts to find the right button on the remote to close the garage door but as it slid into place, he reversed down the drive and was away. Anyone watching now would assume that Dowie was on his way to his office.

Jimmy drove less than a mile, down a narrow lane and to a patch of waste ground. He'd watched the area and knew that no one went near it. A developer had bought the land, intending to build fifty or so homes on it, but planning permission had been refused and the ground had been left to its own devices while the owner appealed the decision. The few people who knew about it used it as a rubbish dump. A couple of old mattresses had been rotting there for months, a sofa too.

He parked the car on the far side of the land, where it wouldn't be noticed for a while, doused the interior with petrol and took a breath. He had three cigarette lighters in his pocket, just in case, but the first threw out a big flame. He tossed it onto the back seat and watched the sudden burst of orange take over. He strode away and, when he turned to look, all he saw was a fireball.

He half walked, half ran back to the Crescent. He climbed inside his van, saw that Dowie was still unconscious, and drove off. His heart was racing.

There was little traffic about. A Status Quo song was playing on the radio and Jimmy slapped the steering wheel to the beat. It was a breeze and he was soon pulling up outside the small terraced house he'd rented.

Surprisingly, Dowie was still out cold. Jimmy thanked whatever god was watching over him.

It wasn't until Jimmy had dragged him out the van

and into the back of the house, and pushed him down a set of steps into the cellar that Dowie began to come round. He was still very groggy so Jimmy had little trouble tying him to a chair.

Dowie struggled in an attempt for freedom but Jimmy just laughed at him while he fixed the long length of rope to the rafter. He slipped it around Dowie's neck.

"The thing is," Jimmy said, standing in front of Dowie and smiling at him, "you're a bit stuffed right now. If you knock the chair over, you're a dead man. Even if you just tip it forward, you'll hang yourself. Still, a clever bloke like you will have worked that out for himself."

Dowie was trying to shout behind his gag. Jimmy ignored him. He double-checked that Dowie's hands were tied securely behind his back and that the ropes binding him to the chair were tight, then he ran back up the stairs, taking them two at a time.

"Be seeing you, Brian." He flicked off the light switch and plunged the cellar into darkness. "By the way, my van's fixed so I won't be needing a new one for a while."

Jimmy was still smiling as he stepped outside. He'd left his car a couple of streets away and he walked briskly to collect it. Once inside, he drove off, satisfied with a job well done.

Home was only five minutes away and he walked into the usual breakfast mayhem.

"It smells of cat in here." He wrinkled his nose at the pungent smell.

No one took any notice of him. Carol was shoving washing into the machine, Matthew was pushing toast down his throat as fast as he could and Ewan was putting his football kit into his bag.

"I said it smells of cat in here."

"Does it?" Carol sniffed. "I can't smell anything. It could be George, though. He peed on the carpet yesterday. He's getting old, poor thing."

Not old enough. But even when George turned his paws, they'd still be stuck with three cats. Carol was cat mad.

Matthew nudged his big brother's elbow. "It's probably Ewan. He always stinks."

"Shut up, moron."

"Who are you calling a moron?"

"Enough," Carol said. "Come on, you'll miss the bus if you don't get a move on."

"Can I get a lift to the cinema tonight, Mum?" Matthew asked.

"Yes, yes—so long as you don't miss your bus."

"And then can I have Chinese takeaway?"

"I suppose so."

"Why can't you get the bus to the cinema?" Jimmy asked. "You can't expect your mum to ferry you around forever."

"It's no bother," Carol said. "Besides, the bus takes ages."

"You could run, Matt," Jimmy said. "I've done five miles this morning. It does you good."

Matthew groaned.

"Petrol doesn't come out the tap, you know," Jimmy said. "It'll come out of your pocket money."

"Oh, Dad, that's so not—"

"Stop arguing, Matt." Laughing, Carol flicked a tea towel at him. "Come on, you nagged and nagged to go on this trip. I want you out the front door in sixty seconds. Both of you. Scram."

Five minutes later, the front door slammed and all was quiet except for the irritating rumble of the washing machine.

Carol poured herself another coffee and sat down at the table. "You're too hard on them, Jimmy."

"And you're too soft. They're both turning into proper mummy's boys. You'll regret it, you mark my words."

"You might regret playing the sergeant major too. They're good kids. Let them enjoy life while they can."

"There's more to life than enjoying yourself."

She snorted at that. "Sure there is. There's getting a job, paying the bills, buying a house, getting sick—they'll find out all about that soon enough."

"And they're being prepared for none of it. They need a lot more discipline."

"That's the army talking. And you're only mad at Ewan because he wants to join the police. You should be pleased. A lot of sixteen-year-olds don't have a clue what they want to do."

"And why does he want to join the police? Because he thinks the sun shines out of my dad's arse. Well, it doesn't. Believe me, it doesn't."

"Then don't try so hard to be exactly like him." Carol finished her coffee and went to the sink to rinse out her mug. As far as she was concerned, the conversation was over.

"I'm nothing like my dad."

"You're exactly like him, Jimmy."

"That shows how much you know."

She probably didn't hear him because she'd gone

upstairs. She did that a lot. It was as if she enjoyed say-ing something that she knew would piss him off and then walking away.

A couple of minutes later, she came back to the kitchen carrying a tall pile of towels. A bag was slung over her shoulder and her car keys dangled from a fin-ger. "I need to go." She dropped a kiss on the top on his head. "I'll see you tonight, love."

She didn't expect an answer so Jimmy didn't give her one.

When the door closed behind her, he walked up the stairs and threw himself down on their bed. The adren-aline had gone, leaving total exhaustion in its wake.

He closed his eyes and thought he might sleep for an hour, but it wasn't to be. He was immediately back with his colleagues, pushing into the hell that was Musa Qala. All they'd needed to do was assert Afghan gov-ernment control in the rebel stronghold. It should have been easy. His pulse started to race again. He could taste sand and dust in his throat. He was there.

He leapt off the bed and raced to the bathroom. He was violently sick, but not before he saw their muti-lated bodies.

As he splashed cold water on his face, he thought of Carol chatting with clients about the latest TV soap as she cut and coloured their hair. He thought of Matthew raving about the latest zombie movie with his chums, and of Ewan telling everyone he was going to be a po-liceman just like his wonderful grandfather.

That bloody cat wandered into the bathroom with his ginger hair standing upright on his arched back. Jimmy lashed out with a towel. "Fuck off and pee somewhere else!"

THREE

"YOU LOOK GREAT," Dylan said.

Bev turned away from the dressing table mirror, mascara wand in her hand, to frown at him. "I look like shit."

"You don't."

She'd lost a little weight since her operation, but she'd also lost that haunted, frightened look. As daft as it sounded, worrying that she might have cancer had affected her far more than *knowing* she had it. Now that she knew what she had to deal with, she was calmer, more relaxed and more likely to smile.

"Wait till I start the chemo and my hair drops out," she said, turning back to the mirror.

He didn't want to think about the course of chemotherapy that lay ahead. These days, he was able to block it from his mind if he tried really hard. Bev was young, fit and healthy—she'd fight this hateful disease. He refused to believe otherwise. "So what's the plan for tonight?"

She applied a coat of lipstick and pursed her lips together. "The usual. Lucy's bringing a DVD over—a romance, I think, in which no one dies of cancer—and I've got the wine. So we'll watch the film, phone for a takeaway, slag you off and get drunk. Well, as drunk as we can on a Thursday night when Lucy has to work in the morning."

"If you need me—"

"I'll whistle. Go and enjoy your pub crawl."

"It's not a pub crawl. I told you, I'm meeting someone."

"You haven't told me why you're meeting up with some old police informer."

He hadn't. The last thing he wanted was for her to start worrying about some maniac out to kill him. Besides, despite his uneasy feeling about all this, it was unlikely that his mysterious caller wanted to do anything more than scare him. If he wanted him dead, he'd have made a move by now. "It's just a job, Bev. There's a bloke recently released from prison who's done a runner. I need to find him, that's all. It's nothing exciting."

"It is if it pays the bills," she said.

Except it wouldn't pay any bills. When it came to Leonard King, Dylan was both investigator and client. He had a couple of paying jobs, though, both looking into insurance claims, so there was a little money coming in. "We won't starve." Not yet.

He walked to the wardrobe, pulled his leather jacket from a hanger and shrugged it on. Returning to stand behind her seat at the mirror, he put his hands on his shoulders. "You do look great, you know." He bent to kiss her. "Right, I'm out of here. Give me a shout if you need me. And don't get too drunk."

"See you later."

As he walked down the stairs, he was aware of the silence settling around the house. Luke was having a sleepover at his friend's house and Freya was staying with Dylan's mum for the night. A lively teenager and a baby could make a lot of noise between them and the house missed them. So did Dylan.

He wondered if he should wait for Lucy to arrive, then decided Bev would accuse him of fussing again, so he put his wallet and keys in his pocket and left the house.

He walked to the rank and took a cab to the White Horse where he'd arranged to meet Archie Bryson.

It didn't take long to spot him, although Archie, a small man, well into his seventies now, blended into the furniture. He was sitting in his usual spot at a table in the corner, an almost empty glass in front of him. In the past he'd always had a hand-rolled cigarette dangling from his lips, and even though the smoking ban had been in place for years, he still looked out of place without it.

It must be six or seven years since Dylan had last seen Archie but he hadn't changed. His dark, slicked-back hair was a little thinner, and he was minus a couple more teeth, but he still wore a collar and tie. It would be difficult for onlookers to believe he'd spent half of his adult life behind bars.

Dylan walked over to his table. "What are you having, Archie?"

Archie looked up and gave him a toothless smile. "Long time, no see. You're looking well, Mr. Scott."

Archie had always called him Mr. Scott and Dylan had given up trying to change that. It sounded like a sign of respect but everyone knew what Archie thought of coppers or ex-coppers. He liked getting cash out of them for information, though. And little happened on the streets of London without Archie's knowledge.

"You too. So what are you having?"

Archie looked at his pint glass. "I'll have a whisky, please, Mr. Scott. A double if it's not too much to ask."

Dylan bought their drinks, whisky for Archie and a pint for himself, and carried them across to the table. "How have you been?" he asked as he sat opposite Archie.

"Mustn't grumble. Managing to keep my head above water. Going straight now, of course. How about you? Odd to think of a bloke like you ending up behind bars." There was no hint of a smirk, only genuine surprise.

"Yeah, well. It was claimed that I used unreasonable force during an arrest."

"So I heard."

"It was all bollocks."

"I guessed it would be. Odd that they kicked you off the force too." Archie wouldn't let the subject drop but he didn't seem to be gloating.

"It suits me. I'm my own boss now so I can do things my way."

"A private investigator no less. I bet that keeps you busy. I suppose it's one of your cases that brings you here this evening?"

"No, this is personal. I'm looking for Leonard King. Remember him?"

Archie always claimed poverty, but Dylan reckoned he could have made a fortune as a poker player. His expression never gave anything away. Never.

"I do," Archie said. "Served time for being caught in a big drugs bust. Was set up along with Max Rickman. Recently released, I hear."

"The very same. Any idea where I might find him?"

"No." Archie took a long swallow of whisky and

paused to savour the liquid flowing down his throat. He put down his glass and licked his lips. "I can tell you you're not the only one looking for him, though."

"Oh? Who else wants him?"

Instead of answering, Archie straightened his perfectly straight tie and preened a little. Dylan took the hint and took two twenty-pound notes from his wallet. "What do you know, Archie?"

"Word on the street is that John Weller wants a chat with Lenny King."

"Who?" The name meant nothing to Dylan.

"Rickman's stepson. His wife's lad by her first marriage."

"Got him." Dylan delved back in his memory. "He'd be—how old now?"

"I dunno. Thirty perhaps. Something like that. He's opened up one of these flashy gyms where you have to be stinking rich to go on one of his running machines. Mercedes driven by stick-thin women fill the car park."

"What does he want with King?"

"Your guess is as good as mine. I don't reckon it's good, though, seeing as how King's gone into hiding."

"This gym Weller owns," Dylan said. "Is it clean?"

"As far as I know. I think his mother owns half of it—Rickman's wife."

"Are they still married?"

"Technically, yeah. He's not likely to meet anyone else, is he? Mind, neither is she when you stop to think about it. And to hear her talk, you'd think she was Cleopatra waiting for her Romeo."

"Juliet?"

"Is it? Yeah, probably. Anyway, I hear she has a bit of male company. Despite everything, she's still a looker and she's a good ten years younger than Rickman."

"Any names?"

"Not that I've heard. Phil Browne's a regular visitor, I gather, but I don't think there's anything in that."

"As in Phil Browne the lawyer?"

"That's him."

Browne was more crooked than any of the people he'd ever defended in court. He was a damn good lawyer if you were lucky enough to be able to afford him. Many a criminal had walked free thanks to his efforts. But even Browne's talent hadn't been enough to keep Rickman from a cell.

"To tell the truth, I always had a bit of a soft spot for her," Archie said, taking Dylan completely by surprise. "She had a lot to put up with and money's not the answer to everything, is it? Well, not in her case. She's always seemed like a fun person, though, despite everything." Perhaps thinking he'd said too much, he cleared his throat and took a swig of whisky.

Odd to think of Archie fancying Rickman's wife, especially when he was old enough to be her father. Still, whatever floats your boat...

"What was the word on the street about King's and Rickman's arrest, Archie?"

"That was the interesting thing." Archie emptied his glass, savouring every last drop of whisky. "Everyone believed they'd been set up but no one had any idea who was behind it. I never heard so much as a whisper as to who might have grassed them up."

Archie toyed with his empty glass and, again, Dylan took the none-too-subtle hint. "Same again?"

"You're a true gent, Mr. Scott."

It was several minutes before Dylan had their drinks in his hand, not because the pub was busy but because the barmaid was more interested in the soap being shown on a small TV above the bar. She'd mastered the art of watching the TV and dispensing spirits measures at the same time, but she couldn't do it at speed.

"Thanks." Dylan took his change from her but her eyes didn't leave the screen.

Archie's eyes didn't leave the double whisky Dylan put on the table in front of him either. He took a slow appreciative sip.

"They say half a million quid was found at King's flat," Archie said.

"Then they're exaggerating." It was a little over a quarter million. "King claims it was planted. Any ideas?"

"Like I said, I've heard nothing. Except that the money was stolen from Rickman."

"Oh?"

"Yeah, that's common knowledge. But as to who set them up, no one knows. It could have been anyone. Someone shifting as much heroin as Rickman was bound to make plenty of enemies along the way. Besides, he's an evil piece of work."

"True." None of this was helping him find King. "What about King's friends? Who are they? I know his wife divorced him so I don't suppose he's hiding out there." According to prison records Pikey had looked at, she'd never once visited him inside. "He's got a couple of teenage boys, though, hasn't he? He must want to see them."

"He might, but I reckon they'll be strangers to him.

His wife would have nothing to do with him after that little lot was found in her flat."

Dylan could still remember Wendy's reaction when the booty had been found. She'd alternated between shock, a raging anger and tears.

"I don't suppose she told the kids what a great dad they had," Archie said. "I bet he doesn't see them now."

Archie could be right, but he'd still bet King would want to see them, if only from a distance. Dylan made a mental note to follow the sons and see if King showed up. "He must have other friends. Other places to go."

"I can't think of anyone special. He won't be able to keep away from the dogs, though."

"Dogs?"

"Yeah, greyhound racing. He's addicted to it. He might be hiding from Weller, but I'll bet he'll still be trackside. Anyway, I can't see Weller worrying him too much. He's barely out of short trousers."

"You said he was thirty."

"Yeah. Just a kid." Archie lifted his glass. "But if I wanted to find King, that's where I'd look. The dog track."

"Are there still greyhound tracks around? I thought they'd all closed down."

"Wimbledon," Archie said. "Every Friday and Saturday night. It's the last track left in London and I expect that'll be gone soon."

It wasn't a lot to go on, but it was better than nothing, and it wouldn't hurt him to look at some dogs tomorrow night.

Dylan pulled another two twenty-pound notes from his wallet and handed them over. "Give me a call if you hear anything, will you, Archie? Anything about King, Rickman or anyone else involved."

"Of course I will, Mr. Scott." Archie gave him a toothless grin. "You know me, I'm always happy to help in any way I can."

FOUR

"THIS WINE'S GONE to my head." Bev switched off the TV and returned the DVD to its case. "Good film, though."

"Hugh Jackman," Lucy said. "How could it be anything else?"

"If only all men were made that way."

"And how is Dylan?"

"A pain in the arse." Bev snorted with laughter. "Hey, we can manage another glass, can't we?" She picked up the bottle and pulled a face on seeing less than half an inch in the bottom. "I'll open another."

She bumped into the wall on her way back from the kitchen but no damage was done. The bottle survived.

"Dylan's okay really. Driving me mad, but I suppose he's on a hiding to nothing. I long for a bit of sympathy from him and then I can't abide him fussing. On the very rare occasions that he wants to talk, I don't. When I want to talk, he's out of here before I've drawn breath. And he's still trying to understand why women can't run marathons twenty-four hours after having a hysterectomy."

"They have no conception, do they?"

"None whatsoever. I'd love to see them cope with childbirth. They're always at death's door when they have a cold." She filled their glasses to the brim with red wine. "So tell me all the gossip. Who's doing what with whom?"

"Nothing's happening. Really, it's all quiet." Lucy laughed at Bev's expression. "I have no gossip at all. Nothing. Zilch."

"Some friend you are."

"You're missing being at work, aren't you?" Lucy said.

"I am, yes. It was lovely at first—well, apart from recovering from a hysterectomy—but I hate not seeing anyone normal. The only people I talk to are doctors and kids. So yeah, I miss the normality of work. I'd love to get up in the morning—"

"Without a hangover?"

"That would be a bonus." Bev grinned. "But I'd love to walk into a classroom and do battle with thirty kids tomorrow."

"It won't be much longer now."

"But before then, I've got the chemo and I hate the thought of my body being pumped full of chemicals. The side effects can be horrendous. I'll die if my hair drops out."

Lucy nodded. "It's scary stuff."

"Terrifying. I'm a nervous wreck. I might not look it with all this wine inside me, but I'm stressed to hell. I'm taking it out on Dylan and the kids too. Dylan—well, you know what he's like. It's water off a duck's back to him. But I shouldn't let it make me snappy with the kids."

"Freya's too young to understand and Luke's old enough to know that when people are ill, they get snappy. Don't feel bad about it."

Bev supposed Lucy was right. No one sailed through

cancer without getting tense and stroppy. Perhaps she was being too hard on herself.

"If you want to be snappy with me, you know where I am." Lucy patted her arm. "Seriously, I'm always here if you need me. You know that, don't you?"

"I do, thanks. I'm okay with you because—"

"Because we're always drunk?"

"No, because I don't have to pretend. You know I'm scared witless, and I don't have to pretend otherwise. With Dylan and the kids, I try to act normal. It's bloody difficult at times."

"Then stop pretending."

If only it were that easy. "If I admit I'm scared, Dylan will panic. As it is, he can keep telling himself that I'll soon be back at work and life will return to normal."

"It will, Bev. You'll see."

Sitting here with Lucy, a glass of wine in her hand, Bev could believe that. She could laugh at her silly fears. When she woke in the early hours, though, everything was different.

It was the same when she was talking to doctors and nurses. They were so calm, so matter-of-fact, that worrying seemed such a ridiculous waste of time. Once she was away from them, though, she wanted to yell at them that she wasn't just another patient, that this was her life in their hands.

No one understood how she felt. The kids couldn't, it wasn't possible. Dylan certainly couldn't. Even Lucy— how could anyone know how she felt?

"Did I tell you that Dylan wanted me and the kids to go away for a while?" she asked.

"No." Lucy frowned. "How do you mean? Go where?"

"That's exactly what I said. Honestly, he's being more weird than usual at the moment. He said he thought I needed a change of scene, and he thought the kids would enjoy it. How he imagined we could just take off, I have no idea. I'd have to come back every ten minutes for all these blasted hospital appointments."

"It sounds a nice idea—an Easter break. I expect he thought you'd relax more away from home."

"Maybe. But he's fussing more too, and it's so unlike him," Bev said. "It's as if he feels he needs to keep watch over me in case I fall apart. It's driving me mad."

The front door opened.

"Talk of the devil," Lucy said. "Unless Hugh Jackman's popping in for coffee."

"God, I wish."

Dylan was shrugging off his jacket as he walked into the living room. "Hi, Luce. Everything all right?"

"Great, thanks."

"We were hoping you were Hugh Jackman," Bev said.

"I was hoping you'd be sober, but you can't win 'em all."

For some reason that escaped Bev, she and Lucy found that unbelievably funny and rolled around on the sofa with tears running down their faces.

FIVE

CAROL WASN'T SURE what woke her in the early hours of Sunday morning. She lifted her head from the pillow and heard George's distinctive purring. He sounded like a cross between a wheezy steam train and a vacuum cleaner.

"I hope you're not going to pee on the carpet again." She pulled the duvet up to her chin and reached out to Jimmy. Except he wasn't there.

She fumbled in the dark for her phone and the display lit up to tell her it was 4:24 a.m. She switched on the light and was about to call out but, not wanting to wake the kids, she got out of bed, pulled on her dressing gown and went downstairs.

She'd expected Jimmy to be sitting in the kitchen with a coffee, or perhaps a beer, but all was quiet.

"Where the hell—?" She went to the porch and counted the shoes that always provided an obstacle course for people trying to get in or out the house. Jimmy's running shoes were missing. "I don't believe this."

As well as being wide awake, she was bloody annoyed now. What sort of idiot went running at four in the morning?

She hated conflict, hated telling Jimmy what he should and shouldn't be doing, but this was ridiculous. No one in their right mind had to run at this hour. It wasn't as if he worked and needed to fit in his exercise before spending a day in an office. He had all day to run. Just like he had all day to paint the sitting room, retile the bathroom, fix the cooker housing and the landing window, and all the other jobs he'd promised to do. Mostly, she had no idea how he filled his days, but he certainly didn't do anything useful.

Not for the first time, she wished he was back in the army. She'd had her own routine then and it had suited her and the kids. She got them to school, opened her hairdressing salon, chatted to her clients about forthcoming summer holidays, new fashions and celebrity gossip, banked her takings and came home in time to make sure Matthew and Ewan did their homework and were ferried to friends' houses or various social events. Life had been simple. Uncomplicated.

Now, with Jimmy home, there was no order to anything. It was ironic that he was the one who liked everything to run with military precision and yet life had been chaotic since he arrived home.

The worst of it was his moodiness, and the way the kids couldn't do anything right. Ever since Ewan had decided he wanted to join the police force like his granddad, Jimmy hadn't had a good word to say to his son. It couldn't be that he had anything against the police—well, other than his belief that they were all lining their pockets—so it had to be that he resented Ewan being closer to his grandfather than his own father. And given that Jimmy was so strict and snappy with him, that wasn't surprising. Jimmy loved to complain that both kids always asked her if they wanted to go somewhere, but that wasn't surprising either. They knew damn well that if they asked Jimmy he'd say no just for the hell of it.

She knew she should make allowances, but it was so difficult. She wasn't good at dealing with mental health problems. She should be, given the number of books she'd read on the subject, but she wasn't. Depression, panic attacks, suicidal thoughts—she'd never experienced anything like it so couldn't put herself in Jimmy's shoes. Whenever she tried, she failed.

It was all so—sudden too. One minute, life had been ticking along happily and the next, Jimmy had been discharged from the army suffering from post-traumatic stress disorder. It had come out of the blue and none of them had adapted well to the change. She'd been thrown out of her depth and felt helpless.

Maybe she should be grateful there wasn't a woman involved. At least, she didn't think there was. She wasn't blind, she knew Jimmy still liked to flirt with anything wearing a skirt, but as far as she knew it hadn't progressed past the flirting stage for a few years.

The last time he'd had an affair, Carol's sister had accused her, probably correctly, of being naive. Any fool would have been able to tell, she'd said. Was it happening all over again? He was spending a lot of nights away again, coming and going at all hours.

It was a little before six when his car pulled up outside, and she was still sitting at the table.

He walked into the kitchen with his car keys swinging from his fingers. "What are you doing up?"

"Wondering where the hell you are."

"I've been for a run." He spoke as if it were the most natural thing in the world.

"In the car?"

He smiled at that. "I drove out to the river and did seven miles alongside that. It's the best time to run—nice and quiet, no one around."

Was she naive to believe him? She no longer knew.

"Don't look like that," he said. "The doctor would give me a gold star. Exercise releases all the happy endorphins. It's good for me."

Then perhaps *she* needed to go for a run because she was far from happy.

She couldn't argue that he wasn't in great shape. He was. Tall and well muscled, there wasn't so much as an ounce of spare flesh on him. He could run for miles and he was strong. The army's fitness regime had kept him in top shape and she wouldn't want him to sit around getting fat now that he was home.

She had to believe him. Either way, there was no point arguing with him and making him angry.

"Let's go to bed," she said. "We can have a lie-in, breakfast in bed with the Sunday papers…bliss."

SIX

DYLAN HAD ONLY spent a few months behind bars so he couldn't say how King was feeling, but the first thing he'd wanted on his release was to be with his wife and kids. King didn't have a good relationship with his ex-wife, so it was said, and so the speed with which she'd divorced him would indicate, but he must still want to see his kids. Children were like an extra limb. They linked one generation to the next. Without them, it was impossible to feel whole.

That belief had Dylan sitting in a red hired Peugeot within viewing distance of Wendy King's house early on Sunday morning. He couldn't use his own car because it stuck out like a—well, like a 1956 Morgan in Daytona Yellow. As much as he loved it, he had to admit that it was worse than useless for surveillance work.

He wasn't sure if King would recognise him after all these years. He kept telling himself that too many years had passed, yet he knew damn well that if someone had helped put him behind bars, he'd recognise them. It wasn't worth taking unnecessary risks so he'd pulled out an old disguise that he'd used a few times in the past. Disguise was perhaps a flattering description for the long brown wig and the rimless, nerdy-looking glasses, but they would help.

Wendy had moved house twice in the years since King's arrest. She'd gone from a flat above a kebab shop that had its windows smashed every other fortnight to this extremely desirable three-storey Victorian semi in Notting Hill that had to be worth somewhere between a million and a million and a half.

When their husbands wound up in prison, wives usually struggled to make ends meet. They didn't, as a rule, end up with a better lifestyle. It was possible that a relative had died and left her some money, or perhaps she'd had a win on the Premium Bonds or the Lottery.

Or perhaps the cash found in the flat at the time of King's arrest had been the tip of the iceberg. Maybe, after all, King had been up to his neck in dealing and had amassed a small fortune that Wendy felt able to spend.

In a perfect world, King would walk up to the front door and his children would race into his open arms. The world wasn't perfect, though, so Dylan continued to wait.

All in all, he'd had a pointless week. Not pointless from the bill-paying side of things because he'd finished and been paid for a couple of small jobs, but pointless from a finding-the-sicko-making-death-threats side of things.

Last night's visit to the dog track had been a waste of time. When Archie had said King liked to be "trackside," Dylan had imagined standing by a rickety fence in the cold and rain with a group of old men in flat caps. He'd never been to a greyhound-racing meeting in his life and the whole experience was a complete surprise. The grandstand was covered, enclosed and glass-fronted, although you could step outside if you wished. There was no shortage of food and drink. Hell, there was even a tapas bar. People were more smartly dressed than he'd expected too, probably because it was a venue of choice for some wanting to celebrate birthdays, stag nights or hen parties. TV screens were everywhere so you couldn't miss your dog racing past the post—or not. But the poor dogs who gave their all week in and week out seemed of secondary importance to the party atmosphere.

It had been a mildly interesting evening but, as King had been nowhere in sight, a waste of time. And that was another thing that niggled away at him. He'd seen a mug shot of King and had found a couple of photos taken at the time of his trial on the internet, but other than that, Dylan was relying on his memory. He wasn't a hundred percent sure he'd even recognise him after all this time. His hair had been dark and quite short. He'd been tall but thin. Scrawny even. On the back of his neck he had a tattoo, the Tottenham Hotspur Football Club emblem with Spurs Till I Die beneath it. If he was wearing a high collar, however, that would be of no help whatsoever.

It was no use. He couldn't sit still any longer. Unfortunately, though, despite having little else to think about, he still hadn't come up with a convincing story as to why he wanted to see Wendy's ex-husband.

He left his car and strolled the few yards along the quiet street to Wendy's house. The small front garden was immaculate. He knocked on the door and didn't have long to wait. A woman wearing an impressive amount of gold jewellery—watch, bracelet, necklace and earrings—opened the door. She was wearing black trousers and a red shirt that showed off her slim figure. Blond hair surrounded an attractive face.

"Mrs. King?" he asked.

"Yes."

"Bill Williams." He gave her a beaming smile, and she looked, unsurprisingly, blank. "My publicist contacted you." Still she looked blank, as well she might. "About the book I'm writing?"

The latter had a suspicious frown marring her attractive features.

"Sorry," he said, "I can see there's been a mix-up. My publicist was supposed to get in touch with you and arrange a meeting. According to her, I'm due to meet you for a chat at—" he glanced at his watch, "—two o'clock. You know nothing about this, do you?"

"Nothing."

"I'm really sorry about this. Let me introduce myself. I'm Bill Williams, the author. I'm currently working on a book about prisoners who've been wrongly convicted and I was hoping to feature your husband's case."

She visibly paled at that but managed to gather herself enough to say, "Ex-husband. And he wasn't wrongly convicted."

"Well, no, but some people think it was a setup."

"Then they're wrong. The police found the evidence. It was real enough, believe me, because I was there when they found it." She began to close the door. "I have nothing to say to you. In case you haven't heard, I'm divorced. I no longer care what Lenny does. It's nothing to do with me."

"Right, I can understand that. And I'm really sorry for any misunderstanding. Perhaps you could let me know where I might find your husband?"

"I don't know where he is. And I don't care."

"He hasn't been to see you since he's been released? You do know he's been released, don't you?"

"Oh, yes, I know. And no, he hasn't been anywhere near. He might be a lying bastard, but he's not completely stupid. After what he put me through, he knows not to show his face anywhere near me."

"I thought—his children. Doesn't he see them?"

"No. They're better off without him." Again, she tried to close the door and again, Dylan pushed against it to stop her.

"I've read up on his case and I think it might make an interesting story. What if it was a setup? What if he wasn't involved with Rickman—other than to be paid for driving? The more I think about it, the more convinced I am that he served far too long a sentence. What if someone proved he was set up?"

"They won't, and it's no skin off my nose either way. Look, I've got nothing to say to you and I'm busy."

"Fine. I'm sorry to have bothered you. If he does get in touch, could you tell him I'm looking for him? My number—"

"He won't." This time, she managed to slam the door in his face.

Dylan was at the end of the drive when he turned and saw Wendy through the ground-floor window. She wasn't paying attention to him. She was too busy talking on her phone. Interesting that she'd felt the sudden need to make a phone call.

Or perhaps someone had called her.

Dylan walked slowly back to his car. He hadn't seen any sign of the children all day and he'd heard nothing while standing on the doorstep. The sun was shining, albeit weakly, so he would have expected King's sons to have been outside making the most of it. Perhaps they were out for the day. If they were, they'd left early. Perhaps they were away for the weekend. Perhaps they were spending part of the school holiday with friends or family. Or even their father.

Wendy King was young, slim and comfortably off so it was surprising that she hadn't remarried. Perhaps she wasn't as anti her husband as she claimed. She might have divorced him for show while being grateful for his having provided financially for the family. Maybe she loved him today as much as she had on their wedding day. For all Dylan knew, he could have been hiding in the house.

At a little before six that evening, a large dark car pulled up outside the house. The driver, a woman in her mid-forties, got out and opened the doors. Dylan watched as two, three, four teenage boys tumbled out and raced to the front door.

An hour later, two of those teenagers followed the woman back to the car and left.

Soon after, Wendy's two sons emerged from the house, took cycles from the house and pedalled away. There was no movement until they returned at a little after half past nine.

All lights in the house were extinguished before eleven o'clock. With everything in darkness, Dylan decided he might as well admit defeat and go home.

MONDAY CAME AND went and Dylan wasted most of it either watching Wendy's house or following her sons to the shops and back.

Tuesday morning found him outside the house for

the third day running. And he was annoyed. Fucking annoyed.

Photographs that had been hand delivered to his office at some point during Sunday night or Monday morning sat on the passenger seat next to him. Thoughts of stable doors and horses bolting came to mind, but a security firm was busy installing cameras at the front door of his office building. Too little too late probably.

The same firm had already installed security cameras at his home. He'd given Bev a cock-and-bull story about getting the system cheap and, thankfully, she'd been too preoccupied to do anything but smile at what she described as toys for the boys.

Dylan had changed vehicles and today's surveillance was taking place from a blue van. He was still wearing the brown wig and glasses. Actually, he thought longer hair suited him.

At eight-thirty, King's sons left the house on their cycles. Dylan followed them. They talked and laughed as they made their way to the nearby park to meet up with a group of other kids. There was no sign of King so Dylan returned to his spot outside Wendy's house.

What felt like hours but was only forty minutes later, the postman walked up the drive and dropped mail through the letterbox.

This was madness, but Dylan was fresh out of better ideas. Archie was no help. Dylan had promised him a lot of cash if he could find King, but even he'd drawn a blank.

"He must be dead," Archie had said. "That's the only thing that would keep him away from the dog track."

Storm clouds gathered and the rain came in biblical proportions at noon. It hammered on the van's roof so that Dylan struggled to hear himself think.

A car pulled up outside Wendy's house, and a well-dressed man, possibly in his forties or fifties, it was difficult to tell, climbed out and headed to the front door. Dylan didn't recognise him, and the photos he managed to take weren't much help. The chap's face was averted, his coat collar was turned up against the rain and he was walking quickly to avoid a soaking. Dylan had a clear photo of the car's registration plate so that was something.

Five minutes later, the man emerged. Dylan clicked away with his camera as the chap trotted back to his car and jumped inside, but none of the pictures would give up the man's identity. Sodding weather.

Minutes turned into hours. He would have expected Wendy to go shopping, visit friends or her hairdresser, or do one of the dozens of other things women did with their spare time, but there was no movement.

He took another look at the photos that had been delivered to his office. One showed Bev and the kids at the front door of his house. Another showed Luke messing around with a football in the front garden. Yet another was of Bev standing inside the house with Freya in her arms.

He'd kill the sick bastard who'd taken them.

A motorcycle roared up the road and stopped outside Wendy's home. The rider pulled off his helmet and—was it King? Dylan couldn't be sure but the man who strode up to the door looked a likely candidate.

A car drove past, momentarily blocking Dylan's view so he didn't see the front door open. It was impossible to know if the man had been welcomed inside by Wendy or if he'd used his own key.

Dylan checked his watch. It was 2:45 p.m. He'd give them five minutes and then confront the pair of them. He'd look pretty silly if it was Wendy's boyfriend or a pizza delivery, but he'd be seriously pissed off if it was King and he missed him.

Less than a minute later, the man ran out the house, pulling on his helmet as he did so, jumped on the bike, fired it into life and sped off down the road at well above the legal speed limit. *Shit.*

Dylan didn't have a hope in hell of catching him. He left the van and marched up to the house. He rang the bell. Nothing. He rang it again. And again.

He tried the front door and was surprised when it swung open. He stepped into a spacious hallway.

"Hello?" He stood at the bottom of the stairs. All was silent. "Hello? Mrs. King?"

He found her in the kitchen.

She was lying on the floor with one leg bent at an awkward angle. Her face was unmarked, but her head was resting in a pool of blood. Dead eyes stared at the ceiling.

SEVEN

DYLAN PUSHED OPEN the door of his local pub. "Hey, it's just like old times."

Pikey wasn't convinced, or particularly happy with the arrangement. "I don't remember the three of us drinking together."

"True," Dylan agreed. "I think we were too busy getting bollocked by a certain detective chief inspector."

"Will you two shut up and buy me a pint?" Frank said. "That's another problem with you soft southerners, you talk too much."

Frank—ex-detective chief inspector Willoughby—walked up to the bar and gave the beers on offer a critical eye. Despite having retired from the force on health grounds, he stood tall and erect. His suit was a perfect fit, and his black shoes had been polished to within an inch of their lives. Frank still had standards.

When Dylan had heard that Frank was making one of his rare visits to London from Lancashire and could spare time for a drink, he'd immediately phoned Pikey to see if he could join them. Dylan had worked several cases in Lancashire—the not-so-sleepy northern town of Dawson's Clough would forever haunt him—and he'd been glad of Frank's help. Pikey, however, had shown no enthusiasm whatsoever for a cosy drink with their ex-boss. Dylan could understand that. When they'd worked together on the force, the arrival of Detective Chief Inspector Willoughby had soon turned into their worst nightmare.

These days, though, Dylan was pleased and proud to call Frank a friend. He was sure that Pikey would soon accept that their boss had changed—mellowed—over the intervening years.

Pikey looked smart in a crisp white shirt and blue tie too. Dylan had gone for the more casual look, or scruffy as Bev preferred to call it, with T-shirt, jeans and a leather jacket that had to be at least ten years old.

He bought their drinks and they took a table in the corner where they could talk without being disturbed or overheard.

His local had changed hands three times in the past two years and a quick look round told him that, yet again, he didn't recognise anyone. It had been a decent pub once but the current owners had tarted it up, started serving food at odd hours and, worse, felt the need to adorn the place with flags and bunting for any old reason. It had been impossible to move for waving leprechauns and inflatable pints of Guinness for the two weeks leading up to St. Patrick's Day. He often thought it a pity that English pubs celebrated Paddy's Day with gusto yet usually ignored their own patron saint. Poor St. George was lucky if anyone bothered to hoist a flag.

"I can only stay for a quick one," Pikey said, "so you'd better get to the point, Dylan. What's going on?"

"There's this for starters." He slapped a brown envelope on the table. "This was hand delivered to my office."

Frowning, Frank opened the envelope and pulled out photographs of Dylan's wife and children. "Christ."

"As you can see, I've dusted them for prints," Dylan said, "but there's nothing. That's not surprising. A kid of five would know not to leave fingerprints."

"And you reckon this is the work of Leonard King?" Frank sounded doubtful.

"Most of the folk we helped put away threatened to get us," Pikey said, "but, of those, only King has recently been released."

"I've been told it's payback time," Dylan said.

"Has this caller made noises about your family?" Frank asked.

"No, but I struggle to believe the calls and the photos are unconnected." He took a swig of beer. "I'd hate to think I had two nutters after me."

"So where's King now?" Frank asked. "Still missing?"

"We'll soon have him." Pikey sounded more confident than he looked. "He's wanted in connection with his ex-wife's murder." He waved a dismissive arm as Dylan tried to interrupt him. "Yes, yes, I know he didn't kill her, but we're still dragging him in."

"Tell me about that," Frank said.

"I'd been watching the house for days, hoping King would show up," Dylan said. "Wendy had a visitor at about ten o'clock yesterday morning. Male, well dressed, probably mid-forties, although I didn't get a good look at his face. Rain was lashing down and he kept his head averted. He stayed for five minutes and then left. I got the car's registration but, guess what. It had been reported stolen from a supermarket's car park half an hour earlier and was later dumped a couple of miles away. Nothing happened at the house until King rode up on a motorbike—at least, I'm fairly sure it was King—at a quarter to three. He was there for less than a minute before he raced off. As I didn't have a chance of catching him, I went inside to question Wendy. I found her on the kitchen floor. She'd been dead for a few hours so there's no way that King could have killed her."

"The doc reckoned she died between nine and eleven," Pikey said, confirming this.

"Did you call it in?" Frank asked, and Dylan nodded.

"I had to. I didn't want her sons returning home to that."

"They're staying with Wendy's mother," Pikey said. "Other than that, I don't know much about it because it's not my case. Everyone's looking for King, though, so we'll soon have him."

"I had a quick look round before I called it in. There wasn't much to see, but it's possible she may have known her killer and let him into the house. But the way the kitchen looked—two stools overturned, knives on the floor—makes me think she put up a fight. There were no opened cupboards or drawers to suggest her killer was looking for something."

"It's a bit bloody odd," Pikey said.

"Too true. But there's a lot of odd stuff going on in King's life right now," Dylan said.

"But why Wendy King? And why now?"

Dylan didn't have a clue. "According to a reliable source, Rickman's stepson is after King. That same source reckons King must be dead if he's managing to keep away from the dog track. Then his wife's murdered—"

"With that little lot going on," Frank said, "you'd think he'd have far more important things to do with his time than try to rattle one of the coppers who helped put him behind bars."

"My thoughts exactly," Dylan said. "But who the hell else can it be?"

"Any other ideas?" Pikey asked.

"None." Dylan had thought and thought and drawn a blank. "My job involves upsetting people. It could be anyone. For a start, I have to pay the bills and to do that, I occasionally have to sink very low and do the worst job in the world."

"And that is?" Frank asked.

"Proving the infidelity or otherwise of spouses." One of his recent cases came to mind. Discretion had been the name of the game and Dylan wasn't even sure that Brad Goodenough knew he'd been investigated let alone by whom. If he did know, though, he'd be pretty pissed off with Dylan. "A chap asked me to investigate the bloke his daughter was planning to marry. He thought the prospective fiancé was after his daughter's considerable bank balance and he was right. The father was relieved, the daughter was broken-hearted and the fiancé was—well, I can only assume he was less than pleased. I'm not sure if he knew I was responsible for outing him, though. And wanting me dead seems a bit extreme."

"The world's full of crazy bastards," Frank said. "Who is he?"

"A chap by the name of Brad Goodenough. But he'll probably be as difficult to find as King. He'd been renting a property under a false name and I gather he's a bit of a gigolo. He has a penchant for rich women."

"Don't we all," Frank said.

"Yeah." Dylan grinned. "I could be wrong, but I bet Goodenough is using yet another identity and eyeing up another rich future wife."

"You need to find out, mate." Pikey drained his glass and got to his feet. "Sorry, but I really do have to go. There's an Easter fundraising thing on at the school and my name will be mud if I miss it. It's good to see you again, Frank. Actually, yes it is good to see you."

"Christ, don't go all soft on me," Frank said.

"No danger of that. Good to see you too, Dylan. I'll keep you posted."

They watched Pikey leave the pub and Frank decided they needed more beer. He chatted to the barmaid for a couple of minutes before bringing their drinks to the table.

"Don't get sidetracked by King," Frank said. "Yes, he threatened to get you when he was sent down, but that holds true for a lot of criminals."

"I know."

"His wife's murder is all sad and tragic, but a team of perfectly capable coppers is looking into that. What you can't afford to do is get wrapped up in King and ignore other suspects. You might be dealing with a harmless crank, but you might be dealing with a bloody psychopath."

Dylan accepted the truth of that. He needed to go through the file of every case he'd ever worked on and draw up a list of possible nutters. It would be one hell of a long list.

"So how's Bev?" Frank asked.

"Oh—you know."

"Yes, I suppose I do." Frank gave him a knowing look. "And how are you coping with it? Burying your head in the sand, I imagine."

Dylan was about to deny the charge, but Frank was right. It was easier to push it from his mind. If he didn't talk about it, if he could stop himself thinking about it—

"Something like that," he admitted.

"So you keep busy." Frank nodded his understanding and obligingly changed the subject. "Tell me about this chap whose engagement you foiled. What's his name again?"

"Brad Goodenough. And no crap jokes about him not being good enough." Dylan took a long, slow drink of his beer. "My very wealthy client's daughter had been dating him for three months. A typical whirlwind romance. On the surface, Goodenough was charming, more than comfortably off and totally besotted with said client's daughter. The truth was that the flat he supposedly owned was rented under a different name—possibly his real name and possibly not. The Porsche he drove was borrowed from an older woman he was having an affair with. He's a charmer. A handsome charmer. Women fall under his spell and he makes the most of it."

"What's he doing now?" Frank asked.

"Charming other women, I imagine. I found out enough—and had photographic evidence of his infidelity—for my client. Given the high profile of my client, he didn't want to press charges and he certainly didn't want any publicity. Instead he had a 'never darken my door again' chat with Goodenough, paid me for services rendered and that was that. End of. At least, I assumed it was end of."

"How much are we talking? Financially, I mean?"

"Millions. My client's getting on a bit and, when he pops his clogs, his son and daughter stand to inherit the lot. The daughter is doing well in her own right too. With her father's backing, she set up her own fashion label. Goodenough has lost out on a fortune."

"There you go then," Frank said. "There's another name for you. So far you have King and Goodenough. Dig some more and I'm sure you'll come up with more names. Just watch your back."

"And on that cheerful note, it must be my round."

He'd hoped Frank would dismiss it, that he'd remind him that people who wanted to scare you made phone calls and sent notes, and those who wanted to kill you did just that. Frank hadn't dismissed it, though, and try as he might, Dylan couldn't shake off his growing sense of unease. Or perhaps dread was more apt.

He had a *really* bad feeling about this.

EIGHT

JIMMY ZIPPED HIS holdall and hoisted it onto the kitchen table.

"How long will you be away this time?" Carol asked.

"Four days. No longer. Well, I hope it's no longer. I'll call you."

"You're spending more time in Somerset than you are at home. Still—" she smiled at him, "—at least it keeps you out of mischief."

"How do you know?"

Laughing, she lifted her hands to his shoulders and kissed him. "It had better be keeping you out of mischief. Seriously, Jimmy, I'm glad you're able to do this. You should be proud of yourself. A lot of ex-army bods think the reservists are beneath them. It's good that you've volunteered to help with their training."

"Yeah, well." He shrugged off the compliment, kissed her back and then grabbed his holdall. "Call me if you need me, okay? Otherwise I'll see you soon."

"Take care, Jimmy. Hey, you've remembered to pack your medication, haven't you?"

"Of course. Stop worrying." *Stop fucking nagging!*

Jimmy marched out of the house with his bag slung over his shoulder. He took car keys from his pocket, flicked the button to unlock the doors and threw his holdall onto the back seat. He climbed inside, fired the engine and reversed out of the drive.

Nickelback's "Rockstar" was playing on the radio and he cranked up the volume and sang along. He felt good. Alive and free. Birds must feel this way every day, he thought. "I'm as free as a bird," he told the radio, and the knowledge made him laugh.

Freedom had been a long time coming. It was exactly a week since he'd taken Dowie, much longer than he'd wanted to keep him. All was good, though. Police hadn't even found Dowie's car yet. In fact, they didn't seem to be taking the bloke's disappearance too seriously. They soon would but, for now, that suited Jimmy.

Because of roadworks, a journey that shouldn't have taken longer than five minutes lasted for over twenty. He parked his car a couple of streets away and walked the rest of the way to Russell Street. After making sure no one was around, he opened the garage door and checked his van. All was as it should be and he went round to the rear of the house and let himself in.

Several flyers for local fast-food outlets had been pushed through the letterbox, and Jimmy dropped them in a black bag he'd filled with rubbish. He opened the cellar door, switched on the light and walked down the stairs. The smell clawed at his belly. It was a mix of damp walls, stale urine and worse.

"Ah, you're awake." He gave Dowie a beaming smile. "I should have provided you with a radio. You've missed some great music."

Dowie groaned behind his gag and his chin flopped down onto his chest.

Jimmy wondered if the rope round Dowie's neck was right. Yes, it must be. If Dowie so much as tipped his chair forward, he'd hang himself.

"I've brought you some water, though. See how I

look after my friends?" Jimmy unzipped his holdall, reached inside and pulled out a litre bottle of water. After unscrewing the cap, he yanked the tape from Dowie's mouth and shoved the bottle between his lips. Dowie coughed and spluttered. "Look at the mess you're getting in. Drink slowly. Breathe. That's it. A mouthful at a time."

Dowie was drinking like a dying man, which he was, and Jimmy took the bottle away.

"Who are you? What do you want? I'll give you anything. Anything."

"You really have no idea who I am, do you? Don't worry, I'll jog your memory soon." Jimmy carefully replaced the bottle's cap before putting fresh tape across Dowie's mouth. He put on three layers, all overlapping, just to be sure.

"I'll be spending the night here," he said. "You'll enjoy that, won't you? It'll make a change for you to have some company."

A fat, solitary tear rolled down Dowie's face.

Jimmy wondered if he'd cope with the smell. He'd called every day, but he'd only stayed long enough to check on Dowie and give him a quick drink of water. The thought of putting up with this stench for any longer made him nauseated. Still, he'd have to put up with it. So would Dowie. This wasn't a luxury hotel with en-suite facilities. Dowie would have to sit in his own shit and piss, and Jimmy would have to try to ignore it.

He pulled up a chair and sat opposite Dowie. "I wonder if the car business is doing okay without you. I wonder how your wife is coping too. Do you think she misses you? Do you think the police are searching for you?"

Dowie groaned.

"Well, let me tell you, they're not looking too hard. She didn't report you missing for days, you see. And why not? Because she thought you set off for the office as usual, then went to Cardiff for a few days to look at a possible new dealership you were thinking of buying." Jimmy clicked his teeth. "Tut, tut, Brian. What a tangled web you tried to weave. Leave the wife behind, spend a few days shagging your mistress and return to unsuspecting wife—a nice plan, but I'm afraid it won't work this time. You see, you won't be returning to your unsuspecting wife."

Indignant noises came from behind Dowie's taped mouth. It was impossible to guess at what he was trying to say. Jimmy didn't bother.

"I expect there have been other women over the years," Jimmy said. "There are women you marry, aren't there, like your lovely wife, but there are also women you must have. You don't love these women, but the sex is refreshingly different, and, hey, it's good to know you can still pull the birds. I know I'm right. I'm sure you love your wife in your own way." Jimmy got to his feet. "Anyway, I haven't come to lecture you on fidelity. Who am I to do that? My point is that the police won't be looking for you. Not yet."

He walked up the stairs and into the kitchen. The sun was trying to shine. It might be a nice day after all.

A crop of dandelions was thriving in the back yard. That was the thing about weeds. Very few plants would fare well between old paving slabs, but dandelions took over and provided a carpet of yellow. He'd have to pull them up. It was a pity, but he didn't want neighbours complaining about seeds blowing into their gardens.

That was unlikely as the house on his left was empty and the one on his right had an untidier yard than Jimmy's. An old man lived in it with an equally old dog. They limped off for walks together occasionally.

Jimmy filled a tin mug with coffee and carried it down the steps to the cellar. He took up position on the seat opposite Dowie and blew across the surface of his drink.

"I would have made you a cup, but you wouldn't be able to drink it, would you?" He took a sip. It was good and strong, just as he liked it. "So what shall we talk about? Me? There's not much to say really. I'm married to Carol—she has her own hairdressing salon. She's good at her job. Pretty too. She hasn't let herself go like some women do. She still takes care of herself." He smiled. "Sometimes her hair is blond and sometimes it's dark. Occasionally, she puts a red streak in it. I think she does that to see if I'll notice. I always do, of course, but sometimes I pretend I haven't."

Dowie's expression was glazed. There was no flicker of life in his eyes.

"Like you, I have two sons," Jimmy said. "Matthew and Ewan. They're good boys really. Well, for teenagers. Kids have it easy these days, don't they? I'm sure yours are the same. It was different in our day, wasn't it? Still, perhaps change isn't such a bad thing."

He finished his coffee and put the tin mug on the floor by his feet. He leaned back in his chair, feeling relaxed and perfectly at ease.

"What else can I tell you? Let me think. I'm what you'd call between jobs at the moment. I was discharged from the army on medical grounds. If I said I was sorry about that, I'd be lying. Oh, there's nothing wrong with me, by the way. Nah, I'd had enough. Simple as that. The army's okay, but there's more to life, isn't there? It's good to be home in a lot of ways. I need to get a job, but not yet. I have things to do first. Are you listening to me, Brian? Are you?"

Jimmy walked over to the really damp part of the cellar and picked up his crowbar. He whacked it against the palm of his hand as he returned to stand in front of Dowie.

"I'll soon make you pay attention."

He swung the crowbar hard against Dowie's knee. Dowie spluttered behind his gag, his eyes rolled and then his head slumped against his chest. Jimmy leapt forward in case he had to stop Dowie hanging himself, but there was no need. He was unconscious. Christ, the bloke wouldn't last five minutes in the army.

Jimmy threw the crowbar aside and went upstairs to the kitchen. He'd get out in the sunshine and pull up some dandelions to pass the time. He hated the waiting.

By four o'clock, the yard was tidy. There was nothing in it apart from two wheelie bins and a black bag filled with weeds.

He was admiring the neat space when his elderly neighbour returned with his dog. It was difficult to tell which of them was closer to death. The chap had to be pushing ninety and the dog was stiff, had a large lump on its belly and had milky eyes.

"You moving in?" the man asked.

"Not permanently." Under normal circumstances, Jimmy wouldn't be caught dead in a place like this.

"What's that?"

"I said not permanently." The bloke was deaf—good. Jimmy could make as much noise as he liked in the basement. "I'll be coming and going for a few weeks."

The chap nodded and limped into his own house with the dog walking stiffly beside him.

At five o'clock, Jimmy wandered down the street and bought fish and chips that he ate from the wrapper as he walked back to the house.

He went to the cellar and thought about giving Dowie more water, but couldn't be bothered. The bloke pissed him off too much. He was snivelling like a baby most of the time. Tears and snot mingled on the tape across his mouth.

"We've talked about me, Brian," he said. "What about you? Let's talk about you, shall we? You're one of the self-made rich, aren't you? You started buying cheap cars that were advertised in the local rag, doing them up and selling them on at a profit. You've done well for yourself, haven't you?"

Dowie's only contribution was the occasional groan.

"There was that accident, wasn't there?" Jimmy said. "Not your fault perhaps, but who knows? If you hadn't been drinking, perhaps that little girl wouldn't have ended up with broken legs. We'll never know, will we? Still, you paid the fine and accepted a driving ban. I don't suppose that meant much to her parents. Or perhaps they were too relieved that she was alive to care about you. If she'd died, you would have been on a far more serious charge. Death by dangerous driving. You'd have done time then, that's for sure."

Dowie's head lolled on his chest and Jimmy gave up on conversation.

The evening dragged. It was tempting to leave early, around midnight, but he managed to stick to his plan.

At exactly two o'clock, he left the house, and quietly took the van from the garage.

As he was driving off, he saw that an upstairs light was on in his neighbour's house. Perhaps it was true that, when you got old, you didn't need so much sleep. Or, more likely, you had to keep getting up for a piss.

The streets were as quiet as they always were in the early hours of the morning and he was soon parking a short distance away from Dowie's house. He pulled on a pair of latex gloves, grabbed his small shoulder bag and kept within the shadows of walls and tall trees as he walked.

The house was in darkness as he'd expected. High up on the front wall, two lights flashed from a white box. Jimmy shook his head in disgust. Any burglar worth his salt would recognise a fake alarm when he saw one. People who saved money by not having the real thing fitted asked for everything they got.

He walked up to the front door, ran his hand beneath one of the tubs of flowers, and smiled as his gloved fingers touched metal. Twice he'd seen Diane Dowie put something beneath this tub and he'd guessed it was a spare key for emergency use. Security at Dowie's car business was as tight as a duck's arse, but his home would be easy for any novice burglar to enter. Jimmy wasn't complaining, though. He'd been prepared to cut glass in the conservatory and gain access that way, but a key was as good as a welcome.

He tried the key in the front door, but wasn't surprised when nothing happened.

He crept round to the back of the house. He'd have put money on it fitting the conservatory door, but he was wrong. It opened the door that led into the kitchen.

He was soon inside the house and he switched on his small torch. It was far too easy. No wonder burglars made such good livings.

He stood for a moment, relishing the silence. The only sound was an irritating tick-tock from the kitchen clock.

He walked soundlessly along the hall. The stairs were thickly carpeted and he climbed them slowly, being careful to put his weight on the outer edge so as not to disturb any boards that might creak.

On the landing, he stood still. Weeks ago, he'd looked round a house that was for sale farther down the road. The layout was identical and he guessed that the door on his right, the master bedroom, would be where Diane Dowie was currently enjoying her beauty sleep.

The door was slightly ajar and he took a step forward and peeped inside. His torch gave him enough light to see a lump under the bedclothes. He didn't want to shine the torch on her face, but he was confident it was her.

He entered the room and stood over her for a moment. She was sound asleep.

When he slammed his hand across her mouth, she woke with a terrified start.

"Don't scream," he warned. "If you make a sound, I'll hurt your children. Got that?"

She nodded, her eyes wide.

He removed his hand just long enough to gag her with an old towel. She struggled, but was easy enough to hold. He took his handcuffs from his pocket and looked around. In the end, he had to drag her from the bed and cuff her to the radiator.

"Not a sound," he whispered.

She nodded again, her eyes like saucers.

He left the room, his steps silent on the thickly carpeted landing, and walked into one of the other bedrooms. He wasn't sure which son was sleeping here because the light from his torch was too dim. They both looked the same, though, and it didn't matter either way.

He checked his knife's blade briefly then ran it through the boy's neck. It was so quick that Jimmy wasn't even sure the boy woke up before he died.

There was blood everywhere and he had to be extra careful as he walked into the next bedroom.

This boy woke up but, again, he was dead almost instantly.

Satisfied, Jimmy returned to the master bedroom.

Diane was curled up in a tiny ball, tears rolling down her face. Her whole body was trembling. She looked scared, vulnerable and far more sexy than he'd expected.

"Don't worry," he said. "I'll go easy on you."

Later, he'd put his knife through her main artery. First, he'd have some fun.

NINE

DYLAN STILL HAD mixed feelings about his office. It had been Bev's idea, and he thought it too big, too flash and far too expensive. It looked good when clients visited, made him appear far more important and successful than he really was. The only other thing in its favour was the view from his first floor window. He wasted far too much time watching the activity on the street, and looking down on the comings and goings at the coffee bar on the opposite side of the road. Today, people were risking the outside tables, a hint that spring had arrived.

He swung his chair away from the window and returned his attention to his computer. His file on Goodenough was small. Very small. It hadn't needed to be anything else, though. Rodney Pelham had contacted him, said he had doubts about his daughter's fiancé and asked him to check out Goodenough. Dylan had watched the bloke, with very little enthusiasm, and soon had enough information to justify Pelham's fears. He'd passed on the information to Pelham, been paid, and thanked his lucky stars that a particularly mindnumbing job was over.

Photos he'd taken stared back at him and, again, he was struck by the size of Goodenough. He worked out a lot and had muscles to prove it. He was a vain man, always immaculately dressed, who often paused to check his reflection in shop windows. Dylan had seen him with two women, both of whom had looked awe-struck to find themselves in his company.

Dylan had also seen him remove a wedding ring. What was that about? Was he pretending to be married so that the women of the moment didn't get any ideas about relationships and a future? Or was he married and about to commit bigamy with Pelham's daughter? Maybe he'd had no intention of marrying her. It was possible he'd been planning to extort money from her or—

Dylan didn't know. At the time, he'd neither known nor cared. He'd had enough information for Pelham and he was happy with that. Now, he began to wonder.

He didn't even know Goodenough's real name.

Dylan tapped Pelham's mobile number into his phone. When it was answered, it sounded as if Pelham was in a wind tunnel.

"Hi, it's Dylan Scott. Are you able to talk?"

"I am, Dylan. Is there a problem? Sorry," Pelham said, "but I'm on the golf course and it's as windy as hell."

"No. No problem." Try as he might, Dylan couldn't picture Pelham on a golf course. The bloke was old and frail. He struggled to walk and there was no way he'd have the strength to swing a club. "I just wanted—"

"Sorry, can you repeat that?"

"I wondered if Brad Goodenough knew that you'd used me to investigate him."

"Goodenough? Um—I'm not sure. I don't think I mentioned your name. I may have. Is that a problem?"

"No. No problem." Pelham said something that Dylan didn't catch. "Sorry?"

"I think I may have referred to you as Mr. Scott when I showed him the photographs."

"Right. Okay, thanks for that."

"Is that it?"

"I'm trying to find him—a different case altogether. You haven't heard from him, have you?"

"I certainly haven't. I made it quite clear that he'd be wise not to show his face round me—or my daughter—again. As you know, he left his flat—owing rent, no doubt—and vanished, thank God."

"Yes. Okay, thanks. How's your daughter, by the way?"

"Still moping, but she'll get over it."

The line was too noisy to endure any more social niceties so Dylan ended the call.

He was no further forward, but he knew he needed to investigate Goodenough a little more thoroughly. As Frank had said, he'd look ridiculous if he was busy investigating King when Goodenough, or whatever his name was, put a knife in his back.

His phone rang and he hit the button to answer. "Hey, Pikey. What's new?"

"I'm well, thanks, mate. Thanks so much for asking."

"You're always well so there's no need to ask. And why wouldn't you be? You have a great life. You're living the dream."

"Ha. Anyway, I thought you'd like to know that King's been found. He's currently helping us with our inquiries into his wife's murder."

"Excellent news." King hadn't killed his wife—

she'd been dead for hours before he turned up at the house—but Dylan was more than happy for him to stay in a cell for a while. If he was locked up, he couldn't stick a knife in Dylan's back. "Keep him there as long as possible."

"It's not my case, but I'll let you know."

"Thanks."

"How are you getting on?" Pikey asked.

"I'd do a whole lot better if I knew what—or who—I was looking for. I'm about to visit John Weller's gym and check that out."

"I had a cursory look into that and it all seems above board. It's probably a case of like father, like son, though. Weller's real father was into every scam going, and a known drug dealer. He was gunned down in front of their house—some sort of territory war— when Weller was twelve years old. I'm not sure how the son would turn out given a father like Weller and then a stepfather like Rickman. Let me know if you find anything interesting."

Dylan promised to do exactly that. He ended the call, grabbed his jacket, picked up his car keys and left the confines of his office.

Traffic was snarled up and it was almost an hour later when he parked his Morgan in the vast car park belonging to Weller's gym. Neighbouring cars were of the pricey variety.

The building was ultra modern. Glass and steel captured the light and threw it back at him.

Stepping inside the building was like boarding a luxurious spacecraft. It was minimalist, plush and reeked of money. He passed a tall mirror, and his reflection caught him by surprise. It wasn't only the wig and the glasses. He looked taller, thinner. It must be one of those flattering mirrors Bev swore they put in clothes shops.

He wandered round the vast reception area and paused to read a poster offering special discounts. If he joined the gym today, it told him, he could enjoy his first twelve months' membership for a special price of only—only?—eighteen hundred pounds.

For that sum, he'd be entitled to six one-to-one sessions with his personal trainer, a check-up with the gym's own doctor, a course of Pilates and use of the facilities whenever he chose.

The young man behind a curving marble desk had finished his phone call and Dylan walked over to him. Up close, it was obvious that the man's tan was fake. He was probably early twenties and his huge muscles rippled beneath a T-shirt bearing the gym's distinctive logo. He was a great advert for the gym, but Dylan still reckoned he could floor him if the need arose.

"Good morning. What can I do for you? If you're thinking of joining, we have a special offer on right now."

"Yes, I've been reading about it," Dylan said. "I was hoping to see John Weller, but I'm really impressed with this place. I need to get in shape and I've had a look at a couple of other gyms. Neither were a patch on this. So yeah, although I'd like to see Mr. Weller, I wouldn't mind a look round while I'm here."

"Just a minute." He picked up a phone, tapped a number and waited. "Hi, I've a gentleman in reception who was hoping to see Mr. Weller. Any chance of that?" He sounded doubtful. "Right. Okay. Hang on a sec." He took the phone from his ear and looked at Dylan. "Can I ask what it's about?"

"It's personal," Dylan said. "If you could say that Bill Williams would like five minutes of his time, I'd be grateful."

This information was relayed to the person on the other end of the phone and Muscle Man's face broke into a smile as he finished the call. "You're in luck. Mr. Weller's out of the building at the moment, but his secretary tells me he's due back in the next few minutes and she's managed to find you a five-minute slot for twelve o'clock. That gives you forty minutes to look round and me forty minutes to convince you to join up. I'm Jason, by the way."

"Excellent. Thanks very much."

That had worked out far better than he'd hoped. An audience with John Weller *and* the chance to snoop round the gym.

Jason led them to a huge room that was Dylan's worst nightmare. Row upon row of static cycles, treadmills and rowing machines promised more pain than a body should have to endure. He liked to keep fit—he didn't, but he liked the idea of it—but he'd never seen the point to this. Of the countless machines, five were in use. In use, as always seemed the case, by young, ridiculously fit people who didn't boast so much as a gram of surplus fat. Most were listening to music through earphones as they worked those muscles. For the price of membership these people could buy a real cycle and get some fresh air and enjoyment from their exercise.

"We're quiet at this time of day," Jason said. "It's a different story in the early morning and early evening. There's nothing like a good workout to get the adrenaline flowing before a hard day at the office, is there? Well, perhaps a good workout to get rid of the stress after that hard day. There's always a machine free, though. Don't worry about that."

Dylan wasn't. Far from it. "Very impressive."

"You've seen nothing yet."

Their next stop was a much smaller room that still boasted some decent equipment.

"We have several trainers and coaches," Jason said, "so you get the same treatment as modern day athletes. These rooms are for the one-to-one consultations. We also offer several classes, catering for everything from strength and condition to dance. We offer kick-boxing, yoga, Pilates, Zumba—you name it, you'll find it here."

They walked on with Jason talking all the while. Dylan was only half listening. He was more interested in the layout of the building and the siting of any security cameras. The latter were rare.

He was shown the swimming pool, the sauna, the massage rooms and the bar.

"This is a short cut back to the reception." Jason pushed open a door marked Private and led the way through a long narrow corridor that had several doors off it.

"Where do all these doors go?" Dylan asked.

"That's just storage. We keep old or faulty machines there, stationery supplies, that sort of thing."

Which didn't explain the need for two security cameras in such a narrow corridor.

"I've never had a need to go in there so I can't say how much stuff is there. You need a card to get in."

Dylan had already noticed that. Interesting.

"So what do you think?" Jason asked as they returned to the room housing all those machines.

"It's very impressive. I'm busy for the next couple of weeks but as soon as that's out of the way, I'll have a serious think about joining."

"You won't regret it." Jason seemed satisfied. At least he wasn't pushy.

Five minutes later, Dylan was being escorted to the first floor of the building by Weller's secretary.

"I'm afraid Mr. Weller has a tight schedule today," she said, "so he can only spare five minutes."

"That's perfect. Thank you. I appreciate it."

She knocked on a door, waited until a voice invited them to enter, and stepped inside. "Mr. Williams to see you."

"Thank you." Weller was another good advertisement for the gym and his tan was real enough. His muscles weren't so evident, but he looked streetwise and mean despite the smart suit and silk tie. He wore a ridiculously large gold ring that drew the eye to the adjoining finger and its missing tip. "Take a seat."

"Thanks. And thank you for seeing me. I'm very grateful." Dylan sat in a blue leather reclining chair opposite Weller. An oblong glass desk covered the space between them. *Very nice.*

"How could I refuse? I'm curious. What can I do for you, Mr. Williams?"

"Bill," Dylan said.

Weller nodded, but there was no invitation to call him John.

"I'm an author," Dylan said, adjusting his glasses. "True crime. I'm currently working on a book about people wrongly convicted." Weller's expression was darkening with each word, but Dylan pushed on. "I'm interested in your stepfather's case. I'm not saying he was wrongly convicted, of course, but there are rumours that the whole thing was a setup. Also, his accomplice, Leonard King, might have been innocent."

"You've come to the wrong place." Weller's words were clipped. "Rickman is nothing to me other than the man my mother was foolish enough to marry. I haven't seen him for years and we were never close. He's a fool who put drugs on the street and he paid—is currently paying—the price."

So there wasn't much love lost between stepfather and son.

"Yes, I appreciate that," Dylan said. "But what about Leonard King? There's a rumour that he was set up, that he hadn't known he was walking into your stepfather's drug factory, that he knew nothing about the cash and drugs found at his home."

Weller smiled, and it had the effect of dropping the room's temperature by five degrees. "Set up? Of course he wasn't. God, who puts these stories around? He stole money and drugs from my stepfather, that much is obvious. It was found in that slum of a flat he called home, for God's sake. Look, all criminals like to protest their innocence, Mr. Williams. And it hardly matters now, does it? He's done time in prison and he's now free to do as he chooses."

"True, but stories of faulty convictions sell books. I'd still like to talk to Leonard King."

"Then talk to him, but all you'll hear is the usual pack of lies about the money being planted at his flat."

"My problem is that I have no idea where he is. Can you help with that?"

"Me?" Weller laughed. "Why would I know where he is? All he is to me is a name."

"You can't even take a guess where he is now?"

"No."

"But you knew he'd been released from prison?"

"I saw it mentioned."

"Where?" As far as Dylan was aware, news of King's release hadn't been deemed of interest to the media.

"I can't remember."

He was lying.

"I saw him," Dylan said, "but by the time I realised it was him, he'd gone. I didn't get chance to talk to him."

"Oh? Where was that?" The sudden but oh-so-casual interest didn't surprise Dylan.

"At the dog track. He's there every Friday and Saturday night. I'll have to go again and make sure I catch him next time." Dylan rose to his feet. "Right, thanks so much for your time."

"You're welcome. And the best of luck finding him." Weller's smile was far more genuine now. "I didn't even know dog tracks existed these days. Whereabouts is it?"

"Wimbledon." Oh, yes, Weller was interested. "By the way, Jason showed me around the gym. Really impressive. I'm thinking of joining."

"You won't regret it. I could be biased, but I think it's the best in London. I work hard to make sure it's the best."

"It shows. You must have good staff. Running a place this size can't be easy."

"It's hard work, but I enjoy it. And now, I'm sorry, but I have an appointment."

TEN

"I THINK WE should get a dog," Luke announced.

Dylan groaned. "I should have guessed it was time for this conversation again. We haven't had it for, oh, at least a week."

"Very funny, Dad. It would be so cool, though."

"Freezing probably," Bev said, "especially in the winter when you have to leave your nice warm bed at the crack of dawn to go walking."

Luke tutted at his boring, ancient parents. "Really, it would be ace. Tom's dog is—"

"—having puppies," Dylan finished for him. "Yes, we know. But you don't even like Tom's dog."

"I do!"

"You said it was a yappy little thing," Bev said.

"It can be. But the puppies won't be like that. Tom reckons the dad will be the Labrador that lives three doors away. He's a great dog."

"That's just it, though, you don't know who the dad will be. It might be another yappy little thing."

Luke shrugged at the logic of his dad's comment. "I still reckon we should get a dog. I'll walk it and feed it and do everything with it."

"Pay the vet's bills?" Dylan asked.

"Of course. So long as you give me enough pocket money." Luke tried another angle. "All kids should have pets. I read about it. It's good for them. I bet, when Freya's older, she'll think you're so mean for not letting her have a pet."

Bev snorted with laughter. "She will not."

"You're not home all day," Dylan said, "so who's going to look after it? And what about when you go to university?"

"I don't want to go to university."

Dylan didn't want them getting into that argument again so he said nothing.

"Why does what I want never count for anything?" Luke asked.

"Because what you want puts demands on other people." Dylan waited for more eye-rolling and wasn't disappointed. "And because your savings wouldn't even run to a can of dog food."

"When I'm finished with all this hospital stuff," Bev said, "we'll think about it. Okay?"

"Really?" Luke asked.

"Really."

"Wow. Way to go, Mum."

"And on that vague promise," Bev said, "it's time you scuttled off to your bed. You've still got homework to do before you go back to school on Wednesday, remember?"

"Don't remind me."

"And don't spend half the night listening to music," she said.

"Okay, okay." It took him a full ten minutes to gather up iPod, phone and earphones, but then he was gone.

"You're not seriously considering a dog, are you?" Dylan asked. "I mean, really?"

"He's wearing me down," Bev said. "He's wanted

one for so long and—well, maybe when this hospital stuff is out of the way, I'll be past caring. Everything will seem like fun." Shadows flitted across her face.

"Do you want to talk about it?"

She smiled, a tight, nervous smile. "There's no point, is there? We've talked about it and talked about it. All we can do now is hope for the best. All eyes forward and trust in the Lord, as they say."

He nodded, and felt the relief wash over him. He hated talking about it. Frank was right in that he preferred to bury his head in the sand. Bev was right too in that they'd talked about it more than enough. They referred to it as *this hospital stuff.* It sounded far better, and much less terrifying, than chemotherapy or radiotherapy. They certainly didn't utter the c-word. Hell, no. That one was definitely off-limits.

"I think I'll catch up on *EastEnders.*" She reached for the TV remote. "I've got three episodes recorded so that should put me in the mood for sleep. It's been rubbish lately."

"Good idea." Dylan refrained from asking why she watched something she described as rubbish. Instead, he switched on his laptop.

The more he thought about Goodenough, the more curious he became. He'd found out easily enough that he was bad news, and certainly not suited to Pelham's daughter, but he had no real idea what the bloke's game was. He hadn't cared until now.

"Bev, have you had any more of those odd phone calls?"

She shook her head, her mind on the soap. "No. Why do you ask?"

"Oh, I just wondered." He didn't want to scare her.

"Pikey was saying there had been a spate of burglaries in the area and I wondered if the two were connected. Probably not, but don't forget to make sure all the windows and doors are locked, okay? They're nicking stuff like TVs, DVD players, laptops—the usual. We can do without the hassle of having to go through the insurance company to replace it all."

"I will." She turned up the TV's volume, which translated as "Shut up and let me watch this rubbish."

He shouldn't be *too* concerned because of the simple fact that, when someone wanted you dead, they killed you. They didn't waste time trying to scare you with phone calls and mysterious deliveries of photos.

Back to Goodenough—

He'd rented a luxury apartment in an upmarket area of the City, all on the strength of two months' rent in advance and a couple of fake references. The name he'd used was Gordon West. He'd taken off, owing rent and, needless to say, hadn't been foolish enough to leave a forwarding address.

"And now," his landlord had said during their brief phone conversation, "the new tenant is moaning because debt collectors are knocking on the door at all hours of the day and night. The bastard bought TVs, leather sofas—you name it, the bastard bought it on these interest-free loans where you don't pay a penny for twelve months. Gas, electric—the bastard owes everyone. Bastard. I hassled him for the rent, of course, but what can you do? The bastard tenants have rights coming out of their ears, but the landlord can do nothing. Do you know, if you go hammering on the bastard's door asking for the rent a couple of times, you can be done for harassment?"

"Yes, so I believe."

"Bastard."

"Indeed. And he definitely left no clues as to where he was going?"

"If he had, I'd be chasing the bastard down myself. I asked the other tenants but they knew nothing about him. One reckoned he worked for one of those escort agencies."

"Really?"

"Yes. The sort where ugly women pay a good-looking bloke to take them out and have sex with them."

"I know the sort. Any idea which one?"

"She didn't know. If she had, I'd have been hammering on the bastard door to get him."

It wasn't much, but it was a start. Dylan had phoned a dozen agencies but wasn't surprised to learn that no Brad Goodenough or Gordon West was registered on their books. He'd check out more, and he'd hang around their offices to see if Goodenough or whatever his name was showed up, but he dreaded to think how many such agencies operated in London.

Dylan stared at his computer's screen, flicking through photo after photo of Goodenough. He hoped inspiration would strike. It didn't, probably because his mind insisted on returning to Leonard King. And Wendy King. And the identity of Wendy's killer.

He forced his mind back to Goodenough. He'd find him. It might take a while but even people who changed their names on a daily basis left paper trails as long as the M1. It was only a matter of time.

ELEVEN

JIMMY LIKED HAVING his own space at Russell Street. The rent was low, which was no wonder when you looked at the state of the place, and the landlord lived in the Midlands. Jimmy had paid rent in advance, in cash, and so long as he made sure future payments were received on time, no one would bother him. It was his personal den.

He reached behind the cooker, grabbed the plans and spread them across the kitchen table. They were held together with Sellotape but were accurate to the nearest millimetre. Scotland Yard. His heart thumped with excitement.

Concrete barriers sat in front of ground-level windows as a countermeasure against car bombs. A concrete wall protected the entrance to the building, and the exterior was always guarded by armed officers as well as a generous smattering of security staff.

But Jimmy had thought of everything. Nothing could go wrong. He was going to blow the building to smithereens. And soon.

After an hour or so, he put the plans away—he'd memorised them long ago—and switched on the TV that he'd bought from a charity shop for twenty pounds. It was an old monstrosity but it worked. He flicked to the news channel. Some idiot in America had run amok with a gun, a train had crashed in India killing scores of people, lifeboats were searching for the crew of a fishing boat off the coast of Cornwall and, finally, came the piece of news he'd been waiting for.

Details were vague because the story had only just broken. He wondered what had taken so long. No names were being released, probably because they couldn't inform the next of kin, but at least there was a story.

He pulled the TV from the wall socket, but that was no good. Even if he managed to drag it to the cellar without damage, he wouldn't get a signal down there. The TV couldn't go to Dowie so Dowie would have to come to the TV. It was an inconvenience but it couldn't be helped.

He switched the TV back on and stood, hands on hips to take several deep, calming breaths. There was no rush. They always milked breaking news stories to death so it would run for hours yet.

Feeling calmer, he walked down the steps and into the cellar. Dowie was barely conscious. What a waste of space the man was. He was pathetic.

Jimmy lashed out with his boot, kicking Dowie on the shin. It made him lift his head slightly and groan. He stank. He was soaked in his own urine and sweat.

Tutting with disgust, Jimmy removed the noose from around Dowie's neck. He released him from the chair, then bound his hands firmly behind his back with a plastic tie.

Jimmy took the gun from the waistband of his jeans and held it to Dowie's temple. "Make a noise, or a sudden movement, and you get a bullet."

There was no response.

"Got that?"

Dowie nodded. He looked as if he didn't care. Jimmy would soon make him care.

He didn't want to use the gun as it would make too much noise, but he liked having it close. Few things beat a gun in an emergency.

"We're going upstairs." Jimmy hauled him to his feet and cursed as Dowie's legs gave way beneath him. "Get a grip. You stink of shit and piss and now you can't even walk. Call yourself a man? You're fucking pathetic."

Still holding the gun to Dowie's head, Jimmy half pushed and half dragged Dowie up the stairs. It took long, frustrating minutes, and Jimmy was breathless when they finally emerged into the main room of the house.

He pushed Dowie onto his knees in front of the TV screen. "A special treat for you tonight, Brian. We're going to watch the telly together. Won't that be fun?"

Jimmy wished he could remove Dowie's gag, but it was too risky. The idiot was sure to make a noise. The old man next door was so deaf he probably wouldn't hear a bomb explode, but it was still too risky. Only an idiot took unnecessary risks and Jimmy wasn't one of those.

He should give Dowie a drink, though. He didn't want him passing out or, worse, dying. Not yet.

Not taking his eye off his captive, Jimmy took a bottle of water from his bag, unscrewed the top and took a swig. "You see, Brian? It's not poisoned."

He laughed as he yanked the tape from Dowie's mouth. His lips were chapped and bleeding, but that was nothing. He put the bottle to Dowie's mouth and squeezed so that water went everywhere. "There you go. Try to drink more slowly, though."

When he'd had enough—when Jimmy grew bored at least—Jimmy took away the bottle, put on the cap, and threw it aside. He grabbed the reel of tape and put three fresh layers across Dowie's mouth. The only response to this was a groan and a few tears rolling down his cheek.

"You're crying again." Jimmy's laughter was scoffing. "What a crybaby you are. I thought you were a man, not a pathetic girl. I ought to see if I can find the cartoons channel for you to watch. Or Disney. Oops, better not. They might be showing *Bambi* and that would set you off again, wouldn't it?"

Still chuckling, Jimmy switched on the TV and flicked through the news until he came to the 24-hour news station. They suffered a full five minutes of boredom as so-called experts discussed the likelihood of finding any survivors from that fishing boat.

"I hope you're paying attention, Brian. It'll get better. Much better."

A couple of minutes later, the scene changed. A reporter stood at the end of Dowie's road. The area had been sealed off and police cars and vans blocked any real view of the property. Cameramen had long zoom lenses and were doing the best they could.

"As yet details are sketchy," the reporter said, "but reports suggest that the bodies of a woman and two teenage boys have been found. A police statement is expected shortly and we'll remain live at the scene to bring you more information as we get it." The camera zoomed a little closer. "Although no formal identifications have been made, neighbours have told us that the house belongs to a Brian Dowie, his wife, Diane, and their two sons."

A high-pitched keening sound, muffled by tape, came from Dowie. He began to struggle but Jimmy had him secure.

"The whereabouts of Mr. Dowie are unknown at this time. We don't believe he's at the property but, as I said, we're dealing with speculation as we await a formal statement from officers at the scene."

Jimmy grinned at that. "I wonder if you're a murder suspect, Brian. No need to worry. The police won't find you."

Dowie spluttered and howled through his taped mouth. He struggled. He tried to kick out. He rocked back and forth on his knees. It was all a waste of energy.

"You're making the whole house smell," Jimmy said. "It's time you went back to the cellar. I'll bring you out again tomorrow when they have more information about your wife and kids. Your very dead wife and kids."

TWELVE

WHEN DYLAN ARRIVED at his office on Saturday morning, the first thing he spotted was the brown envelope lying on his desk with the rest of his mail. The other envelopes, all from people trying to sell him things he didn't need and couldn't afford, went straight in the bin. The brown envelope, hand delivered, was opened very carefully.

Inside was a single colour photo of Bev and the kids. Bev was carrying Freya and looked about to strap her in her car seat, and Luke was laughing at something Bev had said. Bev had turned and was looking straight at the camera.

Unless Dylan was very much mistaken, the picture had been taken at the same time as the others. Bev was wearing the same clothes.

He slipped the photo and envelope into a plastic evidence bag. "Bastard!"

Pikey had called yesterday afternoon with the news that Leonard King had been released without charge. Apparently, he had a rock-solid alibi for the time of his ex-wife's murder that CCTV footage had backed up. Was it coincidence that, shortly after his release, Dylan received another photo?

The photo could have been delivered any time between five-thirty yesterday afternoon and nine o'clock this morning. Meaning that Dylan had a mere fifteen and a half hours of video footage from his new security camera to look through.

Thankfully, he had time to spare. The Gunners didn't have a game this weekend so he could waste the whole day. No change there...

He made a coffee and sat at the computer to watch the comings and goings outside his building's entrance. His first floor office was opposite one that had recently changed hands. A dentist was setting up a private practice and was in the process of upgrading the space. As it was a rushed job, tradesmen were working long into the night. They might help stave off the boredom.

The camera gave him a good view of the mailbox, as he'd intended, and should have captured anyone putting an envelope inside it.

He'd been through about two hours of footage when Frank called.

"How's it going, Dylan?"

"Badly." He told Frank about King's release and about the photo delivery. "King was a fairly harmless small-time crook, but he's spent the past eight years behind bars mixing with the lowest of the low. Who knows what happens to a bloke like that? His anger will have had plenty of time to fester. Maybe he's spent those years dreaming about revenge on those he holds responsible. Like me."

"It's possible."

"It is, and I don't like it. I can't do anything about it either because I'm too busy watching Bev and the kids. I can check a few things out while the kids are busy, and while Bev's at the hospital or something, and that's it. I told you I tried to persuade her to go away, yes? That would have been easier all round, but no, she wouldn't have it. Anyway, I'm getting someone on the case, someone to keep an eye on them. There's a chap I know, an investigator—"

"I'm not doing anything."

"Sorry?"

"I'm not doing anything, Dylan. Christ, I never am these days. I can easily spend a few days in the City. In fact, I could do with a change of scene."

"Are you serious?"

"Of course. I'll throw a few things in a bag and get the next train south. Now. Today. Just find me a B&B or a cheap hotel nearby and I'll sort out a hire car."

Dylan didn't know what to say. He'd feel far happier if he knew Frank was keeping a watchful eye on Bev. On the other hand, the fact that Frank was worried enough to leave his Lancashire home did nothing to lessen his unease.

"It's probably nothing to do with King. It's more likely to be some crank out to scare me." He didn't know if he was trying to convince Frank or himself.

"It's possible. There's no point taking chances, though."

"No. Well, why not stay at our place then? I can tell Bev you're down in the City to—"

"Oh, no. She's got enough on her plate right now. I can easily check into a nearby B&B."

"It'll be fine. Really. She'll be glad of the company." And it would be so much easier to keep an eye on her and the kids.

"Are you sure? Then tell her I'm down there trying to catch up with old colleagues to organise a reunion.

But will she really be okay about it? It would make life easier, but I don't want to put her out."

"Truly, she'll be glad of the distraction. I'll put it to her and see what she says."

"Okay. If she doesn't like the idea, and I wouldn't if I were her, find me a B&B nearby, will you?"

"I will." Dylan was still a little lost for words. "Thanks. I really appreciate this, Frank."

"I should be thanking you. A bloke can get thoroughly sick of kicking his heels all day. And don't worry, no harm will come to Bev while I'm on watch."

Dylan knew it. He could think of no one he'd trust more. "Thanks, Frank."

As soon as he ended the call, he called Bev.

"Hi," she said. "You okay?"

"I'm good. I've just had Frank on the phone. He's coming down to London for a few days to catch up with old colleagues and arrange a reunion. He asked me to recommend a B&B or a cheap hotel."

"What? But why doesn't he stay with us? We've got room—well, until your mum stays over. Even then, one of them could have the sofa."

"I did suggest it, but he thought you had enough to deal with. He didn't want to intrude."

"Tell him that's nonsense. I'd love to have him here. Tell him the spare room's ready and waiting for him."

"Are you sure?"

"Of course. I adore Frank, you know I do. He's such a gentleman, isn't he?"

"Oh, yeah." A gentleman who'd reduced many a hardened criminal to tears.

"I'll give him a call myself and tell him we're expecting him."

"That would be good. Thanks. So what are you up to today?"

"Not a lot. A bit of tidying up—well, a bit more if Frank's coming. The house is a tip."

"The house is fine. Don't overdo it. You're off work because—"

"I know, I know. Don't worry, I'll take it easy. Your mum's here and she'll make sure I do."

His mum being there was the reason he'd felt able to come to his office this morning, although God knows why he thought the presence of a stoned old woman would keep the nutters at bay. He felt as if a weight had been lifted from him now. He hadn't realised how much he'd been worrying about Bev's and the kids' safety until Frank had offered to keep an eye on them.

He returned to his video footage with renewed enthusiasm.

It was tempting to skip the early hours as he couldn't imagine anyone delivering mail before seven or eight in the morning. However, he plodded on.

At a little after five-thirty, the security light came on as a man approached the building. He took something, presumably a brown envelope although the image wasn't clear enough to see, and put it in the mailbox. He stood back, lifted his covered face to the camera, and waved a gloved hand. Arrogant, conceited sod.

"I'll get you, you bastard," Dylan muttered.

He viewed the footage a dozen times or more, but learned little. His early morning postie was wearing dark running trousers and trainers, a dark hooded top, a balaclava and gloves. He could have been black or white, old or young. Yet he walked with a confident swagger and didn't have the gait of an old man. On the contrary, he looked fit.

He paused the footage and stared at the screen. Then he ran down the stairs from his office and into the shared reception area.

"You don't have a tape measure I could borrow, do you?" he asked the girl behind the desk.

"I do, but it might take me a while to find it." She hunted through the drawers in her desk, pulling out old magazines, toffees, several bottles of nail polish and a hair brush. "Here it is."

She handed over a chunky metal tape. Dylan was impressed. "Thanks."

He went outside and measured the distance from the bottom step to the sign that listed the offices inside the building. By his reckoning, the man who'd delivered the photo was six feet two.

He returned the tape and went back to his office. Even if the six feet two was accurate, it didn't help a lot. King was tall. So was Goodenough. So were thousands of people.

He supposed he'd ruled out very short suspects. Not that he'd had any of those.

He rewound the footage and watched it again. And again. Did it look like King? This man appeared broader. It had been a chilly night, though, and King would look bulkier beneath several layers of clothes.

God, he hated mind games.

He grabbed the photo of Goodenough from the chaos on his desk. He was broad shouldered, but was he the man who'd delivered that envelope and had the cheek to wave at the camera? It was impossible to say.

Dylan hunted down his ridiculously long list of escort agencies in the area and took off. Anything had to be better than sitting at his desk.

He managed to waste the morning and most of the afternoon going from one agency to the next, showing people his photo of Goodenough, waiting for the inevitable head shaking, thanking them and going on his way.

Then, just as he was thinking of calling it a day, the routine changed. This stunningly gorgeous girl wasn't shaking her head.

"Yes, I know him. That's Chesney." She tapped the photo. "He's no longer on the books, though. He left a week ago. In a way, it's a pity because he was very popular and good for business."

"Chesney? Do you have a surname?"

"Marshall. Chesney Marshall."

"An address?"

"Probably, but I can't give you that." She looked worried. "Has he done something wrong?"

"Not that I know of but I really, really need to find him."

"Hang on a minute." She looked through records on her computer, tapped her fingers on the desk and then seemed to reach a decision. "Here." She scribbled down an address on a square of paper and handed it over. "If anyone asks, you didn't get that from me. I shouldn't do it, but hey, he wouldn't do me any favours."

"Oh? Didn't you get on?"

She clearly regretted her words and actions. "Not particularly."

Dylan gave her a sympathetic smile. "I can't say I'm a fan either. He's a bit too full of his own importance for my liking."

"That's it exactly. He thinks he's God's gift to the universe." She warmed to her theme, just as Dylan had hoped. "He'll be utterly charming so long as he thinks there's something in it for him. If there isn't, he won't give you the time of day. I don't meet many of the escorts, there's no need as it's all done by phone or online, but he was always coming here for a moan. He couldn't believe that he wasn't getting many bookings. We told him he was getting more than anyone else, but he still complained. And then, when women did book him, he sometimes didn't turn up. He always claimed something more important had come up. He was only here a couple of months and I was glad to see the back of him. I'll tell you something else," she said, dropping her voice to a whisper, "his name isn't—" She broke off, realising she'd said far too much.

"It's okay. I didn't think it was Marshall."

"I overheard him on the phone once," she said. "He didn't know I was there, and I heard him call himself by something other name. I can't remember what, something unusual, but it certainly wasn't Chesney."

"Goodenough? Brad Goodenough?"

She looked surprised. "That's it, yes."

"What else did he say during that phone call?" Dylan asked.

"I can't remember. Nothing that registered. It was just the way that he used that different name. What a poser."

Dylan nodded. "Perhaps he didn't want people to know he was working for the agency."

"Perhaps."

"Was he in a relationship? Seeing anyone?"

"He's married. At least, that's what he said. Never

mentioned her—well, not very often. Sometimes, if he was in a good mood, he'd jokingly call her the boss. If he knew he'd got a sexy woman to spend the evening with, he'd say the boss wouldn't like it if he got up to any hanky-panky."

"And did he? Get up to any hanky-panky?" Dylan had assumed that was the whole point.

She shrugged. "I don't know. Officially, our escorts don't offer any sexual favours. We cater for visitors to the City mainly, women who want to go out for a meal, take in a show or simply see the sights with a handsome, intelligent man. But if the escort chooses to make a bit of cash on the side—well, that's up to them."

"What's the going rate? The official rate."

"One-fifty an hour. Eight hundred for a full day."

"You're kidding me. Hell, I'm in the wrong job. I reckon if I got in shape—"

"No need to worry about that. Believe me, we've got a lot worse than you on the books."

Dylan wasn't sure if he should take that as a compliment or not. "You don't know his wife's name or anything?"

She shook her head. "You said he'd done nothing wrong. Why are you so keen to find him?"

"I'm helping someone out. If by any chance you bump into him, could you ask him to give me a call. Tell him it's about Miss Pelham. And tell him there's money in it for him." He handed her his business card.

"Oh, my God. This is serious, isn't it?"

"No, not really."

"I've never met a real P.I. before."

"You haven't missed much." Dylan began to cough. An irritating cough that simply wouldn't stop. "Sorry."

"Are you all right? Would you like a glass of water?"

"I'd love one," he managed to gasp between coughs. "I had a cold and I'm damned if I can get rid of this cough. Sorry."

"I'll get you a glass of water. Won't be a tick."

She went, as Dylan had guessed she might, into a small room that backed off this minuscule reception area. He'd assumed she must have tea—and coffee-making facilities somewhere.

Still coughing, he made the most of her absence by leaning over the counter to look at the computer screen. Goodenough's details were still visible. Dylan only had a few seconds, just enough to take a picture of the screen showing the names and addresses of two women who'd booked time with Chesney. Both addresses were local, despite most clients supposedly being visitors to London.

"There you go." She returned and handed him a large glass of water.

"Thanks." He coughed once more and drank the water. "And thanks for your help with Chesney. I appreciate it."

"You're welcome. And you didn't get that address from me, okay?"

"What address?"

She was grinning as he drained the glass of water. He thanked her again and left the building.

Rush hour traffic would make the trek across the City impossible in his car, so he parked it and took the Underground. He knew, as sure as he knew that night followed day, that Goodenough wouldn't be at the address she'd given him. He couldn't afford not to check it out, though.

He'd thought Goodenough was married, thought he'd seen him removing a wedding ring. So what was his game? Presumably he used a fake name and found rich women to charm, promised them a happy-ever-after, got as much money out of them as he could and then scarpered. He wouldn't be the first to make a living in such a way, but that sort of lifestyle didn't fit with death threats. People like that lived on a diet of hope. They were chancers. They were too busy charming everyone they met in the hope that a friendship would be financially rewarding to bear to a grudge. They were greedy but they weren't dangerous.

Much to his amazement, he arrived outside the property in time to see the man himself. Goodenough was climbing into a taxi. Dylan waved his arms and shouted, but the cab sped off. If he'd come in his car—

If he'd come in his car, he'd still be an hour away.

Sod it.

At least he knew Goodenough was at this address, though. It was one of several exclusive apartments that boasted good security. Places like that didn't come cheap.

Sod it.

There was nothing else for it. He might as well make the return journey across London and get his car.

As he walked to the Underground station, he phoned Bev.

"Frank's just arrived bearing wine," she said. "We're about to crack open a bottle."

"Lucky you. I'm jealous. I'll be home late, by the way, so don't bother waiting up."

"What are you up to? Have you got another woman in tow?"

"Ha. You're more than enough trouble for me. I'm still looking for this chap. I told you about him. Take good care of Frank, okay?"

Dylan would have liked to go home and mull things over a glass of wine or a couple of beers with Frank but, unfortunately, he had more important matters to attend to.

THIRTEEN

THE GREYHOUND-RACING TRACK was even busier tonight because a hen night was in full swing. About fifty females of assorted ages, all loud and all wearing pink sashes with Tart, Slapper or similar slogans emblazoned on them, were getting more and more drunk. Men flocked around them and it was doubtful that the girls would need to buy any drinks.

Dylan had a pint and immediately wanted another. That was the thing about alcohol, though. If you didn't want another, there was no point to it. He thought of his Morgan, decided that a drink-driving charge was the last thing he needed—apart from a nutter out to kill him, of course—and bought what had to be the most expensive bottle of water in London.

His day hadn't been a complete waste of time. Frank had arrived, and that was something Dylan wouldn't forget in a hurry. He owed his one-time boss. He'd also discovered that the crazy delivering photos to his office was around the six-feet-two mark, and he had another alias for Brad Goodenough as well as an address. He'd even seen the bloke briefly. All in all, he'd had a reasonable day.

He walked around, sipping water from his bottle, watching everyone. Some serious money was being placed on the dogs' backs. A race started every fifteen minutes or so and Dylan wouldn't have minded a share of the bookies' takings. He couldn't see the attraction for anyone else, though. The track was 480 metres long, the speeding dogs became a blur and the race was over in seconds. Why bother?

It was more interesting watching the hen party. The bride-to-be almost screamed the place down when she backed a winning dog.

The last race of the evening was about to start when Dylan spotted the man he'd come to see. He pushed his way through the crowd to stand face-to-face with John Weller.

"What a surprise," Dylan said, offering his hand.

"Oh, it's—" Weller feigned thought as they shook hands. "It's Williams, isn't it? Bill Williams?"

"That's right. What brings you here?" As if he didn't know.

"It's all your fault." Weller spoke with forced merriment. "Like I said, I thought the dog tracks had died out years ago. After speaking to you, I thought I'd come along and have a look for myself. I must say, it's quite an experience."

"It certainly is."

"What about you? I suppose you're still looking for Leonard King?"

"I was, but I've just seen him."

"Oh? He's here then?" Sharp grey eyes scanned the crowd.

"He was. He left about ten minutes ago so I'm afraid you've missed him."

Weller shrugged. "I'm not the one looking for him." *Yeah, right.*

"I suppose you've heard the latest," Weller said. "His

ex-wife was killed, and he was taken in for questioning."

"He can prove he wasn't involved."

Weller shrugged again. "I suppose he can. They released him pretty fast. It makes you wonder, though, doesn't it?"

"How do you mean?"

"He treated her like dirt. That's what I heard anyway. So tell me, is he going to spill all and help with your book?"

"He isn't keen. It seems he has other things on his mind. Between you and me—" Dylan leaned in close, "—he thinks someone's after him."

"Like who?"

"Your guess is as good as mine."

"Perhaps he's right. Scum like him make a lot of enemies. Anyway, good to see you again. If you'll excuse me—"

"Of course. Enjoy the rest of the night."

"You too."

Weller headed back to the bar and spoke to the two heavies who'd been keeping a watchful eye on their boss. Weller had a quick drink, and the three left together.

IT WAS ALMOST midnight when Dylan parked his car on the drive, took off his wig and glasses, and walked into his house. Bev and the kids were in bed and Frank was nursing a glass of whisky while he watched the TV news.

Dylan took off his jacket and threw it over the back of the armchair. "Thanks for coming, Frank. I owe you."

"Rubbish." Frank turned down the TV's volume. "It makes a change for me. Oh, I'm helping myself to your whisky, by the way."

"I'll join you." Dylan's attention was caught by the news item. "Brian Dowie? That name rings a bell. What's that about?"

"His wife and teenage sons have been found. Murdered. He's vanished into thin air and is currently a murder suspect. What's left of his car has been found on waste ground. How do you know the name?"

"I don't know."

"He has his own car sales business. Quite successful, I gather," Frank said. "Other than that, there's not much information about him."

"Perhaps we've bought one of Bev's cars from him in the past then. I rarely forget a name." He went to the kitchen for a glass and the bottle and tried to conjure up a face to put to the name. Brian Dowie wasn't a particularly common name, yet Dylan couldn't place it.

He refreshed Frank's glass, poured himself a generous measure of whisky, and sat to tell Frank of the day's events.

"So Archie was right about Weller wanting a word with King," he said. "There was no other reason for him and his heavies to be at the dog track."

"And if that's the case," Frank said, "would King really bother with you when he's busy hiding from Weller?"

That thought had crossed Dylan's mind several times. It didn't feel right. And yet, apart from Goodenough, who was another who seemed unlikely to waste time threatening him, he was out of ideas.

"Bev and your mum are off to some Easter parade

tomorrow," Frank said, "so I'll keep a close eye on them. From a distance, of course. I'll be far enough away not to alert Bev and close enough to see if any sicko follows them."

"Thanks. I can't tell you how much I appreciate this. And thanks for reminding me that it's Easter tomorrow. I have flowers and chocolate in the car."

He'd bring them inside later. First, he refilled their glasses and they settled down to talk over old times. There was nothing like two ex-coppers for putting the world, and especially the modern police service, to rights.

"Gone are the days when a copper could go out and bag a criminal," Frank said. "And don't even get me started on human rights."

Dylan knew their views on that particular issue were in tune. "Your average crook has more rights than I've had whiskies, and your victim—"

"—has none at all. Yep, that about sums it up. The world's gone mad."

FOURTEEN

APART FROM THE fact there was less traffic on the roads than usual, it was impossible to tell it was Easter Sunday. Dylan had seen a few of the faithful gathering outside a church in their finery but, for most, it was just another day.

Dylan was back at Goodenough's flat, but there was no sign of the man himself.

"I rarely see Chesney," one of his neighbours said, "and I'm at home most of the time. He's often away for days on end, sometimes a week or more. He seems nice enough, though. No trouble. Very quiet. The perfect neighbour, really."

"When you see him, would you ask him to give me a call?" Dylan handed over his card. "I have money to give him—not mine, I hasten to add—and he's proving difficult to find."

"Of course. It could be days or even weeks before I see him, though."

"I understand." Dylan thanked her and tried another neighbour. This one, an elderly man, wasn't quite as impressed by Goodenough.

"An odd chap," he said. "You can talk to him for an hour and still have no idea where he comes from, what he does for a living—nothing."

"Talk to him often, do you?" Dylan asked.

"Good Lord, no. He must work away and use this as a weekend or holiday home. He's rarely here."

"You've no idea where he might stay the rest of the time?"

"None at all. I saw him once at Euston Station. He was catching the train north to Manchester. He was looking a little—well, shabby, to be honest. He had a large holdall with him too. Perhaps he works up north."

That sounded unlikely.

No one knew anything about Goodenough, or Marshall, and Dylan left the building no wiser.

He headed to the home of Victoria Shelby. According to the escort agency, she'd attended a show with Goodenough and had paid a ridiculous amount of money for the privilege.

He found the address easily enough—a vast home set it its own gardens—and sat outside. For once, he didn't have long to wait. A woman, probably early fifties, soon emerged, climbed into a silver BMW and drove off. Dylan followed.

They drove for about five miles, until she parked near the Underground station and headed for the trains. By the time Dylan had found the only other available parking spot and raced into the station, she was already at the machine buying a ticket.

He banged his hip against her. "I'm so sorry. I was busy looking at the map."

"It's fine." Her voice was refined and slightly breathy.

"Hey, do I know you?" He rubbed his chin. "I'm sure we've—ah, I've got you now. You're a friend of Chesney's."

Her eyes widened with surprise. Or embarrassment. "Well—"

"I saw you with him not so long ago. I was with my wife. It was my wife who wanted to see the show."

"Ah." Definitely embarrassment.

"I don't suppose you've seen him in the last couple of days, have you? I've been trying to speak to him, but he's not returning my calls. I hope he's all right. I'm getting a little concerned."

She blushed an attractive shade of red. "I haven't. Sorry."

"He's a character, isn't he?"

"Yes." She gave him a tight smile. "Sorry, but I'm in a rush."

"Will you be seeing him—?"

"No."

"Ah. I see. I'm sorry it didn't work out for you. You looked good together."

"Sorry, I can't help you." The machine spewed out her ticket and she dashed off to the trains.

Dylan chalked that up to a waste of time and crossed the Thames to a very different property. This one was a modest semi with a beautifully tended but minuscule front garden. *Garden* was too grand a word as it was a small square of concrete. A mass of brightly coloured flowers blossomed in attractive pots of different heights though.

According to the agency's computer, twenty-six-year-old Janice Filgrew lived here. The same Janice Filgrew who'd paid for three hours in Goodenough's company.

He sat in his Morgan watching the property for a couple of hours and was rewarded when a young woman of around the right age emerged with a canvas shopping bag dangling from her arm. She stopped to inspect the flowers by her front door, removed a couple of faded blooms and dropped them on another pot. Satisfied, she put her shopping bag over her arm and strode along the street.

Dylan followed at a distance, all the while wondering why the hell this young woman bothered with escort agencies. She was slim and attractive with a curtain of blond hair cascading over her shoulders. He had nothing against men or women using escort agencies but he couldn't help thinking it smacked of desperation. Janice Filgrew had no need for such measures.

They'd been walking for about half an hour but hadn't travelled far. She kept pausing to look in shop windows, most of which were closed for the Easter holiday, and spent around five minutes chatting to a young Asian girl she met.

She stopped outside a greengrocer's, where the pavement was crammed with stalls laden with fresh fruit and vegetables. Dylan ducked into a nearby phone booth and watched her pick up a wire basket and fill it with oranges that she squeezed to test for ripeness, bananas that it took her a full five minutes to select, and apples. With the wire basket hanging heavy on her arm, she checked out bunches of flowers that had been put in large buckets of water. She finally chose a colourful arrangement and went inside the shop to pay.

Either there was a long queue or she stopped to chat because it was several minutes before she stepped into the sunshine again. When she did, she began walking back along the street toward Dylan's phone booth.

The pavement was crowded and she was walking on

the edge, close to his phone booth, to avoid pedestrians. He timed it perfectly. As she drew level, he pushed open the door and rushed out. The door missed her, but he startled her.

"So sorry," he said. "Are you all right?"

"Yes, fine." She laughed. "You gave me a fright, that's all."

"Sorry," he said again. "Hey, don't I know you?"

She gave him a wary look. "I don't think so."

"You look familiar and I never forget a face. It'll come to me."

She looked even more worried as he fell into step with her.

"Got it." He gave her a triumphant smile. "I saw you with a friend of mine. Chesney."

"Chesney?" Her face lit up. "You're a friend of his?"

"Acquaintance. Funnily enough, I've been trying to speak to him for days and he hasn't been returning my calls. I called at his place yesterday too but there was no sign of him. I don't suppose you know what he's up to, do you?"

"I don't, but it's odd that you should mention it. He promised to call me, and I've been getting a little worried myself." She chewed on her bottom lip. "I hope he's all right."

"I'm sure he is. Perhaps he's visiting family for Easter and hasn't thought to tell us. You know what he's like."

"Yes." It was clear that she didn't.

"Here. Let me." He took her shopping bag from her.

"Thanks."

"Chesney was changing jobs the last I heard," Dylan said, "so perhaps he's busy with that."

"He might be. To tell the truth, I haven't known him long." They moved apart to avoid a woman pushing a buggy while hanging on to a toddler. "I met him while I was out running," she said when they were side by side again. "He knocked me off my feet—literally."

"Oh?"

"Yes." She was positively glowing at the memory. "I usually go for a morning run by the river. That particular morning, I was running one way, and he came round the corner from the opposite direction and collided with me. He knocked me flying. He picked me up, dusted me down and insisted on buying me a coffee. We chatted and—well, we just sort of clicked."

Dylan nodded his understanding, but wasn't sure whether to believe her or not. He would have staked his life on her being genuine if he hadn't known for a fact that she'd paid good money to see him.

"I'm not sure he'd agree with that," she said, "but I knew there was some connection between us. You just get those feelings sometimes, don't you?"

"Yes, I suppose you do." Love at first sight? Bev would have enjoyed this. It was straight out of the trashy romance books she read.

"We chatted over coffee, then went our separate ways. I couldn't get him out of my mind, though. All I knew was his first name and that he sometimes worked for an escort agency."

"He's quit that job now."

"Yes, he said he was going to. Anyway, I went online and rang round them all to see if they had a Chesney on their books. It took ages but I eventually struck gold. They wouldn't give me an address or phone number for him, understandable really, so I had to book a meeting with him through the agency."

"Ah." By his reckoning, she'd paid five hundred and forty quid for that meeting.

"We met up and had a wonderful time." Her expression became nauseatingly dreamy. "Like I said, I knew there was a connection between us. We have so much in common—music, films, books, even a love of chocolate ice cream—and we just hit it off. There was a spark, you know?"

"I know." He didn't. "So you saw him again?"

"That's just it. He said he was going away for a few days and would call me the moment he returned." The worried frown was back. "It may be that he's away longer than he anticipated, but I can't help wondering if something's happened."

Dylan felt a rush of sympathy for her. He'd bet his life that any spark had gone unnoticed by Goodenough—or Marshall, or whatever his blasted name was. He would have sussed that Janice wasn't wealthy enough to bother about. Flirting with women was what he did best, it was part of the job, but only the very wealthy would receive a follow-up phone call.

"I'm sure he's fine. He travels a lot, so—" He shrugged.

"Yes, I know. He has itchy feet. That's why he joined the army. I wonder—do you think he's lost my number? I didn't get his which, with hindsight, was pretty stupid of me."

"He may have lost it, I suppose. He's not the most organised of people, is he?"

"That could be it. I wonder, if you manage to get in

touch with him, would you give him my number? Oh, I'm Janice, by the way."

"Of course I will." He juggled her shopping bag and took his phone from his pocket. "If I put it straight on my phone, I won't lose it."

She rattled off her phone numbers, landline and mobile, and Dylan duly noted them.

"He might—well, I don't know how to put this," Dylan said. "Did he tell you about his last girlfriend?"

"No."

"Things didn't work out," Dylan said. "He doesn't have feelings for her or anything like that, but I gather someone caused trouble for him—for her too. Did he mention anything about that?"

"Nothing at all. No."

"Reading between the lines, I think the girl's father got involved and decided he wasn't suitable for his daughter. I gather Chesney was pretty angry about it. He didn't tell you?"

She gave a sad shake of her head. "No."

"I expect he's forgotten all about it then. Not to worry. I'll make sure he gets your phone numbers."

"Thanks so much." They reached her house with its sunny array of flowers. "This is where I live."

"Right. Well, good to meet you, Janice. I'll tell him to get in touch with you." He handed over her shopping. "Take care."

He wanted to tell her she wouldn't be hearing from Goodenough, or Chesney, and he wanted to tell her that she deserved one hell of a lot better, but there were no words that she'd believe so he walked back to his car and drove off with a growing hatred for Goodenough.

He hadn't learned a lot. Goodenough was often

away. No surprise there. He was ex-army, he ran by the river, presumably close to Janice's home as she also ran there, and presumably near a coffee bar. And that was the sum of it.

Goodenough was a particularly callous individual but Dylan couldn't imagine him making death threats. He certainly couldn't see him as a killer. Perhaps if he were being paid well—but no, that didn't make sense. If you wanted someone killed, you could walk into any of a handful of pubs in London and get the job done for next to nothing.

Of his two suspects, neither of which he could actually find, King had to be the most likely. He'd never killed anyone to Dylan's knowledge, but he'd served time for waving a gun in a shopkeeper's face. A scared shopkeeper would, quite rightly, hand over his worldly goods so it was impossible to say if King would have used his weapon.

But where to find him…

He was still convinced that King would find a way to see his kids. The pull of flesh and blood was too strong to be ignored for long. They were staying with Wendy's mother so, as he had nothing better to do, and as he was fresh out of better ideas, he drove to her address.

It was an old and slightly shabby bungalow with a well-cared-for, if uninspiring, front garden. An eight-year-old Volvo sat on the front drive waiting for someone to clean it.

Dylan had been watching the property for close to two hours when a text message came through. "Your kids have had their faces painted, received eggs from the Easter bunny, followed a brass band and are now home. No oddballs around. I'm back at your place opening a bottle."

Dylan wished he could join him.

Half an hour later, two boys emerged from the property. They didn't go anywhere, just sat on the low garden wall and talked. Dylan's heart went out to them. Losing a mother to illness was one thing, but how the hell did kids cope with knowing their mother had been murdered?

They weren't outside long. Still looking aimless, they went back inside and closed the door behind them.

Just as Dylan thought he might as well go home and share that bottle with Frank, a man walked smartly along the pavement and turned into the driveway. Leonard King!

Dylan couldn't believe his good fortune.

He waited. Each minute seemed to last an hour, but according to the dashboard's clock, King was only inside the house for thirty-two minutes. He came out, alone, and strode down the street.

Dylan jumped out of his car and followed. He was damned if he'd lose King this time.

King walked at a brisk pace and Dylan had to half jog to catch up. Finally he drew level. "Leonard King?"

King stopped in his tracks, looked behind him and looked back at Dylan. "Who wants to know?"

Dylan knew a moment's relief. King might want him dead but he didn't recognise him. A wig and a pair of glasses wasn't much of a disguise but, thankfully, it was doing its job.

"Bill Williams." He put out his hand. It was ignored. "I've been looking for you for a while now."

"Why?" King stepped forward—Dylan would put

him at six feet two, the same height as his anonymous postman—and glared at Dylan. "Who the fuck *are* you?"

"Bill Williams. I'm writing a book—"

King laughed at that, and seemed to relax a little. "Go and write the fucker then."

"It's about people wrongly convicted. Rumour has it that I can include you in that category."

"Does it?" King carried on walking.

Dylan fell into step with him. "There's money in it for you."

King stopped. "How much?"

"That depends."

"On what?"

"On how good your story is, on whether I'm convinced you were wrongly convicted, if you can toss out the odd name."

"Oh, I've got a good story. Talk money. You must have a figure in mind."

"It'll run to several thousand."

King seemed slightly more interested. But nervous. He kept looking behind him. Maybe he was expecting Weller to leap out of the bushes. "How many thousand?"

"Like I said, it depends."

"What would I have to do to get the money?"

"Tell me your story."

"How long till the money came through?"

"A month maybe."

King shook his head. "So I *might* get some cash, yeah? And I *might* get it in a month, yeah? Fuck off."

"I might be able to get it to you sooner. As I said, it

depends on how good your story is. I've heard things about you. And about Rickman."

"Like what?" King's eyes had narrowed to small black slits.

"I'd rather hear your side of things."

"Okay. Let's do it. Not here, though."

Dylan couldn't believe this. King was either desperate for money or desperate to hear the things Dylan had heard. He'd be disappointed on both counts. "Where are you living?"

"Like I'm going to tell you that." King's lips curled into a sneer. "Out in the open. The park."

London was full of parks. "Which park?"

"Follow me."

King must be the only bloke on the planet who could call the small patch of green, not much bigger than Dylan's front lawn and with four benches provided, a park. It was a circle of grass almost hidden from the road by a few trees.

King chose a bench that offered a good view of the four exits. Dylan sat beside him and took out his phone.

"How do I know I'll get the cash?" King asked, somewhat belatedly Dylan thought. "For all I know, I'll give you your story and you'll fuck off."

"You'll get the cash. I'll give you small amounts—" Dylan took out his wallet and counted the contents. He kept a tenner back for himself and gave the rest to King. He must be mad. "There's a hundred and sixty there."

King took it, counted it and laughed. "That's it?"

"It'll have to be enough for now. And if you don't tell me more than I already know, you won't get a penny more." He switched on his phone's voice recorder and hoped it lasted. Not that it mattered. It was only for show. "I'll be recording this, okay?"

"Suit yourself."

"Off you go then," Dylan said. "Start at the beginning. Tell me why you were at Rickman's drug factory the night you were arrested. And what about the coppers who turned up? How come they were detectives? I heard the police got a tip-off about a domestic dispute so why didn't a couple of uniformed officers investigate it?"

"Bloody hell, you expect me to tell you all that for a piddling hundred and sixty quid? You've got to be kidding."

Dylan shrugged. "Tell me something else then. Anything. But make it good or there won't be any more cash."

King traced a pattern on the grass with his shoe. "Rickman wanted a driver and I wanted some quick cash. That's why I went to his place. I knew he was dealing, and I guessed what he wanted me to deliver, but I didn't know the scale of the operation. I'd been there about ten minutes, hearing about the job. It wasn't as easy as I'd thought—it meant making big deliveries—but the money was good. Then these two fucking coppers showed up." He spat on the ground, narrowly missing Dylan's shoe. "Bastards. The cocky fuckers thought Christmas had come early. I'll get 'em, you have my word on that."

Don't count on it, sunshine. "Can you remember their names?"

"Oh, I can remember all right. Detective Sergeant Pike and Detective Sergeant Scott. Pike was a big ugly bastard but it was other who nearly fucking killed me.

Thanks to him, I had two busted ribs and I nearly lost an eye."

Hell hath no fury like a crook wronged. "Police brutality? Why didn't that come out in court?"

"Because my lawyer knew we'd get nowhere. The law looks out for its own."

That was a laugh. Dylan had served time for so-called police brutality. King did get a couple of broken ribs for his trouble and, yes, he had a bit of a shiner too. When you're expecting to find a husband and wife having a tiff and instead, stumble across a big bloke wielding a samurai sword, manners tend to be forgotten.

King was lying, though. The story of how he came to be at Rickman's drug factory was too neat. It was the same story he'd told over and over again. Word for word.

"So you're going after those coppers?" Dylan asked.

"Too right."

"Isn't that a bit tricky with John Weller after you?"

"Who says he's after me?"

"I do. What does he want with you?"

"No idea." Another lie.

"Maybe he's after the cash that everyone believes you stole from Rickman. The quarter million."

"Yeah. Maybe."

"But that was his stepfather's cash and they don't get along, do they?"

"No."

"How did the cash end up in your flat?"

"It was stolen from Rickman, along with a stash of heroin. Stolen and then planted. I was framed."

"But who'd steal from Rickman?"

King's lips curved into an evil sneer. "Wouldn't you like to know?"

"Yes, I would." He'd prefer to know what King was doing to get revenge on the two detectives who'd arrested him that night, but he was curious.

King got to his feet. "I'll meet you here Tuesday night. Maybe. Bring some cash and I'll tell you more."

"Hey, come on, give me a name. So far, you've told me nothing I don't already know."

"You want to know who stole that cash? Then I'll tell you. The same person who tipped off the coppers to go to Rickman's place that night."

"And that was?"

"As I said, bring some cash on Tuesday and I'll tell you."

"Aw, come on."

"Seven o'clock Tuesday night." King checked all entrances to the park, got to his feet and strode off without a backward glance.

FIFTEEN

"HEY, CAROL, DO you remember the last time I was in here and I was telling you I hadn't seen your Jimmy since he'd come out of the army? Well, you'll never believe this, but I saw him the very next day. What a coincidence."

"Did you?" Carol was rushed off her feet this morning. Her new assistant hadn't turned up so she was having to cope on her own and, worse, she'd made a complete cock-up and was overbooked. The salon was usually busy before Easter and quiet after but this year had proved the exception. She could do without Violet's constant chatter this morning but, as one of her best customers, Violet always received service with a smile, even if that smile was delivered through gritted teeth. "Are you having the same colour, Violet?"

"Please. Maybe with a bit of ash blond thrown in. It looked good last time, didn't it?"

"I'm glad you liked it."

Carol mixed the colour and gave a new customer an apologetic smile. She'd already forgotten the girl's name. "I'll put Violet's colour on and then I'll be with you. Sorry about the wait."

The young girl smiled. "It's okay. There's no rush."

It was just as well because Carol was running very

late and, with the double booking, she'd struggle to catch up.

"I didn't see him to speak to," Violet said. "Your Jimmy, I mean. He was coming out of the fish-and-chip shop and I was on the other side of the road. Funny that, though, wasn't it? Just when I said I hadn't seen him."

Carol idly wondered what he'd been doing eating fish and chips. He was always home for his meals and he didn't have much of an appetite these days.

Then she thought back to Violet's last visit to the salon and knew the woman was mistaken.

"You're wrong, Violet. The last time you came in, Jimmy was away in Somerset."

"It was him, all right. I might not have seen him for a while, but I'd recognise him anywhere."

Carol laughed and slapped the colour on Violet's hair as fast as she could. "I'm telling you, he was in Somerset."

"And I'm telling you he was coming out of the fish-and-chip shop on Russell Street. My sister lives there and I was on my way to visit her at the time."

Carol was aware of the silence in the salon. Only the hum of the dryer was audible.

"Perhaps he has a double," Carol said. "Whoever you saw, it wasn't Jimmy. Put your head forward. That's it."

Thankfully, the new customer was only booked in for a cut and blow dry so that shouldn't take long. The girl's hair was long and naturally blond, and looked to be in good condition.

"Here," Violet said, "I hope I haven't put the cat among the pigeons."

Violet was an incorrigible gossip and would love nothing more than a juicy story.

"Not at all. Perhaps I'm muddling the dates." She knew she wasn't, but it wasn't worth arguing with Violet. The woman would never admit to being mistaken. "Right, let's get you under the dryer."

"You hear such stories these days, don't you?" Violet wouldn't shut up. "I was reading about a man who had a whole other family. Really, he used to leave one family, saying he was going away on business, and then visit his other one. Five kids he had, two with one wife and three with the other, and both women were completely ignorant. Fifteen years it had been going on. Honestly, you can't credit it, can you?"

"Amazing," Carol murmured.

"Not that I'm saying your Jimmy's up to anything," Violet added.

"That's a relief." Carol laughed, though it took great effort. Some clients she loved to see. They chatted about everything under the sun so that it felt more like a social occasion than a job. Violet, though, had always been difficult, a gossip who loved to stir up trouble and pretend that she was a good, caring soul who wouldn't say a bad word about anyone.

Carol switched on the dryer, hoped it boiled Violet's brain, and checked her appointments diary for her new customer's name.

"Now then, Mandy, if you'd like to come over here, I'll get you shampooed. Just a trim and a blow dry is it?"

"Please." Mandy put down her magazine and sat by the basin. "I only want about an inch off. Just to tidy it up really."

Carol turned on the water, waited until it was the correct temperature and began to wash Mandy's hair. It was a job her assistant should have done. The girl had only been working with her for a fortnight and already she'd phoned in sick twice. Carol hated any sort of confrontation, but she'd have stern words with her. It wasn't good enough.

"Men usually have it easier, don't they?" Violet said.

"How do you mean?" Carol asked.

"Like that chap I was telling you about who had two families on the go. It's easier for men to leave the wife and kids behind and go somewhere else. The wife's the one who keeps everything ticking over. Men can walk out the door, say they're working late or going away on business, and have affairs or do whatever else takes their fancy."

"I suppose it is." Carol had given up smoking three years ago but she still kept an emergency supply upstairs. She might just light up in way of celebration when Violet walked out the door.

"Not that I'm saying your Jimmy's having an affair," she said. "It makes you wonder, though, doesn't it?"

"It doesn't make me wonder, Violet. He was in Somerset when you thought you saw him. Jimmy's only obsession is helping with the reservists' training. You're not too hot under there, are you?"

"No, I'm fine. Well, if that's what he's told you, I can't argue, can I?"

She could and probably would. Carol ignored her and towel dried Mandy's hair before showing her to the chair farthest away from Violet.

Carol chatted to Mandy as she trimmed her hair

and dried it. She was a nice girl and Carol hoped she'd come back.

It was time to wash Violet's colour out, trim her hair and dry it. The end was in sight.

Carol chatted about everything from shoes to holidays as she worked, anything to shut Violet up. It seemed to work. Violet told her about the holiday she'd had in Egypt last year, a subject that kept her busy until Carol held a mirror behind her so that she could see the back of her head.

"How's that?" she asked.

"Perfect. That's lovely. Thank you, Carol."

Violet had paid and was putting on her coat. "You should ask your Jimmy where he *really* was when you thought he was in Somerset. Sounds to me like someone has been telling the odd lie or two. Right, I'll be off then. Thanks, Carol. See you next time."

Carol was too nonplussed to think of a cutting reply before the door closed behind Violet. The damn woman was the absolute limit. She'd go to her grave believing she'd seen Jimmy coming out of that fish-and-chip shop and no one would convince her otherwise. Certainly not the wife who went to bed with him every night and woke up with him every morning. Oh, no, the woman who admitted herself that she hadn't seen Jimmy for years wouldn't be convinced.

The stupid, meaningless exchange left Carol in a bad mood for the rest of the morning. In a way, it was fortunate that she was busy, but even chatting to her clients didn't take her mind off Violet's stupid comments.

She tried to think of practical things, like what she'd cook for dinner, but then wondered if Jimmy would eat anything or if he'd call at that fish-and-chip shop again. Not that he had. No. Violet must have been mistaken.

She wondered how she'd feel if he *was* having another affair. Relief was the first thought that sprang to mind and, feeling guilty, she pushed it aside. She wouldn't be relieved. She'd be as hurt and as distraught as the last time.

She supposed she couldn't blame Violet entirely. After all, the thought that he might be having another affair had crossed her mind the night she'd woken and found him absent. Had he really been out running? Or was he seeing someone else?

The sex thing crept into her mind. There was a time they'd made love three times in the same day but, like all married couples, she supposed—not that she'd done a survey on the matter—the sex had dropped off to once a week, then once a month. It had to be two months, probably closer to three, since they'd last made love. If she made advances, he'd claim to be too tired.

Damn it. Jimmy was her husband, the father of her children, and Violet was nothing but an old gossip.

So why was she doubting her husband and beginning to believe the old gossip?

Perhaps Violet *had* seen him coming out of that fish-and-chip shop, but on a different day. It was possible. Not only possible, it was a far more likely explanation. Most of the time, Carol had no idea how he spent his time so he could easily have been there. She didn't have a clue where he was right now or how he was spending his morning.

She vowed to keep a closer eye on him in future...

SIXTEEN

THE TABLES OUTSIDE the café gave Jimmy a clear view of Gerry Lowell's office. More people than usual were sitting outside to enjoy the warm April sunshine with a tea or a coffee, but he wouldn't miss anyone who entered or left Lowell's building.

Jimmy nursed a cup of sweet coffee. It was weaker than he liked, but it was okay. He was only passing time anyway. His table was in the shade but he didn't mind.

Though he sat with his legs crossed at the ankles, looking relaxed, his mind was busy. He'd memorised every inch of Scotland Yard and he had the bomb. Well, almost. It was nearly there. One day soon, he'd blow the place to smithereens. He couldn't wait.

The downside was that the building was packed with civil service staff. Unbelievably, they now outnumbered the police by two to one. The victims would be unknown to him. That was unfortunate, but there was nothing he could do about it. It would make the whole world sit up and take notice, and that was the important thing.

He'd spent hours gazing at the twenty stories of anonymous stainless-steel-clad office block. It was being sold off soon, although he couldn't imagine anyone would want to buy it. People didn't realise it was such a crap building. All they saw was the revolving

sign that news reporters always stood beside to deliver
their stories. It revolved fourteen thousand times a day
apparently, but who the hell cared? Inside the hallway, the so-called eternal flame had flickered for years
alongside the names of all officers who'd died while
on duty. When Jimmy's plan came to fruition, they'd
be able to add a few more names to that particular list.

He forgot the inhabitants of Scotland Yard and mentally ticked off everything he knew about Lowell. On
the surface, Lowell was happily married to Janette. It
was his second marriage and he had three kids. The
two teenage girls from his first marriage lived with
their mother, and he had a seven-year-old daughter,
Emily, from his second marriage. It was odd then, at
least Jimmy thought it odd, that Lowell hung around
gay bars. He'd leave his office, spend an hour or so in
a nearby gay bar, making a drink last an hour, watching the other customers, and then he'd go home to his
wife, daughter and dog, a springer spaniel named Sam.

Home was a large five-bedroom house which, judging by the number of hours the cleaner worked, was
spotless. Caterers were employed when the Lowells
held one of their regular dinner parties. They enjoyed
a good life.

Lowell's business was above board, supposedly.
He'd started in a low-key way, lending small amounts
of money here and there. Business had taken off,
though, and over the years he'd made a fortune. When
the banks wouldn't lend them money, people went to
Lowell. He was a good talker and easily convinced
people that his extortionate interest rates were reasonable given the risks he took. Countless people had
lost their homes to Lowell. A lot had lost everything.

Lowell didn't care about that. He was too busy enjoying his perfect life with his perfect family.

Jimmy had a quick flick through the newspaper he'd bought. There was little of interest in it, just a couple of paragraphs about Dowie. Police were still appealing for information regarding his disappearance. His burned-out car had been found and, although the article was short on information, it seemed to Jimmy, reading between the lines, that police believed Dowie had done a runner, burned his car, returned to murder his family, and set off for a new life.

They'd never find him. Jimmy would make sure of that.

He folded the newspaper and finished his coffee. It was five minutes to one, almost time for Lowell to take a lunch break. Jimmy ordered another coffee and a chicken salad sandwich. It arrived at the exact moment that Lowell emerged from his office.

"Thanks." The waitress scurried away and Jimmy watched Lowell stride the twenty yards from his office to the café.

Jimmy bit into his sandwich, then watched, horrified, as Lowell stopped beside his table.

"Do you mind?" Lowell asked.

Jimmy looked around. This was out of the ordinary as Lowell always—*always*—took an inside table. Now, Jimmy's was the only table with empty chairs. He did bloody well mind, but what could he say? "Be my guest."

"Thanks." Lowell pulled out the chair opposite and sat. "This good weather soon has the outside tables filling up, doesn't it?"

Jimmy nodded and picked up his newspaper. He

didn't want conversation. He needed to observe. As he pretended to check the evening's TV-viewing schedule, he took a calming breath. It didn't matter where Lowell sat. Not really. Usually, it took him around twelve minutes to eat and drink, and then he strolled back to his office. Today would be no different—except he would spend those twelve minutes in Jimmy's space.

The waitress came over. "Hello, there. What can I get you?"

"You're looking particularly lovely today, Carmen. I'll have the usual, please." He gave her a smile and a wink and she walked off with a definite sway to her hips.

So Lowell was on first-name terms with the staff. So what? As he'd been having lunch here for so long, that wasn't surprising.

Jimmy had always loathed the man's conceit. Hated his arrogance. He wouldn't be so bloody sure of himself when Jimmy had finished with him.

The "usual" was soon brought to the table. A prawn sandwich with side salad and a large cappuccino.

Jimmy could remember the first time he saw Lowell. Even two decades ago, Lowell had been convinced that he had something special, some gift that people couldn't resist.

Lowell wouldn't recognise Jimmy. Jimmy never forgot a face, though, and the one opposite him was little different to the one he'd seen all those years ago. On that first meeting, a crowd of around twelve had been gathered in a pub. Lowell had taken up position on a barstool and everyone had stood around him, acting as his audience. He'd called everyone mate or buddy as he'd told jokes and shared amusing anecdotes. People had wanted to be his friend. Jimmy hadn't. He'd hated him even then.

As Jimmy ate his sandwich and sipped his coffee, Lowell took his phone from his pocket and hit a single button.

"Hi," he said when his call was answered. "Everything okay?"

Jimmy listened as Lowell chatted about domestic matters for a couple of minutes. Presumably he was talking to his wife.

"Okay, sweetheart. I'll see you later. I have a meeting that could go on a bit but, with luck, I'll get away by seven. See you then."

Lowell ended the call and returned his phone to his pocket. He ate his food, drank his coffee, and signalled to the waitress for his bill. He left the cash on the table, with a generous tip, got to his feet, nodded and smiled at Jimmy, then strode back to his office.

All in all, he'd been away from the building for fourteen minutes. Nothing unusual about that.

Jimmy would bet that, despite what he'd said, Lowell would get away from the office by five-thirty or six at the latest. He'd then spend an hour in the gay bar down the road before going home.

Jimmy would be watching. He'd watch Lowell's every breath until it was time to make his move.

SEVENTEEN

AFTER AN UNSEASONABLY warm day, the temperature had dropped dramatically and Dylan wished he'd had the sense to bring his jacket. He wasn't sure King would show up, and the idea of sitting on this bench with the chill breeze biting through his shirt wasn't appealing.

King seemed to have fallen for his far-fetched story of being a writer, but Dylan needed to be on his guard. If King discovered his true identity—

He'd cross that particular bridge when he came to it. For the moment at least, King would be too busy hiding from Weller. At least, Dylan hoped he would.

Dylan was early but he'd wanted to see if anyone was keeping an eye on King and, more important, logging his own movements.

The circle of grass—Dylan refused to call it a park—was deserted, apart from a pair of pigeons hunting for crumbs. Away from the green, on the other side of the spindly trees, people rushed from office to bar to home. Car horns blared, and an ambulance's siren shrieked. Buses and taxis ferried people around the City. People were too busy getting on with their lives to pay the grass or Dylan any attention.

Six o'clock came and went. As did six-fifteen. At twenty-five past, King appeared from nowhere and sat beside him.

"You got the cash?"

"I told you, I can't get any until I know if your story's worth printing."

"Fuck you!" King jumped to his feet.

"Wait. I've got a small amount—think of it as a down payment. Five hundred."

"Five hundred? Are you fucking joking?"

"You get to take it whether your story's worth writing or not. Look at it this way, if you have as much to tell me as you claim, it'll make a great story that I'll be able to write up quickly. If it's that good, believe me, my publisher will want it in the bookstores before you know it."

Sighing dramatically, King sat again. "Let's have it then."

Reluctantly, *very* reluctantly, Dylan took the cash from his wallet. It grieved him to hand over five hundred pounds for nothing. Well, probably for nothing. King *might* tell his story, and he *might* tell the truth, but that was unlikely to help Dylan.

King counted the money, grunted his thanks or disgust—it was difficult to tell which—and pocketed it.

"So the cash found at your flat on the night on the arrest was definitely stolen from Rickman?" Dylan asked.

"Yep."

"Who took it? Who the hell would be brave enough to steal from Rickman? How did they do it? And who made the call to the coppers that night?"

King sneered. "Who do you think?"

"If I knew that, I wouldn't be asking. Come on—this is bullshit."

"My ex-missus."

"Sorry?"

"Wendy."

"Your ex-wife set you up?"

"Yep."

"Are you sure?"

"Oh, yes, I'm sure. She didn't take the money herself, someone else did the dirty work, but she hid some of it where the filth would find it, along with the heroin. And she phoned the cops."

Dylan leaned back on his bench. It was feasible, perhaps. That call had been made by a woman. "But why?"

"To make some money for herself and to get rid of me. Two birds with one stone, you could say."

"She got her husband, the father of her kids, put away?"

"Yep."

"What proof do you have?"

King's head jerked up. "Proof? You want fucking proof? I can't give you that, can I? She's dead. You do know she's fucking dead, don't you?"

"Yes. Who killed her? Did you have anything to do with it?"

"Of course not. I could have, though. God, if I could have got my hands on her—but no, I had nothing to do with it. I have no idea who did it."

"What about Weller?" Dylan asked. "He's after you, so maybe—"

"Who says he's after me? I don't know nothing about that."

"Oh, believe me, he's after you."

"Like I said, I don't know nothing about that."

"Maybe he thinks you stole that money from his

stepfather. Maybe he went to Wendy's house looking for you."

"Dunno."

As soon as Weller's name was mentioned, King clammed up. Why?

This was madness. Who killed Wendy King, who stole money from Rickman, and King's innocence or otherwise was of no interest to Dylan whatsoever. Yet he was intrigued. He'd always been a sucker for a story.

"So," he said, "you're telling me that your then wife, Wendy, stole money and heroin from Rickman, with an accomplice, and then made an anonymous phone call to the police about a fictitious domestic dispute in the knowledge that you and Rickman would be caught red-handed?"

"Yep."

"I heard that it was less than two minutes between that anonymous phone call being made and those two coppers turning up?" He knew that was true because he and Pikey had been so close to the property in question.

"Yeah. Two detective sergeants no less. Like they'd go and sort out a bloody domestic, eh? Of course, everyone fell for it because London was in chaos that night. There were bomb scares and God knows what else going down. We thought those two bastards got lucky. If we'd been dealing with a couple of plods, we could have sorted it."

"How?"

"Rickman had weapons there."

Including two samurai swords. "Guns?"

"Knives. We'd have sorted it."

"Killed them?"

"Yep. If that's what it took."

"So why didn't you kill the detectives? What's the difference?"

"The bastards were too quick for us, that's why."

Too quick and too experienced. In short, too bloody good.

"So you're out to get them now?" Dylan asked.

"Yep. Well, Max is. It's Max really. I'll be right behind him, though."

"Hang on a minute. What do mean? Max is inside. What the hell can he do?"

King tapped the side of his nose. "He has contacts on the outside. Lots."

Dylan didn't doubt it. All the same—

"Years have passed," Dylan said. "How do you know those coppers are still around. Maybe they've retired, maybe—"

"They're still around. One's still a copper."

"What about the other?"

"He gave it up soon after, so I heard. He's a private investigator these days."

Shit.

"Sounds a bit odd to me," Dylan said. "I mean, why, if Rickman's so keen to get them, hasn't he done anything about it before now? Let's face it, he's had years to plan his revenge and it's not as if he's been busy with a demanding social life, is it?"

That sneer curled King's mouth again. "Like I said, we fell for it."

"Fell for what?"

"We thought it was coincidence that two detectives turned up. It's only recently that we've found out."

"Found out what?"

"The bastards were in on it."

"What?" Christ, he'd heard it all now. "You reckon the detectives who arrested you were involved?"

"Yep."

"How? Why?"

"Why? To get their hands on a share of the loot, that's why. You show me a copper and I'll show you a fucking crook."

"Okay. So how?"

King took a pack of cigarettes and a lighter from his pocket and took an age to light one. He inhaled and blew out the smoke. "A couple of months before I got out of prison, Max's missus was at a nightclub and she heard a couple of blokes talking about it. They were saying that, as soon as I was out, I'd be sure to get the truth out of Wendy—the truth being that she—and one of those coppers—set me up."

Unbelievable.

So unbelievable that Dylan was almost lost for words. Almost. "So Rickman's wife overhears a bit of gossip in a nightclub's toilets—"

"She was at the bar."

"Wherever. She overhears a bit of gossip and Rickman—and you—take it as gospel and decide that those two detectives stole cash and drugs from Rickman and set you up?"

"Give me a better idea. How the hell would that cash have got to my flat if Wendy wasn't involved, eh? Who else would have known that I'd be at Rickman's place that night, eh? And those coppers—they had to be involved. Otherwise a couple of plods would have turned up."

Put like that—

"That's your lot." King stood up and tapped the cash

in his pocket. "If you want more, you need to pay up. The next instalment costs five grand. Up front."

"Hang on a minute. When you said Rickman had contacts, that he was out for these coppers, what do you mean? What's he doing?"

King tapped the cash in his pocket again. "Same time on Thursday night."

"How many times have you spoken to Rickman since you got banged up?"

"Eh?" King looked confused.

"I'm wondering how you know what Rickman's thinking of doing?"

"I've talked to him often enough. Like I said, if you want more, be here the same time on Thursday night."

He strode off, looking left and right and over his shoulder as he did so.

Dylan wanted to go home and share a drink with Frank, but he had no choice but to follow King.

It was easier said than done. Every time a bus came into view, he expected King to leap on it, but King kept on walking, all the while checking over his shoulder, ducking into shops, walking into the Underground stations and taking a different exit. They walked for three-quarters of an hour until King suddenly ran into a Tube station and jumped onto a train as the doors closed.

"Shit." Dylan had lost him.

BY THE TIME Dylan stopped the car on his driveway, he was more than ready for the drink he'd been promising himself all day. His mind was still reeling from King's fictitious offering. He'd give a lot to know who'd started the story about him and Pikey being involved in the mess that was King's life.

He pushed open the front door and waited for the noise to greet him. All was quiet.

His mother, dressed in long skirt, T-shirt and cardigan in every colour of the rainbow, was sharing the sofa with Frank. No one else was around.

"Talk of the devil," his mum said. "I was telling Frank how it's a miracle you ever came into the world."

Dylan groaned. Once she got started on the horrors of childbirth, or the horrors she'd had bringing him into the world at least, there was no stopping her. Dylan swore he could walk his way through a degree in gynaecology.

Frank was grinning, but he hadn't heard the story a million times already. Besides, he had a glass of whisky in his hand and Vicky Scott was far easier to deal with when alcohol was being consumed.

"That's why he's an only child, Frank. I wouldn't want to go through that again. And can you imagine inflicting two like Dylan on the world?" She cackled with laughter.

Dylan had given up trying to work out who his father might be, but he'd often wondered what life would have been like if his mother hadn't found herself in lone parent mode. Given that she'd spent her time smoking marijuana and drifting from one commune to another chanting Love and Peace, it could be anyone. A waiter in Turkey, a bullfighter in Spain—anyone.

She drove him to the edge of insanity, but for a reason that had always eluded him, he loved her dearly. And he had to admit that it was useful to have a willing babysitter at the end of a phone. A crazy dope-smoking babysitter wasn't every parent's dream, but it didn't seem to have harmed his kids. Yet.

"Where is everyone?" he asked.

"Bev's having a lie-down, Freya's fast asleep and Luke's staying the night at Tom's."

"Is Bev okay?" The question sounded ridiculous as soon as it left his lips. She was having treatment for cancer. How the hell could she be okay?

"Fine. Just a bit tired. So how's your day been?"

Like mother, like son. Neither of them were comfortable discussing Bev's illness. Both were quick to change the subject.

"Boring," he said. "So who needs a drink? Frank?"

"I'll have a small one with you."

"I'm nipping out for a smoke," Vicky said.

"Great idea, Mum. I love you more when you're stoned."

"Ha." With bangles and beads jingling, she walked out the room.

"Sorry about that, Frank. I did tell you she was mad, didn't I?"

"She's a star," Frank said.

"That's one word to describe her. Insane is another."

Frank grinned. "You could have done a lot worse."

"I could have done a lot better too. I'll nip up and see Bev and then I'll be back with the bottle."

He took the stairs quietly—that was another thing, he always tiptoed around now that Bev was ill—and pushed open the door to his bedroom.

There had been no need for the softly, softly approach because Bev was sitting up in bed wide awake.

She smiled and laid her book aside. "Hello, love. You had a good day?"

"Boring." He leaned across the bed and kissed her. "You?"

"Yes, it's been good. As your mum's here, I thought I'd come to bed for a bit of peace and quiet and a read."

"Good idea." He'd have been relieved to hear it if she hadn't looked so pale and exhausted. "I'll have an early night too. I'll be up soon."

She nodded, still smiling. He couldn't tell if the smile was forced or not, but he guessed it was. She was great at putting on a brave face but he knew the other emotions—like the depression and the abject terror—were never far from the surface.

"Meanwhile, I'd better go and supervise our guests. Mum's getting stoned, Frank's getting drunk—"

She laughed at that, and the carefree sound took him by surprise. "Getting drunk's the only option when Vicky's getting stoned."

"True. I might have to join him."

When he left Bev, he checked on Freya. She was lying on her back, her arms thrown out wide, an expression of pure happy innocence on her face. God, he loved her.

He envied her too. How wonderful it must be to have no knowledge of cancer, of death threats, killers and drug dealers. Mind you, spouting gibberish to every passing dog, cat or pigeon probably became a tad boring after a while.

He left her door slightly ajar and went downstairs to the kitchen for the bottle of whisky and a glass.

His mother came back inside at the same time. She made herself a cup of some herbal concoction that she'd brought with her, and settled down to flirt with Frank while she drank it.

It wasn't the first time Dylan had noticed that she had to flirt with anything in trousers. She'd been a very attractive young woman and age had done little to mar her looks. She'd never been a great one for makeup, and although more wrinkles were evident these days and her hair was grey, she still had a certain charm and vivacity.

"Right," she said, getting to her feet, "I'll love you and leave you."

"Do you want a lift home?" Dylan asked.

"Good grief, no. I'm not in my dotage yet." She grabbed a cavernous bag and slung it over her shoulder. "Good to see you, Frank. Night, both."

Dylan was still smiling when he heard the door close behind her. "I think you could be in luck there, Frank."

"She's a star," Frank said again.

"Yeah, well, don't panic. She's not the marrying kind."

"Me, neither," Frank said immediately—which, given that his three marriages had ended in the divorce courts, wasn't strictly accurate. "So what have you learned today? Anything useful?"

"I know that the latest rumour is that me and Pikey—one of us or both of us—was supposedly involved in setting up Rickman and King."

"You're kidding."

"Nope. Some bastard has put that story about, and Rickman's supposedly out to get us."

"So Rickman's responsible for these death threats?"

"I don't know, but it seems more likely than King. That bloke's all talk. He might have shown a bit of bravado at his court hearing and threatened to get the two coppers who arrested them both, but I think he's got his hands full avoiding Weller."

"And Rickman?"

"According to King, Rickman's wife overheard someone talking about how Wendy King, the late Wendy King, stole the cash and heroin that was found at her place. Her accomplice was one of the coppers who turned up at Rickman's place after she made the anonymous phone call."

"Who's putting that about?"

"I don't know, but the timing more or less fits. King said this came to light a couple of months before he was released—about the time that Bev first had those weird phone calls."

"Then it's time to make this official," Frank said. "Get the law involved, Dylan. They can see who Rickman's talking to while he's on the inside."

Dylan didn't want to involve the police. He might ask Pikey for a few favours, off the record, but no way would he go grovelling to the force for help. He could manage this on his own.

"That bit of info cost me five hundred quid." And was possibly worth it. "King wants more cash, naturally. I was expecting him to suggest we meet tomorrow night, but he must have something on because he told me to meet him on Thursday. I need to find him and see what he's up to tomorrow."

"Where's he hanging out?"

"That's just it. I don't know. He meets me on a bench close to his in-laws' place—where his kids are living. Where he goes during the hours of darkness is anyone's guess."

"So you need to get him before Weller does."

"Yes. I can only assume that as Weller is after King, and as Rickman is after me, stepfather and son don't speak a lot. That fits with what Weller told me. I don't suppose he wants his father's bad name tarnishing his fully above board business."

"Is it above board?"

"I shouldn't think so for a minute."

"Anything else?" Frank asked.

"Not really, no. I can't find Goodenough, or whatever his name is, but I can't see him bothering with me. I've more or less dismissed him."

"Hmm." Frank took a long swallow of whisky. "Rickman's a seriously nasty piece of work, Dylan."

"I know."

"If he's after you both—"

"I need to warn Pikey."

"Yes. And you need to find out who he's in touch with on the outside. You need to do it fast too. If Rickman wants revenge, he'll take it. You'll be a dead man."

Dylan knew it. He hadn't been too worried about King, he could handle him, but Rickman was a different matter altogether. He'd kill anyone, or have them killed, without batting an eyelid.

Dylan decided a refill was called for.

EIGHTEEN

DYLAN HAD BEEN at his office less than five minutes when the phone call came.

"Mr. Scott?"

"Ah, it's you again. Yes, I'm still here. Still breathing."

"You won't be for long. Time's running out, Mr. Scott."

Dylan stood at the window, but there was no one outside using a phone, loitering or looking suspicious. There were no distinctive sounds on the line, and the voice was too muffled to offer any clues.

"Says who?" Dylan asked.

"Says me. You're a dead man walking."

"Is that so? And what—shit!" The call was over.

There was no one in the street below who looked to be doing anything other than rushing from A to B. No one was paying any attention to his office, no one was stuffing a phone into their pocket—there was no one of any interest whatsoever.

His mobile rang and a quick glance at the display showed him Pikey was calling.

"Hey, what a lovely surprise. How's life treating you, Pikey? Well, I trust?"

"That's more like it. You see? Even you can be polite when you try. Thank you, I'm well. Or I would be if some bastard wasn't accusing me of being a dirty copper and setting up Rickman and bloody King."

Dylan knew how he felt.

"It's odd that it's taken so long for the farfetched story of our involvement to come out," Pikey said. "And it's bloody coincidental that it's come out at the exact time that King's released."

"That's exactly what I thought. I smell a big rat."

"Yeah. Me too. Anyway, no one of interest has visited Rickman lately. His wife sees him, but that's about it. Oh, and Phil Browne, every crook's favourite lawyer, visited him twice. Other than that, nothing."

"Phil Browne. According to a reliable source— that'll be Archie—he's spending a bit of time with Mrs. Rickman too."

"Yeah?"

"Yeah."

A thoughtful silence filled the phone line but produced nothing of value.

"And King claimed he was staying with a mate temporarily." Pikey gave him the address. "I doubt there will be any sign of him there, but you never know."

"Okay, thanks for that. Let me know if you hear anything else."

"I will. You do the same. And watch your back, Dylan."

He intended to but, before he could do that, he needed to watch hours of surveillance video. No envelopes had been delivered overnight but it struck him as odd, and more than a little coincidental that the phone call telling him he was a dead man walking had arrived so soon after he'd arrived. Someone must have been waiting for him.

He went through the images as quickly as possible. If there were more boring tasks, he didn't know what they were.

The men refurbishing the soon-to-be dental practice in the office opposite finished work at eleven. Between then and one in the morning, dozens of people walked past the building on their way home from clubs or theatres. No one paid his office any attention.

At a little before two o'clock, a young man laughingly pulled his female companion into the shelter of the wall. They kissed—and kissed. The chap soon had his hand inside the woman's blouse. His other hand was lifting her skirt and sliding up her thigh. Just as Dylan thought he was about to witness a session of hot sex by his office door, the woman said something that looked to be a promise, grabbed the chap's hand and dragged him away.

He skimmed more footage but little happened between the hours of two and five o'clock. It was shortly after that the City began to come slowly to life.

He was almost done and was expecting the next item of interest to be his own arrival at his office door when he saw him. It was a little after nine o'clock, around thirty minutes before Dylan arrived.

The man stood tall. He walked up to the main door and tried the handle. It was locked. The receptionist that people who rented the offices paid good money for obviously hadn't turned up yet.

The man stepped back from the door and stood to gaze at the building for a few moments. Then he strode off.

There was no mistaking his identity. It was Brad

Goodenough. Or Chesney Marshall. Or whatever other damn name he'd taken a fancy to.

"Bastard!"

THERE WAS A forlorn bench outside the ugly block of flats where King had claimed to be staying with an old mate. Dylan sat on it and watched the building, but his mind was racing in never-ending circles.

He had no idea what he was doing here. He'd dismissed Goodenough as a possible suspect, but he'd been there, as bold as you like, standing outside his office.

Frank had warned him not to get so obsessed with King that he ended up with a knife in his back. Perhaps he should take note.

Yet here he was, waiting for King to make a move.

What else could he do, though? He'd spent most of the day looking for Goodenough but the bloke was as elusive as King. Both men were hiding—one from a possible killer and the other from debt collectors and scorned women.

Both were doing a bloody good job of staying underground too. London made a great hiding place.

He didn't know for sure that Goodenough was threatening him. Yes, he'd been standing outside his office that morning, shortly before he'd received that phone call. And yes, he'd probably delivered the photos of Dylan's family. Probably. It was difficult to tell. Photo deliveryman had kept his face covered and had waved at the camera. Goodenough had stood there in broad daylight and hadn't so much as glanced at the camera.

He didn't know that King was threatening him either. In fact, he was fairly sure the bloke was too pre-occupied.

As for Rickman, there was no knowing what fun and games he was organising from his prison cell. He believed that he'd been robbed and set up by two coppers. Yep, he was likely to be pretty pissed off about that. And an angry Rickman wasn't someone to mess with. He had an unnerving penchant for samurai swords, for a start...

"Are you looking for some action?"

Dylan dragged his gaze from the concrete building and looked up into the young face of a blond-haired girl whose skirt wasn't worth the effort. "Yes, but not the sort you're offering, love. Besides, my wife can hear me thinking from five miles away. Sorry."

"Suit yourself. You know where to find me if you change your mind." She tottered off on ridiculously high heels to offer action to some other guy.

By the time darkness began to descend, Dylan had been offered great sex, at a price, by three prostitutes. And that was the height of the excitement.

Lights spilled out from shops and with the glow from streetlights and car headlights, it seemed darker—and later—than it was.

At a little after seven-thirty, Dylan thanked whichever god was smiling on him because leaving the concrete rabbit warren was none other than King. A dark hoodie kept his face hidden but Dylan knew it was him. He darted across the road, looking this way and that, like a cornered animal.

Dylan followed, grateful for the chance to stretch his legs and do something. The streets were busy and he had to stay closer to King than he was comfortable with.

They went to the Tube station. Once King had bought his ticket, he headed off for the Central Line. Dylan bought his own ticket and raced after him. He spotted King jumping on a train. Dylan managed to get in the next carriage before the doors closed and the train rumbled on its way.

He could still see King.

Five stops later, they abandoned the train. No wonder King had an affinity with greyhounds. He moved like one. He was wiry, lean and fast.

They walked along streets, caught a bus and walked along yet more streets, these becoming increasingly run-down.

Dylan didn't have a clue where they were heading, only that it was one of those neighbourhoods where you needed to be armed and in company, preferably the company of a few prizefighters.

When they came to a disused factory, Dylan crouched behind a low wall, the only thing offering protection from view. King, however, walked across the square of concrete between the long, low buildings. He paced. Up and down. Up and down.

Long minutes passed, about thirty of them, before a large dark car drove slowly through the factory's entrance. Dylan thought there were four men inside.

King stood in the glare of the headlights, his feet wide apart as he tried for a Billy the Kid look.

This was going to get ugly, Dylan was sure of it.

The two men who'd been sitting in the back climbed out. The bulkier one was carrying a holdall. They left the doors open and walked over to King. Once facing him, they leaned against the bonnet of the vehicle.

Dylan wasn't close enough to hear what was being said, but it was only a very brief chat before King snatched the holdall. He slung it over his shoulder and began walking away, his steps getting ever quicker.

The shorter man pulled out a gun and fired. His aim was impressive and King dropped to the ground like a stone. He was clutching his side and managed to crawl a few inches.

The man with the gun raced up to King and, like Dylan, heard the approaching police siren. The chap grabbed the holdall, raced back to the car and jumped inside. The vehicle sped away in a cloud of dust.

Three police cars, lights flashing and sirens blaring, raced through the gates, the tyres sending up a shower of gravel. All they found was King lying on the ground. The car was long gone.

Dylan didn't hang around. There was no need. Officers would get King to the nearest hospital or the mortuary, depending on which was appropriate. Either way, Dylan guessed his meeting with King had just been cancelled.

NINETEEN

"I'M BORED NOW," Jimmy said. "You're tiresome, tedious and you stink to high hell. You've been here for almost a fortnight, Brian, and you've outstayed your welcome. It's time to say goodbye."

There wasn't so much as a flicker from Dowie to indicate that he'd even heard.

Jimmy lifted the crowbar and whacked it against the side of Dowie's head. He heard Dowie's jaw break. Or perhaps it was his skull.

"I said I'm bored now."

Nothing.

Jimmy didn't have time for chitchat anyway. He had too much to do.

He ran up the stairs and outside to the garage. His first job involved the back of his van. He'd brought a roll of industrial-strength polythene sheeting and he covered every surface with it.

Next, he took the dozen heavy-duty black plastic bags he'd bought into the house. His chainsaw sat in the yard primed for action.

While carrying it into the house, he saw that a few drops of petrol had leaked. He gave it a quick wipe and hoped it didn't let him down.

"Doing some work?" a voice asked.

Jimmy spun round to see his elderly neighbour peering over the wooden fence that separated the two yards. Nosy bugger.

"I'm getting it ready to take to a friend's house. He has some logs to chop up for next winter."

The chap nodded, but said nothing. The deaf old sod probably hadn't heard.

"Can't stop," Jimmy said, and he hurried inside, clutching the chainsaw to him.

How deaf was the old chap? The saw made a hell of a lot of noise, and if he heard it, he'd know Jimmy wasn't chopping up logs.

It didn't matter. The old man would be taking his dog out soon—you could set your watch by them—and Jimmy would do it then. Meanwhile, he'd relax with a coffee. He'd drink it in the yard so he could see when man and dog set off.

He took one of the kitchen chairs outside and sat on that as if he were enjoying the sunshine.

He wondered briefly what Carol and the boys were doing. He'd guess that the boys were waiting for Carol to finish at the salon before asking her to take them to tonight's entertainment. She was far too soft with them. He'd have to start spending more time at home and instilling some discipline in them.

Their grandfather, Jimmy's dad, thought they were the best kids ever born but he'd change his mind if he saw them on a daily basis. "Nancy boys," he'd call them, just as he'd called Jimmy. He'd ask them if they were gay, just as he'd asked Jimmy.

Jimmy loathed the bloke. He was civil to him for his mum's sake, but he hated him. Hated him.

Even now, he could hear his mocking laughter. "You? In the army? You won't last five minutes. Or perhaps you will. I've heard it's full of gays now. They're that desperate, they're letting anyone in."

If he could see him now, if he could see the wretch in the cellar, he wouldn't be laughing. He wouldn't call him a nancy boy then.

Jimmy wished it was his father in the cellar. He'd love to have the conceited, cruel bastard at his mercy. He'd give anything to hear him beg.

The door to the adjoining house banged closed.

"Off for a walk then?" Jimmy said.

"The dog can't go far these days," the old chap replied.

Neither of them could go far. The short distance they travelled always took them an age, though.

Jimmy watched until man and dog were out of sight. Then he went back inside, picked up the chainsaw and descended to the cellar.

"Like I told you, Brian, it's time to say goodbye. I hope all your affairs are in order." That made him laugh, but Dowie didn't seem to appreciate the joke. There was no reaction, not so much of a shudder.

Jimmy put a finger to Dowie's neck. There was no pulse. The skin was cold.

"You useless fucking twat. Jesus. You wouldn't last five minutes in the army." Jimmy was furious. He'd intended to have fun with Dowie. There was no hope of that now. "Useless fucker. Just give up, eh? The going gets a bit tough and you give up and fucking die. That's great. Just fucking great."

Thinking about it, Jimmy supposed he wouldn't have had much time for fun anyway. He needed the job done before his neighbour returned.

He untied the ropes from around Dowie's neck, arms and legs and Dowie dropped to the floor.

Jimmy checked for a pulse again, but it was no use. The bloke had been dead for hours.

He pulled the cord on his chainsaw and gave a little smile of satisfaction as it growled into life. He'd known it wouldn't let him down.

Sweat poured off him as he worked. It wasn't as easy as he'd thought it would be. He had to stop twice to vomit. The smell was unbearable too. He'd seen worse than this in Afghanistan but, all the same—

He carried on with the task. His heart thumped. Sweat dripped into his eyes.

When the task was done, he put the body parts into the black plastic bags, tied them securely and carried them, one or two at a time depending on the weight, to his van.

He locked the house, jumped in his van and drove off with the windows open.

His first idea had been to dump Dowie's body in the Thames, but it was too busy. Instead, he'd decided to drive to the coast. It was ages since he'd been to the seaside and he was looking forward to it. Perhaps he'd visit Brighton. Or maybe he'd go to Beachy Head, where everyone went to commit suicide. He could throw Dowie off the cliffs.

It would be late when he got there, but he liked it better that way.

He'd drop Dowie into the sea. Piece by piece.

TWENTY

DYLAN PICKED UP his phone and tapped in Mrs. Rickman's number.

"Hello?" She answered on the second ring.

"Mrs. Rickman?"

"Yes." There was a frown in her voice.

"My name's Bill Williams. I don't know if you've heard but I'm a writer, and I'm currently researching a book about criminals who've been wrongly convicted."

"I've heard."

He waited for more but nothing was forthcoming. Presumably her son had spoken to her about him.

"I was wondering if I could have a chat with you," he said. "About your husband and Leonard King. Obviously, I know your husband wasn't wrongly convicted, that he was dealing drugs, but rumour has it that both men were set up." There was a long, long silence. "Mrs. Rickman?"

"You can't pay attention to rumours, Mr.—?"

"Williams. Bill. I know that, but I've heard a few things recently that make me wonder."

"Like what?"

"That's what I'd like to talk to you about."

Another long silence.

"Perhaps I could buy you dinner." He'd be broke at this rate. Or more broke. "I can tell you what I know and then you can make up your mind whether or not to talk to me."

"Okay," she said at last. "Les Deux Salons. Seven o'clock this evening. I'll make the booking."

"Right. Good. Thanks. See you there."

She cut the connection before he'd finished the sentence.

He looked up Les Deux Salons on the internet. As it was in Covent Garden, the French restaurant was apparently *the* place to go for pre-theatre dining. Thankfully, it didn't look *too* pricey. A burger at McDonald's would have suited Dylan better but at least she'd agreed to see him.

He thought about calling Pikey to see if there was any change in King's condition, but he knew Pikey would call him if there were.

King would live. He'd lost a lot of blood and had needed an operation to remove the bullet, but he was probably in the safest place.

His story was that he'd been heading to a boxing club he'd joined when two men had stopped a car and accosted him. He claimed to have no idea why they'd picked on him or what they'd wanted.

It was all bollocks, of course. King had been waiting for those men, and Dylan would bet his life that the holdall had contained money or drugs.

Police had been looking into Weller's affairs, which was why they'd been so interested in the vehicle involved and why they'd reached the scene so quickly. The car belonged to Weller. He'd reported it stolen, had a watertight alibi, as did all his staff, and was totally in the dark as to why it might have been used in such a manner.

It was all nice, neat and convenient. And it was complete bollocks.

Dylan wished he could get out of his office. Work was continuing at a pace in the soon-to-be dental surgery across the corridor, and it was difficult to think straight with all the noise caused by workmen hammering and banging. Soon, the noise would be of the dentist's drill variety and Dylan wasn't sure which was worse.

He couldn't escape, though, because he needed to look through hours of footage taken from the cameras outside his home and office. It was a job he could only do for an hour or so at a time. Any longer and his brain went numb and saw what it wanted to see rather than what was actually there…

Les Deux Salons was better than Dylan had expected in many ways. The menu was more tempting and varied than he'd found in other French restaurants. Or perhaps he was simply hungrier than usual.

He was a few minutes early but, true to her word, Mrs. Rickman had make a booking and Dylan was quickly shown to their table. He didn't have long to wait.

The breath left his body in a shocked whoosh when he saw her arrive. He recognised her face from old photos he'd seen, but he hadn't realised she was in a wheelchair.

He stood up as the waiter escorted her and her chair to their table. "Er—good to meet you, Mrs. Rickman. Thanks for seeing me."

She was fifty-two but she clearly tried to hide that fact behind well-cut blond hair, expertly manicured fingers and carefully applied makeup. Her trim figure suggested that this evening wouldn't be as expensive as Dylan had feared. She was wearing a simple black dress, a gold necklace, gold watch and two diamond stud earrings.

"As you're buying me dinner, you'd better call me Sarah," she said when her chair was in the most comfortable position.

"Thank you. As you know, I'm Bill."

He wondered what she saw when she looked at him. A bloke whose brown hair needed a good cut and a bloke who had no taste whatsoever when it came to buying spectacles. At least, he hoped that's what she saw. Better that than a bloke whose wig was slipping.

Either he was staring too hard or the shock was still etched across his face because she gave him a knowing smile. "Don't worry, Bill, it's only my legs that are knackered. The rest of my faculties are in perfect working order."

"Ah. Right. Sorry, I didn't mean to—I didn't know."

"Really? You haven't done your research very well then, have you?"

"Apparently not."

"An accident," she said. "I was still in hospital when Max went to trial."

How the hell hadn't he known? Thinking back, Archie had said something that should have alerted him. *"Despite everything, she's still a looker...money's not the answer to everything, is it? Well, not in her case."*

He remembered Rickman's trial, but he couldn't remember hearing that the bloke's wife had been in hospital.

"What happened?" he asked.

She gave a small smile and said, as if she'd had to explain it too many times in the past, "I was hit by a car."

"Oh?"

"A hit-and-run driver. We never did find out who was responsible. I'd probably had too much to drink so perhaps it was my own fault. Now then, let's look at the menu."

The trouble with meals—at least, the trouble with meals when women were involved—was the time it took to get down to the important conversation. Men could discuss business while eating fish and chips in the street, or over a plate of pie and chips in the local pub, but women insisted on making a song and dance of it all. Bev was exactly the same.

It took an age for Sarah to choose a wine to drink while she perused the menu. She ordered a third-of-a-bottle carafe of white wine. "That way, I can sample the other wines as the evening goes on," she said.

If it took her that long to decide on the first carafe, they'd be here all night. She'd also be very drunk if she went through the entire list. Still, that probably wouldn't be a bad thing. There were few things better than alcohol for loosening tongues.

He ordered a beer to pass the time.

He declined a starter but she insisted on having beetroot salad with crumbled goat's cheese or some such thing. Then came the ordeal of ordering a main course. Dylan ordered the duck, and after a great deal of deliberation she settled on what had to be the most expensive thing on the menu, grass-fed veal chop.

She was reasonably good company, though, and,

under different circumstances he would have enjoyed himself. He could see why Archie was a tad smitten.

However, Dylan needed information from her and it was difficult when she insisted on talking of TV programs, films she'd seen recently, mobile phones and everything else.

"I've always loved the cinema." She was downing wine as if it were about to be banned from the land and was already a little tipsy. "It's always been my treat. Of course, it's not the same these days. When I was a teenager, you could barely see the screen for smoke. Now that smoking's banned everywhere, you have to endure people eating popcorn, chocolate or ice cream. People never used to talk during a showing either."

"I rarely go to the cinema," he said, "so I wouldn't know. I prefer to watch films on TV. That way, I can pause it to get a drink and watch it when I feel like it."

"It's not the same, Bill."

"No, I don't suppose it is. More convenient, though. You don't have to get dressed up to go out—"

"You don't have to get dressed at all," she said, her eyes meeting his.

She was flirting with him. He was ten years younger, which ought to mean he could do better, but a small part of him was flattered. The sensible part of him was curious as to why she'd bother. Clearly, she wanted something from him.

When she took a mouthful of grass-fed veal, he took a breath and launched in. "So you knew about the book I'm working on. I suppose your son told you?"

"He mentioned it, yes. Not that he's interested," she said quickly. Too quickly? "Him and Max have never been close. Not Max's fault. Not John's really. John idolised his dad and never really got over losing him. Or never got over seeing me with someone else. It's not that he's jealous exactly—it's more that Max was a stranger to him, just someone who came to live with me."

"Does he have a family of his own?"

"John? No. He hasn't married. There's only me." She smiled proudly at this.

The bloke was thirty.

"I heard—and I've heard so many rumours that it's difficult to know what's truth and what's fiction—but I heard he was after Leonard King."

There was the briefest of pauses as she sought her answer. "No. Why would he be?"

"I don't know. Maybe he wants the money that he believes King stole from his stepfather."

"I don't know who's told you that, but it's ridiculous. John knows Lenny didn't steal it. And as I said, John doesn't care about Max. They never grew close, it's as simple as that. He hasn't even been to see Max inside. Not once."

"So he's not looking for King?"

"Of course not. It's ridiculous."

"One of John's cars was involved in something, wasn't it? King was shot and I heard—"

"The car was stolen." Her tone was icy. "Someone was out to make it look as if poor John was involved. He wasn't. Of course he wasn't."

"But it's not surprising that people believe it to be the case. After all, a lot of money was taken from his stepfather and if he believes King stole it—"

"He doesn't. Even if did, why bother? John's doing

all right for himself." Her face was crimson as she spoke and Dylan knew she was lying.

"With the gym, you mean?"

"It's actually a health and well-being centre, but yes. He studied business at college, you know. He has his head screwed on the right way and is doing really well."

Dylan didn't believe her. He'd have to get hold of the accounts. "You own half of it, don't you?" he asked.

"Yes." Her tight smile thawed the icy glare a little. "That's how John likes it. Me and him doing everything together."

"Ah. And I suppose it gives you something to pass the time until Max is free."

"That's it exactly. Besides, I want an income too, you know. It hasn't been easy since Max was arrested."

He'd assumed she could live out the rest of her days in comfort on the fortune Max had made before he was sent down. Perhaps that wasn't the case.

"Of course," she said as if she could read his mind, "everyone thought Max was coining it in. He wasn't. That operation he was involved in—and I knew nothing about that, trust me on that one—was new and he didn't make much money at it."

"And yet someone stole half a million quid from him?"

She gave him a sharp look. "It was a quarter of a million."

"I heard half a million. I heard that the police only found some of it."

"Who told you that?"

"Is it true?"

"I have no idea. In any case, it didn't really belong to Max. It was money he owed. We never had that sort

of money." She was looking distinctly rattled now—
and drunk.

He ordered more wine for her.

"You'll have me tipsy, Bill."

That was the idea. Not that he wanted to be responsible for her getting hit by speeding cars.

He let her concentrate on her food and wine and
was surprised when she ordered a dessert. She looked
like a woman who counted calories. He was impressed
with the food and the service, though, and would bring
Bev here one night. She'd love it.

"So who made the phone call to the coppers the
night Max and King were arrested?"

She snorted at that. "That's easy. Who wanted her
husband out of the way?"

"Sorry?"

"Think about it," she slurred. "Lenny's marriage
was on the rocks and Wendy wanted him out of her life.
She knew he was seeing Max that night. She knew that
if she called the cops, they'd both go down."

"Wait a minute. You mean Wendy King knew what
Max was doing while you didn't."

She flushed at that. "Oh, I had a vague idea. The
same as she did. We knew each other, you know. In
fact, it was me who introduced her to Lenny and Max
in the first place. We used to be quite good friends.
She wouldn't have known the scale of it, the same way
as I didn't, but she'd still have known that they'd get
sent down."

"It seems a bit extreme. Why didn't she just divorce him?"

"Because she was a weakling."

"So as soon as he was behind bars, she divorced him?"

"She was free to do as she pleased then, wasn't she? Wendy had no intention of standing by her man."

"So she made the call to the police? She stole the money from Max?"

"Along with someone else, yes."

"Who was that?"

She leaned in close to whisper. "A copper. He stole the money, she hid it at her place, and the next thing is that Max and Lenny are arrested. Wendy's copper friend was first at the scene."

She leaned back in her seat, delighted with her work of fiction.

"That's some story. How did you find out? About Wendy and the copper, I mean."

She tapped the side of her nose. "I've already said too much."

"What was the copper's name?" he asked.

"What?" She frowned at him. "I don't know. One of those who turned up at Max's so-called factory that night, that's all I know."

"I bet Max is pretty angry about that. Why hasn't he appealed? If there's a bent copper involved—"

"God, you're naive. What would be the point of that? The law looks out for its own. They're all on the take—from the coppers pounding the beat to the high court judges."

"What's he going to do, then? Presumably he wants his money back."

"I'm sure he'll sort it when he gets out." She sighed dramatically. "There's still a while to go before that happens, though. Still, we have to keep cheerful. Me and John manage. We get by. I visit Max as often as I can but it's not the same, is it?"

"No."

Her phone alerted her to a text message. She took it from her small handbag and checked the screen. The font was large enough for Dylan to read it—just. *See you later?*

"Excuse me, I'll just—" She tapped in three letters, pressed the send button and returned the phone to her bag. "Now then, I think I've probably said too much. Let's talk of other things. Tell me about you, Bill. Are you married?"

"Yes."

They talked of a family that Dylan invented while they drank their coffee and he was soon helping her into a taxi. Not that she needed much help because she was an expert with her wheelchair.

He was pleased to hear her ask the driver to take her to her home. He soon found another taxi and headed in the same direction. He was curious as to who she might be seeing later.

He let the taxi go and hung around outside her house watching lights go on and off in different rooms. Less than thirty minutes later, another taxi pulled up. A man climbed out, handed the driver a couple of notes, and trotted up the drive to Sarah's impressive home.

Dylan recognised him immediately. It was every crook's favourite lawyer, Phil Browne.

TWENTY-ONE

"GET ME ANOTHER BRANDY, will you, Phil? You'll have one with me, won't you?"

Sarah's first job on arriving home had been to pour herself a glass of brandy. She'd had quite a bit to drink at the restaurant, but she still felt in need of something to soothe her nerves.

"How's Lenny?" she asked. "Have you heard?"

"He's fine." Phil handed her a glass. "Never mind him, how did your chat with Bill Williams go?"

"I don't know." She wheeled her chair into the lounge and stopped it close to the radiator. The room felt chilly this evening. "He knew how much cash was found at Lenny's place, he knew John's car was involved in Lenny's accident and yet—one thing struck me as odd."

"Oh?"

"He didn't know about this." She slapped her wheelchair. "You'd think any writer worth his salt would have known, wouldn't you?"

"That's interesting."

"I told him about Wendy and those coppers being involved—" She took a sip of brandy and paused to enjoy the warmth running down her throat. "I don't think he was convinced. And he seemed too interested in John for my liking. I told him John had nothing to do with Lenny's shooting, but I don't think he believed me."

"Few people would." Phil sighed heavily and sat back on the sofa. "You need to have a good talk with John. I mean it, Sarah."

"I will. Truly, I will."

"You keep saying that and nothing happens."

"It's difficult. If I say anything to him, he thinks I'm criticising him. He's always been too sensitive, you know he has."

Phil rolled his eyes. "For Christ's sake, Sarah, this is serious. He's not twelve anymore. The way things are going, he'll be glad to get thrown in prison because it'll be the only way he'll have a roof over his head. Apart from everything else, he's got about as much business sense as a Labrador puppy—"

"Phil!"

"It's true, Sarah. Open your eyes. If it was his money, fine. It's not, though. He's taking you down with him. And you're sitting back and letting him."

Sarah had heard it all before. "I'll speak to him."

"Make sure you do."

Sarah had been friends with Phil for more years than she cared to remember, but she knew he'd never understood John. She doubted he ever would. John was a good boy, a good son, and if he did have problems, it was only because life had dealt him such a rough deal. He'd idolised his father, as had she, and he'd never recovered from seeing him gunned down in front of his own home. Nor had he recovered from the shock of seeing her with someone else. He'd hated Max from the moment he first saw him.

Phil stood and paced the width of the room. "So did this Williams bloke seem genuine to you?"

She was glad of the change of subject. "Of course he did."

"It just seems bloody odd to me. No sooner do you tell Max that Wendy and those arresting officers were responsible for setting him up than this writer appears out of the blue."

She smiled at that. "You've got such a suspicious mind, Phil."

"Too right, I have. And it's stood me in good stead all these years." He swallowed some brandy and returned to the sofa. "Max is being too bloody quiet for my liking too. And he swears he had nothing to do with Wendy's murder."

"Maybe he didn't."

"Get real, Sarah."

She'd hoped Phil would soothe her frayed nerves, but, as was so often the case, she was going to have to find words to calm him down.

"Maybe he didn't," she said again. "Max knows the end's in sight. Three months and he'll possibly be out. He's behaved himself while he's been inside and they always take pity on prisoners who are sick. If he'd wanted revenge on Wendy, which I'm sure he did, he'd have wanted to dish it out himself. It's the same with those coppers. When he gets out, they'll need to watch their backs."

"And what if, like Wendy, they're mysteriously killed *before* he gets out?"

"It's not Max's style. He hates people doing his dirty work for him."

"What a fucking mess!"

Sarah heard the distant echo of her grandmother's voice. "All men are trouble, Sarah, love. You mark my words." How Sarah had laughed. She'd been fifteen or sixteen years old at the time and boys had fascinated her. She'd liked them big and strong, brave and daring. Handsome too, of course. Trouble? Yes, they'd been trouble. Without exception, the men in her life had brought her nothing but problems.

Except John. When the midwife had put her beautiful boy in her arms for the first time, Sarah had thought it impossible to feel so much love. She would have died for that little scrap of humanity. Willingly. And nothing had changed.

Phil drained his glass. "I need to go. It's late and I still have a load of work to do. I'll call you tomorrow, okay?"

"Yes. And I will speak to John. Promise."

"Make sure you do." He dropped a kiss on her forehead, sighed heavily, and left.

The silence of the house settled around her. She hated it. As a child, she'd been used to a house full of noise and laughter. Laughter or fights. She still hated a quiet house.

She switched on some music and Janis Joplin's voice soothed her for a few moments. It didn't really help, though, so she turned the volume low, grabbed her phone and hit the button.

John answered almost immediately with a slurred "Hi, Mum."

"Hi, darling. Sorry it's so late, but I needed a chat. You okay?"

"Sure. You?"

"Better now." No matter what problems life decided

to throw at her, the sound of John's voice always made her feel better. She would always have John, no matter what. She'd make sure of that.

"Anything wrong?"

"No, nothing's wrong. I've had a busy evening. First, I had dinner with the writer, Bill Williams. That was okay, I suppose, but he seemed a little too interested in you for my liking. Well, interested in your car."

"I told you."

"I know, darling. I know. It's fine. Then Phil called round and—"

"Oh, here we go. Money, money, money."

"He's a bit worried about the business, darling, that's all. We need to sit down and talk about it, don't you think? We're losing too much. We can't afford it."

"I know what I'm doing. This is just short-term. I told you that. We'll soon be raking it in."

"I tried to explain that to him."

"I know he means well, and I know he's been a good friend to us, but his ideas are outdated. Look, I'm shattered. Why don't I call round in the morning? We'll have breakfast together, shall we? We can talk then."

Sarah felt all the tension leave her. "I can't think of anything I'd like more."

"I'll do that then. Love you, Mum."

"Love you too. And don't worry about Phil. Or Max or Lenny. Everything will be fine, darling. I'll make sure of it."

"I'm not worrying. And there's no need for you to make sure of anything. I told you, I'm sorting it. Leave it to me."

TWENTY-TWO

JIMMY DIDN'T TAKE risks so he was never sure what made him follow Lowell into the bar. It was crowded for a Thursday evening, and noisy, so it was unlikely anyone would notice him. He bought himself a drink and sat on a stool at the end of the bar.

There were two women at a table in the corner. At least, Jimmy believed they were women. Their hands were small and there was no sign of an Adam's apple on either of them, so he assumed they must be as they appeared. Other than that, the bar was packed with men aged anywhere between twenty and sixty.

Lowell was at the bar laughing with two men who were ten years younger than him. His companions were dressed casually, but Lowell didn't look out of place in his business suit.

Minutes passed and then Jimmy noticed that Lowell was no longer laughing. His two friends wore expressions that were a little menacing. The taller one was leaning in to Lowell's face as he spoke. Lowell was leaning back, trying to placate them.

Freddie Mercury's voice was belting out of the speakers so Jimmy had no idea what was being said. Hell, he couldn't even hear the conversation between the two men standing next to him.

He felt uncomfortable in gay bars and usually did

his best to avoid them, but Carol and her friends often had a night out in this area. She said women could enjoy themselves without men trying to chat them up. She claimed they could drink, dance and generally have a good time without feeling threatened. Loads of her friends were gay—well, they would be as most of them were in the hairdressing trade.

Lowell and his two chums walked away from the bar and out toward the back of the building. Jimmy had no idea what was there. Another bar maybe? The toilets?

He was finishing his drink, thinking maybe they'd left and that it was time he went home, when Lowell's two companions returned. There was no sign of Lowell.

The taller of the two was laughing and rubbing his knuckles. They bought more drinks. The shorter man had his hand round the other chap's waist, his hand wandering lower, as they chatted over their drinks.

Curious, Jimmy drank up and left the bar as if he were heading to the toilets. Another door was marked Fire Escape. He pushed it open and saw that it led into a narrow alley where crates of empty bottles were stacked.

At the end of the alley, struggling to his feet, was Lowell.

Jimmy hesitated. He didn't like taking risks and this wasn't part of the plan.

He chewed on his bottom lip. Plans were made to be changed. Think on your feet, that was what had been drummed into him.

He wandered over to Lowell. "You okay, mate?"

Lowell looked up, fear in his eyes and blood dripping from a nasty cut on his face. There was no hint of recognition. Jimmy hadn't expected any.

Lowell nodded and managed to get to his feet before slumping back against the wall.

"I've got a van outside," Jimmy said, proud of how he could think so quickly. "There's a first aid kit inside. We'll get you cleaned up, shall we? That's a nasty cut."

"Thank you." Lowell's voice was shaky. He looked as if he were about to burst into tears.

"Come on, put your arm around my shoulders. It's only round the corner." He nodded back at the bar. "It would be quicker that way, but I'm guessing you don't want to meet up with those two again."

"Thanks. They thought—I wasn't—" He tried to walk, but couldn't put any weight on his left leg. "My ankle. I think it might be broken."

Of course it wasn't broken, for Christ's sake.

"Lean on me," Jimmy said. "We'll get you to the van, clean you up and give you a minute to get your breath."

It took ten minutes to get Lowell to the van. Ten bloody minutes to walk a couple of hundred yards.

Thankfully, there were few people around and those rushing along the street where Jimmy's van was parked kept their faces averted. They probably assumed Jimmy was escorting a drunk to safety. They didn't want to get involved and that suited Jimmy just fine.

Jimmy unlocked the van and opened the back doors. "Get in here." He gave Lowell a gentle shove. "No one will see you. We can get that blood off your face and get you a taxi home. Or to the hospital to get that ankle checked out."

Unlike Jimmy, Lowell wasn't thinking on his feet.

He wasn't thinking at all as far as Jimmy could tell. He lunged himself into the back of the van and half sat, half lay against the side of the vehicle.

"Here's the first aid kit. See?" Jimmy unhooked the red metal box. It was empty, but he smashed it against the side of Lowell's head. Again. And again.

Lowell was out cold. Jimmy tied his wrists behind his back, tied his ankles and covered his mouth with tape. He couldn't take any chances so he wrapped him in an oily blanket that had been lying in the back of the van when Jimmy bought it, and tied that around him.

Deciding Lowell was as safe as was possible, Jimmy climbed out of the back of the van and into the driver's seat. Going home was an inconvenience but it had to be done. He had no gear with him and he needed to make his excuses to Carol.

Traffic was stop-start because of endless roadworks and when he eventually got home, he couldn't get on his driveway. "Shit."

His father's car was parked right in front of the house, leaving no room for Jimmy's van.

He'd bet his father had turned up out of the blue. It wouldn't have crossed his mind to check that a visit would be convenient. He'd know better. He'd know that Jimmy would never find a visit from his father welcome.

Still cursing, he parked the van on the road and strode into the house.

His father was sitting with his feet under the kitchen table as if he'd moved in. "Jimmy."

Jimmy nodded, but didn't bother speaking.

Carol was leaning back against the dishwasher, a cup of tea in her hand.

"Something's come up," he told her. "I'll be away for the night. The training—Ed's sick so they've asked me to stand in. I couldn't really say no, could I?"

"Again?" Carol let out her breath on a long-suffering sigh. "The kids have got sleepovers and I wanted us to go out."

"Tomorrow night," he said. "I'll be back as soon as I can tomorrow. It looks like you've got company anyway."

She flashed Jimmy a warning look before turning a sweet smile on his father. "What about it, Dad? Do you fancy a couple of beers down the local? I could do with getting out for an hour."

"I'd be delighted, love."

"There you are then," Jimmy said, struggling to keep the temper from his voice. "You've got an old man for company. He'll be able to tell you tales of life on the beat."

"Less of the *old*," his father tried to joke, but Jimmy ignored him.

"I'll throw a change of clothes in a bag." He raced up the stairs and grabbed a few essentials.

When he returned to the kitchen, it was obvious from the way the conversation suddenly stopped that they'd been talking about him.

"What's with the van?" his father asked. "That's a waste of money, isn't it?"

Whose fucking money was it to waste?

"I need it for the training. There's a lot of gear to carry."

"I'll come out and have a look at it. I bet I could have got you a better deal from my mate."

"I got a good deal." No way was his father seeing

the van, not while Lowell was lying in the back. "I need to go."

"No proper job yet then?" his father asked.

"Too busy with other things at the moment." Jimmy felt his jaw tighten. "There's plenty of time."

"If you want to be kept by your wife, then yes, there's plenty of time. Most men wouldn't be happy with that, though. They'd feel embarrassed."

Jimmy glared at Carol, and she flashed him another look that warned him not to pick a fight.

"I'm going." He didn't even bother to give Carol the usual goodbye kiss. He just went, slamming the door after him.

Once in the van, he felt the tension leave him. He liked to be alone these days. People couldn't nag him and he could think clearly. Yes, he was much happier with his own company. The best thing to do was forget that his father existed.

He drove to the terraced house and put the van in the garage. Darkness was falling, but he sat in the van for another hour, waiting until it was completely dark, before he hauled a now conscious Lowell from the van and into the house.

Judging by the way it dragged along the ground, Lowell's ankle might be broken. Jimmy didn't care one way or the other.

He was heavier than he looked, though, and sweat was pouring off Jimmy when he finally got him into the cellar and shoved him into the chair that Brian Dowie no longer needed.

He missed Dowie. Still, the fish off Beachy Head had hopefully enjoyed a tasty meal.

Jimmy went through the same routine with Lowell

as he had with Dowie. He made sure he was tightly bound and gagged, then fixed the noose around his neck.

"Push the chair forward or backward and you're a dead man," Jimmy told him. "Got that? We don't want any accidents, do we?"

Jimmy, happy that his captive was safe, went upstairs to the kitchen and made himself a coffee. He had to drink it black because he hadn't got any milk in. That was the trouble with thinking on your feet. Although you got the important things right, it was all too easy to forget the small stuff. It didn't matter, though. Black coffee was okay.

Everything was fine. He'd been thrown off-kilter having Lowell handed to him like that, and he was always rattled at the sight of his father. But he'd sorted it. All it meant was that Lowell was in the cellar a few days earlier than anticipated. That was no big deal. It simply gave Jimmy more time to enjoy him.

He went down the steps into the cellar. He'd scrubbed the place with gallons of bleach, but it still stank. It was a sickening mix of Dowie's excrement and fear. He was glad he didn't have to spend too long down here.

He pulled up a chair and sat opposite Lowell. The bloke looked more angry than scared. His eyes bulged from their sockets.

"Oh, don't worry," Jimmy said. "I'm not another gay basher. Mind you, those blokes who did you over didn't look as if they were either. What was all that about? Did they accuse you of teasing them? Did they resent the fact that you only went in that bar to see what was going on before you went home to your wife?"

Lowell groaned and spluttered behind his gag. At one point, Jimmy thought the bloke was choking.

"You don't recognise me, do you? No one does." Jimmy drew an invisible pattern on the stone floor with the toe of his boot. "I'll tell you my name, Gerry. Still Gerry, is it? Or, now that you think you've made it, do you prefer to be called Gerald? Gerry's an all right sort of name, isn't it? It's not a gay name. Anyway, as I said, I'll tell you my name. Perhaps with a hint or two you'll remember me, eh?"

Jimmy suddenly became aware of the old dog barking next door. He'd never heard him bark before but the dog sounded as if he were taking on half a dozen intruders.

Jimmy left Lowell and went upstairs to investigate. He stood in the lounge with the lights off and soon saw the cause of the disturbance. Three young lads, about sixteen years old, were kicking a couple of empty tin cans along the pavement.

They soon moved on and the dog was quiet again. Jimmy was surprised that the old animal had heard them or cared about them.

Jimmy returned to the cellar and resumed his seat in front of Lowell.

"Are you sitting comfortably, Gerry?" Jimmy chuckled. He took the small knife from his pocket and ran the blade along his finger. He'd been meaning to sharpen it for ages but that was something else he hadn't had time for. It was too blunt to cut butter but he'd have to persevere with it. It was either that or go back upstairs to the kitchen and he couldn't be bothered.

He knelt in front of Lowell and cut the shirt and

jacket from Lowell's arm. Hacked was a better description as the blunt knife was as good as useless.

He flung the material to the floor, eyed up Lowell's tanned arm—courtesy of a recent holiday in Greece—and mentally planned his design.

"Tell you what, we'll have some fun with this," Jimmy said. "I'll spell out my name but it'll be a bit like Hangman." He spluttered with laughter. "Hangman. That's good, isn't it? There's you with a noose round your neck and we're about to play Hangman."

Jimmy's burst of laughter lasted a full two minutes, until he had to wipe the tears from his eyes. Lowell didn't get the joke.

"Didn't you ever play that game?" Jimmy asked. "You get a number of blanks—imagine you got five dashes followed by five dashes and had to guess the missing letter. Okay? Say your first guess was S. Now, if the other person filled in the first letter of the first five dashes and then the third and fifth letters of the second five dashes, you might take a guess at Stone Roses. You got that? Hey, I'm sure you've played the game before. The thing is, with my game, it'll be a little different. I'll give you a letter, right? Then you have to guess at my name. I'll give you the letters randomly, though. So, you tell me when you're ready to take a guess and, when you've got it right, I'll stop giving you the letters."

He ran the blade of the knife along his thumb. "The blade's not very sharp. Sorry about that."

He put the knife to Lowell's arm and cut at the skin. Lowell protested behind his gag as the blood oozed.

"Look, I've apologised about the knife, okay? It's not my bloody fault I ended up with you earlier than

I thought. Christ, look what you've made me do. That looks a mess."

Jimmy carved some more, wiped the blood away, and carved some more.

"I know, I know, it looks like a wonky *O*. Well, it's not. It's a *D*, okay. That's your first letter. *D*. You have a think, Gerry. Meanwhile, I need to get out of here for a bit. This cellar stinks."

Jimmy needed fresh air. And food to settle his stomach. He'd walk along to the fish-and-chip shop and see if they had any chicken. He really fancied chicken and chips.

TWENTY-THREE

DYLAN WAS HAVING BREAKFAST—a strong black coffee—when Bev came downstairs. She was wearing her dressing gown and a tired expression.

"You okay?" he asked.

"Fine. Just tired. Shattered in fact."

"Didn't you sleep?"

"Like the dead, but I'm still tired."

"Do you want a coffee?" he asked. She looked as if she hadn't slept for a week. There was no colour in her face apart from a dull grey. "Or shall I make you a cup of tea?"

"I don't know what I want."

"Go back to bed," he said, "and I'll bring you a coffee up."

"No, I'll drink it down here."

He poured her coffee and put it in front of her. She looked ill—she *was* ill.

"What are your plans for the day?" she asked.

"Oh, this and that. There's plenty to keep me busy." His reply was deliberately vague because the truth was that he didn't have a plan. A chat with Goodenough would be good if, and it was a bloody big *if*, he could find the bloke.

The man he *should* be watching was Rickman. Yet Rickman was safe enough behind bars and it was impossible to know who he was speaking to on the outside. Visitors to Rickman were rare, his wife was the main one, but who knew what phone calls he made?

Issuing orders to have someone killed would be easy enough for a man like Rickman.

And yet—Dylan was certain that, for Rickman, this would be personal. He'd want to do the deed himself. He'd want to unleash his fury on the people who'd conned him in person. Besides, if he wanted someone killed, he'd have them killed. What would be the point of the scare tactics? Why bother making phone calls and having photos taken? It simply didn't add up.

What a bloody mess. Rickman, King and Goodenough all had reason to want him to suffer. Of the three, however, only one, to his knowledge, had been spotted outside his office. Goodenough.

Goodenough had to be responsible for the stupid phone calls, but Dylan couldn't picture him as a killer...

"What about you?" he asked.

She gave him a wan smile. "I'll probably sleep all day. Mind you, if I do that, I'll be awake all night."

Dylan wouldn't bet on that. She looked as if she needed to sleep for days.

"I expect it's the stress of all this hospital stuff," he said. "No one sleeps properly when they're stressed."

"Could be." She didn't sound convinced. "Anyway, I can go back to bed anytime. Your mum's coming over this morning."

"Good."

She walked to the window and gazed out. "It's going to be another nice day. I might sit in the garden and read a book." She drank half an inch of coffee and then groaned. "It's no use, love, I'm going back to bed. I'll see you tonight." She leaned across and dropped a kiss on the top of his head. "And I promise I'll be awake by then."

Dylan sorted the kids out—not that Luke needed any sorting out other than a few prods and reminders that time was passing quickly. Freya too, was in a particularly sunny mood and needed little other than a few smiles.

Frank came down for breakfast, looking his usual wide-awake self, then Dylan's mother arrived and Dylan decided he might as well leave them to it.

As he had no better plan in mind, no plan at all in fact, he drove to Goodenough's flat. The upside was that he didn't have to wear a disguise when hunting Goodenough. His wig was a good one, but he still didn't trust it to stay put in the gentlest of breezes and God knows what a heavy downpour would do to it.

He rang the bell with C. Marshall written beside it and received no answer. He rang a random bell, and an elderly woman answered the intercom.

"Hello," Dylan said, "I'm trying to get hold of Chesney Marshall. You wouldn't happen to know if he's around, would you?"

"I saw him come in about ten minutes ago," she said. "You'll have to try his bell again. Mind you, if he's in the shower, he won't hear you. I know I don't. The bells aren't very loud at the best of times. Sometimes, I don't even hear mine over the radio. I keep saying they should do something about it."

"Okay, thanks. Sorry to have troubled you."

Dylan tried Goodenough's—or Marshall's—bell again. Still no response.

He decided to sit in his car for a while and then try again. Perhaps, after all, Goodenough was taking a shower. Or perhaps he was ignoring all strangers at the door in case they turned out to be debt collectors or worse.

Less than two minutes later, Goodenough emerged from the building. He wouldn't have had time to leave the shower and dress so that particular explanation was out.

He jumped in a car, about twenty grand's worth of sleek, dark grey Alfa Romeo, and drove off.

Dylan followed. He couldn't afford to keep hiring cars, but definitely needed another. He supposed he could use Bev's Vauxhall while she wasn't using it, but he liked his own car. The speedometer had stopped working long ago and, as yet, he hadn't got around to having it fixed so he didn't know when he was breaking speed limit (frequently) or how many miles his beloved car had done (one hell of a lot).

Thankfully, traffic rarely moved quickly in London and he was able to keep a safe distance behind Goodenough's car while still keeping him in sight.

Twenty minutes later, Goodenough drove into a multi-storey car park and Dylan followed. Dylan parked at the far end, got out of his car, and followed Goodenough down the steps to street level.

As they walked, Dylan realised they were heading in the direction of Pelham's daughter's shop—or boutique as she liked to call it. She was rarely there as she liked to concentrate on her designs and the business side of things and leave staff to concentrate on selling her outrageously priced fashions.

They walked on until, sure enough, Goodenough ducked inside her boutique.

Dylan stayed back, pretending to be engrossed in the expensive houses offered for sale by a nearby estate agent.

At least it explained why Goodenough hadn't contacted Dylan about the money he supposedly wanted to give the bloke. If he was still in touch with Cass Pelham, he'd know damn well there was no money.

Minutes dragged by until Dylan began to wonder if he'd missed Goodenough. He'd expected the bloke to walk in, ask if Cass was around, be told she wasn't and go on his way. Perhaps he'd used the back entrance.

Twenty-five minutes later, Goodenough emerged. He was straightening his tie which struck Dylan as odd. Well, unless he'd had hot sex with whoever was manning the shop.

Dylan was torn between following Goodenough and venturing into the shop. He watched Goodenough head back in the direction of the car park and he opted for the shop.

It was a double-fronted property with silver lettering spelling out Cass Pelham's name. In one window was a dress—no price shown because if you had to ask you couldn't afford it—a handbag and a matching pair of shoes. In the other window was a tasteful display of more handbags and silk scarves.

He pushed open the door and stepped inside the plush interior. On the rare occasions he'd had the misfortune to shop with Bev, he'd seen her fight her way through rail after rail of clothes. Here, there were only a few items on display. There wasn't a price tag in sight either. There was certainly nothing so tacky as a Sale sign.

A young slim woman stepped through a door wearing a bright smile.

"Hello. May I help you?" she asked.

It was Cass Pelham. Her father had said she was heartbroken, but she didn't look it. She looked disgustingly fit, well and happy. Her smile was genuine, her eyes bright and full of life.

"I don't know. My wedding anniversary is coming up and I wanted to buy my wife something—different." Dylan had a mental picture of bills piling up and money flying out. "It's no use me choosing her a dress or anything like that as I'd be sure to get it wrong, but I thought perhaps a scarf or a bag or something."

"What a lovely idea. Would you like to look around?"

"Thank you." There was hardly anything to look at. "I don't suppose you could help me choose."

She smiled. "I'd be delighted. What can you tell me about her age, her skin and hair colour, the colours she likes to wear—"

All he wanted was a confounded scarf. And he didn't really want that. "She's forty, blond, fair-skinned and she wears—well, a lot of blue. And black." He'd never really thought about it before.

"Right." She began running her hands through a rail of silk scarves.

"Are you married?" he asked.

"Not yet." She gave him a bright smile. "Soon."

"Ah, congratulations. A pretty girl like you—what's taking him so long?"

She chuckled at that. "It's not him. Brad would

happily whisk me off to the registry office at lunch-time but, well there are other things to consider, aren't there?"

"Without exception," he agreed. "I can't begin to tell you the problems my wife and I had when we announced our engagement. We've been married for ten years now, but wow, we ruffled some feathers. Her father wasn't keen on me and—"

"Really?" Her interest was piqued. "We have a similar problem. I keep thinking we should marry and let other people live their own lives, but Brad thinks we should wait until—" She let the sentence hang in mid-air but Dylan could guess only too well that Good-enough wanted to wait until Pelham died, until his will was read and he had confirmation that Cass Pelham was indeed worth a small fortune.

"My wife and I didn't have the patience to wait." Dylan smiled at her.

"And did her father come round to the idea of your marriage?" she asked.

"He died, I'm afraid. Oh, it wasn't the shock of his daughter marrying me," he added. "He'd been ill for some time."

"I see." Her hand stilled on the scarves as she mulled this over. "Our case really is very similar, you know. Brad has always felt—well, a little inferior. I come from a wealthy background and Brad thought that, to get me to see him, he had to pretend to be living a very different life. Silly really. I'd marry him tomorrow if all he possessed was the clothes he stood in."

"He lied to you?" Dylan tried to sound outraged.

She gave a tiny shrug. "He led me, and my father

of course, to believe that he owned property—well, it wasn't really a lie, was it?"

Um, yes.

"All he wanted," she said, "was for me and my father to think well of him. I keep telling him that it's the person that counts, not the possessions, but it's hard for him. He had a difficult start in life. You see, his mother died when he was young and his father was a strict disciplinarian. He believed Brad should join the army and, although Brad did, and was good at his work, it was never what he wanted. He's not an army sort of man, if you know what I mean. But he's done with all that now. As for the rest, the pretending, we've sorted it out."

Dylan's heart wasn't exactly bleeding for Goodenough. Thousands of kids had difficult childhoods. Thousands of boys ended up in the army because either their parents thought it was a good idea, or they wanted to get away, or they simply thought it would be fun to see the world. They soon realised there wasn't much fun to be had in places like Afghanistan and got out of the army as quickly as possible while still blaming their parents, their teachers or the world in general.

"I'm glad to hear it. And is your father happy with the arrangement?"

Her silence said everything.

"You haven't told him, have you?" Dylan said. "Well, I can't say I blame you. Believe me, I know how difficult these things can be."

"It's not that," she said, and her eyes seemed unable to drag themselves away from the sight of her shoes. "He—he had a stroke on Monday night."

"I'm sorry to hear that."

"He'll recover." She tried to smile. "He's a fighter. And I have Brad. We'd split up but, on hearing about my father, he came to see me. We're together, we're happy, we have each other."

"That's it exactly. Look at me, happily married for ten years now and I wouldn't change a thing."

Her expression cleared. "I'm happy for you. Really happy. In fact—" She selected a pale pink scarf and handed it to him. "Take this for your wife."

Dylan looked it over. It was as nice as all the others and, given that it had the Pelham name on it, Bev would love it. He only hoped his credit card could take the strain.

"Thank you. How much—?" He reached for his wallet.

"Take it." She waved his hand away. "Really. You've made me feel so much better. When Brad and I have been married for ten years, I'll think of you and your wife. I hope you'll have many more happy years together."

"Oh, I couldn't possibly—"

"Of course you could. I hope your wife approves of my choice."

"I'm sure she will. Thank you. Thank you very much."

"It's been my pleasure."

The scarf was wrapped in pink tissue paper and put into a small bag that bore the distinctive Cass Pelham logo.

Dylan left the shop feeling all kinds of a deceitful prick.

Not as deceitful as Goodenough, though. That bastard had lied his way out of a difficult situation and into a very lucrative one. He was a chancer. He'd heard that Pelham's demise might be a little more imminent than he'd thought and had worked on the daughter. Easy when you had charm by the bucketload.

Dylan still felt awful, though. He'd left a vulnerable young woman back in that shop. He could so easily have told her that he was the man who'd uncovered Goodenough and shown him for the lying piece of shit he really was. He could have told her that there were plenty of honest, decent men out there but that Goodenough wasn't one of them. But she wouldn't have believed him. Love—or lust—had a lot to answer for.

So would Goodenough, with his life back on track and expecting to fall into a very comfortable lifestyle in the near future, waste time sending death threats? On the other hand, Dylan hadn't received either a phone call or a photo for a few days.

Coincidence?

Heading back to his car, he decided to stop for a strong coffee. There was also the matter of food, as his stomach persistently reminded him, but nowhere around here offered a good fry-up.

He ducked into a trendy coffee bar and ordered a coffee. He gave the food a cursory glance but it was too small, too trendy and, mostly, too sweet. There wasn't so much as a bacon butty in sight.

A quick glance through the free newspaper provided little of interest. The world was in its usual mess. No change there. He was informed that his carbon footprint should be uppermost in his mind. Yeah, right. With China opening a factory on an almost hourly basis, his recycling the odd whisky bottle or walking half a mile now and again instead of taking the car would make not a jot of difference.

He leaned back in his chair and took his phone from his pocket, intending to scroll through his contacts and see if inspiration came. What he saw was five missed calls. Sod it. He'd switched his phone to silent overnight and forgotten to switch it back on.

The first call was from Archie. "Usual place. Seven o'clock."

Interesting. Perhaps Archie would provide some information and much needed inspiration.

The second call was from Frank. "Give me a call when you pick this up, mate."

The third was from Frank, but no message had been left.

The fourth and fifth messages were also from Frank. On the last call, he'd left a message. "Nothing to worry about, Dylan, but Bev's been taken to hospital. Your mother's gone with her, as has Freya. Luke's in school so he doesn't know. Not that there's much to know. Nothing to worry about. It's a precaution, that's all. Give me a call, eh? Or get yourself to the hospital and find out what's happening for yourself."

Dylan got to his feet, dropped some money on the table, and was heading out of the door when one of the waitresses grabbed his arm. He was about to point out that he'd paid the bill—

"You forgot this, sir." She held out the bag and whistled as she spotted the Cass Pelham logo. "Very nice."

"Thanks." He grabbed it and ran.

TWENTY-FOUR

CASS PULLED ON a pair of jeans and a pink cashmere sweater. The day had been long and frustrating, and she wished she could curl up in front of the TV and do nothing.

Brad pushed her hair back from her face. "Your father would understand if you gave the hospital a miss this evening, sweetheart."

"I know he would, but I'd never forgive myself. And it's not a hardship, is it?"

"It is when you've had a difficult day. But I know you. Nothing I say will keep you away from his bedside. However—" he tried to sound stern "—you're not leaving here without some food inside you." He took her hand and pulled her to the kitchen. With his free hand, he dragged out a stool. "Sit."

She laughed. "I don't have time, Brad."

"No arguing. I'll make you one of my famous cheese-and-tomato sandwiches."

Cass watched him carefully grate cheese and slice a tomato. She loved having him in her kitchen, loved the way he made her feel so precious.

"Enjoy." He put her sandwich in front of her, gave her a long sweeping bow and withdrew.

"Thank you. Seriously, Brad, thanks for being here. It means a lot to me."

"Eat."

"When Dad's better…" she began, but he waved her words aside.

"As soon as you've eaten, I'll drive you to the hospital. Would you like me to wait for you?"

"No. You go home. I'll get a cab back. I'll call you when I get in, shall I?"

"Are you sure you don't want me to wait? I don't mind." He tapped his fingers on the counter. "It's so difficult while we live so far apart. If we lived together—"

"Brad, I—"

"I know, I know." He put a finger to her cheek. "I know, sweetheart, and I don't blame you. After all the stupid things I've done, I really don't blame you for not trusting me."

"Brad, no! You know it's not that. Of course I trust you. We've been over and over this." She was appalled that he could think such a thing.

"Yes, we have. Sorry. It's just that I don't feel very trustworthy."

"It's Dad," she said, knowing he couldn't understand. "Until he's better, I don't want him getting in a state about us. I hate lying to him and, by not telling him that we're back together, I feel I am lying. But you know I trust you, darling. I'd trust you with my life."

He tried to joke. "But not with your bank account."

It wasn't even close to funny and she couldn't raise a smile.

"Hey, I'm being an idiot," he said. "Sorry."

"Let's just leave things as they are for a while."

"Of course." He took her hand and stroked it. "It's my own stupid fault for telling all those lies. At first,

I thought I had to impress you. You were—*are* the most beautiful woman I've ever seen. Even now I have to pinch myself to make sure I'm not dreaming. If I hadn't pretended to be someone I'm not, maybe your father would have been okay with me. Who knows?" He sighed. "Anyway, there's no point going over old ground, is there?"

"There isn't," she said, "and it really doesn't matter. I trust you with everything I have, Brad. Truly. And Dad will too. As soon as he gets to know you better."

"I hope so. I just wish I could make your life a little easier right now. It's so difficult when we live at opposite ends of the City."

"You do make my life easier." Smiling, she pushed her empty plate away. "That was the best sandwich I've ever had."

What Cass wouldn't do was upset her father while he was so ill. She felt bad enough because he didn't know she was seeing Brad again. He'd worry himself sick if he knew Brad was at her house.

On the other hand, she was a grown woman and she wanted Brad. She'd like nothing more than to come home to him this evening, spend the night in his arms, make love and wake with him in the morning.

She loved him and she wanted to marry him. She *would* marry him. Just as soon as her father could be persuaded to accept him.

"Come on, sweetheart. Let's get you wrapped up. It's chilly outside." Brad held her coat out so that she could slip her arms into the sleeves.

They stepped out into the cold night air, and Brad held her close to him as they dashed the few yards to his car. He held open the door for her and, once she was seated, closed the door and ran round to the driver's side.

"It'll soon warm up," he promised as he fired the engine.

She didn't care about the cold. She hardly noticed it, in fact. Her mind was too full of Brad and the way she loved everything about him.

"I'm seeing my lawyer tomorrow," he said.

"Why? About what?"

"I want something in writing, something that says I can't get and won't accept a penny of your money."

"Brad, don't be silly. There's no need for that."

"There is. For my own peace of mind."

"There's no need."

"I won't hear another word about it," he said. "My mind's made up."

He stopped the car at the lights and Cass watched a young couple cross the road in front of them. They were arm in arm, wrapped up against the cold, and laughing into each other's faces. They looked as if they didn't have a care in the world. How Cass envied them.

Brad was soon stopping the car outside the hospital's main entrance. "Are you sure you don't want me to wait here for you?"

"Quite sure." Cass opened her handbag, took out her keys and handed them to him. "Stay at my place tonight, Brad."

Her father wouldn't know and she needed him. That was all there was to it.

"Are you sure?" he asked.

"I'm sure."

She leaned across to kiss him, then left the warmth of his car.

The stuffy atmosphere of the hospital soon filled her nostrils and she took the lift to the third floor and her father's room.

She didn't want to upset him, so she wouldn't mention Brad to him until he was strong enough to deal with it, but when that day came, she'd stand firm. She loved Brad and she was going to marry him. It was high time her father stopped treating her like a child.

She wanted a husband and children. Grandchildren too, one day. That was her choice, not her father's.

TWENTY-FIVE

ARCHIE WAS LATE. Dylan couldn't remember that happening before. It wasn't that Archie had a thing about punctuality, it was just that he was always sitting at the same table in the pub. Dylan imagined him being sold along with the fixtures and fittings when the pub changed hands.

Dylan bought himself a much-needed pint and sat at what he thought of as Archie's table to wait.

Trade was slow for a Friday night. A pub fifty yards down the road was offering karaoke plus a free supper so perhaps everyone was there.

The pub cat, an enormous black creature, stalked round the room, tail held high as it tried to find strangers to terrorise. The regulars knew better than to reach out and stroke it. The owners had named it Sam, but customers knew it as Slasher.

Dylan's beer barely touched the sides of his throat as it went down and he returned to the bar for a refill. His heart was still racing.

Once back at the table, he had to take a few steadying breaths. He'd be glad when Archie arrived to take his mind off everything.

When he'd arrived at the hospital, Bev had been sitting up in bed, reading a magazine, and looking slightly better than she had this morning, although the

dazzling white pillows and sheets could have been responsible for creating an illusion of her having more
colour in her face. They were keeping her in overnight
for observation and a scan was lined up for the morning. She seemed calm—calmer than Dylan at least—
and was more concerned about the kids than anything
else. Not for the first time, Dylan thanked God that his
mother had decided to up sticks and move to London
to be nearer to them. Dylan was a lot of things but do-
mesticated wasn't one of them. He'd have to try a bit
harder in the future because he didn't want Bev worrying about the kids on top of everything else.

"Ah, Mr. Scott. Sorry to keep you waiting." Archie
slid into his seat and looked expectantly at Dylan.

"I wondered what had happened to you, Archie. I
thought you lived in that seat."

"Now that would be a nice thought. No, I've had a
few errands to run." He cleared his throat. "It's thirsty
work."

Dylan took the hint. "What are you having?"

"That's very generous of you. I'll have a double
whisky if it's no trouble. And a pint of whatever you're
drinking. It'll save you going up to the bar again."

"You're all heart, Archie."

Dylan still had half a pint left but he bought himself another. As Archie said, it would save him disturbing the barmaid again. He could leave her in peace to
watch TV.

He'd left his car at home and would catch the Tube
back. Or take a taxi. Either way, he could have a drink
or three without worrying about driving. Visiting times
were over at the hospital, Luke and Freya were in the

capable hands of his dope-smoking mother—everything was fine.

"You're a true gent," Archie said when Dylan put his drinks in front of him.

Dylan sat opposite. "So what do you know, Archie? Anything interesting?"

"Just something that struck me as odd." He took a long drink of whisky. "It's about John Weller and his being after Lenny King."

"And?"

"Well, it's a funny lot of it. Rumour has it that Weller promised King money. Seems he wanted to pay him for something."

"Yeah. I'd figured that."

"Oh." Archie looked disappointed.

It was obvious that King had been lured to that factory car park with the promise of cash. Or drugs. His attackers had even allowed him to take the holdall before the bullet hit.

"But pay him for what?" Dylan asked. "Why would Weller be paying King?"

"I don't know, but there's another thing. I heard that Sarah Rickman was broke. Now, as she owns half of that flashy gym, it suggests to me that Weller can't afford to pay anyone."

Dylan had heard similar noises. It seemed that staff at the gym hadn't been paid last month.

"I saw Sarah Rickman," he said. "I didn't know she was in a wheelchair."

Archie looked at him as if he were crazy. "Why else do you think she missed Rickman's trial? She was in hospital at the time. The accident, if you want to call it that, only happened about a month before Rickman and King were arrested."

Dylan hadn't given her absence at the trial any thought. He'd been too concerned about seeing her husband sent down for a good stretch. He couldn't remember reading newspaper reports about her accident either.

"She was hit by a car, I gather," he said.

Archie pulled a face at that. "She was. And not by any old car."

"How do you mean?"

"Well, now, I don't know this for sure. It could be nothing more than idle gossip, and normally, I wouldn't take any notice of it, but—well, there was a rumour going around that it was Rickman's car."

"Rickman's?"

"Yes. As I say, that could be nothing more than a bit of juicy gossip."

"What? An accident?"

Archie shrugged. "I can't answer that either. The story going around was that she'd had enough of Rickman and was leaving him. He took exception to the idea and—well, either he misjudged things or—or he deliberately ran her down. I don't suppose anyone will ever know the truth. Mind you, I can believe it. Rickman's always been an evil bugger when he gets the drink inside him. Bad enough sober."

"What makes people think she was planning to leave him? I thought they were devoted to each other."

"So she'd have people think. But then, if someone put me in a wheelchair, I wouldn't have a bad word to say about them in case they came back to do a proper job."

Dylan didn't think Sarah Rickman was the type of woman to be cowed by her husband. He'd thought she had more sense. On the other hand, most people found it safer to keep on the right side of Rickman.

"What about Phil Browne?" Dylan asked. "You said she'd been seen in his company, right?" Dylan had seen that for himself.

"So they say."

"What's all that about then?"

"From what I've heard, they've been friends for years. If I'm remembering right, they were neighbours and went to the same school. I mean, we're talking years here. Now, whether they're just friends or whether—well, you know. Although, with her in a wheelchair—" Archie took a thoughtful sip of beer. "I'm not sure what sort of works and what doesn't, if you get my drift."

"I get your drift, Archie." Given the way she'd been fluttering her eyelashes at him, Dylan would guess that everything "worked" fine.

"Perhaps he just keeps her company now and again," Archie said. "I don't suppose she saw much of him when Rickman was around because he's one jealous bloke. As they're friends, he probably wants to make sure she's doing okay while Rickman's inside."

"That's a cosy picture you're painting there," Dylan said. "Browne's more crooked than a spiral staircase."

"That's as maybe but I wouldn't mind swapping bank accounts."

Dylan wouldn't either. "Have you got one, Archie? A bank account?"

Archie grinned and winked. "No way. I don't trust them buggers. No, I can take care of my own money, thank you very much. I've no need of banks. Not that I have much to worry about. Still, as long as I can eat, drink and sleep under a roof of sorts, I'm content."

And rob the odd electronics store. Archie had a dark fascination with TVs, DVD players and anything else he could offload quickly.

He thought about what Archie had told him. It wasn't much, and certainly not worth the cash he'd have to hand over to keep him sweet.

"So basically, Weller tried to kill King after having offered him cash for something?"

"My gut says he's up to something and I always listen to my gut. It tells me when I'm hungry, when I'm thirsty—"

"Same again?" Dylan asked, already on his feet.

"Like I say, you're a real gent, Mr. Scott. They don't make them like you anymore, that's a fact..."

TWENTY-SIX

PHIL WAS IN the outer office, signing a couple of letters his secretary had printed out, when Dylan Scott walked in. For a moment, all Phil could do was stare at him. What in hell's name was he doing here?

"Long time no see, Mr. Scott," he said at last. "Did you want to see me?"

"Just a quick chat, Phil."

"You'd better come inside. I can spare you a couple of minutes."

Phil's office was considered old-fashioned by some, but it offered an impression he liked. A mahogany desk almost sank beneath the weight of dusty tomes. Yet more books lined one wall from floor to ceiling. The carpet was quality, but well-worn. Everything about the office shouted old school, respectable and trustworthy.

"How are you doing, Phil?" Scott asked. "Still keeping the guilty on the streets?"

Phil smiled at that. Insults had never bothered him. "Have a seat."

Scott sat in an old, worn leather captain's chair. The mahogany desk separated them.

"How's civilian life treating you?" Phil asked. "You're a private investigator these days, I believe."

"I am."

"It was a shame—what happened to you, I mean.

It always worries me when good police officers are brought to their knees by criminals. If you'd come to me—"

"Even you couldn't have got me off that charge, Phil."

"You'd be surprised."

"The powers that be needed to show Joe Public that complaints about their officers, no matter how bloody farfetched those complaints might be, are taken very seriously indeed. Even you can't compete with police politics."

Phil merely shrugged, but he would have liked to have taken on the system. He could have won Scott's case, he was sure of it. He knew a few in high places who weren't averse to the odd handout. Everyone had their price.

That was history, though. Scott had been thrown in a cell and served his time. Phil was more concerned about the present, and, more specifically, what the hell Scott was doing in his office. "So what can I do for you, Mr. Scott?"

"A writer wants to talk to me," Scott said. "A chap by the name of Bill Williams. I wondered what you'd heard about him."

Williams was a damn nuisance. They could do without him—and Scott for that matter—sniffing around. "Me? Why would I know anything about him?"

"Because he's spoken to your clients and friends. I gather he's interested in Rickman's and King's arrests all those years back. A little bird told me that he'd had a chat with Rickman's wife too. You're friendly with her, aren't you?"

Phil took his time answering. "I've heard he's asking questions, yes. So what? It's no big deal. Let him write his book."

"He seems to be under the impression that the officers who arrested King and Rickman that night were somehow involved."

Phil smiled at that. "Were you?"

"You know damn well we weren't."

"I wasn't there, Mr. Scott. All I know is what my client told me, and he claims he was set up by someone. Maybe it was you."

"Cut the crap, Phil. No coppers were involved and you know it. Now, tell me, why is this being stirred up now? Why is Williams on the scene now? Why has a story suddenly emerged about coppers being involved? Why now?"

"I've no idea." That was partly true. He had no idea why Williams was hunting down a story for his book.

"What about your client's wife? You're friendly with Mrs. Rickman, aren't you?"

"We go back a long way, yes. I knew Sarah long before Rickman married her."

"You were her first husband's lawyer, yes?"

"I was. God rest his soul."

"And I bet you're her son's lawyer too."

"I am." Weller, the stupid, spoiled little brat, was causing him headaches on a daily basis.

Scott leaned back in his chair, hands linked behind his head. "When people start asking questions about me, Phil, I start asking a few questions of my own. And what do I come up with?"

"You tell me."

"I hear rumours about your client, John Weller,

being after King. I hear he promises King money. I hear he shoots—"

"Oh, come on." There were many times when Phil wished Weller had never been born. Covering up his stupidity was becoming a full-time job. Albeit a lucrative one. "My client's car was stolen. Shortly after being reported as stolen, it was used in an incident involving Mr. King."

"So someone's trying to frame Weller?"

Phil shrugged. "Or it was plain coincidence. Who knows?"

"Right, have it your way. I also hear rumours about your friend, Mrs. Rickman, and the car that put her in a wheelchair."

"Oh?"

"There's a whisper on the streets that Max was driving that car."

"I don't know where you get your gossip from, Mr. Scott, but that's all it is. Gossip. Now, if there's nothing else, I have a meeting I need to attend." Phil rose to his feet and gathered up a pile of random files from his desk.

Scott was also on his feet. "I have a busy schedule myself, Phil. People to see, questions to ask. This writer chap, he believes my life is in danger. He reckons someone—someone like Rickman or King perhaps—is seeking revenge."

"Then I suggest you watch your back, Mr. Scott." Phil ushered him out of the room. "I don't know anything about it. And I need to get to my appointment. Good seeing you again, though."

Phil closed the door behind him and stood at the

window where he had a good view of the street below.
He was still watching Scott stride briskly along the
street when he called Sarah's number.

TWENTY-SEVEN

"HERE." CAROL THRUST a newspaper at Jimmy and jabbed a finger at an item ringed in red ink. "That would be perfect for you."

Jimmy read the notice under Situations Vacant. "Security? In a department store?" He tossed the newspaper on the table. "You are joking, I assume?"

"No. What's wrong with that? It would be easy enough. All you have to do—"

"Is walk round lingerie and homeware all day waiting until someone slips the odd bra or saucepan lid into their pocket. No, thanks."

"The pay's not bad."

Jimmy grabbed the newspaper, read it again and threw it back on the table. "It's only just above minimum wage."

"Yes, but that's not bad these days. And it's sensible hours. No silly shifts or anything. I think you'd be good at it."

"A chimp would be good at it given an hour's training."

"But the money would be useful and—"

"Is that all you think I'm good for? The best that I can do?"

"No, of course not. But until something better comes along—"

"I'll starve first."

"Oh, thanks very much. So me and the kids have to starve along with you, right? Just because you're too stubborn—"

"I said no." Jimmy refused to argue about it. No way was he applying for a job that useless old men always ended up doing.

Carol slammed a saucepan full of potatoes on the hob, then pushed past him to get plates ready to be warmed. Her lips were a tight line of anger.

"I'm out tonight," Jimmy said. "I'll be late so don't bother waiting up."

"Nice that some of us can afford to go out. Matt? Ewan? Are you doing homework?"

A chorus of "Yes" drifted through from the lounge. They wouldn't be doing homework. They'd be larking around, winding each other up until a fight broke out. Carol couldn't see it, though. To her, they were saints in the making.

"Have I got time for a shower?" Jimmy asked.

"Yep. No job, no life, no kids to deal with, no meals to cook, no washing to do—you've got all the time in the world, Jimmy."

He hated her when she was in this mood. And all because he refused to apply for a dead-end job in a crumbling old department store.

He didn't bother to reply, but ran up the stairs, pulled off his clothes, tossed them on the floor, and switched on the shower. After a second or two, he stepped under the hot water and waited for the tension to leave his neck. He rolled his head, left and right, and shrugged his shoulders to loosen them. As the day's grime was rinsed away, he began to feel better.

By the time he'd dried off, pulled on clean jeans and T-shirt, he felt almost human. Sometimes he wondered if he'd ever wash away the sweat, sand and grime of Afghanistan. It had seeped into every pore. But better not to think about that.

Carol and the boys talked all through dinner as if he didn't exist. They talked of school, of a film that was being shown on TV later, about the neighbour's cat beating up George every time he put a paw outside, about whether Birds Eye fish fingers were better than other brands and a whole host of other stuff. They laughed, they talked—he might have been invisible.

Part of him was annoyed, bloody annoyed, but another part was grateful to be left alone. It gave him time to think, and to look forward to the evening ahead. All the same—

"I am here, you know," he said.

A silence fell over the table.

"Cat got your tongue?" He grinned at that. "Well, we've got enough cats. See if one of them has walked off with your tongue."

No one laughed. They all stared back at him as if he'd escaped from the nearest lunatic asylum. That had to be Carol's fault. She was poisoning his children against him. He could imagine what she told them—that he was happy to let her work but wouldn't get a job himself, that he didn't want them hanging around with their grandfather—

He put down his knife and fork. "This is great fun, but some of us have things to do. I'll see you all in the morning."

He grabbed his holdall and left the house to three

polite goodbyes. All the tension returned to his neck and shoulders as he climbed in the car and drove.

As usual, he parked some distance away from Russell Street and walked the rest of the way. He was about to check that his van was still safe in the garage when he realised his neighbour was trying to attract his attention.

"I hope you haven't had an intruder," the old man said, "but I heard noises coming from your place this afternoon. I wondered if I should call the police. Wasn't sure what to do."

"No need for the police." Noises? What the hell was he on about? Only Lowell could make a noise and if he moved, he'd hang himself. "I've got an old generator I've been playing around with. It's a bit noisy. Sorry about that."

"Ah. I wondered what it could be."

"Just ignore anything you hear. There will be a bit of that because I'm doing some work on the old place before I move in full-time. As for intruders, there's nothing here worth pinching."

"Right. I thought I'd better mention it."

"Yes. Thank you. But there's nothing to worry about. Goodnight."

Still cursing his nosy neighbour, Jimmy let himself in and went straight to the cellar. The sight that met him stopped him in his tracks. Lowell had managed to tip the chair over so that he was now lying on his side. He must have been struggling because he'd kicked over an old oil drum.

He wasn't kicking now. Nor was he dead. How the hell had he managed to tip over the chair without hanging himself? Jimmy was sure he'd tied that noose properly. Yet it dangled from the ceiling. Useless.

"You've been making some noise, I hear," Jimmy said. "Too quiet down here for you, eh? I knew I should have left a radio for you. What do you like to listen to? Arty crap like they have on Radio Three or Four? Radio One perhaps? Jazz? Blues? Or perhaps you're a Planet Rock type?"

Jimmy heaved Lowell and chair back into position. Lowell was far from dead. Anger sparked in his eyes.

Dowie had been a soft touch. He'd spent most of his time down here in tears, the great big baby. Lowell was different. He was furious and determined. Jimmy would have to make doubly sure he was secure. Not that he could go far. The cellar door was always locked so even if by some miracle he managed to untie himself, he wouldn't get out of the cellar. Even so, Jimmy felt a little unnerved.

He put more ties around Lowell's wrists and ankles and stuck more tape around his mouth. After checking and double-checking that the noose was correctly positioned, he sat in his chair opposite Lowell and tried to relax.

What with Carol being moody about jobs, his father calling at the house whenever he felt like it, being forced to bring Lowell here earlier than he'd planned—it was no wonder he was feeling the stress.

Everything was under control, he reminded himself. He was in charge. It was fine.

"Right, we'll forget about the noise you made for now. But don't do it again, okay?"

Lowell's response, muffled by his gag, was a low guttural sound like something a trapped wolf might make.

"Calm down," Jimmy said. "Everything's okay. We're going to carry on with our game. So, what do we have? Just a *D* and that *D* looks like an *O* because you made me get it wrong."

Jimmy had sharpened his knife and he ran it lightly across his thumb.

"Tell you what," he said, "we'll pretend it is an *O* to make it easier. Forget it was ever a *D*, okay? From now on it's an *O*. Got that? And now I'll give you another letter."

Jimmy put his knife to Lowell's arm and began to cut. The *D* that was now an *O* was a mess. The skin was red and swollen around it and it looked nothing like the vision Jimmy had seen in his mind. Perhaps it was simply taking longer to heal than he'd thought. Or perhaps the knife had been too blunt. This letter would look better.

"Now, I appreciate you can't see your arm, but I'll tell you what the letters are and, when you guess correctly, I'll let you see my handiwork. Is that a deal?"

Blood dripped onto the cellar floor as he slowly, carefully, carved the letter *D*. This was much better. He made it deeper and wider than the *O*.

He moved away from his handiwork to look into Lowell's face. His eyes were red and streaming yet his anger almost burned Jimmy.

"You're different to Dowie," he said. "He was as quiet as a lamb. I could have done anything to him. Well, I did. But there was no fight in him at all. What a useless waste of space. Still, it's come good in the end. He's at the bottom of the sea now—food for fish and whatever else lives down there. A shark or two might be fighting over him for all I know. That's good, isn't it? It's nice to know he served a purpose after all."

Jimmy returned to his work. He wiped the blood away with the flat of his hand. The *D* was perfect.

He realised his mistake and raced up the stairs to scrub his hands clean. Lowell might do more than watch the gays. He could be HIV positive for all Jimmy knew.

He pulled on a pair of latex gloves and returned to his task.

"I'm going to have to redo that *O*," he said. "It's a mess. Probably because my knife was blunt."

He worked away until the *O* was the same size and depth as the *D*.

"Tell you what, I'll give you another letter today. A bonus letter. Okay? Another *O*."

This letter was slightly less impressive because Lowell was drifting in and out of consciousness and Jimmy grew bored. It would suffice, though.

When he'd finished, he sat down in front of Lowell again. It fascinated him to see Lowell angry and defiant one minute and unconscious the next.

As soon as he was conscious more often than not, Jimmy walked around the cellar floor, thinking.

"So how do I stop you making noise down here? Ah, I've got it."

He hunted through his metal toolbox until he found his hammer.

"If you can't put so much pressure on your feet, you won't be able to topple the chair, will you?"

Lowell shook his head from side to side and made furious noises behind his gag.

Jimmy ignored him. He lifted the hammer and slammed it down on Lowell's right foot.

There was a brief noise—bones cracking, Lowell's muffled cry—before Lowell passed out, slumped over and would have tipped the chair again if Jimmy's reactions hadn't been so quick.

That was the problem. Lowell was heavier than he looked and the chair wasn't sturdy enough.

It took him over an hour to get Lowell where he wanted him, jammed in the corner of the room so that the wall stopped him toppling to his right, and the old boiler protected his left side. Jimmy covered the boiler with blankets so that in the unlikely event of Lowell somehow managing to bash it, the sound would be muffled.

Setting up the noose in the corner of the room proved tricky but, finally, all was as it should be.

It was almost two o'clock. Time to go home.

TWENTY-EIGHT

DYLAN HATED HOSPITALS. The smell, a disturbing mix of disinfectant and overcooked vegetables, would cling to his skin for days.

King's ward was in the old part of the building where Dylan wouldn't have been surprised to find that consumption and bubonic plague were still rife.

"The last bed on the left," the nurse said.

Dylan strode along the ward, trying not to look at the sick men taking up beds, and was grateful to reach King's bed. At least King looked healthy enough, apart from bandages around his bare chest. Given the way that bullet had floored him, he'd made an amazing recovery. In fact, he looked better than he had when Dylan had last spoken to him. He was relaxed. Perhaps he felt safe here.

"Look who it is," King said. "Have you brought money from your publisher?"

"I don't have a story yet. I've brought you some grapes, though." Dylan put them on the cabinet by the side of the bed and pulled up a chair. "What happened then?"

"Dunno. I was off to the gym when two blokes—"

"What really happened?" Dylan didn't have time for the fictitious version. He'd already heard it. "I was there. I saw you waiting for them, I saw them hand over a holdall, and I saw the guy shoot you."

King thought for a moment, then seemed to shrink a little against the pillows. "Weller said he owed me some money. I don't know what he was talking about. It was a setup."

"You believed he was giving you money? Why would he do that?"

King shrugged. "I dunno."

Dylan helped himself to a handful of grapes. Fruit wasn't his food of choice, in fact there were times when he thought he was allergic to it, but he was starving and it was better than nothing. "What do you know about Sarah Rickman?"

King visibly jumped at the question. "What does she have to do with anything?"

"I'm curious. I've been doing some research for the book and I've heard strange rumours about the car that hit her and put her in a wheelchair being driven by her husband."

"That's nothing to do with me. How would I know what happened? If she says it was a hit-and-run, then I take her word for it."

"I think she's lying."

"So you reckon Max ran into her?"

"I do."

"So what's it to do with me?"

Something about this conversation was making King edgy. "You tell me."

"Who's saying it's anything to do with me?" Oh, yes, King was definitely agitated. "They're fucking lying, whoever they are."

"She was friendly with your wife, wasn't she?"

"So?"

"I heard she was planning to leave Rickman, and that Rickman took exception and ran her down. Perhaps he'd been drinking. He's fond of a drop, I hear, and a lot say he's not a bloke to argue with when he's drunk."

"Perhaps he had been drinking. Perhaps she had. I don't know nothing about that."

Dylan helped himself to more grapes. He was convinced King was lying. "So what happens now?"

"I get out of here—tomorrow, if I'm lucky."

"So soon?"

"Yeah. It was just a graze. Nothing serious. The shock was the worst of it, but I'm as good as new now."

King was one lucky man. Dylan had thought he'd been heading to the mortuary. "What happens when you get out?"

"Nothing."

"What about those bent coppers who landed you in trouble in the first place?"

"Yeah. I'll get them."

"How?"

"Don't you worry about that. They're fucking dead."

"I thought Rickman was dealing with them."

"It doesn't matter, does it? Either way, they're fucking dead men."

"What's Rickman doing about it?"

King frowned. "I don't know. I haven't spoken to him."

Dylan finished the grapes while they talked but it was obvious that King wouldn't tell him anything of interest.

"I'll be seeing you, Lenny. Meanwhile, keep dodging the bullets."

He was glad to escape the ward, and even more pleased to step outside into the sunshine and head away from the old part of the hospital, past the gleaming glass and chrome of the main building and to the car park.

It was time he visited Bev. For a bloke with such a strong aversion to hospitals, he was spending one hell of a lot of time in the blasted places.

It wasn't that he was squeamish. He'd seen too many gun and knife wounds for that. He'd seen dead bodies and attended post-mortems. True, he'd fainted at his first post-mortem and the smell was something he'd never forget, but he'd learned to cope with them. Sudden death didn't bother him too much. What he found so unsettling about hospitals were the number of near-death people being moved around in wheelchairs or on trolleys, and patients strolling around attached to intravenous drips. He'd even seen one chap sitting in a wheelchair outside the main building, holding on to a bag of something being intravenously fed into his system, while smoking a cigarette. Madness.

It didn't take long to drive to Bev's hospital but it took an age to get his bearings. The building was a vast sprawling place, and Bev's room was on the opposite side to the car park. She had her own room, not because they were paying a fortune for it, but because all other beds had been taken.

He collected his car park ticket and ventured inside, then realised belatedly that he was still wearing his Bill Williams disguise. He returned to the Morgan, removed his wig and glasses and shoved them in the glove box before going back to the building.

Signs led everywhere—cardiac unit, urology department, X-ray, antenatal—and he was soon lost again. After walking what felt like miles, he finally found himself following the yellow arrows to the oncology unit.

Hushed voices came from Bev's room. He recognised his mother's voice, then Bev's, and another female was talking. He stood for a moment, gathering his breath and pinning a nonchalant smile on his face.

"I don't want Dylan told." Bev's voice wasn't hushed now. In fact, she sounded almost hysterical.

He didn't hear any response, but Bev's voice came again, loud and harsh. "Because he's bloody useless, that's why. You know as well as I do, Vicky, that he'll go into complete panic mode. The thought of coping with two kids on his own—God, he'll be on the next plane to bloody Australia."

Dylan's smile vanished. What the hell was she talking about? He'd coped with the kids loads of times. Bloody useless? He'd never heard such rubbish.

He would have pushed open the door and said as much, but he heard his mother's voice. "He has to be told, love. It's not fair to keep it from him."

"And I will tell him," Bev said, "but not now. Not yet. He'll need to be told—carefully. He's managed to convince himself that I'm young, fit and healthy and that, after a couple of sessions of chemo, I'm going to be running marathons for the rest of my days."

He wanted to move, either walk into the room or walk away, but he couldn't. His muscles refused to obey the simplest of commands.

"How can I can tell him that the bloody cancer has spread, that I might only have a couple of months to live? I can't. Not yet. In fact, if anyone so much as whispers the bloody word *terminal* to him, I'll kill them. He's my husband, and I know how to deal with him. I'll break it to him slowly and gently."

There was a brief silence until Bev said with feeling, "I could kill for a bottle of wine right now. Make that two bottles. I warn you, as soon as I get out of here, I am going to get totally and utterly wasted."

Dylan heard his mother start to cry.

The sound, one he'd never heard before, galvanised him into action. He turned on his heel and strode back along the corridor, not knowing where he was going, only knowing he had to escape.

He saw a door marked Toilets and pushed it open. Thankfully, it was deserted. He threw cold water on his face but it didn't help. He dashed into a cubicle and spent the next few minutes throwing up. Sweat soaked into his shirt. His heart was thumping out a crazy rhythm.

He couldn't think straight. Nothing made sense. Somehow, he had to walk into Bev's room as if everything were normal.

He couldn't do it.

Christ, she was right. He *was* bloody useless.

Dylan was throwing more water over his face when an elderly man opened the door and stepped inside. He frowned at Dylan. "Are you all right?"

No. I've never been less all right.

"Fine. Thanks." He left the toilets, strode along endless corridors until, more by luck than judgement, he managed to escape the building and find his car.

He was hunting through his pockets for change to pay for the parking ticket when some semblance of sanity returned and he knew he couldn't avoid Bev forever. He might be bloody useless, but he wasn't a coward. Not too much of a coward, at least.

He leaned against his car for five or ten minutes, trying to talk himself into action, mentally practising the smile he'd wear and rehearsing the cheery chat he'd deliver when he walked into that room.

This was crazy. He'd spoken to doctors, several of them, and none had so much as hinted at anything like this. If they were hinting at it now—well, sod it, he wouldn't believe them. They'd get a second opinion. And a third and fourth, if necessary. Bloody National Health Service—they'd probably mixed her records up with someone else's. It wouldn't be the first time that had happened. Even if they hadn't—they would beat this thing and nothing would convince him otherwise.

Feeling slightly reassured, he squared his shoulders and aimed for a casual stroll into the building. The floor insisted on coming up to meet him and he collided with the wall twice. He couldn't even walk straight let alone talk.

He was soon lost again and had to ask for directions.

"Follow the yellow lines," a cheery orderly said.

He did, and he was soon outside Bev's room again. All was quiet. He opened the door and walked into the room. There, that wasn't too difficult.

Smiling—at least he hoped it looked like a smile, because it sure as hell didn't feel like one—he sat on the edge of her bed.

"Oh, you're here," she said. "I bet your mum ten pounds that you wouldn't show up today."

"What? Why wouldn't I?"

She grinned. "I happen to know that the Arsenal game's being shown on TV. A pity I lost my bet, but thank you for coming. So how's your day been?"

A voice, one that didn't sound like his own, came from goodness knew where. "Pretty boring. What about yours?"

"About the same. They're letting me out tomorrow—well, assuming I pass muster when the consultant does his rounds..."

TWENTY-NINE

WHEN LUCY BREEZED into her room, Bev wondered if she'd ever been so pleased to see anyone. "What are you doing here?"

"Checking out the hunky doctors. What else?" She dropped her bag on the chair and hugged Bev. "Dylan said you were being discharged today. Is that right?"

"Yes. Any minute now, with luck. I'm just waiting for the doctor to sign me off."

"So what happened?" Lucy sat on the edge of the bed, and held Bev's hand. "How come you had to be brought here in such a hurry?"

"Oh, I felt a bit off when I woke up and—" It was trying to smile and talk at the same time that did it. A huge sob stuck in her throat and her voice refused to do anything useful.

"Bev?"

She shook her head, unable to speak. She lifted her arms, put them around Lucy's neck and howled. She'd known that if she started to cry, she wouldn't be able to stop. And she couldn't.

"Whatever's wrong?" Lucy rocked her back and forth, as if she were a child. "Hey, come on, Bev, it's not the end of the world."

"Oh, Luce, you're a star!" A laugh escaped her, and she almost choked. She dragged in a couple of shuddering breaths. "It *is* the end of the world. My world, that is."

Lucy pulled back to look at her. "What do you mean? What's happened?"

"The cancer's spread. The operation couldn't get all of it, we knew that, but we thought, hoped at least, that the chemo would—" She had to pull in another deep breath. "Anyway, it's spread. It's aggressive. There's nothing they can do. It's just a matter of time."

Lucy's grip on her arms was painfully tight, but welcome. "Oh, Bev. God, no wonder Dylan looks a wreck."

Bev shook her head. "He doesn't know yet. Until I can talk about it without going to pieces, I can't tell him."

Bev felt awful now. Her best friend knew and her mother-in-law knew but her husband, the man who should be first to hear the news, hadn't a clue.

She couldn't tell him, though. She'd have to be strong for him, pretend that she could cope, that they could all cope, and she couldn't do it. Not yet.

"They shouldn't have told you," Lucy said. "They should have told Dylan instead. Why would you want to know something like that? Why couldn't they lie?"

"Because I told them I wanted the truth. No matter how awful."

"Are they sure?"

"Yes."

"How long?"

"No one knows. It could be months or even a year or so." Said like that, it didn't sound too bad. It wasn't today or tomorrow, or even next week.

Lucy began to cry and it was Bev's turn to console her.

"Look at the state we're in," she said. "God, if we're like this sober, what will be like with a case of wine inside us? And I promise you this—at the very first opportunity, we're going to get legless on wine from the best vineyard known to man."

"Absolutely." Lucy sniffed, grinned and sobbed. "No more cheap plonk for us."

"Or perhaps we should stick to champagne. Do you know, I've never been sick or passed out on champagne? Wine, yes. Champagne, no."

"Apart from at Acer's wedding."

"Extenuating circumstances," Bev said. "That was just plain weird, wasn't it? I still can't believe we'd been listening to his woes for almost three years. Three years! All those boyfriends, remember? They came and went and we had to pick up the pieces and tell him that, one day, he'd meet the right bloke."

"I know," Lucy spluttered with laughter although tears still ran freely down her cheeks. "And do you remember how he turned up and handed us the wedding invites? And how we thought Susan must be a misprint for Fred or John?"

"And it turns out she looks like a supermodel and is stinking rich. That was the poshest wedding ever, wasn't it? A complete waste of money, and totally over the top, but just wonderful. Every time I paused for breath, a waiter poured me more champagne. Bliss."

"And Dylan had to carry you to bed."

"Yes, because I couldn't master the stairs." Bev smiled at the memory. "Happy days."

Lucy squeezed her arm. "We'll have more of those yet."

"Of course we will." She handed Lucy a tissue, and

grabbed one for herself. "A lot more." Although not nearly as many as she'd like.

"And we'll drink—hell, I know what we'll do. We'll have a weekend in Paris and drink champagne. My treat…"

THIRTY

DYLAN HADN'T SLEPT. He hadn't even dozed for more than a couple of minutes at a stretch.

The kids had spent the night at his mother's place—she'd offered and he hadn't had the strength or inclination to argue—Frank had gone to bed early, probably because Dylan wasn't in any mood for chat, and Dylan had rattled around in the house feeling more alone than he had in his life.

Alone, and in a state of complete panic…

Now, he was standing outside Goodenough's building. He hadn't rung the doorbell, there was no point because he doubted Goodenough would answer. Instead, he was hiding behind prickly green shrubbery beside the front door.

For all he knew, Goodenough could be on one of his many trips away from home. He didn't know what else to do, though, and he couldn't stand to be at home, so he was waiting—ready to hammer the truth out of Goodenough if necessary.

As for everything else—he couldn't think about it. The feelings of helplessness were too overwhelming. He was supposed to take care of his family, to protect them from danger, yet this—

He knew he had to confess to Bev that he'd overheard, he knew he must persuade her to see another specialist, one who knew what he was talking about, and he knew he had to stay alive. Some moron threatening him when his family needed him was not an option.

Hours passed. Residents came out of the building, presumably heading for shops or offices, but there was no sign of Goodenough. The longer he waited, the angrier Dylan became. He was angry at the world in general.

The door opened and there he was. Goodenough stood for a moment, as if marvelling at the beauty of a cloudless blue sky, or perhaps he was merely counting the days until he got his hands on Cass Pelham's money.

Dylan grabbed him and slammed him back against the wall—hard.

"What the hell—?"

"I would have rung the bell, but I thought you'd ignore it again."

"What? Who are you? What do you want with me?"

"You know exactly who I am."

"What? No, you've got the wrong man. I don't know who you want, but it's certainly not me. I've never seen you before in my life."

If Goodenough was telling the truth, and Dylan wouldn't trust him as far as he could throw a double-decker bus, that was disappointing. The man currently topped his admittedly pathetic list of suspects.

"Then I'll have to introduce myself. Let's go inside and talk," Dylan suggested.

"But I can't—"

Dylan slammed him into the wall again. "Don't fuck with me, sunshine. Not today. You would not believe the mood I'm in. Even *I* don't believe the fucking mood I'm in. Get inside. Now."

"I don't know who you are—"

"You'll soon find out. Inside." Dylan pushed him back toward the building's main door. "Keys."

Goodenough took a bunch of keys from his pocket and opened the door with fingers that shook.

"We'll go to your flat," Dylan said.

"You really think I'm going to allow you into my flat?"

"I certainly do." Dylan gave him an obliging shove in the direction of the lift.

"Right, that's it. I'm calling the police."

"Good idea, Mr. Goodenough. Or is it Mr. Marshall? Call the police and save me a job."

Goodenough appeared to have a change of heart, just as Dylan had expected, and opened the front door.

The flat was large and airy, and furniture was of the designer-tag expensive type. A huge flat-screen TV took up most of one wall. Audio equipment was discreet and would cost a fortune.

"Nice TV." Dylan gave it a tug, checking that it was firmly fixed to the wall.

"Don't—" Goodenough grabbed him.

"Why? Isn't it paid for? No, I don't suppose it is." Dylan yanked at a CD player, sending cables flying, and threw it on the floor. "I don't suppose that was paid for either."

"Stop! For Christ's sake, stop! Tell me what you want."

Dylan paced around the room before standing at the window to admire the view.

"My name's Dylan Scott." He swung around but

Goodenough's face remained convincingly blank. "I'm a private investigator. But you know that, don't you?"

"Of course I don't know it. I told you, I've never seen you before. You're confusing me with some- one—" His expression changed. "Oh, wait. Ah, yes, I've got you now. You're the man who supposedly has some money for me."

So he'd received the message from someone. The helpful girl at the escort agency perhaps. "That's right."

"There is no money, though, is there?"

"No. There's no money.".

Goodenough squinted at him. "You're the chap Cass's father employed to check up on me."

"Right again."

"So what do you want with me now?"

Dylan took a grainy black-and-white photo from his jacket pocket. It was slightly crumpled, but Good- enough was easily recognisable. "I want to know that this isn't you standing outside my office?"

Goodenough checked out the image, then looked at Dylan as if he were insane. "That's me standing out- side a building wondering what happened to the travel agent's office."

Travel agent? The travel agent that had moved prem- ises two months ago? The travel agent that had operated from the soon-to-be dental practice office?

"Which travel agent?"

"Lounden's." Goodenough handed back the photo.

Dylan didn't believe him. He'd studied those CCTV images time and time again and he was convinced that Goodenough had been looking at windows, at secu- rity, trying to fathom out the best way to gain entry.

"I'll ask again—what do you want with me now?" Goodenough's shrug was impressively careless.

If Goodenough wasn't threatening him with imminent death, then Dylan didn't want anything from him. What did it matter if he owed money to more people than could fit in Wembley Stadium? What did it matter if women fell for Goodenough's charm and willingly gave him their worldly goods?

It didn't. Or it shouldn't have. Yet, Dylan had a mental picture of a smiling young woman giving an expensive silk scarf to a stranger. "I want to hand you over to the nearest judge," he said. "Fraud. Deception."

"Now, look—"

"What's your real name, by the way? I'm sure a judge would want to know. It's not Goodenough, is it? It's not Chesney Marshall—"

"Do you want money?" Goodenough asked.

Dylan laughed at that. "I'm probably one of the few people in the country who doesn't want money from you. Which, considering you don't have any yet, is somewhat fortunate, isn't it?"

"So what *do* you want? Look, I've done nothing wrong. I occasionally work for an escort agency because I need the money, and because I'm not proud of that, I tell people that my name's Chesney Marshall. I haven't cheated anyone. I owe a couple of people, true, but they'll get their money. I've told them that."

"When?"

"What's it to you? Why don't you tell me exactly what you want?"

"I want you to keep away from Cass Pelham for one. In fact, if you go anywhere near her—"

"What's it to you?"

"She deserves better. She's a decent person, from a decent family, and what you're planning is theft."

"Theft? I'm planning to marry her. We've cleared up all misunderstandings. I simply told a few lies—"

"Told a few lies?" Dylan gave a snort of laughter that didn't quite manage to conceal his anger. "You've used a fake name and obtained money by false pretences. You're planning to make wedding plans, get your hands on her money—and then what? Go back to your real wife? I'm assuming you're married?" His ring finger was bare but Dylan was still convinced he'd once seen him remove a gold wedding band. "Save your lies. I'll find out for myself."

Goodenough looked too confident and smug for Dylan's liking so he grabbed him by his shirt and slammed him against the wall.

"I'm feeling in a very generous mood." That was a lie. "I can't be bothered with you and your greed, and I'm giving you the chance to get out of my sight. Preferably out of the country. I'm going to be watching you like a hawk, though, and if you go within a hundred yards of Cass Pelham, I'm taking you straight to the law. Is that clear?"

They both knew the law would struggle to touch him. Any half-decent lawyer would see to that.

Dylan gave him a punch in the ribs that had him doubled over. "Is that clear?"

Goodenough gasped and nodded. "Yes."

"Get back to your real life. It'll be a lot safer for you." Dylan punched him again.

"All right. All right."

He must have hit him harder than he'd thought because Goodenough slumped to the ground.

"I'll see myself out," Dylan said. "And don't forget, I'll be watching your every move from now on."

Dylan walked out of the building convinced of two things. One, Goodenough was a coward, one who could happily use scare tactics and send death threats, but he wasn't a killer. Two, he should have left him with a few less teeth.

THIRTY-ONE

JIMMY HAD ALWAYS been fascinated by the way other people lived and he was enjoying every moment of being in Lowell's home.

As a kid, he'd had no real friends. Other children had fallen into two groups, one that his parents disapproved of and the other made up of kids who took great delight in bullying the copper's son. His dad had been a strict disciplinarian, one who'd never believed in giving Jimmy credit for anything. If Jimmy was awarded an A in schoolwork, his dad would demand to know why it wasn't an A+. If he was caught reading anything his father considered frivolous, he was ridiculed. If he attempted to wear any clothes that were vaguely fashionable, he'd been deemed a nancy boy.

Jimmy's mother, older than her husband by eleven years, had grown up in a vicarage and took her religion very seriously. She was more gentle with Jimmy but certainly no fun. She was too busy striving to keep her husband happy—meals on the table the second he walked into the house, neatly pressed shirts to wear, a tidy house, well-kept garden—to take much notice of Jimmy.

In Lowell's house, on the other hand, there was evidence of a much-adored-but-spoiled child. Samples of the brat's artwork—brightly coloured daubs—were held against fridge and freezer doors with magnets. Her bedroom was a mass of soft toys. She had an iPad, lots of books, a wardrobe crammed with clothes, and photos of the dog stuck to the walls.

It was a shame about the dog, but Jimmy had been left with no choice. The spaniel had been friendly enough—too friendly, in fact. Instead of objecting to finding a stranger in the house, it had insisted on wagging its tail and jumping at Jimmy in excitement. Putting the rope around the dog's neck had been simple enough. It was a shame, but the animal hadn't suffered for long. Jimmy had carried the dead weight into the field at the back of the house and placed him under a tree.

The master bedroom was huge and dominated by a super king-size bed. Given the amount of time Lowell spent hanging around gay bars, Jimmy wondered if it saw much action.

A walk-in wardrobe, bigger than Jimmy's own bedroom, housed rails of clothes—Lowell's on the left and his wife's on the right. The clothes bore labels from designers that even Jimmy had heard of. Some were protected by dust covers and some were still in dry cleaner's bags.

One dressing table, Lowell's, held only a hairbrush and two dishes, one for loose change and one for cufflinks. The other was covered in creams, potions, lipsticks, makeup brushes and a host of other beauty products. It also held a framed photo of Lowell and his wife on their wedding day, along with several of their daughter at various ages.

Jimmy wandered downstairs and into a second living room. This one housed an upright piano and he guessed the little girl would be having lessons. Lined up on top of the instrument were a dozen framed photos of the happy, smiling family. Jimmy picked them up and looked at them in turn.

A sudden clatter made him jump. He crept to the front door and gave a small laugh of relief when he saw the flyer from a nearby pizza store. From the side window, he saw a young woman, a bag slung over her shoulder and a couple of dozen leaflets in her hand, walking down the drive.

Jimmy fancied a cup of tea, but that would be pushing his luck too far. Or would it? He'd just have to make sure he washed the cup thoroughly.

He filled the kettle and switched it on, then hunted through cupboards until he found a box of Earl Grey teabags. He made his tea, added a touch of semi-skimmed milk, washed the spoon and returned it to the drawer, and went into the lounge to sit and enjoy it.

This was as good as having sex in the open. The risk of being caught more than tripled the pleasure. Years ago, he and Carol had often enjoyed sex in the great outdoors. That had stopped, though. Carol always had an excuse at the ready—usually the kids, or the weather, or a headache. A pity. Still, there were plenty of women willing to oblige where she refused.

Having finished his tea, he returned to the kitchen and scrubbed the cup clean.

He took his camera from his pocket and flicked the on switch. It was only a cheap one but the flash was decent, the pictures were acceptable and, most important, he could put it in his pocket. His SLR would have been much better, of course, but it was far too bulky to carry around.

For his first picture of the kitchen, he used the self-timer and captured himself standing by the breakfast bar. He moved on, snapping everything that caught his eye. He was careful not to use the flash near the windows as he didn't want busybodies wondering what was going on. It was unlikely as they would assume Mrs. Lowell was at home.

He had fun in the bedroom. When her underwear was spread across the bed and arranged to his satisfaction, he took several arty shots. He was pleased with the result and couldn't wait to download them to his computer.

He'd just finished returning the scanty items to the drawers when he heard the front door open and close. "Fuck!"

Careful not to make a sound, he crawled under the bed. For all the hours the cleaner spent at the property, she clearly didn't believe in vacuuming under beds. The dust was thick. Jimmy hoped to God it didn't make him sneeze.

He heard voices—adults, females—drift upstairs.

"Sam? Sam, where are you?" He could tell Mrs. Lowell was calling the dog. "Sam?" There was the rattle of something that could have been a tin of dog biscuits. "Sam, come here!"

The other woman said something that Jimmy didn't catch.

"No, he'll be fine. He must have dashed out when we came in. He does that, but he doesn't wander far. He'll soon come back and there's no point shouting at him because he's gone deaf."

There was more conversation that Jimmy didn't catch, then Mrs. Lowell was speaking again. "Christ,

I don't know what to do. I know something awful has happened, I know it. The police know it too. They're taking it very seriously."

"What about the hospitals, love?" This woman sounded older. Her mother perhaps?

"All contacted again this morning. Nothing." There was a sob in her voice. "What will I tell Emily? She keeps asking where he is, and I keep telling her he's had to go away to work and will be back soon. How can I tell her that her dad's—gone?"

Jimmy didn't catch the other woman's response.

"Every time the phone rings—every time the doorbell goes—I think it's the police coming with bad news. I know it's coming. I know he's dead."

The older woman made soothing noises as Mrs. Lowell wept for her missing husband.

Mrs. Lowell was a looker and Jimmy would have been more than happy to console her.

It was no use, he couldn't stay under the bed. The dust would make him start coughing, and it was too claustrophobic.

The door to the en-suite bathroom was ajar. Was it too risky? The small room offered no real hiding place but it was unlikely she'd take a bath or shower until her companion left and, if either of them needed the toilet, they'd use the downstairs cloakroom or the family bathroom. It was a little dangerous perhaps but he was in the mood for taking risks. In any case, he couldn't stay under the bed.

The bathroom had a pleasant enough smell—fresh pine, he'd guess. Here, the cleaner did her job because it was spotless. The chrome gleamed as did the white porcelain washbasin and shower tray. He draped a dark blue towel over the glass shower screen and hid behind that. She might wonder about the towel but, by then, it would be too late.

During the hour or so he spent in the shower, the phone rang fourteen times. It was impossible to hear their voices now, but Jimmy guessed that journalists were eager for news on her missing husband. Perhaps the police were calling to say there was no news.

The shower was too uncomfortable and Jimmy knew he must revert to plan A. A bit of dust wouldn't hurt him. Christ, he'd swallowed enough of the stuff in Afghanistan. He wasn't thinking about that, though. Instead, he'd look forward to the pleasure ahead.

Before taking up position beneath the bed, he quietly opened the bedroom door and stepped out onto the landing. When he looked down, he saw her. She was carrying two cups to the kitchen but she didn't look up.

She was exactly his type. Tall, slim, elegant—classy. Pert breasts that weren't too big or too small. Long, long legs. It was her class that appealed, though. She was graceful in speech and movement. God knows what someone like her saw in a bloke like Lowell. Still, there was no accounting for taste. Later, he'd show her what a real man could do for her. He grew hard at the thought.

It was thinking about her body, about her hair, and the way she moved, that made him forget all about the dust beneath the bed. He lay perfectly still, his eyes closed, fantasising about her. He could even imagine the way she might smell. Fresh, sexy and classy.

He lost all sense of time. It could have been minutes or hours before he heard the front door opening and closing. The other woman had gone. Jimmy was alone in the house with Mrs. Lowell.

He could hear the chink of crockery being put in the dishwasher. The radio was switched on and almost immediately switched off again.

He held his breath as he heard her light tread on the stairs. Then she was in the bedroom, standing only inches from him. He could see the black high-heeled shoes she wore.

The bed sagged as she lay down. Then he heard her begin to cry.

He couldn't remember the last time he'd wanted a woman this much. Only a mattress separated them now and it was almost more than he could bear. His longing was a physical ache, one that he could do nothing about yet.

He had no idea where her daughter was. Perhaps she was staying with her grandparents. For all he knew, someone might be bringing her home any minute. He couldn't take any risks and would have to stay where he was until Mrs. Lowell settled down for the night.

But to have her so close, to hear her breathing—

The phone rang again and she snatched at the extension on the bedside table. She didn't say anything, just listened, and then slammed it down. He'd bet it was a journalist eager for a story.

The phone kept ringing and she kept sobbing.

Then she got off the bed, left the room and padded downstairs. A door opened. "Sam? Sam? Where are you?"

Darkness eventually fell, but it felt like hours before she finally came upstairs again. She went to the bathroom and he heard the shower running. She was making herself ready for him.

Soon, he promised himself. Very, very soon.

She returned to the bedroom and let her towel drop to the floor. He could see her feet, small and perfect with the nails painted a pale pink.

Finally, she got into bed and switched off the lamp. Jimmy was surprised she couldn't hear his heart hammering. No matter how he tried, he couldn't steady its racing beat.

He gave her an hour or so, but he could tell she wasn't sleeping. No way could he wait any longer.

He slid out very quietly from under the bed. All was in darkness, but he'd memorised the layout of the room. He was safe enough.

He climbed onto the bed and she let out a scream before he managed to clamp his hand against her mouth. She was naked, which took him by surprise. He'd seen silk nightdresses when he'd looked through her drawers and he'd expected her to wear one of those. He'd been hoping for the sheer lilac one and he felt let down.

He lay on top of her, one hand against her mouth, and the other fumbling with his trousers. She struggled, but she was a lightweight and easy enough for him to control.

"We're going to have some fun," he promised.

He struggled one-handed to pull his jeans around his knees and soon pushed himself inside her. Still she struggled. Her legs kicked out, her arms pummelled his back.

He didn't care. He had to be inside her. He pushed, deeper and deeper, ignoring her muffled protests.

Sweat poured off him as he thrust into her. It dripped off his forehead onto her.

"You're spoiling everything, you ungrateful cow," he said. "Stop struggling and enjoy the moment."

He lost his erection—her fault—and he had to slap her about a bit.

He fumbled about in the dark for the lamp and finally managed to switch it on. "That's better. I can see you now."

She continued to fight him, her eyes tightly shut, her face contorted into a mask of horror.

He rolled her over so that she was lying on her stomach, her face in the pillow. That was much, much better. He was soon hard again, and he took her from behind.

When he'd finished with her, his overriding emotion was disappointment. Her lack of reaction had been pathetic. He wished he could leave her on the bed and walk out of the house.

There was no point getting sloppy, though, so he dragged her into the bathroom. She screamed all the way, but Jimmy was past caring. He held onto her while he filled the bath. When he considered it deep enough, he lifted her into it, pushed her head under the water and held it there until she stopped struggling.

It didn't take long. In fact, the old dog had put up more of a fight. Still, she hadn't suffered…

He returned to the bedroom, stripped the sheets from the bed, carried them downstairs and put them in the washing machine. When he was satisfied that the machine was doing its work, he left.

He stepped out into the cool night air, checked his pocket for his camera, and drove home.

THIRTY-TWO

DYLAN ALWAYS FELT as if he were stepping into a fantasy land, one where fairies lived happily at the bottom of the garden, when he walked into his mother's flat. Bells tinkled and pieces of glass danced in the light as the door opened and closed. Everywhere was a rainbow of colour and there had to be at least a hundred candles dotted around the place. At least she'd be okay in a power cut.

"What are you doing here? Is Bev all right?"

"You know how Bev is, Mum. And so do I." They fought their way past a stone pixie and what Dylan called a disgusting feather thing and she called a dream catcher into the kitchen. "I overheard her telling you that if anyone so much as mentioned the word *terminal* to me, she'd kill them."

"Oh." Her hand reached out to clutch at his arm and her eyes suddenly swam in a pool of tears. "Oh, Dylan."

"Don't start crying," he warned her. "If you start, I'll have to join you."

She wrapped her arms around herself and bit on her bottom lip to keep all signs of emotion locked in. "We'll get through this, love."

"We will. I've made an appointment for her with a Mr.—a chap whose name I've already forgotten and can't pronounce anyway. Sri Lankan. An expert.

Wednesday at ten o'clock." He couldn't seem to string a sentence together and was aware of his words coming out like gunfire. "It might be best if you came along. Is that okay?"

"Of course. This chap—he's a private consultant?"

"Yes. It'll be expensive if she needs a lot of treatment but, to be honest, I couldn't give a flying fuck about that. Sorry."

She shrugged off the apology for his language. "I couldn't give a flying fuck either."

She reached for a joint, already rolled and sitting in a pottery ashtray, and lit it. Dylan was tempted to join her but he knew from experience that the drugs didn't work.

"We'll get by. We can sell this place—" She gestured to her flat. "I have some savings too. Not a lot, but it all helps. So long as Bev gets well again, we'll get by."

"Yeah."

"I don't know why she doesn't want you told."

"Like she said, I'm bloody useless. She's right, I am. The thought of having to stand by and watch her suffer—" he shuddered, "—terrifies me."

She nodded, having known that already.

"Or coping without her," he said. "I can't even begin to think about that."

"I know, love."

Dylan paced the small, cluttered room and wished he could take off and run for miles.

"The doctor was nice," she said. "He promised that, these days, no one will die in pain."

Dylan shrugged that off. How the hell did doctors know? They weren't the ones dying.

"As for the kids," he said. "Freya's too young to know what's going on, but God knows what the news will do to Luke."

She took a deep drag on her joint, but not before Dylan had noticed the fresh tears that sprang to her eyes.

"I don't suppose there's any alcohol in this place?"

"No, sorry. Oh, wait. Actually, yes, there might be." She got down on her knees and opened a low cupboard that looked to contain nothing but pots and pans. "Here you go. A bottle of brandy leftover from Christmas." She handed him a bottle that was covered in dust. "It doesn't go off, does it?"

"Who cares?" As he couldn't find a glass, and as she was too busy smoking her cannabis and fighting back tears, he poured a measure into a thick white mug and took a swig.

"Have you told Bev that you know?" she asked him.

"Not yet. Tonight," he said vaguely.

"Yes, you need to. Especially as you've made this appointment."

"How's she been with you, Mum?"

"Oh—worried about how you and the kids will manage. Reasonably okay. A bit detached, if I'm honest. It's as if it's all happening to someone else and she's just going through the motions. Denial, I suppose. How's she been with you?"

"She's going around the place with a forced cheerfulness that's driving me insane."

"She's making a diary for Freya and Luke—one each, I think. She wants to make sure they remember her when they're grown up."

For a second, Dylan thought he was about to vomit.

The moment passed and he took another drink of brandy to settle his stomach.

"All we can do, love, is remain positive. Perhaps this Sri Lankan chap will come up with something. Although as the cancer's spread—but there, we don't know what they can do these days, do we? They can cure all sorts of things. Modern medicine is filled with miracles."

Dylan hoped so. For all their sakes.

"I can't really stop, Mum, because I've got a load of stuff to do. I just wanted to tell you about the appointment on Wednesday. Come over to our place, will you? We'll leave about eight-thirty. No, make it eight o'clock. Traffic will be murder at that time of day."

"I'll be there."

"Thanks." He emptied his mug and immediately wished he could empty the bottle. "I know I don't say this often enough, but I do appreciate you being around and helping out all the time."

"Struth, don't go all soft on me. It's mutual, love. I appreciate being able to treat your house like my own and see my grandkids whenever I want. There's not many daughter-in-laws who'd be so—so good. Bev's one in a million, you know."

He nodded, but didn't feel able to comment on that. "I'll see you on Wednesday."

He strode out, and managed to catch his head on that bloody stupid feather thing before knocking his knee against the stone pixie. Any burglar who broke in here deserved a sodding medal.

FOUR HOURS AND several strong coffees later, Dylan was being searched extremely thoroughly before being allowed to see Max Rickman.

It was difficult to say whether Dylan hated prisons more than hospitals or vice versa. Both places gave him the creeps. Here, the smell wasn't of disinfectant and rotting vegetables, it was male sweat, testosterone and pure undiluted evil.

The majority of the other visitors were women, many with children clinging to their hands. He'd never thought prison a good place to bring children, but he'd never thought it right that fathers shouldn't see their kids either.

As soon as he spotted Rickman—a model prisoner by all accounts—he was taken back to that arrest, and those samurai swords. He'd had no doubt at the time that Rickman would have taken great pleasure in using them. He felt the same now. There was something dark and malevolent about Rickman. Thankfully, however, there was no spark of recognition in his expression. In fact, there was nothing. His eyes, a dark brown, were like mirrors. All you saw when you looked into them was your own reflection. There was no emotion in them. Nothing.

"Bill Williams," Dylan introduced himself. "Author. I'm writing a book—"

"I know who you are." Rickman's voice was one long wheeze from years of chain smoking.

"I assumed you would. Your wife or stepson will have mentioned the book I'm writing, yes?" Rickman didn't answer so Dylan ploughed on. "My problem is that all I'm hearing is rumours. I need facts and—" he gave Rickman a smile, "—who better to talk to than you?"

"What facts?"

"The night of your arrest, Leonard King was only there to discuss a driving job with you, is that right?"

"He was there. That's all that matters."

"And you were both caught in the act because someone—and I've heard rumours to suggest that the someone was King's wife and a couple of police officers—set you up. Is that right?"

"That's right."

"And those same police officers, detectives, turned up to arrest you both. Yes?"

"That's right."

Dylan gave another smile. "I wouldn't want to be in those coppers' shoes when you get out."

Rickman's face was totally expressionless. "Me neither."

"How long is it till you get out, by the way?"

"I'm in front of a parole board in a couple of months."

"That's good then. I've heard you're a model prisoner—you should do okay."

A cruel, cold sneer tugged at Rickman's mouth. "Yeah."

"I imagine you'll be straight after those coppers when you get out?"

"Yep."

"Or will you get them beforehand? Wendy King—well, someone's already got to her, haven't they?"

"Yeah." Still Rickman's expression gave nothing away.

"Not your doing, was it?" Dylan smiled, trying to make light of the question.

A nerve twitched in the man's neck. "Nope."

Dylan wasn't sure whether to believe him or not. He

had the best alibi in the world but Dylan wouldn't be in the least surprised to learn that Rickman had decided he wanted revenge on Wendy.

So how long before he wanted revenge on the two detectives he believed were involved?

"It was your wife who found out about Wendy and the coppers, wasn't it? And only recently. I spoke to her—your wife, I mean—well, you'll know that. Funny how the truth has taken so long to come out."

"Shit always floats to the surface."

Actually, it didn't, but Dylan wasn't going to argue with him.

"I knew," Rickman went on, "that all I had to do was bide my time and wait for someone to talk. I'm a patient man. And I'm safe enough here." That cruel half smile again. "There are too many people making sure I don't meet with a sudden—accident."

Dylan didn't have to wonder if this man was capable of driving a car straight at his wife. He knew he was. "Talking of accidents, there are more rumours floating around. About your wife and the so-called hit-and-run driver."

Rickman's expression darkened. "Like what?"

"Like it was you who drove the car. Like she was leaving you for someone else."

"Yeah, well, we all know where that story came from, the little shit that is John Weller."

"Your stepson? Why would he start rumours like that?"

"Why? Because he's a little shit." That, as far as Rickman was concerned, was reason enough. "Look, there's no story for your fancy book. I was arrested,

I've served my time, almost, and that's it. If anything needs sorting, I'll sort it."

"Have you started sorting it? Have you warned those coppers that you're out to get them?"

"Why bother? They'll find out soon enough."

Dylan had thought from the start that Rickman would do his own dirty work. It was personal for him, and he'd enjoy doing it himself.

"Was it one copper or both of them? I mean, were they both in on the act?"

"Both."

Which didn't explain why Dylan had received death threats and Pikey hadn't.

They talked for another hour, but Dylan heard nothing he didn't know. He was glad when it was time to leave.

"Good luck with the parole board. Your wife, I know, is hoping you'll soon be free."

"Oh, she certainly is."

It was there again, that cruel, dangerous sneer, the one that said a lot of people needed to watch their backs when the model prisoner was released from his cell. Including Sarah Rickman.

DYLAN WAS GLAD to escape the confines of those prison walls. He ought to go home and talk to Bev, but he was a great believer in not doing now what you could put off till later.

He drove across the City to Sarah Rickman's house. There was more to her relationship with Max Rickman than met the eye, he was sure of that.

He rang the bell, heard it echo through the house,

and waited. Just when he was about to give up, he saw movement through the small glass pane in the door.

The door swung open and she was smiling up at him from her wheelchair. "Well, hello. This is a nice surprise. Come on in."

The words were welcoming enough but the smile looked forced. "Thanks."

He stepped into a wide hallway and followed her wheelchair into a large sitting room. The air outside was strangely oppressive for April, but all her windows were open and the room felt pleasantly cool.

Oak floorboards were well polished and cream sofas were inviting, but the furnishings had a tired look to them. Everything looked a little worn and shabby.

"What can I do for you, Bill?"

"I've had a chat with your husband," he said.

"Oh? How is he? Still bearing up? I haven't seen him for a fortnight."

"He seems well enough. I gather he has a meeting with the parole board soon."

"Yes. Fingers crossed it goes well for him."

"Indeed. You must be counting the minutes."

"Of course." The reply was automatic, but she wrung her hands together as she spoke. "So what can I do for you?"

"I'm having a few problems with the story," he said. "I keep hearing odd rumours. For instance, there's a rumour going around—well, it's about your accident."

"What about it?" She didn't wait for an answer. Instead, she gave him a bright smile. "There's not much to say about it. I'd had too much to drink, and decided I needed some fresh air." She gave a tinkling little laugh that echoed around the room. "That's the silliest thing

to do when you've had a few drinks. I walked down
the drive and out onto the road, and, the next thing I
know, I'm waking up in hospital."

"Who called the ambulance?"

"Sorry? Well, John. Why do you ask?"

"Your son?"

"Yes." She was frowning. "Why does it matter?"

"He was with you?"

"Yes. We were all here—me, Max and John."

A noise came from upstairs. It had sounded as if
something—a book perhaps—had been dropped.

"The cleaner," she said with a rueful smile.

A remarkably quiet cleaner. One who hadn't made
a sound until that point.

"Getting back to your accident, you didn't see the
car or the driver?"

"No. Like I said, I'd been drinking. It was all my
own fault."

"Rumour has it that you were planning to leave
Max. Is that true?"

"Of course not. Why would I?"

Dylan could give her a dozen valid reasons, number one being that the bloke was a homicidal maniac.
"Rumour also has it that Max was driving the car that
put you in hospital."

She gave a scoffing laugh. "People love to gossip,
don't they? What Max did was travel with me in the
ambulance and hold my hand. Not that I knew about
that at the time, of course."

"And it was—how long before Max and King were
arrested? A month?"

"A little less. But what does any of this have to do
with the book you're writing?"

"Nothing really. I'm merely trying to sort the facts from the rumours. Anyway, I won't keep you any longer. At least I know the truth about your accident, although, as you say, it's not pertinent to the story."

She showed him out and seemed relieved to see him go.

He didn't go far. He crept around the side of the house and stood close to one of those open windows. That cleaner had been far too quiet for Dylan's liking.

He heard Sarah's voice, but it was coming from the hallway and was a little indistinct. It sounded something like "You can come out now."

Two voices now, Sarah Rickman's and a male. They became clearer as the two walked into the living room.

"He knows, Lenny," Sarah Rickman said. "He knows everything—about the accident—everything."

Well, well, well. Call Dylan a bluff old cynic but he couldn't imagine King being too hot with a vacuum cleaner.

"Of course he doesn't. He can't," King said.

"Idiot that I am, I told him John phoned for the ambulance. The question took me by surprise and I wasn't thinking straight."

"So what? He knows nothing."

"Christ, what a mess. What are we going to do?"

"I've told you what we have to do."

"How the hell can we?" Her voice was filled with despair. And fear. "If anything happens to Max—"

"It's him or us."

"Don't be such a bloody fool, Lenny. Whatever happens, it's going to be us. If anything happens to him, we're dead, and if—"

"Not if it looks like natural causes. Suicide, perhaps. Or a heart attack. Yeah, a heart attack will be best."

"It'll never work."

"It will. Trust me."

"I'm scared," she said, her voice so soft that Dylan struggled to hear.

"There's no need," King said. "Trust me."

"No, it's no use. When he comes out, I'll have to carry on playing the devoted wife. I won't see you, Lenny. I won't be able to."

"Trust me."

There were muffled sounds, then King's voice came loud and clear. "I have to go, sweetheart. I'll call you later, okay?"

Dylan needed to go too. He ducked down and walked to the back of the house, where he was better hidden and where anyone leaving the property wouldn't see him.

It was a stupid idea as King left by the back door. Dylan dashed back to the side and breathed a sigh of relief as King went on his way, looking as furtive as ever.

WHEN DYLAN WALKED into his house, the first thing he saw was a small suitcase at the bottom of the stairs. Damn. He'd forgotten Frank was having to return to Lancashire.

He walked into the kitchen and found Bev and Frank laughing about something over a coffee. It shocked him to see Bev carrying on as if everything were normal, and it was impossible to reciprocate.

He bent to kiss the top of her head. "Good day?"

"Lazy," she said. "Do you want a coffee? Frank and

I are deciding what we'd do if we could be prime minister for the day."

"My first job would be to print some money." Dylan made himself a coffee. "Then I'd start sorting out the mess that this country's in. I can't see that it would take above an hour either."

"My thoughts exactly," Frank said. "All it needs is someone with some common sense—something that's sorely lacking in our politicians."

"They're too greedy. Which reminds me," Dylan said, "I've booked your car in for a service tomorrow, Bev. It'll be interesting to see how much that robbing mechanic charges this time."

"About half what he'd charge me," Bev said with amusement.

"True. What time does your train leave, Frank? Do you want a lift to the Tube station?"

"It's all sorted, thanks, mate. The taxi's booked. I'll be back late on Friday, if that's okay."

"Of course it is," Bev said. "It's lovely having you around. Who knows, perhaps some of your good manners will rub off on Dylan."

"Sorry, Bev, but I think that's a lost cause."

They chatted about the mundane, and Dylan didn't get chance to update Frank on his day because the taxi arrived and he was gone.

Not that there was much to update him on. Sarah Rickman had been convinced he "knew." She was kidding herself there because Dylan hadn't a clue what she meant. He was still reeling from the shock of King being in the house, King calling her sweetheart…

And why was she so upset that she'd told Dylan that it was her son who'd called the ambulance?

He had no idea.

Luke spent most of the evening chatting to his friends on Facebook. Why he gained pleasure from that when he'd see them in the morning, Dylan didn't know. Freya, after a sleepless night, was catching up on her beauty sleep.

Luke finally went to bed and Dylan knew the time had come for The Conversation.

"Do you want a glass of wine?" he asked Bev.

"Yes, why not? Thanks, love."

It took him far longer than necessary to pour Bev a glass of wine and fix a whisky with ice for himself. He carried their drinks into the lounge.

"Thanks," she said.

She looked brighter, had more colour in her face, but that was the drugs at work. Powerful drugs that she seemed to take on an hourly basis.

"So," he said.

She looked up. "So?"

"I've made an appointment for you to see a specialist. An expert." That hadn't been too difficult. "Wednesday morning. Ten o'clock."

"Why?"

Twice he started to speak, and twice the words lodged behind a huge lump in his throat.

"I know, Bev," he said at last. "I was at the hospital and I overheard you saying to Mum that you didn't want me told."

"Oh, Christ."

"You're right, of course. I am bloody useless, but—"

She clasped his hand in hers and her grip was surprisingly firm. "I did want you to know, of course I did, but I thought the shock—you know. I thought I could build up to it gradually. Sorry."

"It's—" He shrugged it off. "We'll see what this other chap has to say, and then talk about it, okay?"

Her smile was the saddest thing he'd ever seen. "There's not a lot he'll be able to say, Dylan. The cancer has spread. It was on the scan for all to see. Your specialist can't change that, can he?"

"We don't know what he can do. We'll talk about it then, okay?"

"Okay." She was humouring him. "It's all right. Really. There's nothing to panic about. It's not as if I'm going to die tonight, or tomorrow. Heck, I could get hit by a bus tomorrow. Or you could. I could outlive you still."

"I know that."

"I'm not going to let it rule whatever time I've got left. What would be the point of that?"

But it *would* rule that life. Dylan knew all about living each day as if it were your last, but that was crap. How could you? How could you be happy, really happy, when you knew your days were numbered? How could he be happy? How could he pretend that he wasn't scared shitless? He couldn't.

"I don't want to talk about it," she said. "When it's sunk in a bit more, then we'll talk."

"And when we've seen the specialist. He's good, Bev. The best…"

THIRTY-THREE

As Luke closed the door behind him, Bev felt a rising of her spirits. Dylan had already gone, taking her car to be serviced and then doing whatever he was currently working on, Frank was in Lancashire, and Luke was at school. It was just her and Freya, and even that wouldn't last long because her daughter had plans for the day.

Right on cue, the back door opened and Vicky stepped inside.

"Hello, love." Vicky immediately picked up Freya and swung her around. "Well, don't you look gorgeous? We'll have a wonderful time, sweetheart. Ooh, I'll enjoy showing you off."

Bev couldn't help laughing. "How old are your friend's grandchildren?"

"Three. Twin girls." She kissed Freya on the forehead. "And I bet they're nowhere near as pretty as you."

"Have you ever thought you're a little biased, Vicky?"

"Not once." Vicky sat at the table bouncing Freya on her lap. "So how's things?"

How to answer that. "Okay. Except Dylan knows."

Vicky nodded. "He called to see me yesterday. I expect it's for the best."

"Maybe. He's made me an appointment with some

specialist or other, so of course he's convinced himself that the man can work miracles. It'll be impossible to tell him there isn't going to be a miracle."

"You never know, love. Best to keep an open mind, eh? We all need to stay positive."

"Yes. Yes, you're right."

"So what are you intending to do today?"

"Enjoy my freedom." Bev laughed. "I love my family dearly, and it's been great having Frank here, he's a true gent, but I am so going to savour a whole day alone. Don't rush back, will you?"

She'd told Dylan she was going with Vicky and Freya simply because he was constantly fussing these days. If she'd so much as hinted at spending the day alone, he would probably have insisted on staying at home with her. She couldn't bear the fussing. She wanted a day that was—normal.

"We'll be back early evening," Vicky said. "About six. Is that okay?"

"Perfect."

When Freya was strapped into her buggy, and they'd checked and double-checked the contents of her bag—Freya always needed enough supplies for an expedition—Vicky hugged Bev tight and set off.

Bev made herself a coffee and relished the silence. No husband, no kids, no guests—no responsibilities. The day was hers and hers alone. It was such an unexpected luxury that she couldn't decide how to spend it. There were plenty of chores that needed doing but they could wait. She refused to squander a single minute of her day.

She'd go out somewhere. The destination wasn't important, but behaving as if she were young, free and single was. She'd drive out—

And then she remembered that she was carless for the day. Typical.

It didn't matter, she could take a taxi. She had no idea where she wanted to go, but she'd simply ask the driver to keep going until she decided. To hell with the cost.

She picked up the phone and was about to check the local taxi firm's number when she spotted the keys to Dylan's Morgan lying next to the fruit bowl. He was so attached to that car, she was surprised he didn't sleep with the keys.

She returned the phone to the cradle. There was nothing to stop her taking the Morgan. He didn't like her driving it, mainly because once, just once, she'd reversed it into a wheelie bin. But hadn't he bestowed all his worldly goods upon her? Of course he had. Besides, she'd be home before him. He'd never know.

She picked up the keys, grabbed her handbag and left the house before she could change her mind. She was free to pass the day as she chose and she couldn't wait.

Sadly, it wasn't possible to leave the hateful disease behind, but she was damned if she was going to let it spoil her day.

She managed to force the Morgan into gear—eventually—and set off.

Why Dylan was so besotted with the car, she had no idea. It drew plenty of admiring glances, but it wasn't as comfortable as hers and the gearbox had a mind of its own.

The sense of freedom was bliss, though, and, without conscious thought, she drove to Hampstead Heath.

It was one of her favourite places, and the fact that this oasis of countryside existed in the City never failed to amaze her. In the early days of their marriage, she and Dylan had spent many happy days here. She could picture them, lying on their backs, gazing up at a blue sky not unlike this one, and planning their future together. Dylan had talked of being a great detective, and she'd seen herself as head teacher of a school where the children came from good families and had been born with a thirst for knowledge.

Then Luke had come along and, of course, they'd brought him here. One of her strongest memories was of bringing him here to fly his kite. The day had been going so well until Luke let go of his kite and they watched, Luke in horror, as it flew high into the sky. He'd cried and cried, all the way home, for the loss of that bright red kite. They'd soon bought him another, of course, but it had never been the same.

She ambled around, enjoying the peace and watching people running, rollerblading, walking dogs, flying kites or, like her, simply enjoying the magic of the Heath. Perhaps, like she'd once done, they were mapping out the rest of their lives.

She felt more relaxed, and more able to cope with whatever the future decided to throw at her, when she made her way back to the car park.

Even the Morgan's gearbox seemed to be in a better mood.

She was less than two miles from home, sitting in a slow-moving line of traffic when, out of nowhere, came a dark grey car. It wasn't driving at speed. In fact, the whole incident seemed to take place in slow motion. Bev even had time to utter a pleading "No!"

It didn't help. The car, being reversed out of a tight parking spot, slammed into the side of the Morgan.

Later, she wondered if her nerves had been as soothed by her wonderful day as she'd thought because her first reaction was to burst into tears.

There was a tap on the window, then her door was opened.

"I am *so* sorry. Really sorry. Are you okay?"

Feeling like Luke when he lost his kite to the Heath's breeze all those years ago, she brushed furiously at her tears, no doubt rubbing her makeup into attractive streaks, and nodded. "I'm fine."

It had to be done. She climbed out and prayed that the damage to the Morgan wasn't noticeable. Oh, God. The dent was fairly small, but a long scratch drew the eye. No way would Dylan miss that.

"I'm sorry," the driver said again.

Car horns tooted behind them as drivers became irate at the delay.

"Look, I'll park up again. If you grab that space there—" He pointed two cars' lengths away. "Park there and we can sort this out. I'll give you my insurance details."

A furious blast on the horn from a taxi driver spurred Bev into action.

Only as she started the engine and moved off did she call herself all sorts of a fool. All the chap had to do was drive away. She was amazed that he didn't.

By the time she'd parked the Morgan, he was there to open the door for her. "Are you sure you're okay?" he asked. "You look so upset. I feel awful."

"I'm fine. It's just that it's my husband's car."

"Ah." She could see that he understood. "Well, it's not as bad as it looks. It is a lovely car, though, and worth a pretty penny, so I can understand your concerns."

He reached into his pocket, then noticed the coffee bar a few doors away. "Let me buy you a coffee. You look shaken, and a few minutes to relax will do you good. There's no point driving away in a state, is there? I'll feel awful. We can exchange insurance details over coffee."

"Okay. Thanks."

As she locked the Morgan and walked the short distance to the coffee bar, it struck her that the Morgan had been damaged by what was quite probably the most handsome man in London. His tall, beautiful body was encased in blue chinos and pale blue shirt. His eyes were also blue, and were framed by long, dark lashes that Bev would kill for. God, but he was gorgeous. If it hadn't been for the thought of explaining to Dylan that his pride and joy was looking more than a little sorry for itself, she might have enjoyed the prospect of a few minutes in this man's company.

The coffee bar was crowded, and they grabbed the only available seats. They had to share a table with a young mother and her child.

While they waited for the coffees to be brought over, he asked her three times if she was sure she was all right.

"My fault entirely," he said. "I was reversing when my phone rang. Instead of ignoring it as I should have, I tried to find it—it had fallen off the passenger seat.

I reached to get it and—" He threw up his hands in apology.

"It's fine," she said.

"No, it was totally irresponsible of me."

Their coffees arrived and, while they drank them, he asked her dozens of questions about her life. He was only making conversation and trying to take her mind off the stupid incident, she knew that, but he seemed interested in her answers, interested in her.

Half an hour flew by in what seemed like seconds.

"It's time I went home," she said.

"Me too. And once again, I'm sorry. Oh, wait—" He slapped his hand to his forehead and took a pen from his pocket. He searched his other pockets, then walked over to the counter and asked for paper. When he returned, he sat down again and wrote, in a very neat hand, his name, address and phone number, as well as the name, address and phone number of his insurance company.

Bev couldn't believe she'd been so wrapped up in his attention that she'd forgotten the need for insurance details. Feeling all kinds of a fool, she wrote out the same information for him.

"It's been a pleasure to meet you, Beverley Scott," he said. "I just wish it could have been in better circumstances. Are you sure you're all right to drive?"

"I'm fine. Really. And thanks for the coffee."

Bev was pleased to complete the rest of the journey without incident. Just as she drove into their road, her phone chirped into life. The display told her that Dylan was calling her. She couldn't answer it while driving so she ignored it.

Their house came into view—and her own car was parked on the driveway. Damn it. He was home.

She hadn't had a chance to switch off the engine before the front door opened and he strode out, his phone still in his hand.

His gaze went from her, to the dent in his beloved car, and back to her. Frowning, he opened the door for her. "Are you all right?"

"Fine." She grabbed her handbag and got out. "And it wasn't my fault."

He put a gentle finger to the dent, as if checking the depth. Then he stroked the long scratch.

"A chap drove into me. He was coming out of a parking space and I was in a long queue of traffic." She inspected the paintwork. "Sorry, love."

"It's nothing much. So long as you're okay, that's all that matters."

She stifled a snort of laughter. Had she not been ill, he would have hit the roof and treated her to one of his long and oft-repeated rants about how women should be banned from the bloody roads. "I've got his insurance details. We'll soon get it sorted."

"Good. So where have you been?" He followed her inside.

"Hampstead Heath," she said. "I've had a really great day—well, apart from the obvious. It makes such a change to have a day to myself that I thought I'd make the most of it."

"You said you were going with Mum and Freya."

"I know, but I changed my mind. I fancied a day to myself."

They sat and shared a coffee, Luke came home from school, and then Vicky and Freya came home.

Bev looked at her family, all chattering at once, and thought how much she loved them. It had been bliss to have a day to herself, but it was good to be surrounded by them all.

It was later, much later, when Bev remembered to give Dylan those insurance details.

"I'll sort it." He took the piece of paper from her and a look of blind fury crossed his face. At least, that was what she thought it was. It was gone so quickly that she wondered if she'd imagined it.

"What's wrong, Dylan? That's everything you need, isn't it?"

"Yes. Yes, it's fine. So tell me again exactly what happened."

She hadn't imagined it. Every muscle in his body was suddenly tense.

"I was sitting in a line of slow-moving cars," she said. "He was reversing out of a parking spot, a really tight one, to try to pull in behind me. But—he explained it to me afterwards—his phone rang. It had fallen into the passenger footwell. He reached across for it, lost concentration and hit the side of the Morgan."

He nodded as she spoke, almost as if he was trying to hurry along the story.

"He was really nice about it," she said. "He bought me a coffee. He said he wanted to make sure I was calm enough to drive home."

"Did he indeed?"

"Yes. That was nice of him, wasn't it? Is there something wrong?"

"No, nothing's wrong." He let out his breath. "Let's just hope that your nice Mr. Goodenough's insurance policy is up to date."

THIRTY-FOUR

"TO BE HONEST, Gerry, I'm bored with this. Hangman's a stupid game and you probably wouldn't guess my name if I give you *all* the letters. You wouldn't remember it anyway. You haven't spared me a thought over the years, have you?"

The stench in the cellar was unbearable thanks to Lowell's excrement. It was turning Jimmy's stomach.

"I've given you an *O*, a *D*, another *O*, an *R*—you're still no closer, are you?" Jimmy was feeling decidedly queasy. "I need some air."

He left Lowell in his own filth and walked up the stairs and out into the back yard. Several deep breaths began to clear the smell from his nostrils, and he started to feel a little better.

The main problem was that he'd grown tired of Lowell. He'd had fun with Brian Dowie, but Lowell was different. Whereas Dowie had been a snivelling wreck, Lowell was angry. Jimmy wasn't experiencing the same thrill or the same sense of power.

Later, he'd look at his plans for Scotland Yard, and that always excited him. Okay, so the building was filled with civilians and perhaps wouldn't make the point he'd intended, but it would still be big news. He could imagine the blanket coverage media crews from all over the world would give him when Scotland Yard was blown to smithereens.

Before he moved on to Scotland Yard, though, he had things to deal with. He needed to move faster. Tonight, he'd get rid of Lowell. He'd enjoy it, of course, but he was eager to move on.

It was strange but, at the time, he'd been a little disappointed with Mrs. Lowell too. Now, though, he got a thrill just by looking at the photos he'd taken. Being in her house, alone with her, had been one of the best experiences ever. Even now, he could smell the dust beneath her bed. He could smell her shampoo, the soap she'd used in the shower—

Police had no clues as to her killer's identity. They made noises about following several leads, but the truth was, they were clueless. The daughter was being cared for by relatives, so they said, but Jimmy wasn't interested in her.

He'd dispose of Lowell tonight, give the cellar a good wash with strong bleach, and get it nice and clean for his next victim. Meanwhile, he'd spend a few more minutes in the crisp fresh air.

His phone rang and, irritated, he took it from his pocket and glanced at the display. Carol.

He almost answered it so that he could tell her not to bother him, but there was no point. She knew that.

He pushed his phone back in his pocket. It beeped to let him know he had voicemail. He ignored that too. It beeped again.

He grabbed his phone and punched the buttons to hear exactly what piece of trivia she thought warranted his attention. That was half the problem between them these days. It would be a different story if he were still in Afghanistan. She wouldn't be able to bother him every five minutes then. Now that he was home, she had to discuss every detail of her life with him.

"Jimmy, it's Matt. He's had an accident on the football field at school. He's okay, but they think he might have broken his leg. I'm at the hospital. Call me when you pick this message up, will you?"

No, he damn well wouldn't. What was the point? He wasn't a surgeon. He couldn't mend a broken leg. If Jimmy were still fighting for Queen and country, he wouldn't be able to drop everything, would he?

Besides, what was a broken leg? Nothing. The injuries he'd seen—many of his comrades would have been happy to escape with only a broken leg.

He pushed all thoughts of his family from his mind and returned to the cellar.

"Tell you what, Gerry, I've had an idea. I have plans for you, but first, I'm going to indulge you. I'm going to show you my photos. Oh, don't worry, they're not the usual boring holiday snaps. You know the sort. 'That's me in front of the Taj Mahal, that's me chatting to the Greek waiter, that's me standing next to a pelican in Cyprus—' No, these are much better than that. You'll like them."

He'd printed out a dozen ten-by-eight-inch pictures. He took the stairs two at a time, grabbed the folder, and returned to sit in front of Lowell. He was too close to the human pile of excrement, but he'd have to put up with that.

"Here—" He held out a photo of himself standing in Lowell's kitchen. "Thinking about it, I suppose they are a bit like holiday snaps. Here I am standing in your kitchen." The idea made him chuckle. "Here's another. This is your dead dog."

He saved the best till last.

"What about this one? This is your wife—she drowned."

Jimmy could hardly hear his own voice over the noises coming from behind Lowell's gag. He was making all sorts of strange, angry protests.

"I didn't touch her," Jimmy said. "Well, I touched her, obviously. To be honest, Gerry, I've had better shags. She wasn't responsive. A bit skinny too. Classy, I'll give you that, but a bit thin for my taste. But I didn't use a knife on her or anything like that. No, after I'd had sex with her, I drowned her. I made it easy for her."

Jimmy wasn't sure if Lowell protested so much that he fell forward or whether the man gave in and pushed himself forward so that the noose tightened around his neck.

Of course, Jimmy could easily have saved him. All he had to do was drag Lowell upright again.

What was the point, though?

Jimmy watched, fascinated, as Lowell drew his final breath. It hadn't taken as long as Jimmy had expected. It was a neat, clean and fairly quick job.

"Thanks, Gerry. You've saved me a lot of work."

All Jimmy had to do now was wait for his nosy neighbour to take his dog for a walk. Then he could fire up the chainsaw.

THIRTY-FIVE

"LET'S GO TO the Heath," Bev said.

"Okay." Dylan edged his way to the inside lane of traffic and took a left turn. "It's a nice day for it."

A nice day for it? What sort of moron would say such a ridiculous thing? The sun was shining from a cloudless blue sky and the spring air was warm, but it was a shit day for anything. Especially a discussion about Bev's health.

They'd left the clinic in silence and Dylan had driven them halfway home without saying a word. The words to convey his feelings simply didn't exist.

"Do you remember the day Luke lost his kite?" Bev asked, and she was smiling.

"Yeah." He tried to return the smile but had no idea if he was successful or not.

"We've had some lovely days there, haven't we?"

"Yeah." Days when the future was all theirs. Days when the biggest problem they'd had to face was finding enough money to pay the mortgage. Days when they'd fought like tigers, then kissed and made up in the best way possible. Days when they'd assumed they'd muddle on through life until old age came to meet them.

Now, halfway to old age, life was shit. Complete and utter shit.

They drove on to Hampstead Heath in silence and, when they got out of the car, Dylan was relieved when his phone rang. He needed to talk to anyone about anything. Anyone but Bev. Anything but the hateful c-word.

"Pikey, how are you doing?"

"I'm in excellent spirits, mate, and I have some good news for you."

"Oh?"

"Yep. You won't believe this but our favourite drug dealer, Max Rickman, is no more. He's deceased. As dead as the wonderful old dodo."

"Dead?" It took several moments for Pikey's words to sink in. "How? What happened?"

"A massive heart attack."

"No way. I've never heard such bollocks."

"I said you wouldn't believe me. It's true, though."

"No. Someone's made it look like that. Someone close to Lenny King."

"I'm not so sure, Dylan. He's had a couple of minor ones in the past year. He's a heavy smoker too."

"I know, but—no, never in a million years."

"Either way, that's the official verdict."

Dylan hadn't told Pikey about the conversation he'd heard between King and Mrs. Rickman. He hadn't told anyone. He hadn't imagined it, though. Somehow, and God alone knew how, King had managed to get the deed done *and* make it look like a heart attack.

"Just accept that it's good news," Pikey said. "I always feel like celebrating when a piece of scum like Rickman shuffles off this mortal coil."

"Me too."

"Anyway, I thought you'd want to know."

"Thanks, Pikey. If you hear anything more, let me know."

"Will do. So what are you up to at the moment?"

He looked at Bev. She was waiting patiently for him to end his call. Her foot was tracing circles on the pavement. "Oh, not a lot. I'll call you later."

Dylan ended the call, switched off his phone and tucked Bev's arm through his. "Where to?"

"Let's walk for a minute or two."

The silence persisted as they walked. What was there to say? Dylan had pinned all his hopes on one of the best cancer experts in the country. Now, with those hopes dashed, he felt adrift. There seemed nothing tying him to the real world. He didn't want anything to do with the real world.

"Let's sit here," Bev said, and he felt his stomach execute a sickening backflip.

They sat, watching the world go by, for a couple of minutes.

"It wasn't all bad news," Bev said.

But it was. There hadn't been the thinnest shred of good news.

"As he said, I could have months yet. Even years."

"I know. And with the treatment—"

"I'm not so sure about the treatment, Dylan."

"What?" He stared at her, convinced he must have misheard. "But of course you are. He said it could prolong—"

"I need to think over what he said. Yes, those drugs might give me a few more months. They might also have me wandering around like a zombie. I don't want the kids to remember me like that. Or you, for that matter."

She slipped her arm through his and rested her head on his shoulder. "Can you imagine how awful it would be for the kids if they had to watch their mother die a long, slow, lingering death in front of them? Yes, I might survive a little longer, but at what price? I want to live, Dylan. I don't want to merely survive."

"You don't know that the drugs would do that to you, for God's sake. They could add years to your life. Surely, that's what you want."

"Not if I'm going to be too ill to be of any use."

Dylan refused to listen to this. "We're seeing him again next week so we'll wait to hear what he says about it. I'm sure he'll make you see sense."

"I need time to mull it over."

She wasn't thinking straight, and Dylan couldn't blame her. She'd soon realise that the treatment on offer could make a huge difference to her life. Not to have the drugs—well, it was unthinkable. It would be a slap in the face for him and the kids. It would feel as if she didn't care about them.

"We'll see what he says." His voice was clipped, but he couldn't help it.

"We will. But I'm fairly certain I won't be taking those drugs."

"For Christ's sake, Bev, that would be crazy. Surely, you'll want to do everything in your power to stay with us."

"Yes, but not at any price. I'll give it some thought, and we'll see what he says at the next appointment."

He wished his mother was with them if only to try to make Bev see reason. Bev, however, had decided that just the two of them should see the specialist. His mother, always willing to go along with whatever Bev wanted, had announced she had plans anyway and wouldn't be able to accompany them.

"Come on." Bev tugged on his arm. "You can buy me an ice cream."

Carry on as if everything were normal? Pretend this hell wasn't happening?

Sometimes, it was easy to do that. Bev was young and clever, funny and witty. She loved her teaching work, she loved him and the kids, she loved going out with her mates and getting drunk. It seemed unthinkable that she could be so ill…

"Okay." Dylan held his tongue. He'd make sure the specialist drilled some sense into her, though.

Meanwhile, he'd buy his wife an ice cream and hope and pray for one hell of a spectacular miracle.

THIRTY-SIX

"SERGEANT PIKE, MAY I have a quick word?"

"It'll have to be very quick, er—" Pikey smiled encouragement to the new constable whose name he'd already forgotten.

"Joanna Fry," she said. "Everyone calls me Jo."

"Keith Pike. Everyone calls me Pikey. Except my wife. She calls me Keith when she's in a good mood, but she'll be calling me all sorts of unrepeatable things if I don't get home PDQ."

"I understand. It's just that I have the list of names you wanted. People seen with Max Rickman over the last couple of weeks."

"Yeah? Jo, you're a star."

Beaming, she handed him a single sheet of paper. "His wife's on the list, and a chap called Browne, that's his lawyer, but other than that—sorry, it's just other inmates."

"That's brilliant. Thanks."

"Are you thinking there are suspicious circumstances surrounding his death?" She looked so hopeful that Pikey laughed.

"No, it's just something someone said. But no, he had a dodgy heart that was sure to give up sooner or later. Thanks for this, though." He folded the paper and shoved it in his pocket. "And now I need to get home or my life won't be worth living."

He was stopped twice more before he managed to exit the building, but then he was driving home. It was only a little after eight o'clock so Sheila wouldn't give him too much grief. She'd remind him a few times that this was her birthday treat, her three-week-overdue birthday treat, but it would be fine.

He strode inside, apology for his lateness on his lips, and thought at first that the house was empty. Every light was on, but there was no sign of anyone.

"Sheila?" He stood at the bottom of the stairs and shouted. "Laura? Kay? Anyone?"

He was halfway up the stairs when Laura emerged from her bedroom, pulling out earplugs and wrapping them round her phone as she did so. "Oh, hi, Dad. I didn't hear you come in." She gave him a high five. "Got to dash. I'll see you later."

"Hang on a minute. Where's your mum? Or your sister?"

"Kay—" The way she said her sister's name was enough to tell Pikey that his daughters were at loggerheads. That was the norm, these days. They fought just for the hell of it. "Kay is out bowling with—wait for it—Lennon Court."

"Lennon. Isn't he the one you—?"

"Oh, Dad. Puh-lease." She tossed back long, dark hair. "She's welcome to him. They make a great pair, I'm sure."

"Right." There was no point arguing but he felt sure Laura had fancied her chances with Lennon. "So where's your mum?"

"You expect her to tell me where she's going?"

There was another toss of her head before she frowned and added grudgingly, "She did mention something. She was going somewhere, can't remember where, but it was close to Bev's so she's probably still there. You know what those two are like when they get together. Hey, I thought you two were going out tonight."

"We are. We're eating out at the new Italian place. It's a late birthday treat for your mum."

"That sounds like fun. Not. The place will be heaving with geriatrics." She reached up to give him a peck on the cheek. "Enjoy. I'll see you later, Dad. Or in the morning."

"What about you? Where are you dashing off to?"

"All the way to Chloe's." She grinned up at him. "Do you want to see me safely across the road?"

"Get out of here!"

She gave a burst of laughter and raced off. Pikey stood at the window and watched her cross the road and run past three houses to Chloe's. Just as Chloe's dad opened the door to her, Laura turned and waved. Pikey had to smile as he waved back.

That was the trouble with kids. One minute they were the cutest things that ever lived, little beauties who hung on your every word, and the next minute they thought they had the answer to life, the universe and every other damn thing.

He switched off several lights—Laura must have grown tired of saving the planet—and was about to go upstairs for a shower when Sheila walked in. She threw a bag on the table in the hall and looked at him as if she'd never seen him before.

"Sheila? What's wrong?" His mind raced with a

dozen possibilities, all of them connected to the crackpot who was threatening Dylan.

"I need a cigarette." She took a breath, strode to the kitchen and pulled open the cupboard door to reveal her not-so-secret stash of tobacco. "When did you last speak to Dylan?"

"Sorry? Well, this morning. Why?"

"And what did he say about Bev?" She opened the back door, lit her cigarette and inhaled deeply. "Seriously, what has he said about Bev?"

"Nothing. He hasn't mentioned her, I haven't asked—why?"

She rounded on him. "So you didn't know her cancer had spread?"

"Oh, no." He hadn't known, and he couldn't believe it. God, poor Bev. Poor Dylan too. "No, of course I didn't know. I would have told you. When did they find out?"

She took a deep pull on her cigarette. "When was the last time he mentioned Bev's cancer?"

"Ages ago." Pikey couldn't remember. "Probably before she had her hysterectomy. It's not the sort of thing you discuss, is it?"

She took another pull on her cigarette before flicking it into the dark night. The brief red glow died as it hit damp grass with a sizzle.

"God, Keith." She closed the door on the night air and slipped her arms round his waist. "They've told her there's nothing they can do."

"What?"

"I know. I can't take it in."

"Who's told them? That's absurd. She's so young."

"They saw another specialist this morning. A private one. Dylan thought—hoped—" She took a breath that turned into a sob. "There's nothing anyone can do."

Pikey couldn't believe it. Dylan had said nothing. Not a word.

"I knew she had chemo lined up," Sheila said, "but I thought that was more a precaution than anything else. I thought it was just to zap any nasty cells left around after the operation. I had no idea."

"Me neither."

"But I don't think they did either. And I suppose we shouldn't be surprised that Dylan hasn't said anything. According to Bev, he's pretending it isn't happening."

Pikey could understand that. He'd probably feel the same. "How is she?"

"Pissed off with Dylan."

"No change there then."

She smiled. "Apparently, apart from pretending it isn't happening, he's fussing around her constantly. She says he won't leave the house unless he knows someone's with her. It's driving her mad."

"Well, that's—"

"So unlike Dylan it's laughable," she said.

He'd been about to say "understandable," but Sheila was right. It was unlike Dylan to treat Bev like an invalid. In normal circumstances, he wouldn't, but these circumstances weren't normal. Pikey wasn't mentioning death threats to Sheila, though.

"I don't know what to say." He was at a complete loss. "To you or to Dylan," he added.

"There's nothing we can say, is there? That's the worst of it. Everyone's so helpless."

He hadn't realised he'd been holding his breath and he let it out on a long sigh.

"You could have a word with Dylan, though," she said. "He'll take notice of you, love. Tell him to give Bev some space. Really, he's doing her head in right now. It's making her feel worse about everything. Will you do that? Will you talk to him?"

"I'll try, but you know what he's like. Once he's made up his mind…" He let the sentence trail away. No way could he tell Dylan to give Bev some space, not when there was a nutter on the loose. Pikey didn't think there was any real reason for concern simply because, when people wanted you dead, they killed you. It was only when scare merchants were at work that you received crank phone calls and photos. All the same, there was no point taking unnecessary risks.

"Thanks, love." She gave him a quick squeeze, then pulled back to look at him. "I'm not really in the mood to go out. Are you?"

He was too shocked to know how he felt. "Not really, no." On the other hand, worrying about Bev and Dylan would help no one. "I'm not in the mood for staying in and moping either. Let's go out. The table's booked and we need to eat. And anyway, who's to say that nothing can be done? Surely, there's always something. More chemo. More radiotherapy. Another operation. Miracles happen every day in hospitals."

"Of course they do," she said. "That's what I told Bev. I mean, she's so young. And so fit."

"Exactly. Come on, we'll go out. We'll raise a glass to Bev's health and hope for some better news soon."

Sheila gave a small smile at that. "Knowing Bev, she'd insist we raise more than one."

THIRTY-SEVEN

BEV ALWAYS LIKED hospital appointments as early in the morning as possible. Until it came to keeping those appointments. She'd felt like death this morning.

Still, it was over now, and she walked out of the hospital and into surprisingly warm sunshine. Frank had driven her here and suggested she meet him in the gardens.

Sure enough, he was sitting on a bench watching everyone with that calm, assessing gaze of his. She wondered if it were a case of once a copper, always a copper. Dylan watched people in exactly the same way.

"Hi," she said, sitting on the bench beside him.

"Everything okay?" he asked.

"Fine. What are you doing? Watching the grass grow?"

"Making the most of this sunshine. It was monsoon-like when I left Lancashire."

"I'm glad you're back." It meant Dylan didn't fuss quite so much.

He looked at her long and hard, as if he expected to see cracks appear. "You sure you're okay?"

"I'm good. Who wants to grow old anyway? The only advantage I ever saw in that was being able to drive people mad by pretending to be deaf. And gathering a collection of decrepit cardigans."

"And smelling of wee."

She snorted with laughter. "You see? The advantages are few and far between."

They sobered as a couple, probably in their fifties, walked past. The woman was inconsolable. She had her head buried against the man's shoulder as they walked, and her sobs were heartbreaking.

Bev guessed the woman had received the same news she had, and she wished she could take her by the hand and reassure her. She could tell her that the shock, the sadness, the terror, the anger and the grief would pass in time. She could tell her that, gradually, a peaceful acceptance would take over.

Bev remembered the doctor telling her something similar. He'd tried to convince her that the mind and body came to a state of acceptance. She hadn't believed him at the time. In fact, she'd told him to fuck off.

"It's not death that bothers me," she said. "That's the easy part. It's the preliminaries that are a tad of a worry."

He nodded his understanding.

"What I dread is being a dribbling vegetable, wetting the bed or worse." She shuddered and pushed the thought away. It wasn't going to be that way. She'd make sure of that. "But at least I get to say goodbye to people, to put my affairs in order, and make my wishes known. There will be no arguments about my funeral because I've written out a list of things I want. There will be a strict dress code for a start. No one, but no one, will be allowed to attend my funeral dressed in black."

"I'll bear it in mind."

"Do that, Frank. I want it to be a celebration of my

life." Bev was adamant on that score. Life had treated her well—a great childhood, a fun time at university where she'd met lifelong friends, a rewarding job, and marriage to a man she still loved with a passion. A man who'd given her the most precious gifts of all, two wonderful children. "I want the best party ever!"

She'd had a good life and she intended to make sure she had a damn good death too. Her life. Her death. That seemed fair.

She hadn't told Dylan yet, mainly because he wasn't ready to hear it, but she'd become a paid-up member of DIGNITAS. As such, and being of sound mind, and having the mobility to self-administer a drug, she could obtain an accompanied suicide in Switzerland.

She might not need it. Many people who contacted DIGNITAS died peacefully in their own homes. It would be there as a safeguard, though. If things got too bad, too unbearable, it would be there. She would go to Switzerland, swallow a lethal barbiturate, fall asleep within a few minutes and drift quietly into death. That was the way to go. It was her chosen way to go.

"Can we do a detour on the way home, Frank?"

"Of course. Where to?"

"There's a shop—"

"Not more cushions."

"No! You've been talking to Dylan too much." She slipped her arm through his as they left the hospital's gardens. "There's a coat I'm going to buy. A fabulous velvet coat. Purple velvet. It's ridiculously expensive, and probably too outrageous for me to wear, but do you know what? I don't give a damn. That coat's mine…"

THIRTY-EIGHT

DYLAN'S FIRST CALL of the morning was at Good-enough's flat and he was more than ready to kill the bastard.

Frank had returned, thank God, meaning Dylan could safely leave Bev's side. Although given her state of mind, she'd probably welcome the odd homicidal maniac in her life. But with Frank looking out for the nutters, Dylan could get back to work. He'd warned Frank that Bev was tired of people fussing around her and had started lying about where she was going and what she was doing. If she hadn't said she was going with his mother to visit friends, Dylan wouldn't have left her alone, and that bastard Goodenough wouldn't have got close to her.

Dylan had called his motor insurance company and told them about the "accident." Unsurprisingly, they hadn't yet been able to trace Goodenough's details. The bloke didn't pay rent, he changed his name as often as most men changed their shirts so why in hell's name would he bother with such incidentals as car insurance?

Dylan hammered on the door to Goodenough's flat and was surprised when the door swung open.

"Yes?" The woman looking at him was probably early sixties—definitely not Goodenough's type—and she had a clipboard in her hand. Looking past her and into the flat, he saw an empty room. The furniture had gone and the walls were bare.

"I'm looking for Brad Goodenough. Chesney Marshall." Dylan felt as if he'd come to the wrong address.

"He's left, I'm afraid. Can I help? I'm the owner of this apartment."

"Left?"

"Yesterday." She nodded.

"That was a bit sudden, wasn't it?"

"Very. He called at my place, paid the rent up to date, returned the keys and left."

Dylan had an even stronger feeling of turning up at the wrong place. If there was one thing Goodenough didn't do, it was pay rent he owed.

"Any idea where he's gone?"

"Not really, no. He's flying to Barcelona, today I think, but that's probably just for a holiday. I only know that because I saw his flight ticket."

"You don't have a forwarding address for him?"

"Sorry. I did ask about his mail, but he said there wouldn't be anything important."

Well, there was a surprise. Not.

Damn it. Dylan had been looking forward to re-arranging Goodenough's face. Still, Barcelona was a decent distance away. If indeed he was going to Barcelona and not just brandishing flight tickets as a front.

"What about his car? Have you any idea what happened to that?"

"Sorry. I didn't even know he owned one."

He probably didn't. Dylan had seen him driving a grey Alfa Romeo which had been hired for two days. The car that Goodenough had conveniently driven into the side of the Morgan had been a grey BMW.

Bev swore she'd written down the registration number correctly, but when Dylan had checked it out, that particular number belonged to a Suzuki that had been scrapped six months ago. When questioned further, Bev admitted that Goodenough had recited the number while they'd been drinking coffee and she'd made a note of it without checking.

As he walked away from the building, despair settled around him. A great investigator he was when he couldn't even keep track of Goodenough's movements.

There was no need to panic yet, though. Frank would be keeping an extra close eye on Bev and the kids, and Dylan could look after himself. They weren't in danger.

He jumped in the Morgan and drove to Cass Pelham's shop. Again, he wasn't expecting her to be on the premises and again, he was proved wrong. This time, though, she wasn't alone. She pulled on a jacket and picked up a light tan leather handbag.

Her assistant approached Dylan with a beaming smile in place. "May I help you, sir?"

"Actually—" he nodded at Cass Pelham who was heading for the door. "I wanted a quick word with Miss Pelham."

Cass stopped to look at him and Dylan could see her trying to remember where they'd met before.

"I came in for a present for my wife. It was our wedding anniversary and you very kindly gave me a silk scarf."

A smile broke out, although she looked exhausted. Dark smudges surrounded eyes that were red and looked as if they'd spent several hours crying.

"Of course I remember. You'd had problems with

your in-laws and have been living happily ever after. Did your wife like the scarf?"

"She was thrilled with it." It was still in Dylan's car because he'd forgotten all about it. "I was passing so I thought I'd call in to thank you in person."

"I'm so pleased. Thanks for taking the time to call in." She tried to give him a smile. "Sorry, but I'm in a rush. I need to visit my father."

"Ah yes, how is he?" Dylan walked to the door and held it open for her. "You said he'd had a stroke, if I remember."

"Yes." They stepped onto the pavement. "Actually, there have been complications. But he's a fighter. I'm sure he'll be okay."

So that was why she looked as if she hadn't slept. "I hope so."

"Thanks. I worry about him, that's all. But I'm sure he'll be fine." That seemed to be her mantra. "And life's not all bad. At least I have Brad. He's moved in with me—until my father's stronger."

So much for Barcelona. "That's good then."

A taxi came into view and she waved frantically until it slowed to a stop. "Goodbye. And thanks for taking the time to call in."

Dylan held the door open until she was inside and heard her ask the driver to take her to the hospital. The taxi pulled away and Dylan returned to his car.

He'd watched Cass's address when working for her father and he decided another trip to Kensington was in order.

It would be quicker to take the Tube, but Dylan couldn't be bothered and the journey didn't take as long as he feared. He was soon parked as near as he could get to the Georgian house behind Kensington High Street. An attractive house, it even had wisteria climbing over its walls. It suited Cass's personality.

He sat in his car and tried to decide on his next move. The house was no doubt alarmed to the hilt so he couldn't break in. He'd have to ring the bell and see what happened. If anything.

He was about to get out of the Morgan and do just that when the door opened and Brad Goodenough emerged carrying two suitcases. He stood them by the door as he locked the property, then he turned and strode briskly away with a case in each hand.

Just as Dylan thought he'd been spotted, Goodenough crossed the road. Then Dylan saw a grey BMW with the registration plates bearing the number Bev had given him.

He watched as Goodenough threw the cases on the back seat.

Dylan left the Morgan and ran across the road. He grabbed Goodenough as the bloke was about to get in the BMW.

"What the—? Oh, it's you again. It's a small world, isn't it?"

"Two small for both of us."

"I'm sorry about your car, but—"

"Oh, please. Don't tell me it was an accident."

"It was exactly that. I did have a small chuckle to myself when I realised it was *your* car, driven by *your* wife, but yes, it was an accident. Nothing more."

"And I suppose you'll be more than happy to tell that to the insurance company and the police."

"Of course. I gather there's some confusion with

the insurance company, but I'll sort that. It was an accident. I apologise, okay?"

"No, it's not okay. It was no accident that had you standing outside my office, it was no accident that saw you drive into my car, and it was no sodding accident that once I exposed you to Pelham for the shit you are, I started receiving death threats."

Goodenough looked impressively shocked. "What the hell are you talking about?"

"I'll explain later. Meanwhile, you and I are taking a little trip. To the nearest police station."

Goodenough jerked back suddenly and delivered a vicious kick that had Dylan staggering into the road and risking death.

Goodenough was quick, too bloody quick, and by the time Dylan had recovered enough to drag in a lungful of air, the BMW had burst into life. Dylan staggered toward it, but it roared down the road.

Shit, shit and shit.

Dylan ran back to the Morgan, which was facing the wrong way, and executed a U-turn that had an orchestra of car horns blasting out. He put up an apologetic hand to the driver behind him and concentrated on catching Goodenough.

He thought he'd lost him but when he was level with the Underground station, he spotted the BMW at the lights. There were only half a dozen cars separating them at the moment.

They turned left onto Earl's Court Road and when Dylan saw the signs for Heathrow Airport, he wondered if Goodenough was taking a trip to Barcelona after all.

They joined the M4 where, for once, traffic was

moving freely. Goodenough was making the most of this rare phenomenon by ignoring all speed limits. Either he didn't know about the speed cameras or he didn't care.

Dylan managed to gain on him, thanks to some lucky gaps in the traffic, so that there were now only three vehicles between him and Goodenough.

Traffic slowed a little as they approached Heston Services. Dylan wondered if he should pull off the motorway for fuel. The Morgan's gauge was worryingly close to empty. If he did that, he risked losing Goodenough. If he didn't, he risked being stranded on the hard shoulder.

His head told him to stop for fuel. After all, there was nothing to worry about where Goodenough was concerned. He was a coward, one who liked to scare people who crossed him, but Dylan didn't believe he was a killer. Rickman, yes. If that crazy bastard had taken a dislike to you, you were dead. No argument. But there was little to fear from Goodenough.

Dylan's head told him all this, but his heart chose to ignore everything and risk being stranded on the hard shoulder.

Traffic slowed to around forty miles an hour and Goodenough snaked across to the inside lane and veered onto the slip road to make up more ground. He put his foot down just as a truck left the service station and obscured Dylan's view—

All hell broke loose.

Drivers slammed on their brakes, hazard warning lights flashed and car horns sounded. Glass smashed and metal crumpled.

Dylan had a split second to swerve to avoid the car

in front, but the driver following him didn't react as quickly and Dylan was slammed forward in his seat as a small Nissan ploughed into the back of the Morgan.

After the carnage, there was an eerie silence.

When he was certain that all vehicles were stationary, Dylan got out of the Morgan and ran back to check on the driver of the car that was currently attached to the rear of the Morgan.

"Are you hurt?"

"I—I don't think so." The elderly woman was badly shaken. "I don't know what happened. It was all so fast."

They both looked up as police sirens were heard. A couple of patrol cars must have been based at the service station and they switched on flashing blue lights to accompany the sirens.

Dylan was itching to see if his assumption that Goodenough had caused the pile-up was correct, but he didn't feel able to leave the old lady on her own. Although she was speaking normally, her eyes looked a little too glazed for his liking. She was probably in shock.

Ambulances were on the scene amazingly quickly and paramedics were soon going from car to car to inspect the wounded.

As soon as he was able, Dylan left the elderly lady with a capable looking young paramedic and ran through twisted wreckage to where Goodenough's car, now missing its roof, was jammed beneath the truck.

He couldn't get close because police were keeping people back. Paramedics were having to hang back, too, which probably meant they were waiting for fire crews with cutting gear.

If Goodenough had survived the impact, Dylan would start to believe in miracles.

THIRTY-NINE

DYLAN'S LUNCH WAS SPECTACULAR. He'd hardly eaten yesterday because he'd been stuck on the motorway, so today he'd dived into a bar offering "home-cooked pub grub" and ordered steak and ale pie with mash. And it was spectacular. There was no other word for it.

He had a pint to go with it. Sadly, as he was driving, he had to refrain from ordering a second.

He refused to feel guilty about Goodenough. Maybe he'd seen the Morgan in his rear-view mirror and maybe he hadn't. It had been his choice to take a short cut on the motorway, though. His choice to break all motoring laws and smash into a truck. His choice to assault Dylan and make a run for it in the first place.

Dylan was idly glancing through his newspaper, his empty glass in front of him, when Pikey rang.

"We still don't have an ID for your Mr. Goodenough," Pikey said, "but I can tell you that he was flying to Barcelona under the name of Andrew Bowson. That's not his real name either, by the way. Not only that, he was taking a lot more than your usual shorts and sun cream with him. In the bottom of one of his suitcases was a very nice stash of jewellery."

Dylan groaned. "Let me guess, jewellery that belonged to Cass Pelham."

"Got it in one. She usually kept it at the bank but

she'd brought it home to get it valued. It was in the safe, of course, but Goodenough had seen her lock it."

"That seems odd, though, Pikey. He'd moved in with her. He would soon have copped for a lot more than a few bracelets."

"Yeah, but these few bracelets were insured for a cool five million. One pendant thing alone was worth over a quarter of a million apparently."

"So he decided to cut his losses, grab a few million pounds' worth of jewels and hide out in Barcelona for a bit?"

"It seems like it. If he'd driven more carefully, he might have made it too."

If he'd driven more carefully, Dylan would have stopped him boarding any plane.

"Two hours it took them to cut him out of his car," Pikey said.

"I know. I was stuck on the motorway for the duration."

Police had needed witness statements, and then Dylan had faced the task of getting his car towed away. This morning had been spent listening to a long list of work needed on his poor Morgan and arranging a hire car for the couple of weeks the work was expected to take.

"There's a suggestion he was ex-army so we'll soon have an ID for him," Pikey said. "As soon as I hear, I'll give you a bell."

"Thanks. Not that it matters too much. He's dead, that's good enough for me."

"Ha-ha. Very droll."

"The gods appear to be smiling on me," Dylan said. "First Rickman's murdered—"

"Has a heart attack."

"Yeah, yeah. Then Goodenough drives his car under a truck. I might have another pint to celebrate the fact that I won't be getting any more death threats."

"You do that. Oh, and if Sheila asks, I've had a word with you, okay? Don't forget."

"I won't. You'll get lots of brownie points, mate, because I can give Bev all the space she needs now…"

Given that he'd eaten a huge meal, Dylan reckoned he could pass a breathalyser test on two pints. He'd risk it.

With his glass full, he tried to get back to his newspaper but it didn't hold his interest. His mind was too busy on other things.

Goodenough was dead.

So why the hell couldn't he relax? Goodenough had been standing outside his office checking out the building, right? No way had he been looking for the travel agent that used to operate from the building. Driving his car into the Morgan—no way could that have been an accident. Of all the cars in London—no, that was taking coincidence to a whole new level. There could be no doubt that Goodenough had been out to scare him. It had worked too, damn it.

Goodenough had been pissed off enough when Dylan put the proverbial spanner in his future plans to play games with him. Payback time. Yes, Goodenough had been responsible for those stupid phone calls and photos. There could be no other explanation.

It was over.

When he left the pub, he returned to his hire car and drove halfway home. Then, on an impulse, he turned the car around and drove to Sarah Rickman's home.

She opened the door to him immediately and, although she was dressed in black as befitted a grieving widow, she hadn't worked too hard on the heartbroken part.

"Hello, Bill. You've heard about Max then. Come in."

Dylan followed her wheelchair into the sitting room. All was neat and orderly. Two empty coffee mugs sat on the table.

"Yes, I heard." He sat down without waiting to be invited. It seemed more polite given that she had no option but to sit. "What's the real story, Sarah? I heard it was a heart attack but we both know that's not right."

"What do you mean?" She didn't give him chance to respond. "It's been on the cards for a while, I'm afraid. There was talk of him having a heart bypass operation not so long ago, but Max wasn't keen. He was a brave man, frightened of no one, but he didn't like the thought of surgery. The doctors told him it was only a matter of time unless he gave up the cigarettes." She reached into her skirt pocket and pulled out a tissue. "And now he's gone." She gave a theatrical sniff.

"So it would seem. And you have no idea who got to him?"

"No one got to him, Bill. He's been ill for years."

"What does Lenny think about it?"

"Lenny? Leonard King? I don't know what—"

"Come on, Sarah. Stop messing around." Dylan stood and strode to the door. "Lenny? You can come out now."

If Sarah Rickman hadn't started shouting hysterically at Dylan, King might have stayed put. As it was, he dashed down the stairs like a knight in shining armour to protect his woman from danger.

"You?" He frowned at Dylan. "What do you want? How did you know I was here?"

The coffee mugs had given him a clue. "It's a long story, Lenny. How about you tell me how you got to poor old Max."

"I've already told you." Sarah didn't give King the chance to respond. "He'd had heart problems for years and it simply gave out. Why, only a fortnight ago I told my lawyer that I was worried about Max's health and wondered how we could persuade him to have the operation."

"For the sake of convenience," Dylan said, "we'll assume that the lawyer in question is your old childhood friend Phil Browne. Yes? And we'll assume that he helped to get the deed done. Yes?"

"How did you know I was here?" King asked again.

"Just a stab in the dark, Lenny. So how did you get to Max? I suppose Phil Browne has a few friends on the inside. Friends that have a reduced sentence thanks to having him as their defence lawyer. How much did it cost? A pretty penny, I'll bet. Although, I don't suppose Max was too popular, was he? Perhaps people were queuing up to put something in his food. It was a neat job, I'll give you that."

"Exactly what are you suggesting?" Sarah demanded.

"I'm suggesting that the two of you, with Phil Browne's help, had Max murdered."

"Rubbish," King said.

"I think it's time you left, Mr. Williams. How dare you come into my home—into Max's home—?"

"I'm only surprised it took you so long," Dylan said. "Of course, with you inside, Lenny, and you playing the lonely wife, Sarah—"

"Get out!" Sarah was frantically circling in her wheelchair.

"And, of course, it must have taken a lot of planning," Dylan said. "After all, Max had warned you, hadn't he? He'd made—what shall we say?—contingency plans. If anything happened to him, or if he was involved in an accident, his men would have killed you both."

"Get out!"

"You're no writer, are you?" King said. "Who the fuck are you?"

"Is that how you ended up in your wheelchair, Sarah?" Dylan asked. "Did he find out about your affair with Lenny? Did you tell him you were leaving him? Did he decide that what was his stayed his?"

He could see from her shocked expression that he'd painted an accurate picture.

"Are you the filth?" King asked.

"Me? Good God, no. Do I look like a copper?" Dylan laughed that off. "Let's just say I have a vested interest in this case. So tell me, now that you've done away with Max, what do you intend to do?"

"We haven't done away with Max, for fuck's sake," King said. "And where we're going now is none of your fucking business."

"What about the night of your arrest, Lenny?" Max asked. "Exactly who did set you up?"

"You know—"

"I know it wasn't your ex-wife and I know those coppers weren't involved. So who was it?"

"How would we know?" Sarah asked. "All I can tell you is what I heard. The same as I told our lawyer, the same as I told Max—I heard that it was Wendy and those coppers. Maybe one of them, maybe both." She was shaking as she spoke.

"Oh, you can do better than that, Sarah. I think you know exactly what happened that night."

"All I can tell you is what I've heard." She took a breath. "Look, me and Lenny have wanted to be together for bloody years. That's not a crime, is it?"

"Not yet."

"I would have stayed with Max—I take my marriage vows seriously. I won't pretend to be sorry that he's dead, but that's not a crime either. And yes, me and Lenny are going to be together. And that's it. There's nothing else for you to know."

"Those coppers had nothing to do with it, did they?" Dylan said.

"Maybe. Maybe not." King shrugged.

They knew. They both knew the truth behind that arrest all those years ago.

They'd both keep quiet too.

"I thought it odd that those coppers were involved," Dylan said. "I've done some checking up on them and they seem straight. Neither of them are living the high life." To put it mildly.

"It doesn't matter," Sarah said. "It's over. Maybe it was Wendy, maybe not. Maybe those coppers were involved, maybe not. Lenny's done his time, Max is gone—it's over."

"You couldn't have known about Sarah's so-called accident, Lenny. Well, you'd have known she'd been hit by a car and was in hospital, but you couldn't have known Max was driving that car. If you had, you wouldn't have gone round to his little factory to talk about a driving job. There was no job, was there? Max was out for revenge."

"I have no idea what you're talking about," Sarah said. "Anyway, what does it matter now? It's over."

She knew, all right. They both did. They weren't planning on talking, though, and Dylan supposed he couldn't blame them.

As he left the house, with the happy couple still protesting their innocence, he echoed Sarah Rickman's words. *It's over*.

Rickman was dead. He'd been murdered, Dylan would stake his life on that, but it was a job for the police, not him. He didn't care one way or the other.

King knew the truth about the night of his arrest so he wouldn't waste his time threatening coppers. No, he'd be too busy taking care of the woman in his life.

Goodenough was dead too, and although Dylan felt sorry for Cass Pelham, he knew she was better off without him. She'd get over him and find someone who was more interested in her than her bank balance.

There were many secrets being buried and many lies being told, but none of it mattered to Dylan. He could relax. It was over.

FORTY

FRANK SLAPPED DYLAN on the back. "You can get back to real work now."

"Thank God for that. I need to do work that stands a chance of paying a few bills." He needed to concentrate on Bev too. They'd see another specialist.

"This could be mine." Frank nodded at the train trundling up to the platform.

"Looks like it. Thanks for coming down, Frank. I appreciate it. Bev's enjoyed having you around too."

"Any time. It's been a nice cushy break for me. Think of me next week trying to knock my neglected garden back into shape."

"Yeah, well, take it easy."

"You too. I'll be thinking of you. You and Bev. I hope—well, you know."

"Yeah." Dylan didn't want to talk about it and he was grateful to Frank for understanding that. "Be seeing you, Frank."

Dylan stood to watch until the train chugged northward. He half wished he could get on it and be carried away. The idea of working in the now-familiar town of Dawson's Clough was unbelievably appealing. Life was lived at a different pace there, people were more open—but if he were there, his problems would be sure to follow.

Thankfully, Bev had slept well last night. He knew that because he'd spent six hours tossing and turning and trying to figure out the conundrum that was Lenny King and Max Rickman.

No matter how often he told himself it no longer mattered, he couldn't abide all the loose ends. And during those sleepless six hours, he'd figured it out. Possibly.

When Frank's train was out of sight, Dylan left the station, returned to his car and drove across the City to Weller's gym. The car park was crowded but Weller's car with its distinctive personalised registration plate was sitting in a reserved spot by the main entrance. Good.

Dylan strode inside the building and was struck again by the high-tech space-age look of the place. Today, a ridiculously tall young woman was standing behind the reception desk.

"I'm going up to see John." Dylan took the stairs two at a time before she had chance to argue.

He stood outside Weller's office for a moment and straightened his jacket. Scruffy T-shirt and battered leather jacket would look out of place in the office, but at least he'd be comfortable. More comfortable than Weller, he hoped.

He took the car key from his pocket, pulled in a deep breath and barged in.

Weller's secretary opened her mouth to speak, realised Dylan wasn't planning on listening, and put her body in front of him to physically deny him access to Weller's space.

Dylan reached around her and pushed open the

inner door. Weller, sitting behind his desk, looked up in amazement.

"I'm sorry, but—I did try to tell him. He gave me no chance," his secretary babbled nervously.

"A quick word, if I may," Dylan said.

"It's fine." With a wave of his hand, Weller dismissed his secretary.

Dylan closed the door after her, and stood, arms folded, with his car key dangling from his finger.

"What can I do for you, Mr. Williams? I can only spare you two minutes, I'm afraid."

"Two minutes is fine." Dylan strode to the window and peered out at the car park below. "It's about your mother. I'm curious about her so-called accident."

Whatever Weller had expected him to say, it clearly wasn't that. "What the devil does that have to do with you?"

"That's how it all started, isn't it?" Dylan stepped closer to Weller's desk and rested his hip on the edge. "You called the ambulance that night, didn't you? That must mean you know exactly what happened. Now, let me take a stab in the dark. Your mother was having an affair with Lenny King and she told Max she was leaving him. Max took exception, and they had a fight. Max turned nasty, she ran, and he mowed her down in his car. You called the ambulance and vowed vengeance on him and your mother's lover. How am I doing so far?"

"I—that's preposterous. I don't know what you're talking about." Weller's face was white beneath the tan.

"Oh, I think you do. Now, let's move on to the night Lenny and Max were arrested. Lenny wasn't at Max's little factory to discuss a driving job, was he? Of course he wasn't. Max had put Sarah in a wheelchair and now it was time to punish Lenny. All poor Lenny knew was that Sarah had been hurt in a hit-and-run accident. He wouldn't have known that the driver was none other than Max. So when Max said he wanted to discuss a driving job with him, Lenny would have thought of the money and gone along. He won't have known that Max planned to kill him. Hey, I bet your stepfather was a dab hand with a samurai sword."

"Get out!"

"Ironically, you had no idea of your stepfather's intention either. All you knew was that the two of them would be together at Max's drug factory. So you decided to kill two birds with one stone and set them both up. That way, both your stepfather and your mother's lover would be out of your life. Or, more important, out of your mother's life. So, unbeknown to you, you probably saved Lenny's life. Amusing that, don't you think?"

"I don't have the remotest idea—"

"You had someone—your loyal secretary probably—call the police and mention a domestic dispute at your stepfather's place. The coppers turned up and found a drug factory, just as you knew they would. Lenny and Max were taken into custody, tried and found guilty, and sent down for a few years."

"This—this is madness."

"So, as far as you were concerned, all was hunky-dory. Until Lenny was released, that is, and you find that he and your mother are still much too close for your liking. So Lenny *really* has to go. You can't find him, though, can you? You visit his ex-wife, Wendy—"

Weller launched himself out of his chair. "Who the fuck are you? You're not a writer. Who are you?"

"You're right. I'm not a writer. I'm not the police either. But to get back to my story, you visited Lenny's ex-wife—"

"So?"

"Her death was an accident, was it?"

Weller turned on a snake-like smile. "You think you're so fucking clever, don't you? Well, I promise you this, you'll never prove I had anything to do with it."

"You're probably right, but let me continue. You eventually find Lenny—probably at your mother's house because that's where he was hiding out—and promise him money. For what, though? That's the question, isn't it?"

Weller grabbed a handful of Dylan's jacket and pulled him close. "It's time you left. Get out. Now."

Dylan pulled himself free of Weller's grasp. "Perhaps you offered him money to leave your mother alone. That's feasible, I suppose. Not that you could actually give him the money, could you? Of course you couldn't. You don't have any, do you? You see, I've been looking into this place." He threw out an arm to encompass the gym. "It's not doing quite as well as you like to pretend, is it? Despite the cash that your mother's ploughed in, you're in debt. I suppose that means she's short of cash too. So perhaps you offered Lenny money to leave her alone, or leave the country. Being skint himself, and knowing your mother didn't have any, he would have jumped at the offer. So you send your henchmen along with a holdall, stuffed with newspaper probably. They have orders to shoot to kill, but they only wound him and—"

"You can come up with all the crap you like but you won't prove a thing."

"Your mother knew you'd set up Max and Lenny, but she couldn't bear the thought of her darling son being sent down, or—and this is probably more accurate—being the victim of Max's or Lenny's revenge. So she invented a tall story about discovering that Wendy King and the arresting police officers were responsible."

"You think you're so fucking clever, don't you?" Spittle landed on Dylan's face. "What proof do you have? None. You have none because there is none. Now get out of my office while you can still fucking walk."

"I don't suppose it matters now, does it? After all, Max is dead. Lenny saw to that. I've no evidence, of course, but I'd bet my life that Lenny arranged that neat little heart attack. And now, with Max out of the picture, King and your mother will sail off into the sunset and live happily—"

"Over my dead body!"

"Ah. So what are you going to do? Make sure your henchmen don't miss this time? That's the thing, isn't it? When you've killed once, it's easy to do it again. You had Wendy killed so having Lenny killed—"

"—will be fucking easy. Too right it will."

"I have to admire you, I suppose," Dylan said. "You set up Max and Lenny and managed to get them sent down—"

"You'll never prove it."

"You had Wendy killed. You put Lenny in hospital—"

"They won't miss next time, you can bet your life on that."

"And you won't rest until he's dead, will you?"

"No, I won't." Weller returned to his desk and, unless Dylan was very much mistaken, touched something beneath it.

"I guess it's time I was going," Dylan said. "As you said, I can't prove anything—"

When the door burst open, the biggest, ugliest brute Dylan had ever seen filled the gap between him and freedom. The chap had no neck. A huge head sat on massive shoulders. A suit jacket was stretched across enormous biceps.

Dylan put the key ring in his pocket and offered up a silent prayer.

"Ah, I've seen you before. You were supposed to kill Lenny King. May I suggest a bit of target practice?"

"Sort it," Weller muttered.

The first punch completely robbed Dylan of air and the second punch was even more vicious. He managed to dodge the third punch, and, better still, kick his assailant where it hurt. While the thug was bent over gasping, Dylan made a dash for freedom.

He smashed the glass on the first fire alarm he came to and, with bells ringing all around him, joined the panicked throng of keep-fit freaks trying to leave the building.

A quick look over his shoulder told him that the ugly brute had recovered and was following—at an impressive place.

Dylan ran on and vowed to get back in training. When you spent half your life upsetting people, it made sense to be capable of outrunning them.

He escaped the building and pulled welcome fresh air into his lungs. He was racing toward his car, but a quick look over his shoulder told him the thug was too close. Instead, he ran across the car park and on to the main road. A few people stopped to stare. Most moved out of the way.

Then Dylan spotted a uniformed bobby and he headed straight for him. Gasping for breath, he stopped in front of him. "Could you direct me to the nearest Tube station, please?"

"Of course, sir. You need to carry on along this road and take the first left. Five hundred yards on, you'll see the entrance."

Dylan saw that his pursuer had stopped. Their gazes locked and, after a moment's hesitation, the thug decided against a chat with the law. He turned and headed back to the building.

Dylan thanked the copper and went on his way. He kept a safe distance from the gym for another hour, then crept back for his car.

The drive back to his office was without incident and once there, with fingers crossed for luck, he took his special car key from his pocket and attached it to his computer.

"You'll never prove it…" The video was dodgy, to put it mildly, but Weller's voice was clear enough.

"We'll see about that, sunshine." Dylan picked up his phone and tapped in Pikey's number. He had to leave a message. "Give me a bell when you pick this up, Pikey. I've got a present for you."

With the satisfaction of a job well done, or a job finished at least, Dylan began to sort out the papers that littered his desk. He didn't actually do anything with them, other than put them in a neat pile in a filing tray, but he always felt better if his desk was clear.

Whether the police would gather enough evidence to build a case around Weller, he had no idea. He no longer cared. Nor did he care about King and Sarah Rickman. It was—finally—over.

He had a couple of jobs to do, jobs that paid bills, but he'd take a holiday of sorts. He'd put his mind to more important matters. First, he'd persuade Bev to see another specialist, or to at least accept the treatment on offer that would possibly give them more time. He'd spend his days with her and convince her that they'd fight this bloody awful disease together. Not only fight it but beat it.

His phone rang and, expecting to hear Pikey's voice, he picked it up without looking at the display.

"Dylan Scott? It's payback time."

FORTY-ONE

DYLAN REACHED OUT for his phone to check the time. 3:18 a.m.

He gave his pillow another thump, but sleep refused to have anything to do with him.

"What's the matter?" Bev asked.

"Nothing. Go back to sleep."

"I might be able to if you'd stop fidgeting. What's wrong?"

"Nothing." *Everything.*

Bev switched on the bedside light. "I'm wide awake now."

"Sorry. Do you want something? Tea? Coffee? Glass of wine?"

"I want you to stop fussing as if I'm an invalid. I'm perfectly capable of getting myself a drink if I want one." She reached for his hand and gave it a squeeze. "And I want you to calm down. Chill out, for God's sake."

"I'm fine."

"Is this anything to do with me not wanting to pump my body full of chemicals and live like a zombie for however long it takes?"

"It's more to do with you refusing to take an expert's advice and—"

"What? Oh, come on, Dylan. That expert said himself that, if it were him, he'd probably feel the same."

He couldn't argue with that. They'd had a long and extremely depressing discussion about the quality of life. "But surely, each day is precious."

"It is. So long as I know what day it is. If I'm a dribbling vegetable who doesn't even know her own name, then no, it's not precious. It's hell."

"You won't be a dribbling vegetable."

"Too true I won't," she said, "because I'm not going down that route."

"Then will you at least see another specialist?"

Her sigh was long and patient. "The scans don't lie."

"Maybe not. I'd still like to see what someone else can suggest."

She gave him a resigned smile. "Okay, I'll see someone else."

And now she was humouring him. "I don't see how you can be so calm and bloody accepting about it. If it were me—"

"If it were you, I'd respect your wishes. As it's me, you can damn well respect mine. And for your information, if I am calm and bloody accepting, it's because I have no sodding choice. My children are going to have to face life without me and I'm fucking angry about that. There are times when I'm scared shitless and—" She leapt out of bed and tore her dressing gown from the hook on the back of the door. "Do you know what I'm going to do now? I'm going to have a drink. A bloody big one. Because, hey, it's not going to kill me, is it?"

"Mine's a whisky," he tried to joke, but she'd already stomped halfway down the stairs and probably hadn't heard him.

Cupboard doors were slammed in the kitchen, a bottle was banged down hard, the kitchen door was yanked shut. Her returning step on the stairs was thunderous.

She marched into the bedroom, scowling, and thrust a bottle of Scotch and a glass at him. "Think yourself lucky I don't bloody throw it at you."

"Thank you, O mighty one."

"Piss off." A reluctant smile forced its way to her lips.

Dylan poured himself an overlarge measure of whisky and took a grateful gulp. Life usually looked better through a whisky-induced haze. "Sorry," he said, as she climbed into bed beside him and took a sip of her red wine.

She groaned. "Don't let's turn this into *Love Story*, okay?"

"What?"

"The book, remember? The film. 'Love means never having to say you're sorry.' She died. Everyone wept buckets. End of."

It meant nothing to him, but it wouldn't have been "end of." People would have been left behind to cope with the fallout.

"My point," she said, "is that I want to remain as fit as I can for the time I have left. That could be months or, more unlikely, years. But however much time I have, I want it to be quality time. I want the kids to be able to remember me as a fully functioning human being. Is that too much to ask?"

"Of course not. But you can't say that you wouldn't

be a fully functioning human being if you accepted the treatment."

"Without a crystal ball, I can't know what the end will be like. I can't see it being good, though." She reached for his hand and gave it a squeeze. "What I'd really like, Dylan, is something quick and easy. A swift bullet through the brain would be good."

"Oh, yeah, that would be great."

She smiled. "At least it would be fast. Or a car accident. Not a messy one, though."

They sat in silence, lost in their own morbid thoughts. Dylan needed to lighten the mood and he knew just the thing. "I've got something for you. Don't go away."

He leapt out of bed, grabbed his dressing gown and went out to his car.

When he returned to the bedroom, Bev's wineglass was almost empty, but her eyes lit up when she saw the bag in his hand.

"Oh, my!" She laughed. "Where did you steal the bag from?"

"I didn't steal it."

He handed it over and she opened her gift as if she were handling the crown jewels. "Oh, my God. This is—this is freakin' awesome." She ran her fingers lovingly across the silk. "This is—wow. This is the best thing ever. It's utterly, utterly gorgeous. Cass Pelham. Wow."

It was a scarf. A pink scarf. Dylan was glad she was pleased with it, but when it came down to it, it was only a scarf.

"How did you get this?" she asked. "I know for a fact that you didn't walk into the shop and buy it."

"How can you possibly know that?"

"Because I know you far too well. There's no way in hell that you'd pay the sort of money this cost."

She *did* know him too well. In his eyes, only a complete idiot would pay more than a fiver for a scarf.

"It's a long story," he said. "But I'm glad you like it."

"Like it? It's simply—gorgeous. The colour is perfect. Wow—what a gift. I love it. Thank you." She wrapped it gently around her neck, smiling like a five-year-old trying on her mother's makeup. "And this is exactly what I mean. What if I were so ill that I couldn't appreciate the pleasure of wearing something so beautiful?"

Dylan stifled a groan. They were back to the subject that would dominate every second of every day. "You won't be."

"Dylan?"

He didn't like the sound of this. "Yes?"

"If I get—you know, in a really bad state—"

"Let's wait and see what happens, shall we?"

"Yes, but if I do, I'm going to Switzerland. An assisted suicide. DIGNITAS."

Dylan felt the bile rise in his throat. No way. He was shocked that she could even contemplate such a thing.

"I've researched it, paid my membership fee and done the paperwork," she said.

He didn't answer. *Couldn't* answer.

"It's expensive but—" She left the sentence unfinished.

"We'll see another specialist," he said, and he drained his glass. "Come on, drink up. We need some sleep."

Car accidents, bullets, assisted suicides—what the hell had got into her?

"And I don't want you grieving," she said. "It wouldn't suit you and it would depress the kids. I've had a great life, Dylan. Celebrate that fact when I'm gone, okay? Don't you dare make our kids miserable. They're the most precious things in the world and they don't deserve that."

"Drink up."

When her glass was empty, she switched off the lamp and settled down. Dylan breathed a sigh of relief as she rested her head on his chest and prepared to sleep.

"Of course," she said into the darkness, "you could save yourself a lot of money and slip some cyanide in my wine."

"Goodnight, Bev."

He could feel her smiling against his skin. "Love you, you grumpy old bastard."

"Love you too. Even when you talk complete and utter bollocks."

FORTY-TWO

DYLAN'S NARROW ESCAPE from Weller's thug had reminded him how out of shape he was, but he'd never felt as determined to go running as he had this morning. Perhaps he'd finally lost his grip on reality and was going mad.

Either way, on only a single cup of black coffee for breakfast, he was doing the five-mile run that, not so long ago, hadn't even left him breathless. Half a mile in today and he was knackered.

A good run would get his thoughts in some sort of order, though, and God knows they needed it.

How could he have got everything so spectacularly wrong?

Goodenough was dead. Definitely. Dylan had seen the fire crew cutting his body from the twisted metal of his car. No way was Goodenough making calls from the mortuary.

Rickman was dead. Medical experts had confirmed that he'd been suffering from heart disease for several years. Dylan believed them, but he was also convinced that King had somehow arranged his swift end. Dead from natural causes or murdered, Rickman wasn't making threatening calls from the mortuary either.

King would spend his future with Sarah Rickman—always assuming Weller didn't get to him first.

Weller.

Weller didn't know Dylan Scott from Adam. He didn't resent the coppers who'd turned up to arrest his stepfather. On the contrary. So it was unthinkable that he might be responsible for those calls. Wasn't it?

His thoughts ran round in a tangled mess, with Bev right in the centre.

Words failed him there too. If he couldn't make sense of those threatening phone calls, he certainly couldn't get on the same wavelength as his wife.

He couldn't put himself in her position, but he felt certain he'd want to cling to every precious moment of life. So what if he threw up a bit? At least he'd be with his family for a little while longer and, during that extra time, anything could happen. One of these days, someone would stumble across a cure for cancer—nothing was so certain, and who was to say it wouldn't be next month or even next week?

And if she thought that he was telling their kids that he'd taken her to Zurich to die, she had another think coming. The idea was preposterous.

He stopped, hands on his knees, to catch his breath, but his lungs struggled to take in the necessary amount of air.

On the opposite side of the road, a newsagent's was doing a brisk early morning trade.

Dylan staggered across the road, grateful he'd had the sense to put some cash in his pocket.

He took a bottle of water from the fridge and held it against his forehead as he joined the queue to pay. He was almost at the till when he saw the newspaper headline.

Police are concerned for the safety of Gerald Lowell (41) who has been missing from his home since...

Gerald Lowell? He'd heard that name before. What was that other name, the one he'd heard mentioned on TV when Frank was there? Brian Dowie. Gerald Lowell and Brian Dowie.

Oh, shit!

He grabbed a copy of the newspaper and paid for it along with his water. Outside, he read the report in full.

Shit!

He punched in Pikey's number but, as was so often the case, had to leave a message.

"Gerald Lowell—missing person—his wife has been murdered. Just seen it in the paper." He could barely breathe, let alone talk. "Brian Dowie—another missing person—his family killed. They were both on the same police training course as me. Give me a ring, mate, will you? I need to know what happened to others on the course."

He'd known Brian Dowie's name was familiar. Two decades had passed but now, he could even picture the bloke. Average looking, had the gift of the gab and, according to the newspaper, had been running an extremely successful car sales business until his disappearance.

Lowell hadn't been average looking. He'd been a tall, good-looking bloke. Overconfident perhaps, a ladies' man definitely, and always ready with a quick retort.

Dylan drank his water and threw the empty plastic bottle in a nearby waste bin along with the newspaper.

He ran on, taking a short cut, and as his feet pounded on the pavement, he tried to think back to that training course. Memories were dim. Over the past twenty years, attendees had been more or less forgotten.

He could remember silly things, like half a dozen of them climbing a creaking drainpipe to a nurses' residence, and wandering around for days with fellow would-be coppers talking in police speak.

A few names came back to him but none that stood out.

Somewhere in the house, wherever Bev kept old, never-to-be-seen-again photos, there was a picture of them graduating. He needed to see the faces and, hopefully, remember the names.

More important, he needed to get home. The last quarter of a mile was taking an age. He must get home. Dowie's wife and two sons murdered, Lowell's wife raped and drowned—

His train of thought was splintered by a cracking pain on his skull. There was a blinding flash of white light. Then nothing.

FORTY-THREE

"HAS THAT BLOODY cat peed on the carpet again?" It seemed to Jimmy that the house permanently reeked of cat piss.

"Probably." Carol scooped George into her arms and stroked him. "I've made an appointment with the vet for six o'clock this evening. I think his kidneys are on the way out."

"It stinks in here."

"It does not."

"Have it your way. I need to go—"

"Just wait five minutes. I need a word with you."

He was too shocked to utter a put-down, but who the hell did she think she was to monitor his movements?

She was busy shooing the kids out of the house, making sure they had everything they needed and handing them an apple each to eat on the way to the bus stop.

"They're old enough to get themselves off to school," he said.

Matthew was limping as if he'd had a leg amputated. He hadn't even broken his leg, just bruised it, but from the fuss he was making, anyone would be forgiven for thinking he'd been fatally wounded.

"They are. And they do." She ruffled their sons' heads. "I just like to send them off with a dash of mother's love." She laughed at the faces they pulled, then gave them each a kiss. "Have a good day, boys."

"See you."

"Bye."

Jimmy might as well have been invisible for the notice they paid him. That suited him. He had other things on his mind at the moment.

When they had the kitchen to themselves—apart from an incontinent cat—Carol went to the tall kitchen unit and pulled out three, four, five bottles of tablets. She slammed them down on the table in front of him. "Discuss."

Jimmy bit back on his anger. Later, he'd make it abundantly clear what he thought of people snooping through his things. Later. Right now, he had things to do.

"I don't need them."

"And the doctor's told you that, has he? No, I thought not." She folded her arms. "I knew there had been a change in your behaviour. Everything was going along okay and then, all of a sudden, you grew snappy with everyone and everything. You're moody, sullen, withdrawn from us all—"

"Oh, don't kid yourself that a few tablets will make me look at the way you mollycoddle those kids and think it's wonderful. You treat the kids—and me— like bloody five-year-olds. You think everyone should do exactly what you want. Well, I've got news for you, sweetheart. Some of us have minds of our own. Now, if you've finished, I need to go."

"Where?"

"It's none of your damn business. I'm sick to death

of this. It's like working in a bloody factory and having to clock on and off every time I move. Bloody hell."

"You're sick, Jimmy."

"Sick of living like this."

"I think we need to sit down and have a chat with your doctor about—"

"*We? We* need to do nothing. You need to go and cut women's hair and I need to get out of this house." He grabbed his holdall. "I'll be back when I'm back."

He marched out of the house, giving the door a satisfying slam as he did so.

How bloody dare she search through his personal possessions? He should have flushed those tablets down the toilet. No way was some Indian doctor on God alone knew what sort of exorbitant salary telling him what to swallow. Doctors collected their money and spent the day writing out prescriptions. It was all too easy. He neither wanted nor needed them. They made him sluggish and sleepy whereas he needed to be mentally alert at all times.

He drove away from the house, but he couldn't relax now. She'd screwed up everything. He had to be in the right frame of mind and he wasn't. He was edgy. Anxiety was beginning to creep in. *Bloody woman.*

Every traffic light was against him. He longed to drive through them all but, knowing his luck, the police would pull him up.

A woman pushing a buggy while hanging on to a small child dawdled across the road in front of him. Jimmy revved the engine and longed to mow them down.

He rolled down the window. "Get out of my way, you stupid bitch!"

When she was finally out of his path, he roared off, but immediately slowed down again when he remembered that he didn't want to get stopped by the police. His nerves were fizzing. He must stay calm.

When he finally stopped the van outside the terraced house that felt more and more like home to him, his hands were shaking so badly he struggled to remove the key from the ignition.

FORTY-FOUR

A SEXY YOUNG nurse leaned across Pikey, treating him to a glimpse of cleavage. Only his shirt and her black uniform lay between his skin and hers. And still all he wanted was to escape.

He hated dentists. Hated them with a passion.

The chair was adjusted so that he was able to move into a sitting position.

"There you go. Just hand these in at reception." The dentist handed him his records, a sterile swab and a list of instructions on what to do following an extraction. "If you have any problems, give us a call, but I'm sure it will be fine."

"Thanks. And thanks for seeing me so quickly. I appreciate it."

"That's what we're here for."

Pikey handed in his records at the desk, paid the bill and left.

It was bliss to be away. Hopefully, he wouldn't have to go near the place for at least six months.

He switched on his phone, saw he had a message, and was about to listen to it when a call from an unknown number came in. "Yes?"

"Am I talking to Detective Sergeant Pike?"

"Who is this?"

"Guess what, Sergeant. It's payback time." There was a gurgling sound, possibly laughter.

Pikey's brain was as numb as his mouth. This couldn't be happening. It had to be a joke. And yet—

"Who the fuck are you? How did you get my number? What do you want?"

"You're the next on my list. See you soon, Sergeant." The connection was cut.

The bloody anaesthetic had numbed Pikey's brain. He couldn't think straight.

He strode along the street and to the car park, calling Dylan's number as he did so. It went to voicemail. "Give me a ring as soon as you pick this up, mate. It's urgent."

He remembered the message someone had left and hit the button to listen. It was Dylan.

"Gerald Lowell—missing person—his wife has been murdered. Just seen it in the paper." Dylan sounded as if he were running a marathon and Pikey struggled to catch it. "Brian Dowie—another missing person—his family killed. They were both on the same police training course as me. Give me a ring, mate, will you? I need to know what happened to others on the course."

Pikey slammed the car into gear and drove out the car park. He tried Dylan's number twice on the short drive to the station, but he wasn't answering.

Shit. This was no harmless crank out to scare Dylan. This was a maniac who'd already killed several people…

The first person Pikey saw when he reached the office was the new constable. Jo? Jo Fry?

"This is urgent," he told her. "I need to see the powers that be but I want you to drop everything and dig out a name for me. Dylan Scott, ex-copper—he attended a police training course with Gerald Lowell and Brian Dowie."

Her eyes widened at the mention of the missing persons. "Is this Dylan Scott a suspect?"

"What? No, of course he's not. I need the names of every other person on that course, okay? I need to know where they are now, I need to know—everything. Okay?"

She was already sitting at her desk and tapping away at her computer.

As Pikey went upstairs, he tried Dylan's number again. And left another message. "Answer your bloody phone, will you? We're probably wasting time chasing down the same info."

He needed coffee to get his mouth functioning normally again and wash away the taste of blood, and he needed every scrap of information they'd gathered on the Lowell and Dowie cases. There would be a ton of paperwork to check out.

He wasted precious time telling the senior investigating officer what he knew, and almost as much time trying to get a coffee from the machine. In the end, a hefty kick had the machine delivering.

"They're coming to look at it later," a voice shouted across to him. "About time too."

"Anything come in overnight?" Pikey asked.

He nodded at the computer. "Be my guest."

While Pikey checked the incident log, his companion chewed on a Mars bar while taking a call from a man who believed illegal immigrants were being housed next door to him.

"I've had all sorts already this morning." He swallowed the last of his Mars bar. "An unidentified flying object hovering over St. Mary's Primary School, a so-called killer dog that turned out to be a Labrador stalking a butcher, another sighting of Elvis. Illegal immigrants being shipped into Russell Street in a white van is about as normal as it's got so far. I suppose I'd better get it checked out."

Pikey smiled and nodded, drank the sludge the machine passed off as coffee, and tried Dylan's number again. Nothing.

As he returned to his desk, the young constable waved at him. "I'm not sure if I've found out anything interesting or not," she said. "I've still got a few more names to check, but there's a chap here, a James Oxford, who was on the same course as the other three. He didn't complete it because he wound up in trouble—drugs. But he lives fairly locally, and he's recently been discharged from the army suffering from post-traumatic stress disorder."

"Have you got an address?"

She scribbled it on a scrap of paper and handed it over. "I'll carry on checking out the others."

"Thanks. I'll see if I can find him," Pikey said. "Meanwhile, give me a call if you find anything interesting, okay?"

She nodded, already concentrating on the task at hand.

"Thanks," Pikey added. "Good work."

Checking out Oxford would give him something constructive to do, but it didn't feel right. Pikey had no connection to that training course whatsoever so why had he been told it was payback time?

FORTY-FIVE

JIMMY FELT A little better when he'd put the van in the garage, and better still when he let himself into the house.

He'd rushed this, simply because he'd been eager to get his man, and he'd made mistakes. He'd merely intended to watch the house, to see what time Dylan Scott left, and had been taken by surprise to see him running back. He'd had to have him. There couldn't be any more mistakes, though. He had to think clearly, slow down, do everything right.

Phoning DS Pike had been a spur of the moment thing and probably a mistake. The thrill of finding his number on Dylan Scott's phone had been too much and he'd had to call him. It was too soon, though, because he knew nothing about Pike yet. Pike would be a crook, he was too close to Scott not to be, but Jimmy needed to know more about him. It didn't matter, though. It might have been a mistake to call him, but it didn't matter. Let Pike worry for a while…

Jimmy took the stairs to the cellar and had to put a hand to the wall to steady himself as a dizzy spell brought the floor rushing up to meet him. Had he eaten? He'd skipped breakfast, that was nothing new, but he couldn't remember if he'd eaten last night or not. It didn't matter. He'd get something later. This was only a quick visit to make sure he'd tied Scott securely.

He had. There was no escape for Scott.

The man looked ridiculously calm. Dowie had spent most of the time crying like a baby, Lowell had almost exploded with rage, and now Scott, damn him, looked perfectly relaxed. Jimmy would soon change that. He'd soon have him begging for mercy. It would be pointless, of course, but Jimmy would enjoy humiliating him.

Scott did have one thing in common with the others. There wasn't so much as a hint of recognition in his eyes. They'd all forgotten him. They neither knew nor cared what he'd had to go through while they—

"You don't remember me, do you?" Jimmy said.

Scott nodded and still looked infuriatingly calm.

"What? You think you know who I am?"

Scott nodded again.

"I don't believe you," Jimmy said. "What's my name then, eh? Tell me."

Fuck it. This was probably a ploy to get Jimmy to remove the gag. It would be okay. No one would hear Scott. Besides, if he started yelling, Jimmy would knock him unconscious again.

He yanked off the tape. "Go on then. Tell me my name."

"James Oxford. It's been a long time, Jimmy."

Jimmy was too shocked to speak. No one remembered him. He'd been forgotten. Left on life's scrap heap.

"How have you been?" Scott asked.

Jimmy couldn't answer. *Keep calm. Keep calm.* He put layer after layer of tape around Scott's mouth.

Then, without saying a word, he walked up the stairs, locked the cellar door and went into the kitchen.

As he splashed cold water over his face, he wondered why everything was going wrong this morning. When had it started?

He hadn't slept properly for weeks now, and seemed to manage easily on two hours a night, so, as he'd been wide awake, he'd decided to drive to Scott's house and watch. All had been fine until, shortly after seven o'clock, Scott had left the house to go for a run.

Jimmy hadn't known if that was usual for him or not. He'd stayed in his van and, when he'd seen Scott returning, he'd taken his chance. He'd whacked him over the head, bundled him into the back of van, and driven here.

Scott had been conscious but very groggy, and had been reasonably easy to tie up.

Once confident he was secure, Jimmy had driven home.

It was Carol. That was when everything had started to go wrong. As soon as he knew she'd been snooping through his stuff, as soon as he knew he'd have to suffer the "you're ill" discussion. He wasn't fucking ill, for Christ's sake. Disagreeing with the general view didn't make you a basket case. He was not ill.

Then on the drive here, traffic had been against him. Scott—he knew him, he recognised him, he looked as if *he* were the one in control of this situation.

Everything was against him today. Every damn thing.

Jimmy made himself a coffee, black because he still had no milk at the house, and carried it outside. A fine drizzle was falling but he didn't care. In fact, he quite liked the cooling effect. He stared up at the dark clouds—one was the shape of a dragon—and drew in slow, deep breaths.

He jumped when what sounded like gunfire turned out to be his neighbour's door closing.

Sweat broke out on Jimmy's brow as he nodded over the fence at the old man.

"Got company, have you?" his neighbour asked.

"What? Oh, yes. We're doing some work."

"I thought I heard you. I was down in the cellar clearing out some old rubbish. Football programs mostly. I've got a lot going back to the 1950s. My daughter tells me I should sell them on one of these World Wide Web places. Well, I don't know about that. I'll leave her to sort it out. It'll save her a job when I'm gone."

Jimmy nodded.

"Well, I'd better take Toby for his walk," the chap said, fondling the old dog's ears. "He can't go far these days—well, neither can I—but he plays up if we don't stick to our routine."

"Right." Why didn't the bloke piss off?

"Dogs are like that, aren't they? They like their routines. Mind you, I suppose people are the same. Do you have a dog?"

"No. Cats. I have cats."

"Ah. I can't say that I'm a cat person. They're independent things, aren't they? Aloof some might say."

"I suppose they are. Anyway, I'd better get back to it." Jimmy marched back into the kitchen to finish his coffee in peace.

The way everything was going today, he might have known he'd get stuck with that old fool. He'd have to remember not to make too much noise in the cellar once the old man was back home, though. Still, for the moment, he could do as he liked.

Feeling better, he drained his mug, put it in the sink and returned to the cellar. It was about time Scott learned the gravity of the situation.

Scott was still managing to look calm. It had only been three hours, though. He was probably still in shock. Or suffering from concussion.

He yanked the tape from Scott's mouth. "So you remember me, do you?"

"Of course. What I don't remember is anything happening that might lead you to do this. I don't remember Brian Dowie or Gerry Lowell doing anything either. Now, a lot of water's passed under the bridge since then—"

"Too true it has."

"But as far as I recall, we got along well enough. What's with all this?" He nodded at his tied feet.

"You think we got along well? Bloody hell, that's a joke. Don't kid yourself that I liked any of you. I've never known such a smarmy, arrogant, conceited load of wankers."

"I thought we were an okay bunch."

"You three—you thought the world was yours for the taking. You thought you'd be police officers until something better came along. It was just a game to you, wasn't it? A way of passing the time. Not me. I would have been a good copper. I was capable, honest, trustworthy—I would have been a decent copper, not like you lot. All bent, the three of you. All dismissed in disgrace."

At last, Scott registered surprise.

"Oh, yes," Jimmy said, warming to his theme, "I've checked up on you. Dowie tampered with evidence—well, it was never proven but you can bet your life he did—Lowell took a backhander, and you—"

"I was a damn good copper."

"You were dismissed in disgrace!"

"Yes, because an evil piece of scum, a habitual offender, came up with the bright idea of claiming I'd used excessive force during an arrest. On paper, I'm a disgraced copper. In reality, I'm not. I was a damn good copper and proud to carry the badge."

Jimmy spat on the ground. "All of you dismissed from the force for not being worthy and yet I—" He could barely get the words out quickly enough. "I would have been good. One of the best. But no, I wasn't allowed to prove it, was I? You three passed everything with flying colours and I never got the chance to prove myself."

"Time plays tricks on the memory, Jimmy, but weren't you arrested for carrying drugs? Wasn't that why you were kicked off that training course?"

"All my life, I've had to hear what a great copper my father was. Well, he wasn't. Oh, he's got the full retirement package and everyone thinks he's a hero, but he did nothing. All those years on the force and he was nothing. Yet, still I have to hear that he was the world's best copper and that I couldn't even get through the training."

"You made a mistake, and you paid the price. That's all. Nothing to do with us."

"Even now that he's retired, he's still the best copper ever. All because he talked some smackhead down from a multi-storey car park. The fucker wouldn't have jumped anyway. He was only attention seeking. But, oh, no, my father talks him down and his photo is splashed all across the newspapers. If it had been me, I'd have jumped to get away from the tosser."

"Your father sounds like a good man."

Jimmy spat on the floor. "So what happened to me? I was forced into the fucking army, that's what."

"Forced? Wow. Who held the gun to your head, Jimmy? Not me. Was it Dowie? Lowell perhaps?"

Jimmy refused to listen to more of Scott's wisecracks. He looked for his crowbar but couldn't find it so he grabbed the hammer and smashed it down on Scott's foot. The smart arse could take that.

"You've got worse than that coming to you. You think you're so fucking clever, don't you?"

Scott was quiet. His foot was probably broken. Good.

Jimmy walked around the cellar, breathing deeply, calming himself, until he felt able to sit opposite Scott.

"It's not that I couldn't handle the army," he said. "I can handle anything. It wasn't what I wanted, though. That's the point. I'm out now, of course. Glad to be away from it really. I mean, why would anyone want to spend their time in a shithole like Afghanistan? What's the point? They're uncivilised bastards—leave 'em to it, I say. What's the point of me getting blown to pieces, eh? What good will that do? It's a shithole. But you're missing the point. The point is that I would have made a good police officer. A bloody good one. Far better than my old man. You three—you had the chance and you blew it. All of you. You were a waste of time whereas I never had the chance. You fucked up. You thought—everyone thought you were superior to me. You weren't. You're all trash. You fucked up big time. You were—"

He dragged in a breath. Scott would think he was crazy if he didn't pull himself together.

"I'm going to get all you coppers." His voice sounded better now. More calm. More in control. "You know Scotland Yard? I'm going to blow the place to smithereens. I've had the plans for a while. As for making a bomb, that's child's play—"

"No, Jimmy. You're not going to blow up anything. The police are on to you. They know you killed Dowie and Lowell. They know what you have planned."

"Liar. You're a fucking liar."

Jimmy wrapped layer after layer of tape around Scott's face. He didn't care if the bloke could breathe or not.

"You're a fucking liar. They know nothing. I've seen them on the TV. Fucking clueless. I know what I'm doing, and I'm going to blow Scotland Yard to—"

A loud bang plunged the cellar into darkness. Jimmy was trembling. Part of him knew that it was only a light bulb that had blown, but the other part of him was rendered immobile. He was back there, back in the hot hell of Afghanistan.

He had no idea where his flashlight was. All he had was a tiny spot of light from a gimmicky torch on his key fob.

He switched it on and, still shaking, stumbled up the stairs to the cellar door. Daylight almost blinded him and he leaned against the wall, taking in long, deep breaths.

When he'd recovered sufficiently, he found his

flashlight and a new light bulb. He left them on the kitchen table. There was no need to waste light on Scott. He could rot in the dark.

FORTY-SIX

PIKEY HAMMERED ON the door to what he believed was Oxford's house. There were no signs of life.

He walked round the back of the house and peered through a window. All he saw was a typical family kitchen. Four photos of two boys were attached to the fridge door with magnets. A trail of crumbs surrounded a toaster. Two plates, a mug and a glass waited to be washed. A pair of trainers had been slung over the back of a chair, a phone charger sat idle on the table, and a small square of fabric embroidered with the words Home Sweet Home hung on the wall.

He tried the back door, then returned to the front of the house and banged on that door again.

"If you're looking for Carol, she'll be at work." The owner of that voice, a dark-haired woman in her late fifties or early sixties, was regarding him with suspicion from the other side of the low wooden fence that acted as boundary between the properties.

"Carol? I'm really looking for James Oxford. Do you know where he might be?"

"No. I don't see much of him. He could be anywhere."

At least he had the right address. "Carol's his wife, yes? Where does she work?"

"Up the road there." She pointed to the top of the

hill where all Pikey could see were more houses like this one. "When the road levels off," she said, "you'll see half a dozen shops on the left-hand side. The hairdresser's is Carol's."

"Thanks. I'll try there."

He drove up the hill and grabbed a parking space outside the various shops. The hairdressing salon, A Cut Above, nestled between the post office and an Indian takeaway.

Pikey went inside. One woman had her hair wrapped in pieces of silver foil, another was reading a magazine under a contraption that Pikey assumed was a dryer, and yet another was having her hair washed by a young girl.

Supervising it all was an attractive woman who came forward with a smile on her face. "Can I help you?"

"I'm looking for Carol Oxford." He showed her his ID and saw the colour drain from her face.

"What do you want?"

"Could we have a word, please? In private?"

She turned to the girl at the basin. "I won't be long. You'll have to cope without me for a minute, okay?"

"Yeah, sure."

"Come with me." Carol took the stairs two at a time and pushed open the door to a tiny room crammed with a small table, a washing machine, towels and cans of hairspray and plastic containers of shampoo. "It's Jimmy, isn't it? What's he done?"

When confronted by police officers, people usually assumed the worst, thought of accidents, and asked what had happened. Carol, however, had asked what her husband had done.

"I'm not sure that he's done anything," Pikey said. "Can you tell me where he is?"

She bit on her lower lip and shook her head.

"When did you last see him?"

"This morning. At breakfast. Before I came here." Her arms were wrapped tight around her body. "What do think he might have done?"

Pikey didn't answer that. "You've no idea where he is now?"

"No. I asked where he was going, but he wouldn't tell me. We had words, you see."

"Oh?"

She leaned against the washing machine as if she needed the extra support. "He's not well. Um, post-traumatic stress disorder, they call it. I found out that he hasn't been taking his medication and—well, we had words. He stormed out the house."

"Okay." Pikey gave her an encouraging smile. "I assume he has a phone? Will you give me the number?"

"He never answers it." She took her own phone from the pocket of her tunic, looked up the number, then grabbed a pen and business card from her other pocket and jotted it down.

"Thanks. Does he have a car? Can you give me the registration number?"

She nodded and wrote down the number beneath his phone number. "He has a van too. He's just bought it and I don't know the number. I can't remember it."

"That's okay. What sort of van is it? Big? Small?"

"A Transit. Old. White. A bit rusty." She sucked in a nervous breath. "He, um, helps with army reservist training and said he needed it for that. For carrying men and gear around." She lifted the lid on a box that said it contained hair colour and pulled out a pack of cigarettes and a lighter. "Do you mind?"

"Go ahead."

"Thanks." She lit the cigarette and pulled the drug into her lungs. "He sometimes does the training in Somerset. Except—" She took another pull on her cigarette. "He was supposed to be there recently, in Somerset. For four days. That's where he said he was. Except—except one of my customers swore she'd seen him coming out of the fish-and-chip shop on Russell Street. She swore it was Jimmy. I told her she was mistaken but perhaps—" Her eyes swam in moisture.

A white van. Russell Street. Hadn't someone called the police about that this morning? Something to do with illegal immigrants?

"Sometimes," she said, "he goes out in the middle of the night. He says he's been running. He says he drives the car to the river and runs along there."

"Okay. Thanks." Pikey handed over his card. "Will you call me as soon as he gets home or as soon as you know where he is?"

She pocketed his card. "It's Afghanistan, that's what did it. There was an accident—a roadside bomb. Jimmy was okay, physically at least, but several of those alongside him were killed. He has terrible nightmares."

"Okay," Pikey said again. "Just call me if you hear from him."

She stubbed out her cigarette and followed him down the stairs. Pikey left her sorting out her customers and pretending to them that all was well. She knew, though, just as Pikey did, that everything was far from well.

FORTY-SEVEN

DYLAN COULDN'T HEAR any signs of movement from the floor above. Perhaps Oxford had left the building.

His eyes had had time to adjust to the darkness, but he still couldn't see anything other than slightly darker shapes. While Oxford had been talking, Dylan had taken note of everything in the room and had mentally calculated distances. The stairs, by his reckoning, were six feet from his chair. Opposite him was the chair Oxford had sat in. To his left was a rusty old boiler that didn't look as if it had been used since Noah built the Ark. About twelve feet from his chair was a large cardboard box and, lying on top of that, was an old hacksaw. It had been impossible to see, even with the light on, if it boasted a usable blade. He'd have to hope so as it was his best chance of escape.

All he had to do was get to it without hanging himself.

What sort of crazy bastard put a noose around his victims' necks? The answer to that, of course, was the Jimmy Oxford sort of crazy bastard.

Dylan hadn't got to know the bloke well enough all those years ago to form an opinion. He'd never stopped to think about him, but he'd seemed a normal young recruit. A bit quiet perhaps. A bit out of his depth and, now Dylan came to think about it, somewhat lacking in social skills. As far as Dylan could remember, though, there had been nothing to suggest he was this fucking crazy.

Dowie was missing presumed dead. Lowell was missing presumed dead. Dowie's wife and two sons were dead, as was Lowell's wife. Dylan was dealing with the worst sort of crazy, the deadly sort of crazy, and he had to get out.

What the hell had possessed him to leave Bev and the kids and go for that senseless morning run? Having received the warning phone call, he should have stayed home to protect them. He'd had too many warnings, though, and he'd believed, wrongly, that time was on his side.

No matter what, he had to make sure that Oxford didn't get to his family. And worrying about them wasn't helping. The only way he could protect them was by getting out of this hellhole.

His only option was to tip his chair back and hope to Christ he didn't hang himself. If he moved forward, or sideways, he'd be a goner. If he tipped his chair backward slightly he might, just might, manage to escape the noose. But if he was wrong—

If he stayed where he was, he was a sitting bloody duck. Soon to be a dead sitting duck. He had no doubt on that score.

His only chance of escape was to tip his chair backward a little. Except he couldn't. The good thing was that his feet—and he was sure one was broken—just about touched the floor. The bad thing was that no way could he tip his chair back a little. Once he exerted any pressure, it would overbalance and take him with it.

Unless, of course, the noose did its job, in which case it was academic anyway.

Nothing ventured—

FORTY-EIGHT

JIMMY WAS FIZZING with excitement. The van's windows were down and he could hear police sirens in the distance. He guessed where they were going and chuckled to himself. They were too late. The deed was done, and the gun was safely hidden in his jacket pocket.

"You're always one step ahead, Jimmy." He slapped the steering wheel with satisfaction as he drove.

Ten minutes later, he drove the van into a car park. He pulled on the uniform of a local courier service—its previous owner no longer had a use for it, Jimmy had seen to that—and sat with the helmet on his lap.

He switched on his new phone and made his first call. No one would be able to trace it. No one would bother. "Any information I give you is confidential, right?"

"Of course."

Jimmy couldn't fault the Anti-Terrorism hotline. Very polite. "It's just that I don't want my family knowing I've called the police," Jimmy said.

"We understand that."

"My sister married a Muslim, you see, and I've had my suspicions about him for a while now. He's bought large quantities of chemicals that he keeps in a lock-up garage, and he's been vague about what he needs them for. Now, like I said, I don't want my family—him especially—knowing I've spoken to you. I've taken photos, though and I've recorded a conversation I heard him have with one of his friends. I'll get those to you."

"That would be—"

"I can't talk now. I'll send the photos and recording to you by courier. They'll be with you within thirty minutes. Shall I just address it to the Anti-Terrorism officers? Or would you rather give me a name or a reference number? I think this needs looking into urgently."

Jimmy ended the call with a rush of satisfaction. He couldn't believe how easy it was. No way would he get into Scotland Yard—breaking into Buckingham Palace and having tea with the Queen would be easier—but he could send a package inside. They checked out everything thoroughly, of course, but it would be too late by then. The very second that the package entered the building, Jimmy would act.

He put the phone in his pocket, bought his parking ticket, checked and double-checked that it was visible to traffic wardens and other nosy folk, then set off for the Underground station with his package.

This was it, the moment he'd been planning for months.

Jimmy pictured himself walking away from the exploding building. He could see himself clearly, walking tall and proud, a cloud of dust and debris engulfing everything in his wake.

When it was done, he'd return to Russell Street and wipe the smug smile off Scott's face. He couldn't wait to tell Scott about his successful day.

Scott wouldn't believe him at first. That didn't matter, though, because Jimmy had the photos to prove it.

FORTY-NINE

DYLAN'S CHAIR WENT back with a crash, and his head hit the concrete hard. His hands, tied behind his back, took a lot of weight, but at least he was free of that noose. Success. All he had to do now was get himself and the sodding chair to that hacksaw.

His wrists screamed in pain as he used his hands to inch his weight across the concrete floor. There was no knowing how long Oxford would be away. Hopefully a long time because it was going to take an age to reach that hacksaw, even assuming he could find it in the dark.

Sweat poured off him. His right foot wasn't painful, more numb, but he couldn't so much as flex it. It had to be broken.

Bastard.

He moved at a sluggish snail's pace toward the far end of the room with his arms about to leave their sockets. His neck was struggling to take the strain.

His chest burned with the effort. In fact, every muscle in his body, except those in his right foot, was protesting. Loudly.

The dominant smell in the cellar was petrol. He'd spotted a chainsaw so perhaps it was that. He could smell bleach too.

He had no idea where he was—he could still be in

London or out in the country, in a terraced house or detached, a shop—not that it mattered. Until he could free himself from the ropes, he couldn't pull the sodding tape from his mouth so he couldn't scream for help. That was assuming there was anyone within earshot.

He wriggled forward, like an upside-down snail, and wondered what he could actually do if he managed to get to the far end of the room where the hacksaw sat. His mouth was out of action, his feet were tied and one was useless anyway, and his body weight was resting on his hands. Getting to the hacksaw was one thing. Being able to do anything with it was something else entirely.

He had to think of something, though, and fast. Dowie and Lowell had probably died in this cellar. Their families had died in their homes. Oxford was one out-of-control psycho who meant business.

What Dylan would do if Oxford came back now, he had no idea. To say his options were limited was putting it mildly. Psychology wasn't Dylan's strongpoint so he couldn't hazard a guess at Oxford's next move. The bloke was certifiable, obviously, but until someone put him in a padded cell where he belonged, there was no knowing what he was planning.

His knuckles touched the remnants of his mobile phone so he knew he was almost at the far end of the room. Oxford hadn't been content to remove the SIM card. Instead, he'd had to jump up and down on the phone like a hysterical five-year-old throwing a tantrum.

Dylan reached the box, managed to knock the hacksaw to the ground and then tipped himself and his chair onto its side. If he could somehow grab the damn hacksaw, and if it had a usable blade, he might—and it was a big might—be able to saw through the ropes.

He didn't think the door was locked. Oxford was too unstable to make a decent job of kidnapping anyone. He'd almost hit the ceiling when that light bulb popped.

Having said that, he'd proved himself a competent murderer. Police, as far as Dylan was aware, were still no wiser on the identity of Dowie's and Lowell's family's killer.

Dylan refused to speculate on that. He had to get himself free and mobile.

Trying to do anything with the hacksaw soon proved a non-starter as the rusting blade disintegrated within seconds. Time for plan B.

He'd noticed an old tap fixed fairly low down on the wall. The tap was rusting badly, and probably hadn't seen water for fifty years, but the pipe might be jagged enough to cut through the ropes around his feet.

He shuffled his way across the damp floor, feeling the wall with his good foot until he found the tap. Luck was with him because the tap was only about a foot from ground level, the same height as his feet sticking out from the chair.

He began a slow sawing motion. His left foot had to do all the work as his right foot was useless. At times it hurt like hell and at other times it was numb. He kept up the sawing motion, although it was impossible to say whether his ropes or the tap would give way first.

He felt the rope give slightly and, encouraged, continued the action with his legs. Persistence paid off when the rope finally gave way and he was able to wriggle his feet free.

The chair was still attached to him, thanks to the

ropes holding his arms behind his back and those around his middle, but he managed to stand on his good foot. He hopped backwards, throwing as much weight as he could against the wall. Every bone in his body hurt like hell, but he knew the chair was flimsy. Piece by piece, it gave way.

With the chair in pieces around him, he was able to free his hands from their ropes. He yanked the thick tape from his mouth, coughed a couple of times, and drew in a breath.

He'd done it. He was free.

He dragged himself up the steps, turned the door handle and thanked the gods when it opened. The light shining along the hallway blinded him briefly but it was oh, so welcome.

His foot dragged uselessly behind him as he shuffled from room to room of what was an almost empty house. Getting up to the next storey was easier on his backside, he discovered, but there was no sign of Oxford. The only things hinting at anyone ever having been in the building was a sleeping bag, several bottles of bleach, an old TV, a jar of coffee and a mug and spoon.

The back door swung open at his touch and he stepped out into a small back yard. In the adjoining yard was the welcome sight of a uniformed copper. He was talking to an old man.

"Hey!" Dylan hopped to the fence.

The young officer was busy talking into his radio but he broke off. "A word, please, sir."

"No time. I'm an ex-copper, Dylan Scott. DS Pike will vouch for me. James Oxford, the man who killed Brian Dowie's family and Gerald Lowell's wife, kidnapped me. He's on the loose and you need to find him fast."

"I told you." The old man prodded the officer's chest. "I told you he was up to no good."

"You've seen Oxford?" Dylan asked him.

"Several times. He drove off in his van a couple of hours ago. He's up to no good. I've known that for a while. That's why I called you lot this morning." He nodded at the young officer. "You took your time doing something about it."

"Do you know the van's registration number?" Dylan asked.

"I already told them that when I phoned. Like I said, I know the letters. TOB. They stuck out because my old dog's called Toby."

"There you go," Dylan grabbed the officer's arm. "Get everyone finding that van and Oxford. I don't know if he's armed, but he's definitely bloody dangerous."

"Sir, I need—"

"And I need to get home. Where the hell am I anyway?"

Police sirens cut through the air. Dylan had to lean on the officer and let him take most of his weight as they made their way to the front of the building.

Three patrol cars raced along the road and pulled up outside the house. Dylan had no idea what they were doing here, but he was relieved to see them. If necessary he'd steal one of the cars and drive it home.

All but one of the officers went past him to search the property. The remaining officer opened his mouth to speak but Dylan didn't give him chance. "Before you ask, no, I don't have time to answer questions. I need to get to my family."

"Dylan Scott? That's being taken care of. A patrol car's on its way. Meanwhile—" he looked at Dylan's foot, "—it looks like we need to get you a hospital."

"Later. I need to get home." Nausea washed over him. He was close to passing out. "Phone. Give me your phone. I need to speak to DS Pike urgently."

"We need to—"

"Just give me your bloody phone."

The young officer found Pikey's number and hit the button before handing his phone to Dylan.

"It's me," Dylan said, as soon as he heard Pikey's voice. "Long story, short version. I've escaped from Jimmy Oxford's cellar, but he's on the loose and he's fucking dangerous. We need officers at our homes looking out for our families, mate, because he's out to get you too."

"It's in hand. A car's on its way to your place as we speak. He called me to tell me it's payback time, but my place is empty, so it's fine. Sheila and the girls are safe enough. But as to where he is…I had a chat with his wife and she mentioned him being seen on Russell Street. She also mentioned a white Transit-type van. When a man called us from Russell Street and mentioned a man in a white van, we put two and two together."

"Yeah, well, he's nowhere near Russell Street now."

"I know. His van's been seen on CCTV. I'm on to it now. So what's his problem?" Pikey asked. "I know he's been discharged from the army suffering from stress, but what exactly is his problem?"

"Coppers," Dylan said. "His dad's a bit of a hero

in the cop world, I gather. Jimmy was chucked off that training course and ended up joining the army, whereas me, Lowell, Dowie—all bent, all a disgrace to the badge. He would have been a good copper, yet he was sent to Afghanistan, blah, blah. The sick bastard has big plans, though. He reckons he's going to blow up Scotland Yard. He almost had a coronary when a light bulb popped in his cellar so God knows how he'd cope with a bomb, but he's crazy enough to try anything."

FIFTY

PIKEY HAD BEEN optimistic when Oxford's van had been spotted on CCTV nearby, but that was ten minutes ago and they had no idea where he was now. He'd drive round for a while. Maybe Oxford had parked up.

What a bloody day. It seemed an age since he'd been lying back in the dentist's chair listening to the creaking, cracking and general protests of a tooth being yanked out of his mouth. At least the pain had died down. Either that or he'd been too busy to think about it.

Still, at least he was safe. Sheila and the kids were safe. Dylan had escaped the lunatic. Officers would have arrived to keep watch on Bev and Dylan's kids just in case Oxford showed up there. Everything was under control.

He drove on, hoping for someone to call him with details of another sighting of Oxford's van, but all was quiet.

He was passing a small car park when he spotted a large white vehicle at the end farthest from the road. He doubled back on himself and drove into the car park.

And there it was. Oxford's van.

He called Jo Fry while he looked at it.

"There's a ticket that he bought at—" he checked his watch, "—only seven minutes ago." He put a hand to the van's bonnet. It was still warm. "It's paid up till the end of the day. There are clothes lying in the passenger footwell. Jeans and a jacket. He must have changed. A disguise perhaps? A uniform? A copper's uniform?"

He looked around him, hoping for inspiration.

"This car park's close to the station," he said, "and that would be—what?—two stops from St. James's Park Station?"

"Are you thinking New Scotland Yard?" she asked.

"We know he's threatened to blow the place up."

"Everyone's on full alert. He stands no chance."

Pikey wasn't so sure. People like Oxford, people with no concern for life, either their own or anyone else's, could do a lot of damage.

"We need every inch of CCTV for this area checked," he said. "I'll bet he's wearing a uniform of some description—most probably a copper's." It would take too long, though. "Is anything happening back there?"

"His photo's been circulated, they're getting a warrant to search his home—"

"That's a waste of time. He shares his home with his wife and two kids. Anything incriminating will be at that place on Russell Street or in his van."

"Forensics are at the house on Russell Street…"

As Pikey ended the call, he had an awful feeling it was going to be a case of too little, too late.

Staring at Oxford's van wasn't helping.

Pikey headed to the station and jumped on the first train to arrive. He'd been right, it was only two stops to St. James's Park. He got off there and walked to New Scotland Yard.

The building looked as it always did, an unattractive

heap of concrete and glass. Concrete barriers protected ground-level windows from car bombs. Yet more concrete sat around the entrance to the building. An uglier building would be difficult to find.

People walked past without sparing the office block or the armed guards a second glance. Three uniformed men stood at the visitors' entrance. All was quiet. Normal.

Pikey didn't feel in the least reassured.

He paced. Beneath the familiar revolving sign recognisable to most people in the world, a man was trying to take a photo of himself on his phone. He was wearing biker's clothes—a courier's uniform—but there was no sign of a motorcycle.

A young man approached him and offered to take his photo.

The biker removed his helmet just as Pikey spotted the large package at his feet—

Pikey hit a button on his phone and was relieved when Jo Fry answered immediately. Later, he'd wonder why he'd gone straight to her but, for now, he just issued instructions.

"I've got him. He's by the sign outside the Yard. I'm going to try and keep him talking but if he recognises me, we're stuffed." Pikey didn't want to think about that. "He has a parcel with him which I strongly suspect is a bomb. Get someone outside now, Jo. But softly, softly, okay? This guy's fucking crazy…"

Pikey ended the call. Why the hell had he thought this morning's dental appointment was so terrible? Compared to this, it had been a picnic.

He was about to walk over to the sign when he spotted a gift heading straight for him. A tall man was wearing a red velvet hat that boasted a bright peacock's feather. A red scarf was wrapped around his neck several times and still almost touched the ground.

Pikey approached him, showed him his warrant card, and grabbed his hat and scarf. "You'll get them back in a few minutes. Meanwhile, stay here and keep quiet."

The chap's eyes were wide with a mix of shock and fear. Pikey couldn't help that. It was the closest he could get to a disguise right now.

With the hat pulled as low as possible, and the scarf looped around his neck, he thanked God for London's many eccentrics and walked toward the revolving sign.

Oxford was taking back his phone and inspecting the photo the stranger had taken. Pikey saw the outline of a gun. Inside pocket, left-hand side. *Shit.*

"Well, just look at you!" Pikey put on an over-the-top, ridiculously camp voice. *Eat your heart out, Quentin Crisp.* "What a fabulous uniform, darling. Do you ever make deliveries to Scotland Yard?"

Oxford looked both appalled and smug. "Of course. Why else do you think I'm here?"

"But, darling, you have nothing to deliver."

Oxford nodded in the direction of his feet. Up close, that package was bigger. About a foot square. "What do you think that is?"

"Ah!" Pikey leaned in close and gave his scarf a dramatic flick over his shoulder. "I tried to get in, but no luck. My father's cousin knows someone who works for the Diplomatic Protection Group—that's one of the Met's specialist branches. They protect 10 Downing Street, foreign embassies—"

"I know who they are."

"Well, I thought I'd be able to get an appointment through him, but no. Not so much as a sniff of the inside, darling. What about you? Do they let you go inside?"

"Yeah. Course. Not today, though. And it's nothing special inside. Just a lot of stupid coppers."

"Would you mind?" Pikey took his phone from his pocket. "I'd love a photo of you and that uniform. Will you humour me, darling?"

"Yeah. Then you can take one of me, right? I've got one, but it's not very good. Half the sign's missing."

"Oh, of course. You first then. Give me your phone."

Jesus Christ. There was no one about. Well, no one who looked armed. No one who looked like a crack marksman. No one who looked as if they knew what they were doing around bombs. Where the hell was everyone?

"Or," Pikey said, "I can take a picture on *my* phone. The camera's very good indeed. We could exchange email addresses, darling, and I—"

"No need. Just take a decent picture on my phone."

Pikey brushed at his hat and gave his scarf another twist. It would be difficult to convince anyone looking at the two of them that Oxford was the crazy one.

No one was looking at them, though. Pikey realised that there was no one in sight. Not a single tourist was waiting to record a news report from the popular spot.

He could either wait for backup or he could overpower Oxford himself and hope to God Oxford didn't detonate that bomb. Oxford was a big, strong bloke, but Pikey reckoned he could handle him.

"What's in the package?" he asked as he took Oxford's phone.

"A bomb." Oxford snorted with laughter.

"Very amusing. Really, what's in the package? I don't suppose you know. It could be important evidence perhaps or—"

"It's a bomb. Hang around if you want a good picture. As soon as this parcel enters the building— boom." Oxford leaned back slightly and frowned. "Hey, I fucking know you—"

Pikey would have introduced himself but he was pushed to the ground with such force that he had to spit out a tooth that was lost on impact.

"Nice hat and scarf, Sergeant." Oxford's face was so close that Pikey could feel the heat of the bloke's breath.

They struggled, and just as Pikey managed to overpower him so that it was Oxford lying helpless on his back, half a dozen arms pulled Pikey away from his prize.

Oxford was lost from his view as eight or ten officers disarmed him.

Blood dripped down Pikey's chin as he got to his feet. Oxford was being dragged away, his arms tight behind his back, his legs cuffed at the ankles. The package sat beneath Scotland Yard's famous revolving sign.

"Let's get out of here before the fireworks start," an officer suggested.

Pikey was more than happy to oblige. Bomb disposal experts could do their thing without his help.

He picked up the velvet hat and long scarf and tucked them under his arm. They'd served him well, but he'd be glad to return them to their rightful owner.

Oxford was almost out of sight now, but he was still shouting. "Give my regards to Dylan Scott!"

FIFTY-ONE

OXFORD'S HOUSE ON Russell Street was teeming with officers.

"I need to get home," Dylan said to no one in particular. One officer had given him a phone to use, but Bev wasn't answering. Luke wasn't answering his either.

The officer returned for his phone. "You need to get to a hospital," he said. "A car's on its way to your house. It'll be there by now. Meanwhile, let's get you out of here. Hop in." He sniggered at his joke.

Dylan got in the patrol car and tried to get his foot comfortable. He couldn't. "Never mind the hospital. Just get me home."

"Are you sure? We can let your wife know that you're in A&E."

"I need to get home." That was becoming his mantra. "When that bastard Oxford is in a straitjacket, *then* I'll go to hospital." And not a second before. Dylan called his home number, but there was still no answer. He called what he thought was Bev's mobile—he wasn't sure he remembered it as it was always keyed into his phone. There was no answer. He called his mother's number to see if Bev was there but, damn it, she wasn't answering either. Luke's phone went straight to voicemail. He left messages telling his family to call him on his new number, but no one was speaking to him.

"How the hell did you find that place?" he asked the officer.

"It was Sergeant Pike," he said. "It was his day off, but he picked up your message and checked out everyone who'd attended that police training course. It didn't take long to find the person deemed to be mentally unstable. Oxford was discharged from the army suffering from post-traumatic stress disorder. A quick visit to his wife, who confirmed he'd lost the plot lately, gave us the registration of his van. She said that he'd been seen in this area." The officer stopped the car for a red light. "Your luck was in because the chap who lives in the adjoining house had phoned in. He'd heard noises and he said he knew there was no one in the house because the man renting it had left. He reckoned the chap was smuggling illegal immigrants into the country. He told us about the white van the chap drove and was even able to give us a partial plate. Ninety-nine times out of a hundred, the two things wouldn't have been connected. Today, they did. Your luck's in, mate."

Dylan leaned back in his seat and closed his eyes as the officer drove. He'd go home and have a stiff drink. When Oxford was caught and was secure in a cosy cell, he'd get himself and his foot to the nearest hospital.

Traffic was almost at a standstill.

"Sod this," Dylan said. "We'll be here all night at this rate. Give us some lights and music, will you?"

"Will do."

When drivers heard the siren and saw the flashing blue lights, they pulled over to allow them to pass. "That's better. Thanks."

The journey still seemed to take forever and all the while Dylan's foot reminded him that he needed to get to a hospital.

He called Bev again, but still there was no answer. She was probably having a bath, in which case she'd ignore the phone. Maybe she'd gone to bed—

It was becoming increasingly difficult to convince himself. She'd be worrying about him. Hell, she might even have called the police herself by now. Or maybe not. When he didn't return from his run, she would have assumed he'd gone straight to the office. She knew he didn't work to a timetable and was used to his coming and going at all hours. She'd nag him for not returning her calls if she'd tried to phone him, but she might not be too worried.

The officer finally turned into Dylan's road. Dylan was vaguely aware of him missing a gear as they spotted the flashing blue lights very close to Dylan's house. They hadn't sent just one patrol car.

"What the—?"

Police officers were outside his house. Tape sealed off his garden.

"Fuck, no!" Dylan had the car door open before the vehicle had stopped.

Unaware of the pain in his foot, he ran as well as he could until he was stopped by a uniformed officer.

"I'm sorry, sir, but you can't—"

"Out of my fucking way." His mouth was dry. His heart was racing at a dangerous pace. "This is my home!"

"Dylan Scott?"

Two pairs of arms restrained him. He heard their voices, but it sounded as if they were coming from a

distance. "I'm terribly sorry to have to tell you this…
arrived too late…"

"No!" He wouldn't listen to them.

.He pushed past them and into his house. The house
that would never feel like home again.

FIFTY-TWO

"YOU SEE?" LUKE SAID, hanging the last strand of tinsel. "It looks like Christmas now. Wait till Freya sees it. She'll love it."

"She'll wreck it," Dylan said.

"Yeah, probably."

"Unless Bozo gets to it first."

Dylan still couldn't believe they had a dog in the house. Nor could he believe the size of the creature.

They'd spotted it, half-starved, shivering and caked in mud, in the garden one late August night. Luke had thought Christmas had come early, because they'd had little option but to bring the creature into the house and feed it while Dylan called the police and local dog warden. The dog hadn't been wearing a collar, wasn't microchipped, and no one had reported one as lost.

"You can't send him to the rescue kennels." Luke had been appalled.

"We'll keep him for a couple of days," Dylan had said, "but you'll have to be prepared to hand him back to his owners."

"But he's starving. Anyone who's let him get in this state shouldn't be allowed to have a dog in the first place."

Luke had a point. The dog's ribs were painfully prominent.

"Perhaps he wandered off and is lost. Someone, somewhere, is probably heartbroken. They'll be hoping he returns to a cupboard full of food and a warm, comfy bed."

"Huh."

Bozo, as Luke nicknamed him, was allowed to stay for a couple of days. They'd taken him for a check-up, and the vet had thought he was around a year old. The vet had also decided he was a Labrador/collie crossbreed. He was mainly black, with white patches on his chest and paws, and looked nothing like either a Labrador or a collie as far as Dylan could see. Apart from being underweight, he was deemed healthy enough, so, when Dylan had handed over a fortune for vaccinations, flea medication and worming tablets, they'd brought him home. All he'd done since was eat—dog food, shoes, sweaters, mail, tennis balls—anything he could get his teeth into.

Now, it was Christmas Eve and, belatedly, they—Luke, really—had provided him with a decorated Christmas tree to eat.

Dylan wouldn't have bothered with a tree, but that held true every Christmas. Luke had been insistent, though, so they'd gone to the local garden centre and bought a huge pine. They'd sold out of anything smaller. Once they'd dragged it into the house, Dylan had scrambled into the loft to bring down the decorations and Luke had spent the past couple of hours decorating it.

It should have looked like Christmas, but it didn't. The tree was where it always went. Every year, Bev had insisted on moving the TV and a coffee table, and putting the tree in the corner. And there it stood now.

Cards were propped here, there and everywhere, and strung across the room on red ribbon as they always were. There were no hat-and-scarf-wearing turkeys or flatulent Santas on the cards this year. All greetings were of the sombre Thinking of You at Christmas type. Bev would have preferred farts and turkeys.

Almost obscured by the cards was a small note. For Bev's funeral, everyone had followed Bev's instructions and worn bright colours. They'd tried to celebrate rather than mourn a life. Children from Bev's school had written short tributes to her, tied them to balloons and let those balloons fly high into the sky. One note had come adrift during its flight and Dylan had picked it up. It said, *Thank you for everything, Mrs. Scott. I'll live my dream and I'll remember you every step of the way. Love Daisy.*

Dylan had been so touched that he'd kept the note. Knowing she'd made a difference to a young girl's life would have meant the world to Bev.

Luke's phone rang. He turned the colour of a Santa hanging on the tree, muttered something about needing to answer it, and went to his room. Bozo had been snoring in front of the fire, but he leapt up and followed.

Dylan could remember—just—the excitement of his first girlfriend. At Luke's age, all he'd thought about was getting laid. He hadn't got laid until he was eighteen, but he'd thought about it constantly.

The landline rang and when Dylan saw his mother was calling, he was tempted to ignore it. Deciding he had nothing better to do, he answered it.

"Good evening, mother of mine."

"Evening, Scrooge. I'm only calling to make sure you collected the turkey."

"I did. I'll shove it in the oven later and set the timer."

"Good. So what have you been doing?"

"Decorating a tree."

"A real one?" She sounded amazed.

"Yes. There are pine needles everywhere but, as yet, Bozo hasn't cocked his leg against it."

"Lovely. I'll look forward to seeing it. My place looks horrible and bare."

"That's the general idea, Mum."

She'd dropped everything to move in with them and take care of them as they'd stumbled, numb with grief, from one day to the next. They couldn't have coped without her. They couldn't now because Dylan needed to work.

Her flat was in the process of being sold and she'd returned to it for a week to empty it.

"You wouldn't believe how many charity bags I've filled," she said.

"Oh, I would."

"Anyway, it's almost done. I'll nip back one day in the holiday to finish off," she said. "Are Luke and Freya all right?"

"Yep. Freya's asleep and Luke's on the phone to his girlfriend."

"Ah, young love. I remember it well. What's she like?"

"No idea. I know her name's Charlotte because I heard Tom teasing Luke about her but, other than that, I know nothing. She could have two heads for all I know."

"You should tell him to introduce her to us over the holiday."

"So you can be nosy?"

"Why else?"

Dylan smiled at her honesty. "I'll suggest it, but he'll probably die of embarrassment."

"Probably. Right, I'm off to my bed. Don't forget to set the oven timer because we'll be in a mess if it's not cooked. It would be the devil's own job picking up takeaways for so many people. There will be the three of you, me, Frank, Pikey, Sheila and the girls, Lucy and her bloke—eleven."

"It'll be good." In some ways, Dylan was glad that so many would be sitting down to lunch with them. And Bev would have loved it. Part of him wished he could drive off to the hills and spend the day alone, though.

"It will. You okay, love?"

"Yep."

"Christmas is a funny time of year, isn't it?"

"Hilarious. You work all year to pay for it, you clutter up the house with decorations, send cards to people you haven't heard from since last Christmas, eat too much and drink too much—yeah, it's hilarious."

"Ha. I'm delighted to hear the festive spirit is alive and well. Okay, I'll see you in the morning. Early. I'm off to bed now..."

When he ended the call, Dylan went online for advice on how to roast a turkey.

The first file he saw when he switched on his computer was Brad Goodenough's. Dylan never deleted anything, just in case, but he decided to file it somewhere else. Before he did that, he opened it for one last look.

Goodenough's real name was Colin Bloomfield. He

came from a good family, had a good education, joined the army, served ten years and left with the Ministry of Defence's blessing. It was then that his longing for the highlife began. Perhaps he enjoyed the freedom of civilian life. He loved people and parties, expensive clothes, hotels and fast cars. He must have thought he was set up for life when he drove away from Cass Pelham's house with a pile of jewellery. He would have known that tracing Brad Goodenough would be a difficult task, and he would have assumed that Cass would make a claim for the theft through her insurance company. Luckily for her, she hadn't needed to. Unluckily for her, the love of her life was dead.

Dylan still didn't feel guilty about that. Goodenough hadn't been making death threats or photographing his family, but he'd been a deceitful, money-grabbing piece of work.

As he closed the file on Brad Goodenough, deceased, he wondered how Cass Pelham would be spending the holiday. Her father was making a good recovery so perhaps she'd spend it with him and try not to dwell on what might have been, or what she thought was going to be.

He wondered how Leonard King and Sarah Rickman would be spending their Christmas too. According to Archie, they were heading to the sunshine and getting married.

"Love's young dream," Archie had said with a scoffing laugh.

Dylan couldn't imagine Sarah living abroad because she'd want to be near her son. John Weller was currently in custody awaiting trial, but he wouldn't be tasting freedom for a long time. Sarah would be back to the ordeal of prison visiting again.

There was still nothing to suggest that Max Rickman had died from anything other than a heart attack and, reluctantly, Dylan had to accept that.

As for Jimmy Oxford—

Dylan left his computer and went to the kitchen to pour himself a drink. He found it impossible to think about Oxford without a bloody big drink in his hand.

For all he knew, Oxford would enjoy turkey with all the trimmings followed by carol singing around a tree. He was incarcerated in a secure psychiatric unit and Dylan had no idea what the inmates did for entertainment.

He'd known of course that any lawyer in the land would prove Oxford hadn't been responsible for his actions. Dozens of reports had been submitted, all from psychiatrists with more letters after their names than in their names, all saying the same thing. Oxford was crazy.

Christ, Dylan could have told them that.

Shoving him in a padded cell was the easy option, though. Responsible for his actions or not, and he'd seemed pretty damn responsible to Dylan, he should be made to pay for what he'd done.

Yet how could he? Oxford could be torn apart limb by limb, something Dylan fantasised about, but that wouldn't help. Nothing could ever make up for what he'd done.

Dylan hadn't needed the autopsy to confirm that Bev's death had been mercifully quick. The surveillance camera he'd had installed outside their home had shown Oxford breaking in and racing out seconds later. Dylan supposed he should take comfort from the fact that she hadn't been raped like Dowie's and Lowell's wives. He couldn't take comfort from anything, though.

Let it go. Eight months had passed since Dylan had climbed out of the hell that was Oxford's cellar and into an entirely different sort of hell. He had to let it go or he'd end up as crazy as Oxford.

He carried his drink into the sitting room and stared at the tree with its hypnotic flashing lights. The room shouldn't feel so alien because it was exactly the same as it always had been—but with a little more dust, dog hair and clutter. The carpet Bev had taken weeks to choose, and was then adamant that the colour she'd chosen was oatmeal whereas this one was biscuit—something Dylan never did understand—needed a good clean. The TV that Bev had always claimed was too big for the room needed a flick with a duster. The cushions, an obsession of Bev's, needed straightening.

He heard a burst of laughter as Luke came down the stairs. There were a few whispered words to end the call and then, still shoving his phone in his pocket, Luke returned to the sitting room.

"Was that the girlfriend?" Dylan asked.

"She's just a friend." Luke's face turned the colour of beetroot again. "So about this film—shall we watch it? It's supposed to be good."

"Yes, why not? Oh, by the way, your gran thought—"

"Don't call her Gran. She hates it."

"Of course." His mother thought it made her sound old and had banned all use of the word. "Vicky says you should bring—Charlotte, is it?—to meet us over the holiday."

"Oh, Dad. That's gross." Luke lunged for the TV remote. "Are we watching this film or not?"

"Yes. I just thought I'd mention it."

"There's no need. Anyway, I haven't got time. It's the party, then I'm going to the bowling alley with Tom. Plus there's the big game on Boxing Day—hey, I can't wait for that, can you?"

"I can't." A game of football on Boxing Day had always been the highlight of the holiday.

"Right, it's starting," Luke said.

They settled down to watch what had to be the worst film ever made. Almost two hours of complete, utter garbage. It didn't manage to take Dylan's mind off Oxford. It didn't take his mind off anything else either. But at least the zombies looked a little more convincing when he'd refilled his glass.

If you enjoyed films where you started off trying to guess the zombie's identity and then realised that the entire cast was made up of the undead, perhaps it wasn't too bad.

In fairness, they probably missed half of it as keeping Bozo from eating the tree before Freya saw it was a full-time job.

"That was rubbish," Luke said as the final credits rolled. "Everyone said it was good too."

"You see that red button on the remote? It's an off button."

"Ha-ha. I used to say that to Mum, but she never took any notice. She *really* watched some rubbish, didn't she?"

Dylan couldn't argue with that. "I think even she would have drawn the line at that pile of dross we just sat through."

Luke grinned. "Probably."

Bozo raced around the room with a piece of tinsel in his mouth. "Christmas is going to feel a bit strange, isn't it?" Luke said.

"Yes. Yes, it is." It wouldn't be the best Christmas ever—how the hell could it be?—but he'd do his best to make sure the kids were distracted, laughing and happy. There would be a house full of people determined to do the same thing. It would be okay.

And later, he'd drink himself to oblivion…

"Do you talk to Mum?" Luke's voice was barely more than a whisper.

Dylan nodded. "All the time. You?"

"Yeah." Luke looked a little embarrassed. "It's a bit silly really, isn't it? I mean, it's not as if dead people can hear us."

"Who knows? Perhaps they can, perhaps they can't. I like to think your mum can."

"Yeah. So do I." Luke picked up Bozo's ball and bounced it across the room for the dog to chase. "Still, we're doing pretty well, aren't we? I bet she'd be amazed if she could see us."

Dylan was completely taken aback by that. He always felt as if he were drowning in treacle, somehow surviving from one day to the next. But, thinking about it, Luke was right. They were doing okay.

Never mind man's best friend, Bozo was every man's worst nightmare, but Dylan would forgive the dog anything because he'd done so much to help Luke come through this hell relatively unscathed. There had been many times during the long, dark months following Bev's death that Dylan had thought Luke would never communicate again. It was Bozo who'd helped him through his grief and, for that, Dylan would be eternally grateful to the dog.

Luke's phone trilled, alerting him to a message. A flush of colour and a smile that was quickly hidden told Dylan that the girlfriend was chatting to him.

Luke tapped a few buttons and hit the send key. "Right," he said, "I'm off to bed. Don't forget to do your Santa thing and put Freya's stocking at the bottom of her bed."

"I won't."

It was ridiculous because Freya was too young to understand, but it was tradition. Even at this early age, she apparently needed to know that Santa had visited. It wouldn't matter to her and Dylan guessed that regardless of the presents she received, she'd smile her way through the day. She was the happiest of souls, constantly smiling.

Dylan owed his daughter. It was Freya who got him through the days, probably because she was so small and so vulnerable that he was always holding her. Some days, he clung to that scrap of humanity as if his life depended on her.

"Hey, it's nearly midnight. Happy Christmas, Dad."

Dylan hugged him. "Happy Christmas, Luke."

Bozo trotted off with Luke, and Dylan was alone. He went to the kitchen, poured himself a large drink and stared out the window into the darkness.

He hoped Bev would think they were doing okay. He hoped she'd approve of what he and their friends and family were doing. She'd wanted them to grab life with both hands and not waste time grieving. She'd wanted them to remember her and be happy.

"What I'd really like, Dylan, is something quick and easy. A swift bullet through the brain..."

On that fateful day, it had been pure chance, a spur-of-the-moment thing that had seen Luke and Freya leave the house to stay with their grandmother. If they'd been in the house when Oxford had turned up with his gun—

Golden sparks lit up the sky as a firework exploded. That lone rocket was followed by several more until the sky was a riot of blue, red, silver and gold.

It was Christmas, a time when people showed goodwill to their neighbour. Peace on earth and all that. Dylan was the world's biggest cynic when it came to religious festivals but even he had to admit that Christmas always brought with it hope for the future.

He lifted his glass. "Luke's right, sweetheart. We're doing okay...I'll make sure our kids have a good Christmas. Which reminds me..." He returned to the sitting room and his computer, and checked out turkey roasting times.

He heard frantic footsteps pounding down the stairs, and Luke's voice. "Bozo? Bozo, no! Don't you dare. Oh, my freakin' God!"

Dylan went into the hallway in time to see Bozo race back up the stairs with something in his mouth. Lying at the foot of the stairs was the turkey. The one-legged turkey.

"How did he get that?" Luke asked in utter wonder. "It was right at the back of the counter. And covered in foil."

"More to the point—"

"Yeah."

They stared at the turkey for a full minute before Dylan picked it up.

"It won't poison anyone," Luke said. "If we give it a good wash, no one will ever know."

"The missing leg might hint that all's not as it should be," Dylan pointed out.

"Isn't there a shop open where we could buy a turkey leg?"

"It's Christmas morning. So that's a no."

"We could tell everyone we got hungry and decided to cook a turkey leg." Luke grinned. "They'll be mad at us, and they'll think we're crazy, but that's probably better than telling them Bozo's had his teeth round their lunch."

"Hmm. Okay, unless we can come up with anything better during the night, we'll go with that one." They celebrated their solution with a high five. "Happy Christmas, Luke."

"Happy Christmas, Dad."

* * * * *